OCTOBERLAND

Book Three of *THE DOMINIONS OF IRTH*

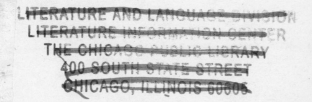

Other Avon Books by
Adam Lee

THE DARK SHORE: BOOK ONE OF THE DOMINIONS OF IRTH
THE SHADOW EATER: BOOK TWO OF THE DOMINIONS OF IRTH

OCTOBERLAND

Book Three of *THE DOMINIONS OF IRTH*

ADAM LEE

ld

AVON · EOS

AVON BOOKS, INC.
1350 Avenue of the Americas
New York, New York 10019

Copyright © 1999 by Adam Lee
Map by John Bergin
Published by arrangement with the author
ISBN: 0-380-79072-6
www.avonbooks.com/eos

Library of Congress Cataloging in Publication Data:

Lee, Adam.
    Octoberland / Adam Lee.
        p.   cm.—(The Dominions of Irth : bk. 3)
    I. Title. II. Series: Lee, Adam. Dominions of Irth : bk. 3.
PS3562.E317028   1999   99-11213
813'.54—dc21   CIP

First Avon Eos Trade Printing: April 1999

AVON EOS TRADEMARK REG. U.S. PAT. OFF. AND IN OTHER COUNTRIES, MARCA REGISTRADA, HECHO EN U.S.A.

Printed in the U.S.A.

OPM   10   9   8   7   6   5   4   3   2   1

For Bel Atreides—
and all like him:
"The people who walked in darkness (and) have seen
a great light."

—Isaiah 9:2

"I form the light and create darkness,
I make peace and create evil;
I, the Lord, do all these things."

—Isaiah 45:7

Contents

Foreworld

AT NIGHTFALL, THE WATER IN THE GARDEN'S MARBLE POOL TURNED black. Its taut surface mirrored a young woman sitting cross-legged on the mossy brink. From her bowed head, long hair spilled in red ringlets over her swollen breasts and her pregnant belly and touched the quiet water with ripples. She gazed forlornly at wobbly reflections of tree-hung lanterns and swaying temple columns.

In this pool, she had worked magic and had created chimerical worlds, a phantom cosmos replete with pinwheel galaxies and motes of planets numberless as gusted pollen. The aeons that carried all the dynasties of evolution in this conjured universe had amounted to merely a few months here in the garden. Still, it was a vast creation, concocted for one purpose alone: to educate her unborn. Within this mirage of happy worlds, she hoped her infant would experience joy and playfulness and a bounty of love.

But something had gone wrong. Ill-shapen, deranged, and malevolent forms had emerged out of the darkness of her dream

and polluted her gentle and antic worlds with disgusting events:
Violence, old age, sickness, and death stormed through her
creation.

Slowly, with grim astonishment, the possibility occurred to
her that this evil was the legacy of the child's father. He alone
had motive for such a cruel intrusion. But she had refused to
step to the edge of this precipitous thought for a long time,
because the implications were too unnerving.

The child's father was a warlord of her people's ancestral
enemies. His capture, alive and unharmed, had been a fortuitous
accident, and with jubilant expectations of peace, her people
offered the warlord's return in exchange for a truce. The warlord's rapacious generals answered with scorn, too consumed
with bloodlust to extend any kind of ransom.

So the warlord had languished, a political prisoner con-
demned to this very garden and its adjoining court. As a novice
enchantress and a minor personage in the house of the suzerain,
she had first laid eyes on him here, while serving those responsible for the captive's interrogation. He had been helpless to keep
any secrets before the onslaught of their persuasive magic, and
very soon they had adroitly manipulated him into revealing
everything they wanted to know. With this timely intelligence,
the warlord's army was quickly repelled, its war machine broken,
and all ambitions of conquest decisively crushed.

After that, she had felt pity for this warrior, whom blind
chance had broken. Despite his humiliating losses, he continued
to bear himself with dignity and oftentimes humor, and in time
she came to befriend him. He was a strangely beautiful man:
tall, with a girl's slender build and a light and delicate gait;
his soft-blushed face, which expressed serene melancholy often
shadowed with disdain, was hardened by two thin lines of determination under the blond mustachios at the corners of his
mouth.

Others of the suzerainty disliked and even feared him, but
for her he was the most truly sincere person she had ever met.

Having witnessed his interrogation, she knew that no magic disguised him. No secret was left undisclosed inside him. He was simply who he was, and she felt more at ease in his presence than among the posturing courtiers in the house of the suzerain. Before long, she took the warlord for her secret lover.

Together they knew a guarded happiness built on stolen moments, until the suzerainty discovered that she was carrying his child. The elders sat in silence. She had shamed her people by conjoining with the enemy.

As punishment, she was exiled, sentenced to take his place as prisoner in this garden, while he was given to the magicians. They plunged him into a profound sleep and carried his entranced body across the sky, hiding him somewhere in the night.

The night—the starless void beyond the titanic ramparts at World's End—had always frightened her. It was her people's ultimate punishment, the black depths where criminals could be safely forgotten. Timelessly suspended in this void, they required no care.

Those whom the magicians sometimes brought back reported frightful deliriums in the lightless deeps. Many claimed that the darkness was a living thing and had owned them while they were inside it. Rarely was it necessary to return anyone to the night ranges twice.

The young woman had wanted to use her magic to find and free the father of her child from this terror. And though she knew that the elders would sit again in silence if she did, she bravely would have defied them for the sake of her unborn. In her heart, however, she saw that her child would suffer from such a drama, and so she had restrained herself from obeying the first impulse of her heart and lived quietly in her garden court.

Only now, toward the end of her term, did she begin to suspect that the warlord entranced in the night was not smoldering in delirium. The darkness did not own him as it had owned the others. Bizarre as it seemed, perhaps he possessed within the darkness powers unknown to her magicians. Perhaps the magic of his fierce people drew as much strength from darkness as her people called forth from light.

How else to explain the cruel intrusion of evil into her spell of spun light? Somehow, the warlord's internal arts had defeated the magicians' trance, and he had reached through the night to enter the dream worlds she had created for their baby's benefit.

The lady of the garden looked up from the reflecting pool and observed the night-held garden. Was he here with her now—that strangely beautiful man, a phantom among the flame shadows of the lanterns?

For a moment, she believed she caught the scent of him, a faint civet on the floral breeze. It vanished. She stretched her legs and gingerly pulled herself to her feet, peering about at the vaults of darkness beyond the columns. Will-o'the-wisps flitted across the black ranks of yews outside the garden, a few blown sparks under the mighty trees, disappearing into the embers of twilight's horizon. Otherwise, nothing stirred.

The lady of the garden sensed something missing in this voluptuous stillness. Gawking about at the leaf drifts around the urns and shrub pots, she retrieved her feather robe from the stone bench where she had dropped it. She drew its warmth about her and stood beside the cage of a tripod lantern, scanning the espaliered garden wall that abutted the trellis gate with its litter of fallen blooms.

"Pixies," she muttered to herself. "*That* is what is missing! There are no pixies here. I haven't seen them in days."

Usually, there were two or three of the impish creatures lurking about, eager to steal the garden's flowers for their elaborate dances in the sedgy fields. But this night, there were no furtive scurryings across the terraced banks of flowers, no eye glints in the velvet dark under the cedar pruning tables, no baby shapes squatting behind the fern sprays that screened the compost bin.

The lady of the garden drew her feather robe tighter across

her enlarged belly. The temple columns of the garden cirque stood around her, graven still and final against the starless dark. Perplexed, she asked as if to a companion in the shadows, "Where are the pixies?"

Flesh Rags

Hope is sour desire.
—GIBBET SCROLLS: 27

IN A WORLD OF HER CREATION

IRTH BASKED IN THE SILVER AURA OF THE ABIDING STAR. AS THE marbled planet turned her hemispheric ocean toward daylight, a sunken continent rose steaming out of the blue depths: Gabagalus.

Rockets flared from launchpads tucked between the green paddies and slick yellow farms of the uplifted land. Their holds were laded with the telepathy-inducing wort cherished as a brew throughout all the worlds. Yet, nowhere in any of the trance dens or shrines among the glittering planets did the dreamdrinkers sense the Nameless One who was herself dreaming them.

Of those few who knew about the pregnant author of the worlds were two lovers enfolded together in their bed on the dark side of Irth: the magus and margravine of Elvre—Reece Morgan and Jyoti Odawl. He was a man of Earth and she a woman of the Bright Worlds, and they knew about the levels of creation.

"Maybe the Nameless One will help us against the goblins," Reece said into the disarray of Jyoti's hair. She lay curled against him in the darkness and her body tensed in his embrace. This was their last night together before Reece returned across the Gulf to the Dark Shore and Earth, hoping to find Dogbrick, his lost friend. And just hours ago, the margravine had received reports that the Goblin Wars had begun again. After a lull of more than four hundred thousand days, the telepathic imps had emerged from their exile in the Mere of Goblins and had begun using their strong minds to control ogres, hippogriffs, basilisks, and trolls and induce them to savagely attack the cities and farmlands.

Learning this, Reece Morgan wanted to stay with the margravine and help her defend New Arwar. This towering city of scaffolded spires and tiered neighborhoods that climbed above the tasseled horizon of the jungle had just been built. Stately palms lined broad boulevards still under construction, and trellises of flowering vines dripped outlandish blossoms over a maze of unfinished lanes and winding byways.

Most of New Arwar was cobbled together from the mountain of rubble that once had been the flying city of Arwar Odawl, Jyoti's ancestral home. In the war with the cacodemons, the city that had once toured the skies of all the dominions of Irth had crashed into the jungles of Elvre—killing all of the margravine's family save her younger brother, Poch.

Before he lost his magic, the magus Reece Morgan had used his power to soften the edge of Jyoti's terrible loss by creating anew the ancient metropolis. His magic from the Dark Shore had been powerful enough to rearrange the heaped debris into a lovely, verdant city vaguely shaped like a flat-topped pyramid. If he could have, he would have restored the dead themselves.

But his magic had been limited to manipulating the physical stuff of the Bright Worlds.

Then, he lost both his magic and his friend Dogbrick to the Dark Shore during their adventure with an old gnome, who served the nameless lady of the garden. Reece felt compelled to go back for Dogbrick, while Jyoti had to stay and complete the construction of New Arwar without magic. Neither of them wanted to separate, but these were responsibilities of the heart that had to be fulfilled.

And now that the Goblin Wars had resumed, Jyoti wanted Reece away from New Arwar—away from Irth entirely. She did not try to dissuade him by pointing out the likelihood that his friend was already dead. Reece would be safer on the Dark Shore, she reasoned, well distant from the terrible events unfolding on Irth.

So when his voice in the dark asked about seeking the nameless lady's help against the goblins, she replied quickly, "You're joking?" She rolled free of his embrace. "Trying to find the Nameless Ones beyond World's End would be even more dangerous than facing goblins."

Reece sighed. If only he still had his magical strength, all this would be so much easier. It pained him to no longer possess the powers he had worked a lifetime to master. As a child, he had scoured libraries and secondhand bookstores for texts on every related subject from astrology to zoanthropy. The astrology would prove useless, as soon as he learned enough magic to journey beyond Earth and the constellations of the zodiac.

But zoanthropy—the arcane lore of human transformation into animal forms—*that* knowledge had served him exquisitely well. At the height of his powers, he had possessed the skills to cover himself in beastmarks.

Ripcat. That was the name he had adopted when he wore the tight silvery fur, the long green eyes, the talons and fangs. . . .

He restrained another sigh. Of that remarkable power, only memory remained.

"What do these goblins look like?" Reece wondered aloud.

"I can show you." Jyoti's reply came from across the bed in the dark, where he heard her clattering among her amulets on the night table. "The Sisterhood of Witches captured a moment with them in a niello eye charm. I pity the woman who sacrificed herself for these images."

Jyoti pressed a cool, glassy lozenge into his hand. "Don't look too intently," she warned, "or you will be spelled."

Reece felt the magnetic tingle of Charm in the lozenge. Charm was the energy of the Abiding Star concentrated like a battery charge inside naturally forming crystals—crystals that, properly cut and shaped by charmwrights, became hex-gems. In turn, hex-gems could be combined, their powers amplified and focused into amulets and talismans designed for specific purposes: energizing power wands, wound-healing theriacal opals, or image-capturing niello eye prisms—as many different kinds of talismanic tools as there were needs for the clever charmwrights to fulfill.

He cupped the niello eye charm in his palm and held it to his eye. Caught like a holographic image within the dark interior, small creatures the size of dolls gazed lazily back at him, their smiles both sad and evil.

Reece sensed dark, anarchic, restless thoughts polluting the curdled brains inside those bulbous heads. And a putrid stench, a rancid reek of cheesy flesh and carnal sulfur, packed the dim grotto where they squatted. Their ricket-sprung limbs twitched as if at the sight of him; for all at once, the grotesque dolls seemed to lean closer, their bald dented heads bobbing, hollow eyes lidded blackly gold as toads' eyelids.

They appeared dazed, concussed, dream hooded, attentive to other voices or beholden only to their own minds' shapeless shape-shifting. In the gray-green smoke of their staring thoughts, he felt his life become a plaything. The inner lives of all people—his life, Jyoti's life, too, the psychic reality of every sentient being—passed before these squalid, grinning things as if provoked out of nothing by their own thoughts, as if reality itself were their imagining. . . .

REMEMBERING DOGBRICK

Jyoti snatched the niello eye charm from Reece's grasp. "Snap out of it!"

He shuddered in the darkness. "My God, they were inside my head!"

"Goblins will do that."

Gasping, he wiped his face with both hands. "I smelled them! Ugly—*deathly* stink!"

"And that's just a Charmed image of them." The eye charm clattered onto her night table. "Pray you never actually confront them."

"How can I leave you here with them?" he asked tensely.

"I'm not alone, Reece." Her voice carried calm strength. "All the dominions of Irth are united against the goblins. We defeated them before—we will again. And when you return with Dogbrick, you will help us."

Dogbrick. The large, beastmarked man had befriended Reece when the magus had first arrived on Irth, disoriented and ignorant, half dead under the fierce rays of the Abiding Star. Ripcat would have perished then and there without him.

Fondly, he remembered his friend—his tawny mane brushed back from a visage cognate with the ferocity of a wolf. There was such human emotion in those orange eyes that Reece had thought of him as human from the first. But that big-toothed, heavy-jawed muzzle of a mouth could roar fury as readily as speak philosophy.

It is big inside a human heart, Dogbrick was fond of saying. Big enough for reality and dreams together.

"I will return as quickly as I can," Reece promised.

Jyoti was relieved to hear the certitude in her lover's voice. She embraced him and for a long moment held wordlessly to his strong frame. After so much loss—the entire Brood of Odawl, all of her name but her brother and herself dead—she clung to him as though this were the only life there was.

And then she let him go. The fact that soon light-years would separate them, quite likely forever, gripped her heart with sorrow; yet she offered to the darkness a smile of somber warmth, remembering the happiness they had shared.

The Charm of her amulet-vest blunted her feelings and his as well. When they embraced again, free of the unbearable weight of grief, his mind roamed ahead to Earth and the quest for Dogbrick, determined to find a way back to Jyoti as fast as possible.

Her thoughts settled on those who could not escape Irth, who had to face with her the goblins and their armies of ogres, trolls, and wild beasts. She wondered grimly how many would survive this latest goblin war. She wondered if she herself would survive. And finally she fixed upon the one person for whom she had to survive, the one person who most needed her, who had always needed her—Poch.

BLIGHT FEN

A BEARDLESS, SIX THOUSAND-DAY-OLD YOUTH, POCH WORE GREEN and black dalmatic robes woven with protective sigils of the most finely spun conjure-wire. His white kid boots, trimmed in witch-fur and studded with hex-gems, warded vipers and poisonous centipedes. Upon his head of henna-colored hair, a turban of glory rags set with rat-star gems imbued his brain with Charm, amplifying his alertness and lending a calm aspect to his wide, squared features. Thus armored against both physical

and psychic harm, the cautious Poch strolled the ramparts above
Blight Fen.

Below him, to one side, ranged the colorful tents of theriacal
fabric where the Peers who were tortured by the Dark Lord
had been healed. All the Peers had departed some time ago,
but their prismatic tents remained as part of the atrocity museum that was Blight Fen. A small blackstone exhibit hall con-
structed with contributions from all the dominions displayed
realistic epoxy statues of the cacodemons, the monsters with
horrid faces embedded in their bellies, who had ravaged Irth
for Hu'dre Vra, the so-called Dark Lord. Few visitors arrived to
see again these slitherous abominations against whose talons
and fangs Charm had been useless. People wanted to forget
that horror.

And so, Blight Fen remained almost entirely unoccupied.
Poch continued here because his role as docent provided him
with a livelihood and a station in society greater than he could
possess anywhere else.

He would not live again under his sister's authority, obedient
to her whims. At least here, on this large marsh hummock
walled in with mangrove palings to keep out swamp beasts, he
was his own lord.

Atop the ramparts, he turned his back on the memorial
grounds and gazed out over the expanse of black water and
boggy holms that extended to the misty horizon of this dominion, the Reef Isles of Nhat. Not long ago, he had suffered here
under Hu'dre Vra—but then fortune had turned what had been
a frightful swamp to a verdant wonderland when the memorial
committee assigned him a special assistant to help him manage
Blight Fen: the apostate witch Shai Malia, herself a Peer, the
niece of this dominion's regent, conjurer Rica.

The atrocity exhibit hardly required two docents, and it was
understood by Poch from the first that Rica hoped to match
her n'er-do-well niece Shai with the margravine Jyoti's otiose
brother and hope for the best. Surprisingly, the two found

themselves to be more than just compatible. Poch and Shai were, from the first, passionate about each other, and after two hundred days together remained stupefied with desire and rarely parted.

Watching the petite woman mounting the rampart stairs, Poch felt a flush of amorous warmth. Like a nymph of night caught by daylight, she moved toward him with ferine grace. Her gray and black witch veils, which she continued to wear even though she had abandoned the Sisterhood more than two thousand days ago, tantalized him with the provocative shades of her dusky limbs and the shadow of her round, olive-skinned face framed in glistening black curls.

"Have you heard yet from your sister?" she asked as he reached to take her into his arms. She extracted the clamshell aviso from the inside pocket of his dalmatic robe and read the message log. "Poch! You haven't even signaled her yet!"

"I don't want to," he whispered against the soft gauze of her veils, suddenly drowsy from the cinnamon scent of her hair. "We don't need her. We can make our own way in the world."

"With goblins and trolls at war with the Peers?" She pushed away and pitched her voice to carry alarm. In the last three days, their aviso had been cluttered with reports of savage troll attacks in all the dominions. "We are unprotected here. We must seek sanctuary in Elvre, in the city of your ancestors."

Poch stiffened. "I'm not going back to New Arwar."

"Why not?" She returned the aviso and both her hands reached from under her robes to massage his shoulders. "You're an Odawl. You've as much right there as your sister. And more, I say."

"More?" He succumbed to her expert fingers, and his shoulders relaxed. "She's the margravine."

"Who abandoned her dominion to adventure upon the Dark Shore. Some margravine!"

"She had to rescue the magus." He nuzzled again against her

veiled hair and breathed the spice of her. "She loves Reece Morgan, as I love you."

"Reece!" Her fingers dug deeper into his muscles, and he straightened with a sudden brightening of pain. "Why is she consorting with this common creature of another order?"

"Shai!" He grasped her strong hands and lifted them from his shoulders. "He's not a creature. He's a man—the man who killed Hu'dre Vra. We all owe him a great debt."

"But he is not of the Bright Worlds," she protested and twisted her hands free. "He *is* a creature of the Dark Shore. How else could he have slain the Dark Lord? I suppose he is worthy of some gratitude—but is he worthy of your sister? You give your sister to this—this alien?"

"I don't *give* my sister to anyone. Jyoti is her own woman." His eyes widened with mock alarm. "And I won't return to Arwar Odawl, because if I do she will treat me like a child!"

"She may once have run your life, Poch, but she will never do that again. Not with me at your side." She slipped her arms around his waist. "If she wishes to risk her life on the Dark Shore and consort with strange beings from there, then I say she should do so on her own. She should abdicate, and you— Poch Odawl—should serve as margrave of Elvre. That is your dominion now."

"My sister's, Shai. My sister's," he repeated.

She edged back, miffed. "Haven't you heard a word I've said, you unreasonable ninny?"

"I hear you, Shai," he replied with a smile and pulled her close to him again. "But I think I would listen better if you were my wife."

Her scowl was obvious even through her veils. "I've told you. I will not marry you until you are margrave."

Gently, he lifted the veils from her face and stared softly into her tapered, ink-dark eyes. "Then I shall ask your aunt Rica to appoint me margrave of Blight Fen."

"Do not jest with me, Poch."

"Never," he promised, pulling her down with him onto the wood planks of the rampart.

BEYOND THE SWAMP ANGEL

WHEN SHAI MALIA GOT TO HER FEET, POCH LAY IN A DEEP SLEEP. Her enchantment would keep him unconscious for several hours. So long as he wore his robes of conjure-wires and his turban of glory rags and rat-star gems, her witch spells were useless against him. But when they made love, he doffed these garments, and gave her the opportunity to employ the ensorcelling skills she had learned as a witch.

While rearranging her veils, she gazed over the black swamp waters, beyond a wall of swamp growth woven from the sordid tanglings of strange parasitic silks, decayed ropes, and tendrils, beyond sepulchral depths of fallen trees and monstrous black roots full of glistening seepings, dripping rot among shifting vapors, to the Cloths of Heaven. These ancient ruins were the oldest upon Irth, and only speculation remained about who had built them and for what forgotten purpose.

Above the span of onyx water brooded the broken coral columns and walls of the immemorial ruins, and to them whispered the witch Shai Malia, "I am coming. I hear your summons, and I am coming. Be patient, my dear ones. I must purge myself first. You do not want me with this fool's child, do you? That is not our promise or our hope, is it? So, be patient, dear ones. Be patient. I am coming to you shortly."

Shai Malia left Poch slumbering on the planks of the rampart protected from the glare of the Abiding Star by the shade of the parapet. She descended to her tent of iridescent theriacal foil, cleansed herself with wort rinses, then donned sturdy garments: knee-high boots, brown canvas slacks, a red blouse embroided with protective glyphs, and an amulet-vest. Over her sable tresses, she wrapped a long gray witch-scarf to keep spiders out of her hair. Then she departed Blight Fen in a scull with a retractable charm-sail.

The scull carried her over the black water past banks of giant medusa trees that stood in ranks dimly retreating among the foggy depths of the impenetrable marsh. Soon, she glided alongside the tarn of inky, percolating water where the Dark Lord's Palace of Abominations had been sunk by the vengeful charmwrights of Irth.

A swamp angel had been set over the site to ward off those speculators who might seek to plunder the sunken pyramid. She paid it no heed. It was merely an apparition, a holographic illusion meant to frighten the uninitiated and to signal an alarm if others violated its territory. Soon, it dwindled out of sight.

Ahead loomed sphinx columns mired in miasmal bog, winding serpent-coil stairways that curled to nowhere, and a tangle of vines and creepers that strangled these ruins of domed porticos and tiled atria. The Cloths of Heaven received her with squawking monkeys and tollings of brightly plumaged birds. She lowered the charm-sail, and the scull skidded to a stop against a broken slab of masonry.

The Cloths of Heaven was haunted. This was well known. Wraiths ravenous for blood heat infested the ruins, and their hollow voices called faintly from the domed vestibules and their archways that dangled with vines and creepers. She would never have dared to enter this doomful place except that the dear ones had summoned her. Briefly, she lifted her gaze to the winged sphinxes atop the corroded pillars and thanked the beneficent gods for guiding her to the dear ones.

When she had first arrived at Blight Fen she had been so unhappy with this remote posting that she had been determined to squat in her tent and gnaw trance roots. But the fool who shared her work proved far more charming and playful than she had dared guess. Her body responded to his with an irresistible yearning, and they enjoyed together the most unconventional gambols and amorous feats. Her only disappointment was his weak will—a will as untrained and diffuse as smoke. He had no psychic strength, no drive to make more of himself than the simpleton docent that fate had elected him. All her attempts to inspire defiance of his sister with the hope that he would take for himself the position of margrave had proved futile. He wanted nothing more than to enjoy erotic mischief with her, and she had resigned herself to play with him for a while before moving on.

And then, the dear ones had summoned her. She was grateful after that for Poch's weak will. It was child's play to put him to sleep at her whim and obey the beckonings of the dear ones. Always, it was the same. They called her here to the old ruins, and she obeyed, gliding over the foggy waterways of the Reef Isles to this gloomy place. They led her, as they did now, under the shadow of the sphinxes, through murky colonnades, and along toppled walls so thick with lichen they appeared melted.

The wraiths did not touch her. They flitted away at her approach, for the dear ones protected her. She moved nimbly over the fungal beds of arched passageways and among broken spandrels and collapsed tiles to a dark cavern. The power wands of her amulet-vest illuminated a felled forest of pillars and a cracked ceiling of sagging vaults upheld by dense ganglia of roots.

Among the crazed shapes of crumbled stone, the dear ones waited. They were none other than the goblins themselves, five of them, doll bodies and warped legs barely strong enough to uphold their bulbous heads. Their sad and evil smiles widened at the sight of her, and the cracked agates of their hooded eyes shone brighter.

Shai Malia knelt in the rubble before them. The cheesy stink of their cankerous bodies did not offend her, for they held her mind in their little hands and passed it around among them. They fingered her thoughts—such delicate thoughts. They were careful with them. They needed her for their war, just as they needed the trolls. Too small and fragile to fight on their own, they recruited help from the cold world around them. They stroked lovely fragrances of summer rain and meadow flowers. They stroked images of babies, wise children of a forgotten realm come to Irth to end the hypocrisy of the Peers, who lived in luxury while so many suffered just to survive. The dear ones would deliver justice to all. And Shai Malia would be their queen—if she would but bring them what they needed now: hex-gems, jewels of concentrated Charm with which they could focus their telepathy and reach far beyond themselves to control trolls and ogres across Irth.

Shai Malia delivered a handful of hex-rubies from her personal cache, and the dear ones filled her with meadow-sweet bliss. They had new instructions for her. The war had begun. The dear ones had sent the fierce trolls into the dominions to topple the Peers, the high-handed ones already weakened by the Conquest of the Dark Lord.

The one who had slain Hu'dre Vra was himself now stripped of his power. He was but a man, an insolent man who had made himself the lover of a Peer. But he was leaving Irth. The time had come for Shai Malia to go to New Arwar and position herself for the coming of the other dear ones, the hundreds who slept through the cold of this world in a remote sanctuary.

This would be their last meeting for a while, an interval in which she would have to use her own cunning and witch skills to prepare a way for them. But though she was on her own, they would not forget her—nor she them. With loving care, they washed her hair in cold fire.

DOGBRICK ON EARTH

HE FELT VERY STRONG. SITTING AMONG THE HEATHERY SWEET FERN of the woods, he gave his strength to the others. They were

like him and yet different. Though larger than he and more
densely furred, they were not as strong, nor could they give
their strength to one another. Quiet creatures, they did not
make the noises he made. They listened. They could hear the
clouds moving overhead. If he tried, he could, too. But he had
to try very hard.

It was easier to give strength to the others and have them
listen for him. He gave them strength, and they found the
food—the sweet berries, the silver thrashing fish, the crunchy
grasshoppers. When they moved over the long rolling country,
he followed. He gave them strength, and they let him come
along.

The ground was brown and soft underfoot among the tall
straight trees with their branches interlocking high above. The
air smelled of resin and mint. The musk of animals flapped like
flags and banners on the wind, helping the others to decide
which way to go. Away from the acrid tang of bear, toward
the fresh scent of rabbit.

There were six others. They were tall and brown furred with
a ruddy sheen to their pelage. His pelt had a tawny color and
a shorter nap, except for his shaggy, blond mane. Also, his face
looked different. In the stone pools of the creek beds, he peered
at his wide, massive jaw and bristly red whiskers. His leathery
black snout glistened with perspiration, and there was a bewildered look in his deep-set orange eyes.

He had a savage face. His black lips pulled back from thick
fangs and serrate front teeth. The others had flat visages and
small, calm, round eyes under sloped brows. And they wore
nothing but their shag, while he wore a gray breechcloth.

At night, the cold descended from the stars. The others huddled in leaf drifts or sat solitary, shivering mildly in their fur.
The cold did not seem to touch him. But he felt a sadness for
the others. And on one particularly chill night, he wove fire in
the air and set it turning gently over the ground. The others

did not like this and ran from him, vanishing like shadows, silently, suddenly. He did not see them again for three days.

In that time, he moved alone through the crowded corridors of the forest. In his heart's small immensity, memories stirred just out of reach. By these felt but unremembered memories, he knew he did not belong with these others. But he had no idea where he did belong or even who he was.

Dogbrick.

The name called quietly to him in his half sleep during an ashen twilight. He sensed that this was *his* name. The others had no names. They knew each other by scent and sight. Drops of rain sang through the needles of the branches as he paced and spoke aloud his name, "Dogbrick—Dog-brick—Dog—Dog—Dogbrick . . ."

That night, while rain sizzled through the trees and he lay curled under the lee of a pine ledge, he dreamt of a city carved into the rock face of a cliff. The city gleamed like black mica, tiers of smoldering factories and tilted streets hewn into the raw rock of titanic sea cliffs. Far below this fuming hive, the ocean surged, its silver tusks flashing. Black dirigibles hovered over the city's heights. Three of the ornately festooned vessels floated near a sky bund of massive trestles, far upwind of the sulfurous smoke. Farther yet, suspended deep within the cobalt fathoms of the sky, other worlds hung like chunks of transparent crystal. Beauty and grace possessed him as he gazed at them. Then, orange mist from the numerous spires and minarets of factory flues covered him in its sour fog.

"Dogbrick—I am Dogbrick," he began to chant the next day, his voice startling birds that chattered and burst into the dawn like gusts of ash from the chimneys of his dream. In the wild silence that followed, he tried to resurrect his memories from the dark pit of sleep. Nothing more emerged. "I am Dogbrick . . . I am."

He wove fire in the air again. The others could not do this, and he thought perhaps that in the fire he might see something that was true to his identity. He stared at the blue and green flames swirling over the rotted logs and pulpy clusters of mushrooms. He stared until the whiskery flames took on an intensity of detail—luminous filaments braiding into translucent veils of fire. And still, he saw nothing of himself.

Frustrated, he kicked the old log to sawdust, and the wispy flames danced away like fireflies. "I *am* Dogbrick!" he shouted, and nothing in the dirty light of dawn or in the cold wind disputed him.

He stopped weaving fire, stopped talking, and just wandered the woods, obscure to himself, content to drift among the sun-filled galleries. When silver storms appeared above the forest canopy, he sought shelter among the rock crevices of the hills and watched rain blowing off the eaves of the forest. He ate leaf and root and what berries he could find.

Then the others returned as silently as they had disappeared. They were suddenly in the forest around him, their smoky scent dry in his nostrils. He gave them strength. He balled it between his palms and tossed it casually to each of them. They were glad for that, and soon they led him to the secret coves beside the running streams where fish waited to be plucked from the water.

They crossed through dark spruce forest, climbed the dry beds of small creeks, and sat on shale ledges under cirrus streams, looking out over a vast country of gray weather and endless woods. Down rocky slopes patched with heather, they loped. Basking under moonlight in their nakedness, they danced. Amorous with animal passion, they rutted. He watched disconsolately, moved to a sadness that possessed him with a vague sense of treachery. He did not belong. None would dance with him, not the way they danced with one another. He began to feel that he was betraying Dogbrick and his dream of the cliff city under the many moons.

When they found a star of ash one dismal morning, the others fled at once, flitting away like shadows. But the pitchy smell, the tar stink that frightened the others intrigued him. He crouched over the cold ashes of the rain-smothered fire and touched the depressions among the pine needles where something had squatted and tended these flames.

Frosty-souled, he recognized this harsh scent. It stirred untouchable memories. He stood and looked for the others. They had walked off into the sprawling fog. If he went after them at once, he might find them again. But the oily smell held him fast. He knew then that Dogbrick wanted to find the animal of this perfume, the fire maker. "I am Dogbrick," he said to the swirling mists where the others watched unseen. "I do not belong with you. I must go now. I must go and find myself."

He turned and walked away from the others. He went where they were afraid to go. Drifting sun streaks among the fog led him through the forest into thinning underbrush and smaller trees. A restless sun swirled inside high mists. Wasps simmered over the vines that wrapped slanted trees. Another exhausted campfire charred the ground with ash and husked walnuts.

Farther on, patches of the sky grew larger, and the clouds turned fleecy. At nightfall, under the dim green of a star, he heard voices singing and laughing. He approached under the colors of twilight to where a fire twinkled. And then, the wind turned and carried to him on the wood smoke a smell he recognized from another world.

THE MAGICAL BEAST

ALL NIGHT, DOGBRICK WATCHED THE CAMPFIRE AND THE SILHOUetted figures around it, ashamed as a thief yet afraid to draw closer. The others feared these fire makers. Yet the scent of them—like pitch, like coal oil, like tar smoke—reminded him of the earlier time he could not remember.

With first light, he crept closer, to see them more clearly.

Dogs barked, yapping angrily. He crouched in the wet grass, paralyzed to his eyes—immobilized by the familiarity of these creatures—these *people*. A man and a woman and with them two pointy-eared red dogs.

The man saw him first and leaped from his sleeping bag with a shout. Dogbrick started and tried to scurry backward, deeper into the grass, hoping to hide himself under the blue scarf of morning. But at the man's shout, the dogs had jumped toward him, snarling.

Dogbrick threw sleep at them. The weariness that had pooled in his limbs during the night compacted easily between his palms, and he threw it directly at the hurtling dogs. They collapsed at once, and he leaped up and turned to flee. The man pointed a stick at him. *No! A gun! A rifle!* The memory of what he saw jolted him the same instant that a needle cartridge slammed into his thigh.

He pulled the stinger from his leg and cast it away as he spun about and ran. Almost at once, a chill dullness spread through his leg and forced him to a limp. By graceless effort, he staggered into the underbrush among the trees. His limbs had become vacant. No matter how hard he willed, they would not move.

He shut his eyes, looked inward, and saw the incandescent smoke of the drug roiling through the red channels of his body. It took all his attention to begin to unravel it, to untangle its paralyzing knots so that his body could stir again.

The man loomed over Dogbrick, pointing the rifle. Unthinking, Dogbrick swung out, surprised that his arm could move and so swiftly. The blow caught the man across the jaw and hurled him to the ground, where he lay motionless. Dogbrick watched from the center of his being as the woman came running.

She was old. Her wrinkled face registered alarm. With frantic hands, she grabbed at the younger one, the felled man, and reached for his throat, then began to pound his chest.

The man's soul had left his body. Dogbrick could see it lying on the leaves, pulsing like a blue ember from a dying fire. No pounding would put it back. He shredded the spellbinding smoke from his throat and rasped, "Stop hitting him. Get his soul."

The old woman sat back on her heels and nearly toppled backward, alarm widening to shock in her staring face.

Dogbrick saw that she did not understand. She had heard him, but she did not see the soul. "I will get it." He tore away the last of the smoke inside him and rose to his knees. With both hands, he gathered the blue soul, throbbing like a giant amoeba, and placed it atop the inert man. It soaked into him, and instantly the body convulsed and gasped for air.

Dogbrick did not wait for the man to sit up and reach for his gun. He backed away into the trees and fled. From among morning's broken light, he watched the man and the woman hugging each other. Later, they stirred the dogs.

A red wagon came for them late in the day—a vehicle on black wheels that crawled speedily over the grassy fields. After much gesticulating by the driver and the man, the wagon drove off with the driver, the man, and the dogs. Only the crone remained behind.

She talked for a while into a slender block box. "An aviso," Dogbrick said aloud, retrieving another memory. "She is in contact with the others."

She prowled the forest at a slow, arthritic pace, searching for him. He kept out of sight. At night, he climbed a tree and watched her in the amber glow of her campfire. After the raveled flames dimmed, and she crawled into her sleeping bag, he threw her his weariness. When he was certain that she was deeply asleep, he approached. From her side, he removed the rifle and the aviso and hid them among the mossy rocks and underbrush.

At dawn, when he gave her strength and she woke to find him sitting in the silver fumes of the spent fire, she sat bolt upright, rigid with fright.

"I won't hurt you," he said, softly as he could.

Her mouth trembled, arduously shaping words yet making no sound, until she found herself saying aloud, "I understand you." Her shivering fingers pulled her red plaid shirt tighter about her. "How? How can I understand you?"

"I am talking to your soul," he answered and splayed his large hand across his furry chest. "Your soul understands me. I don't know why. The others did not."

"Others?"

"In the forest. The big ones. Hairier than me."

Her face brightened. "Sasquatch. You've been with Sasquatch? Are you not a Sasquatch yourself?" She gestured excitedly at the rucksacks leaning against a tree. "That's why we're here. We came looking for Sasquatch. . . ." She began fumbling with her bags, looking for her camera and her recorder.

"I am not one of them. Anyway, you won't find them down here." Dogbrick jerked a thumb over his shoulder. "They're deeper in the forest. They keep to themselves. They won't let you see them."

The crone's face tightened, squinting as if to see him more clearly. "Who are you?"

"I'm Dogbrick," he replied with certainty, then shook his long head. "I—I don't remember more than that. The others—the Sasquatch—they found me. About twenty days ago. Can you tell me where I am?"

"Canada." She found the recorder, and her shaking fingers checked that the tape cassette was in place.

He gawked about at the stands of birch and morning's adept yellow clouds. "I don't know this place. I think I'm from some-where else."

"I think so, too." The old woman's thick-jointed fingers struggled to push the buttons on the recorder, and the machine slipped from her grasp. Her cheeks puffed out in exasperation, and her wide eyes shrilled at him. Flustered, she crossed both hands over her chest. "I'm Mary Felix. I'm an anthropologist—a scientist, someone who studies societies, peoples of every culture. But I've never seen anyone like you. May I—may I touch you?"

Dogbrick extended his hand. When they touched, she felt his wet fur and knew she was not dreaming; he felt her as well, the life of her, the warmth in the same ash of which they were made. He sensed her heart giving out from her swollen longings. "You've lost someone—your husband."

She snapped her hand away. "How—how do you know?"

"I don't know—I feel it." He rubbed his hands together. "He died of a blood-burst brain, not long ago, less than a thousand days. You are lonely. . . ."

Mary Felix stood up, the bony legs in her green denims shaking. "My husband died of a stroke two winters ago. What magical beast are you? How can you know all about me and not know yourself?"

Dogbrick lifted his fierce face toward morning's brightening lavender. "I want to know. I want to remember. But I can't." His orange eyes fixed on her. "Will you help me, Mary Felix?"

"I don't know that I can." She edged closer to him, and once past the screen of wood smoke she smelled his strange scent— a jasmine fragrance, silken as a tropical breeze. "This is truly an extraordinary discovery for me. Do you understand? You must. Please—come with me. Let me show you to my colleagues."

"No, Mary Felix." Dogbrick shook his mane, and the balmy redolence that wafted from him made her sit down under a sudden weight of rapture. "I have felt through your soul to the sickness of your world. I won't go there."

THE COVEN

OCTOBERLAND WAS THE NAME OF THE COVEN. EVEN IN JULY, THE meetinghouse smelled of leaf smoke; yellow and red leaves drifted along the inside perimeter of the wooden building's one circular room with its shagbark boards and its floor of knotty planks rubbed smooth by many seasons of round dances. Corn-silk poppets hung from the rafters along with bines of ritual herbs and chains of faces carved into apples and shriveled to totems of anguished visages, amber souls strung on a silent scream and lifted from ultimate night.

Crimson paint precisely outlined a large circle around the room and a pentagram within. A tall block of pentagonal obsid-ian stood at the center, an altar bedecked with swaths of tat-tered moss partly overlaid by fabric of midnight blue and embroidered with silver crescent moons. An urn squatted atop the altar on a hammered metal dish, flanked by fat black candles and fronting the black smile of a silver knife bound to an ebony haft with copper wire corroded green. A stave of knobby wood leaned against the altar, cankerous with galls, resinous cracks, and membraneous gills of scalloped fungus.

No windows penetrated the walls of furry bark. But when the ram's-head knocker sounded and the door opened, the skyline of Manhattan sprawled below, a canyon of stone towers and sunlight-smashed glass. Dim wails of sirens and bleating car horns drifted up from the distant streets.

The meetinghouse had been crafted from the interior of an abandoned water tank atop a thirty-storey building in midtown.

Nox, the coven leader, entered wearing a hood mounted with the fanged face of a panther and robes of black taffeta like sooty cobwebs. At the altar, hands like burnt spiders folded back the cowl and exposed a long, bald, age-blackened skull. His mummified face consisted of a charred twist of nose, hollow cheeks, and fluted lips stretched taut to a permanent sneer show-ing antique teeth, tiny and discolored as maize kernels. Adder eyes split light in agate bands, and vertical pupils flexed to watch the twelve coveners file in and close the curved door behind them.

The coveners dropped their colorful, heraldic mantles and stood naked before their lord. They were six affluent couples,

consisting of three individuals from each of the four Adamic
races—Afric, Aryan, Asian, Amerind—all in their prime, all dis-
playing glowing health and physical pulchritude. That was the
gift of their lord—a bounty of beauty and wealth. That was
why they served him.

Each had been less before coming to Octoberland. Each had
a story of impoverishment, loss, and despair. Nox had healed
every one of them. Now they flourished. The city was their
playground. And for this privilege, they served Nox with utter
devotion.

The coven lord asked little of them. Once a month, at the
dark of the moon, they came to the meetinghouse late in the
afternoon and danced for their lord, singing the barbarous
chants he had taught them. That was all. That—and the secrecy. None was permitted to breathe a word of Octoberland
to anyone outside the coven. If this oath was broken, Nox
knew. Within the month, the violator and those who had heard
the secret suffered terrible accidents. They did not die; they
survived to suffer lingering malignancies, mute of all but their
cries.

Nox had won this power over generations—centuries. He
had begun as a cupbearer in the temple of Tiamat among the
fig-tree terraces on the river Tigris seven millennia ago. He had
learned his magic from the steppe wanderers, the nomads of
the Baltic highlands, the wayfarers of the star plains, who had
mapped the celestial byways and first trapped heaven in a circle.
They themselves were the inheritors of knowledge from the
horizon walkers of earlier millennia, the builders of the stone
circles of the far north, where the cold fires, the auroras, could
be culled from the sky during the long nights and trapped in
the secret precincts, the sacred places, the first shrines.

Using that ancient understanding, Nox and his occult workers—mathematicians, astrologers, magi—discovered again the
long-forgotten power of twelve. They were the hieratic ones
who relearned how to divide the circle of the sky into twelve

houses. And they assigned the circle the 360 stations of reckoning. They were also the ones who differentiated the day into twenty-four hours, the hour into sixty minutes, the minute into sixty seconds. All this to better control the magic inherited by them from the builders of the first shrines, the masters of stone, who had learned how to trap the cold fires and direct them by the power of will.

Nox mastered the energy of the planet's slow turning through the starry dark. With the help of others, he became adept at gathering the cold fire and circulating it through his body. He and the others became immortals—of a sort. They aged more slowly. Disease could not touch them, for the cold fire burned away all illness. Only accident—only the blind god Chance—remained immune to their power and occasionally betrayed them to the blind god Death. One by one over the millennia, the others who shared his magic had died, slain by freak accidents.

Chance had not left Nox untouched, either. Seven thousand years of exposure to the random batterings of the sun's fire had damaged him. Slowly, slowly he had aged, so that now he was shriveled to a ghastly black skeleton, hairless, his dry ligaments rending leathery, crackling sounds with each movement. But no pain touched him. The cold fire in his bones radiated a power that fused him to the very aura of the planet, the magnetic might of the spinning world itself. If he continued his magic rituals, he would never die. But in time, he would wither to a disembodied wraith divorced from physical contact—a fate of immortal sentience and hopeless hungers that reared up before him more frightful than death.

To avoid this diminishment, he had founded Octoberland several centuries earlier. His dancers helped him circulate the cold fire in the ritual manner that extended his awareness into the astral sky. From there, he could gaze out across space-time for magicians of other worlds.

Nox knew that such magi existed, because such a one had

appeared on Earth much earlier when Nox was but a thousand years old. Duppy Hob arrived as an exile from a higher order of magic, a realm at the very beginning of time. Nox had learned much from him about the Abiding Star and Charm— but Duppy Hob was a dangerous master, full of strange and unpredictable knowledge. He was the one who doled out to the kings the mysteries of science so that he could build his enormous Charm-accumulators: at first, the pyramids and obelisks and then the cities themselves—vast amulets designed to harness power for that vengeful exile.

To protect himself, Nox had avoided the stranded magician yet stayed alert to his whereabouts. He knew that in time others would come from the Bright Worlds. Eventually, he would win from them the Charmed magic to amplify his power and help him discard his flesh rags and reclaim his youth.

And so, each month he called together his dancers, wove the cold fire into bodies of light, one for each of the coveners. These were their personal angels, designed to watch over them and work magic for the coven. And each of them took turns observing the heavens, watching the Gulf.

Thus, he saw at once when the others came for Duppy Hob. They disappeared with the devil worshipper, back to the radiant worlds in the fiery glare of creation. But one remained behind. Lost or forgotten, that one wandered the northern wilderness— and Nox was determined to learn more of him.

THE VOICES OF THE FLOWERS

MARY FELIX, WITH A RUCKSACK SLUNG OVER HER SHOULDER, FOL-lowed Dogbrick through the trees and over the scattered stones of a rattling creek. "The others are coming back for me," she had warned him. "We must go where they won't find you." He led her deeper into the sunless woods, to a hollow hung with moss gray as hag's hair. "I should leave a note. They'll keep searching for me."

"Go back." Dogbrick kept walking. "I will find myself on my own, somehow. Go back to the others."

"Wait—you walk too fast for me." Mary panted, her muscles aching, and hurried to his side. "I want to stay with you. I want to help you find out who you are. I'm an anthropologist. I've got to understand. For my own sake, I want to know who you are."

"I am glad for your help, Mary Felix." Dogbrick moved relentlessly over the gravel banks, avoiding the mud, leaving few prints. "But I have felt your people, and they frighten me."

"Slow down—please!" Mary clutched at her aching side, huffing for breath. "I'm not—not trying to capture you—or trick you. Look—I'm not even taking pictures—or recording your voice. I feel your fear. You can trust me. Just slow down. Let me come with you." She stopped walking and called after him. "I don't want to go back. I have nothing to go back to. I'm alone. Like you."

Dogbrick stopped and turned. Seeing how frail she looked and hearing the sharp note of despair, he experienced her sadness. He nodded, balled strength between his palms, and tossed it to her.

The warmth filled her muscles with vigor, and she bounded alongside him as he strode among immense ferns. "What have you done to me?" She laughed and skipped like a child. The heavy rucksack that had been hurting her shoulder now felt light as paper. "I could run for miles!"

"I gave you strength."

"How?"

Dogbrick shrugged and clambered over the ramparts of roots and under twisted beeches splotched with lichen. "I don't know exactly."

Mary Felix took his blond-furred arm. "I think you should know."

He stopped and leaned against a tree. This small old woman, watching him through a haze of awe, spoke a plain truth that made him ache. The more he tried to remember, the emptier he felt, until he virtually throbbed with hollowness. A frightening futility closed on him, as if he were shrinking. Abruptly, he shoved away from the tree. "I can't remember anything."

"Well, you remember meeting me."

"That just happened."

"And before that?"

He shoved through the ferns to the grassy verge of a brook, a wider swerve of the creek they had crossed below. The brown muscle of a fish shifted among the reeds under his shadow. "I remember the others."

"Tell me about them."

They sat on the thick grass, watching the current splice among the rocks, and he told her about the others, the ones she called Sasquatch. She had endless questions, craved the most minute details, and they sat a long time talking. Slowly, he followed the clews of his memory back to his first awakening, under a cedar where sunlight lay like sawdust atop the bracts and needles. "I remember gliding down shimmering layers of blue—but I don't understand what I remember. I think I was—I was flying through the air. I was flying."

"You're a magical creature." Mary Felix stared at his beast-marks with open wonder. "Why can't you fly now? Have you tried?"

"No."

"Try."

Dogbrick stood and willed himself into the air. A blue light rayed through him, as though he had become suddenly translucent as smoke and perforated by moonbeams. For an instant, he saw the pale bluffs under him and geese on the flyway arrowing above shreds of cloud. Far below, woods spilled among the hills—and he spotted the red wagon again, tiny with distance, followed by two green vehicles on a road like a pale thread.

All at once, he was back beside the murmuring brook and Mary Felix on her knees, mouth agape.

"You disappeared!" She reached out and grabbed his big hand, wanting to reassure herself of his solidity. "Where did you go?"

"Into the sky," he said in a hush of surprise. He glanced around at the spilling brook and the fern walls, and though he saw that he was in the same place, he felt he had arrived somewhere new. "They are coming back for you. I saw them. The red wagon that came yesterday—"

"The Land Rover." Mary hastily got to her feet and turned to look at the trees and bracken that screened the lower slopes. "I told my research assistant to bring help. We thought we had found a Sasquatch. When they find I'm not there, they'll come looking for me."

"Do you want to go back?" Dogbrick pressed his palms together, gathering strength. "I'll give you what you need to get down there quickly."

"No, I've already told you—and I mean it—I want to go on with you." Her face almost seemed to glow. "This is the most amazing thing that's ever happened to me."

"I am going to move quickly, back into the deep woods. You can come with me if you want. But, Mary Felix—I don't know where I am going."

"I don't care. Let's go!"

He gave her strength, and they traveled swiftly past the hedged banks of the brook, over mossy tumble stones, and into the green woods' depths that were smoking with pollen and sun shafts. By mid-afternoon, they reached a glade of feathery grass patched with blue flowers, a clearing bright and unearthly under the dark wall of evergreens. Here, they paused.

"Are you hungry?" Mary reached into her rucksack for the bag of granola and the tins of herring she carried.

She froze.

Her hands—how different they looked! The wrinkled flesh had smoothed. The liver spots of age had faded entirely away. "My God!"

Dogbrick paid her no heed. He was listening to the flowers. They were hard to hear, because bees hummed among them. Clouds sizzled softly overhead. The wind ransacked the trees. And Mary Felix kept jabbering.

"I know I'm awake—but I feel I'm dreaming." She rummaged in her rucksack and came out with a small mirror with a hole in its middle for flashing sun signals. In its bright surface she saw a woman she had not seen in thirty years—herself, her loose gray hair chestnut brown again, her wrinkled face smooth as a teen's and freckled. "Can this be? Can this really be?"

"Listen!" Dogbrick hushed her with an uplifted hand. "The voices of the flowers . . ."

She heard nothing but the wind in the pines and fell to her knees in astonishment. "I don't believe any of this!"

Dogbrick began to step forward, then paused. The flowers were not singing, he realized with a chill. He heard the voices of invisible people, chanting words he did not understand.

A figure appeared in the clearing—a translucent figure of a scorched-looking man, bald, with skin seared black. Adder eyes watched intently. The deathly look in that charred face with tiny, discolored teeth frightened Dogbrick, for he had seen this phantom before, in the misty hours of the forest coves with the others, who had stared and not seen. He hurriedly wove fire in the air and whipped the flames at the apparition.

The ghost vanished in a blue glare and thunder trembled underfoot.

"Did you see that?" Dogbrick asked and turned to Mary. But she had seen nothing. She was gawking at herself in a small mirror and fingering her face.

"You made me young!"

"Not me." Dogbrick spoke distractedly, searching the clearing for further signs of the evil wraith. "The strength I've given you did that. But don't worry. It won't change you anymore now that you're as strong as you can be."

THE ROAD TO MOÖDRUN

REECE MORGAN DEPARTED ARWAR ODAWL AS A PASSENGER ON A convoy of lumber freighters bound for Moödrun. He wore an amulet-vest festooned with every kind of device the margravine could convince her charmwrights to bond with conjure-wire: amber power wands hugged his ribs, collarbones, and spine; hex-rubies patterned a spiral over his liver, protecting him from poisons; sanctum-panes of platinum patched his solar plexus providing energy to overcome fatigue; tiny scarabaeus mirrors glinted like sequins in spiral designs meant to warn of peril and ward off enchantments; buttons of witch-glass served also as revelation prisms that would expose invisible entities; theriacal opals covered his kidneys, ready to heal him if he were wounded; rat-star gems lined the inside of the vest, amplifying his mental functions; and niello eye charms covered his shoulders, acting as powerful ocular lenses for seeing at a distance. With the aviso tucked into the inside pocket of this sturdy vest, he could contact Jyoti at any time, and the barb gun holstered at his back offered an added measure of personal protection.

Yet even with all this charmware, he was not adequately guarded against the harsh rays of the Abiding Star. As a man of the Dark Shore, he lived in jeopardy of charmstroke from overexposure to the radiance of creation's light. That was why, when he had first arrived on Irth, the magic he possessed then had instinctively fashioned for him a protective body of light, an animal form adapted to thrive in the radiance of Charm.

Ripcat's bestial strength and feral agility had protected him not only from the Abiding Star but also from most predators. The loss of magic had deprived Reece of that protection, and now he had to wear a cowl of tinsel to reflect the glare that could kill him outside the sanctuary of cities and Charm-powered vehicles.

On the convoy, Reece rode in a passenger trailer connected between the lading beds of a freighter, and the other travelers barely paid him any heed. He was a clean-shaven man of average stature, with sandy hair and a visage blunt as a boxer's. At first glance, he had the unassuming appearance of a city maintenance worker in his mantle of tinsel, brown trousers and sandals—until he moved. Then, one noticed the feline flow of his motions, the tensile spring of his step: remnants of his beast-marked days.

Reece shared the bluewood trailer and its several sleeping berths and small galley with three violet-haired ælves, master charmwrights all, who were departing Arwar Odawl because the margravine could no longer afford their services. They were bound for the rocketpad at Moödrun and an ether ship that would return them to their homeworld of Nemora.

Along the way the convoy picked up a fur trader, a witch, and a noisy group of lyceum students—aspiring jungle botanists and herb merchants—completing a tour of the dominion. The fur trader and the students filled the only other trailer in the convoy, and the freight manager asked permission of the ælves and Reece for the witch to ride with them.

No one objected, and a sturdy woman shrouded in traditional black and gray veils entered. She sat at the oval rose-glass window where Reece gazed forlornly past tapered trees at the epoxy statues of cacodemons his lost magic had created. "You are the magus of Elvre," she observed at once in a tone of surprised delight.

Reece nodded glumly. He was preoccupied with memories of all that had fallen away from him—Jyoti, Irth, magic—and apprehensions of what lay ahead—the search for the charmways, the passages that tunneled through space and connected remote areas and that could quickly return him to the Dark Shore and the uncertain search for Dogbrick. . . .

"You seem grim." The witch opened her hand and revealed a bliss-prism long as a finger. "Touch this between your eyes. You'll feel so much better, no matter your troubles."

Reece declined with a polite but vague wave of his hand and did not budge his stare from the garden of demons. Then, the convoy lurched into motion, and the flap of his tinsel-embroidered mantle swung open, revealing his jammed amulet vest.

"By the Mistress of the Worlds, you don't need my puny prism!" A laugh sparkled from under the obscuring veils. "You are endowed with enough Charm for a village! As well you should be, for you are Reece Morgan! The man from the Dark Shore. Slayer of the Dark Lord!" She turned to the three ælves, who stood on the deck of the observation bubble regarding the gruesome collection of cacodemonic statuary. "This is the hero who saved Irth from those monsters. Are you aware of that?"

The ælves muttered briefly among themselves, then retreated to their sleeping berths to avoid the garrulous witch.

"If you please, sister, I don't crave attention." Reece moved to rise and go to his own berth, but she took his sleeve.

"Forgive me, magus." With her free hand, she parted the veils from her face and revealed a patchwork of scars, one eye lost, the disfigured flesh sunken into the socket like melted wax. "I have dwelled in the House of Rue, and I am perhaps too loud in my admiration of your victory over those who did this to me."

Reece sat down heavily. "I'm sorry. I—" A question displaced his apology. "Why has not Charm healed you, sister?"

"Because I *am* a sister among the Sisterhood of Witches." She folded the veils back into place. "I am devoted to healing others, who have wounds as bad or worse than mine. What theriacal opals and analeptic pearls the Sisterhood gather we use for others, not for ourselves."

"Surely, there must be enough Charm for all."

"It will take thousands of days to rebuild all that the Dark Lord destroyed, magus. And now—now is no time for my vanity. The goblins believe that the dominions are weak enough to be vanquished. They have come back from their exile to rouse the trolls against us! You've heard?"

Fear brightened in him at the recollection of the drowsy-lidded dolls with their bulbous heads and filthy, warped bodies. "I'm aware."

"Is that why you travel to Moödrun, to protect Elvre's greatest harbor from the trolls?"

Reece's hands flopped helplessly in his lap. "I have no more magic. I can't protect anyone."

"No!" The witch twisted in her seat. "But then, of course, that is why you are so staunchly outfitted with amulets. Your magic is exhausted. Forever?"

Reece frowned. "Don't trouble yourself about me, sister. There are too many others who need your good help. Save your strength."

"I understand." The witch nodded and adjusted the veils across her face. "You deserve your privacy. Forgive my intrusion. But I cannot help my inquiries. As a witch, I am obliged to serve the welfare of all beings—even the magus of Elvre!" She sidled closer and spoke in a confidential whisper. "You don't have to answer me. Strange as this must seem to you, given your skepticism of me and given my eagerness to know you, we already *are* expressing the very ideals of my Sisterhood: pessimism of the intelligence, optimism of the will."

ATTACK OF THE TROLLS

THE WITCH INTRODUCED HERSELF AS "ESRE, IRTH-HEALER"—AND seeing that she was not going to leave him alone, Reece amplified the Charm from his amulet-vest until a smile lifted his heavy features. He sat deeper in the upholstered seat, and they chatted amicably about the Dark Shore and the Sisterhood until nightfall.

Then Esre proved herself an exquisite cook. Even the ælves, who usually preferred their own cuisine, partook heartily that night of her spiced salad and braised fish-tubers and were at her side in the morning helping prepare honey-berry flummery.

Along the highway, the convoy occasionally stopped to stack the lading beds with timber from the jungle dominion's lumber camps. The journey went slowly, and there was ample time for Reece to reflect on his fate. He knew he would never catch up with his past, never achieve again the marvels that his magical powers had wrought. His life had slowed down. Gradually, he came to see that his quest for Dogbrick was equally a search for the clarity to accept the common man he had become, to begin again.

A passionate quiet enclosed him, and he examined his imperfect heart. He saw then that he expected to find himself on Earth because he belonged there. Now that he was no longer a magus, his ambitions fit the boundaries of the Dark Shore better than they did the magical possibilities of Irth. Only Jyoti had kept him here—and would bring him back. And perhaps in a future day when the happy sorrow of her building New Arwar was complete, she would consider living for a while in his world. . . .

By the time the parabolic arches of Moödron's sky bund hove into view above the torn canopy of the jungle, Reece had overcome the melancholy that had plagued him since leaving Jyoti. The wall of the jungle looked impossibly huge, and the treetop city of Moödron seemed bigger yet, as if mortal dreams could transcend even the divine.

Reece had booked passage on an airship that would drop him by glider into the Spiderlands. The charmways there, he hoped, would return him to the Dark Shore. But after he departed the convoy station and strode across the lumber-yards and through the market crowds toward the sky bund, chaos erupted.

The bough streets atop the giant trees and the scaffold roads that rayed across the upper storeys of the jungle swirled with frenzied throngs.

"Trolls!" people screamed, amulets clattering on their tunics and frocks as they jostled one another, desperate for escape.

Reece spotted the invaders climbing from the jungle floor along the boles of massive pilaster trees. The metallic-skinned creatures clawed rapidly up the tendrils and ivy of the tree trunks, only slightly hindered by the charmfire from the city's soldiers. Viper-cowled rangers took up positions in the hanging-garden balconies and fern terraces and loosed hot crimson bolts from their firecharms, not daring to use stronger charges for fear of damaging the tree buttresses or igniting a conflagration.

The red flares of energy smashed the bolt-eyed trolls, exploding them to gory shards. But their severed limbs continued to climb. Unscathed trolls threw the severed heads of their comrades onto the balconies, and the bodiless fangs snapped at the soldiers and the panicked citizens. Trolls on lianas swung from the jungle into the city and with swipes of their razor claws disemboweled shrieking people.

Swept along by the terrified mob, Reece found himself squeezed into the metal cage of a sky bund lift. The pulleys hoisted the cage out of the jungle treetops and into the blue day, among the trestles of the sky harbor. At the top, the cage gate swung wide, and the people rushed madly for the nearest dirigible gondolas, wild to flee the assailed city—only to find that the trolls had already scaled the girders of the sky bund. Clawed arms swinging like scythes, the predators lunged onto the ramp ways, cutting down everyone in their path.

Horrified by the monsters leaping over one another to bury their snarling snouts in the ripped bodies of their victims, people threw themselves over the guardrails and plummeted into the jungle below. Reece unholstered his barb gun, but the metal projectiles only inflamed the already vehement beasts, and they rushed him with raging howls.

A claw strike ripped away his mantle and amulet-vest in one stroke. Bare-chested and with a breathless scream in his throat, he confronted the furious troll, whose claws were entangled in his torn garments. He fired a barb directly into one of its glaring eyes, and it wrenched away shrieking.

Reece charged across a ramp that led onto the nearest gondola. But no sooner had he entered than the dozens already inside heaved against him, stampeding to get out. Trolls had shimmied up the guy wires and entered through the open cargo bay. Reece turned to flee, and hands grabbed him and pulled him away from the hatch. He twisted about and faced the scar-slashed face of Esre, her witch veils pulled asunder by the flailing crowd.

"Stay!" she commanded, then quickly began to herd the passengers off the gondola.

Heart writhing in his chest, Reece watched as three trolls hacked at the last of the passengers, severing heads, splitting breastbones to expose purple bundles of trembling viscera. "Esre—get out!"

From under her veils, the witch drew a compact firecharm and with lethal precision felled each of the three blood-frenzied trolls with shots that struck directly between their eyes. Esre moved with surprising agility for a woman of her sturdy frame and easily rolled the twitching corpses out the cargo bay. As Reece turned to signal for the others to return to the gondola, she jerked him aside and pulled shut the hatchway.

"There are more trolls out there!" Reece shouted. "Let the people in!"

With a deft strength that toppled Reece, Esre spun him away from the hatch and onto one of the cushioned benches where a lopped limb lay. "Don't move," she ordered hotly. "I don't want to have to hurt you."

Aghast, Reece watched the witch crouch in the open bay and

use her firecharm to blast the guy-line bollards. The gondola lurched, and the dirigible rocked free of its berth.

When Esre disappeared into the pilot's turret, he ran to the hatchway, hoping to fling the portal open so that others could jump onboard. But already the gondola had separated from the ramp way, and the ejected passengers stood at the brink, screaming and sobbing while trolls descended upon them.

A dull vibration announced the activation of the prop engine, and sharp pops signaled that the witch had used the control panels to disengage the last of the mooring wires. Through the long windows, Reece watched the sky bund swing away and flickers of cloud rush past.

Esre returned to the passenger cabin, her veils back in place. "Sit down." She pointed to a bench whose squabs were untainted by blood. She spoke while she moved around the cabin picking up body parts and tossing them out the open cargo bay. "I was sent for you. Have you surmised that yet? The Sisterhood's eyes in New Arwar informed us that you were leaving for the Dark Shore—leaving us even as the goblin wars are returning." With a grunt, she rolled a headless corpse out the bay. "We can't have that. You are Irth's greatest magus."

"But I'm not!" Reece remained standing, hands fisted with frustration at his sides. "I told you already. I have no magic. None."

Esre tossed another body through the open floor hatch, then knelt and spun the crank wheel in the hull that closed the bay. "You are a man of the Dark Shore. That means you are of a different gradient of Charm, a colder gradient. That is why you held Duppy Hob's magic so very well. And that is why you will hold our magic just as well."

"Hold your magic?" Reece moved toward the witch. "You sacrificed all those people back there to use me? Do you think I'm going to comply after that?"

Esre straightened her disheveled veils. "Comply—" she shrugged "—or be made to comply. Either way, you will serve the Sisterhood—once more, a hero of Irth."

Wife of Darkness

This is our curse: for every yes, a no.
—GIBBET SCROLLS: 28

BEAUTY WITHOUT CRUELTY

THE MARGRAVINE STOOD AT THE LIANA-COILED RAILING OF AN observation tier, surveying the steep boulevards and switch-backing avenues of her nearly vertical city, New Arwar. Grief spoiled her appreciation of the enormous work that had already been completed. What had been ruins five hundred days ago was now very nearly a whole city again: Flame trees lined the streets, colorful birds roosted among the floriate eaves, and blossom fragrances wafted on Charmed winds. Yet, though the lovely, antique buildings of yore had been restored by magic, she knew that this metropolis would never fly again. The cost of the hover charms necessary to hoist the city exceeded the expected income from all Elvre's exports for the next fifty thousand days.

Jyoti missed having Reece at her side, to share her sorrows for what had been lost and to encourage her faith in what could yet be accomplished. No talisman could replace him. Even without his magic, he was for her the wonder of what the future offered. With him beside her, she had felt somehow that all things were possible, and his absence portended dire times. She wanted to believe that he would return, but she could not quite convince herself that when he did return, she and New Arwar would be here to greet him.

A gloomy atmosphere shrouded the city. News of troll and ogre attacks from every dominion had frightened the populace, and people went about their daily business with evident anxiety. Many had already abandoned New Arwar and decreed it cursed. Those who had come to settle had been enticed by prebuilt, mortgage-free residences in Irth's most venerable estates. They had been adventurous enough to dwell where many thousands had so recently perished. Yet, dauntless and aspiring as they were, few had the courage to believe that this settlement, isolated in the jungle, was defensible against trolls and goblins.

A gentle knock turned the margravine around to face a compact woman in a black utility uniform, the cowl folded back from a bronzed, burnished, square face. Her short-cropped silver hair, stiff as bristles, heightened the angled planes of her head. "I have news from Moödrun."

Jyoti signaled her to advance, and the short woman entered with the silent grace of a shadow. This was Nette, a weapons master from the Brood of Assassins. The wizarduke, Lord Drev, had hired her to protect the margravine the day that he had learned Reece had lost his magic. "I have already heard the aviso reports from Earl Jee," the margravine said, trying to preempt a tedious report of loss and destruction. "I am aware of the damage to the sky bund and the great numbers of casualties suffered before the trolls were repelled."

"The attack was arranged to coincide with the arrival of Reece

Morgan at the harbor city." Nette paused a moment for this to sink in before adding, "The magus was their objective."

"He is not among the casualties," Jyoti countered at once. "He's missing. Has he been found?"

Nette shook her head. "He is not dead. The trolls failed their goblin masters."

The margravine tilted her head skeptically. "If the goblins went after him, why did they wait until he reached Moödrun. They could have assaulted the convoy on the highway."

"The convoy was too well armed. And it would have been more obvious that the magus was their target." Nette spoke matter-of-factly, her tone conveying her certainty in this assessment. "The goblins do not want us to know that he is a threat to them."

"How is he a threat?" Jyoti asked quietly, suppressing the anxiety within her. She wanted to touch a power wand in her amulet-vest and increase its soothing flow of Charm through her body, but she restrained herself, not wanting to show weakness before her hired guard. "Reece has no magic. How can he threaten the goblins?"

The assassin watched Jyoti through the shaded slits of her recessed eyes. She heard the harmonics of worry in the margravine's voice and read the hesitant movements in her hands. By these subtle signs, she was well aware of the Peer's flush of anxiety for her lover—the man she had let go to return to the Dark Shore, the man who could prove vital once again to the salvation of the dominions. "I am merely interpreting the behavior of our enemy, margravine. I do not yet understand the full import of their actions. But my brood's assessment of the troll nests in the jungle around Moödrun clearly indicates that the trolls were in position to attack the harbor days before they did. The goblins restrained them until the magus arrived."

Jyoti considered this a moment, then said, "Earl Jee tells me that the airship Reece had booked to carry him into the Spiderlands was destroyed, but he was not on board."

"That is true." Nette motioned for Jyoti to move away from the observation tier railing. "You must not expose yourself to weapons—or to the strong sight of niello eye charms. Assassins and spies abound during these unsettled times. You have no heir, and your brood's position among the Peers is only as secure as your person."

Jyoti frowned. Out of respect for the wizarduke, she had accepted Nette as her weapons master, but she disliked being told what to do. Her grandfather, the renowned warrior Phaz, had trained her from childhood in the ancient fighting techniques, the acrobatic exercises from the far-gone times before Charm, when survival depended upon using the body as a weapon. She felt competent to protect herself. "My brood is not entirely dependent on my survival. I have a brother—"

"Poch," Nette finished for her. "I am well aware of your weakling brother."

Jyoti glared at the assassin. "Your effrontery is insulting. Are you trying to infuriate me?"

Nette shook her head slowly, with restrained exasperation. "You are a proud woman. And you have a right to your pride. You are heir to a noble lineage. The privilege of Charm has not been squandered on you, for you possess beauty without cruelty, power without arrogance, and hope with little delusion. I am honored to serve you. When the wizarduke secured my services, I was skeptical. You had lost everything—your brood, your capital, your wealth, and the magic that might have restored it. I believed your survival among the rapacious scavengers of these dire times unlikely. But in the hundred days I have been with you, I have seen that you are far stronger than most Peers. You have not been softened by a lifetime of Charm. Your illustrious grandfather trained you well. You are resilient enough to thrive on adversity. But—and I say this with no malice— your brother is not. He is a weakling. Charm alone keeps him alive—and so he is vulnerable to every manipulation of Charm."

"And the point of this analysis?" Jyoti asked coldly, her harsh stare not relenting.

"My point is simple." Nette turned her hands palm upward to show her sincerity. "You are the last of your brood. The hope you cherish of reviving Arwar Odawl depends entirely on one fact—your survival."

WHO IN A NIGHTMARE CAN HELP HERSELF?

POCH ARRIVED AT NEW ARWAR IN A CHARMPROP GLIDER PILOTED by Shai Malia. The chrome-winged vessel was the first airship to be admitted into the sky above the reconstructed city since the margravine had returned to create her isolated capital. A small crowd had gathered on the champaign beyond the city's circuit road to watch the glider loop out of the thermal towers of clouds and land on the grassy plain under the dark wall of the jungle.

Henna-red hair tousled by the windy flight, Poch looked jarred and frail as he disembarked, yet the crowd cheered him. He had survived the Dark Lord's torment in the Palace of Abominations to care for the wounded at Blight Fen, and he was respected as the noble brother of the dominion's margravine. He offered a feeble wave in answer to the boisterous shouts from the fur trappers, lumberjacks, and city workers who had gathered to greet him after hearing his flight reports on their avisos.

Shai Malia stepped down from the pilot's pod, and a baffled murmur rippled among the onlookers as the veiled woman followed Poch into the waiting van that Jyoti had sent for them. Rumors had circulated that Poch had become demented because of having him tortured while a prisoner of Hu'dre Vra and that he required the ministrations of a witch to hold on to his sanity. The sight of the petite woman in gray and black veils confirmed this suspicion. When the charmored van pulled away, the bystanders watched in respectful silence, their concerned faces reflecting in the silver-tinted windows.

"They pity me," Poch groused. He squirmed in his seat to peer out the wraparound windows at the quiet group of well-wishers retreating in the distance. "They think I'm an addle-brained casualty of the Conquest."

"They are in awe of you." Shai Malia contradicted him. "You are a heroic survivor of the Dark Lord."

"They cheered until they saw you." A dark look troubled his pale, wide face. "They think you are my healer. I told you we should not have flown in. We should have come by caravan and entered the city quietly."

"We could well be troll scat by now if we had," Shai Malia retorted, parting her veils to show Poch her frown of displeasure. "You realize the goblins are at war with the dominions, and they are looking for vulnerable Peers. Your sister herself told us to fly in."

"All the more reason for us to have come overland." Poch pouted. "I won't have her managing me. I'm not a child anymore. If you would marry me, I could show her I am my own man. An adult. And those gawkers would not now be whispering about my sanity."

Shai Malia softened her look and took his chin in a soothing hand. "I will marry you, Poch. We are meant to be one forever more. But first, you must take your place as margrave."

Poch glanced nervously at the driver's compartment, where a burly guardsman handled the van's steering yoke, separated from his passengers by a smoked-glass partition. "Hush, Shai. We are in Jyoti's court now."

"She cannot hear us." With a blue-enameled fingernail, she tapped the quartz pendant of hearken fetish at his clavicle. "Why do you wear all these amulets if you're not going to use them? See. The quartz is cloudy. No one is eavesdropping. And besides, what is there to hide? You deserve to be margrave. You endured torment in the Palace of Abominations while your sister hid in the wilderness. And after the fall of Hu'dre Vra you stayed on Irth to heal his victims, while your sister traipsed to the Dark Shore, abandoning her responsibilities to adventure beyond the Gulf. How dare she call herself margravine?"

Poch silenced her with both hands upraised. "Please, Shai. Don't breathe a word of these thoughts again. I agreed to come here with you to save ourselves from the trolls and the goblins, not to usurp my sister. I don't want anything of hers. I want my own."

"Then, you must take it."

"Not from her. She may be overbearing toward me at times, but I must remind you that she has had to be both mother and father to me since Arwar fell." He turned a disconsolate look out the window at the steeply graded streets cloistered by stately trees of fiery blossoms. The city looked oddly familiar, the lean, gingerstone buildings as ornately chiseled with sylvan scrollwork as the houses of his childhood, yet too new, too young to bear the ennobling patina of moss, lichen, and ivy. He regretted coming to this unhappy simulacrum of his ancestral home. "We're just here until the goblins are crushed. Then, I'm going back to Blight Fen. I'm happy there as a docent. If you want to come back with me—as my wife—you're welcome. Otherwise, you'd best find your own way. Do you hear me, Shai?"

"You move me when you are strong, Poch." With an impish grin, she kissed his cheek and then pulled her veils over her glistening black curls and dusky face. The van had rolled to a stop before the bluewood colonnade of the margravine's manor, and the hatch door swung open.

Jyoti appeared to Poch virtually unchanged by her active status as margravine. With her streaked hair gathered into a topknot, she was dressed as casually as when their parents were alive and she enjoyed sand-sledding with him. She wore a simple amulet-vest of power wands and eye charms over a blue bodysuit, and apart from the hard-eyed woman in assassin's black at her side, there was no sign of her position as the dominion's ruler. The siblings embraced warmly, and she whispered to him, "You've been away too long."

After they parted, Jyoti nodded coolly to Shai Malia. "Your aunt was a dear friend of our parents. I am glad for this chance to get to know the niece of the conjurer Rica."

The margravine did not wait for a reply from the veiled woman but took her brother by the arm and escorted him into the main hall—like the rest of the city, a replication of what had stood before the Conquest, replete with buttressed walls, recessed windows, and great crossbeams in the vaulted ceiling four storeys above their heads.

Poch listened absently to his sister's happy prattle about having him home and gazed up at the levels of balconies and viewing arcades. As a boy, those niches had been occupied by the members of their brood—uncles, aunts, cousins—who were bound by blood fealty to his parents. But now strangers gawked down at him—charmwrights, merchants, and trade brokers, the extensive commercial entourage that his sister had gathered about herself to finance the building of New Arwar.

"I hear we're broke," he said, interrupting the margravine's enthusiastic exposition on the reclamation of the capital from ruins. "Dig Dog Ltd. underwrote all this—" he waved his hands vaguely at the shadowed carvings, alcoves, and crannies illuminated by long, dusty shafts of light from the distant clerestories—"all this historical construction, and now that Dogbrick has disappeared, the capital brokers want to foreclose."

Jyoti stopped in her tracks and flicked an uneasy look at the veiled woman. "We'll discuss that later, Poch."

"Sure, why not put it off?" He nodded and lifted a dismayed face toward the balconies of strangers in their spidersilk robes and opulent amulet tabards. "I don't blame you, Jyo. Not one bit. Everything we once had is gone. Only this mirage is left. And even that's fading. I don't expect you to have any answers. It's just something that's happening, and it can't be stopped."

He leveled a hard stare at her. "Who in a nightmare can help herself?"

BLACKNESS BURNING

Nox strolled down Broadway on a sultry summer night. With his time-scorched head tightly wrapped in a turban and a caftan draping his lanky body, he drew little attention among the diverse, ethnic crowds basking in the neon auras of the storefronts. Sometimes, dressed more elegantly but just as muffled, he attended the theater, the ballet, the opera. But this night, he chose simply to walk and look at the people streaming through the shining darkness. The flow of life stimulated him, reminding him what he strove to attain: life, life eternal, and the purpose of life—desire and its fulfillment.

He watched lovers clinging to each other; babies snug in pouches harnessed to their parents; toddlers in strollers or riding on obliging shoulders; children scampering; adolescents prowling; adults conversing on street corners and in sidewalk bistros; and the old people, the geriatric ones that time had worn away to dismal shapes of their former selves.

He was such an old one. He remembered his first pangs of decay in the palaestra of Mycenae, where the heads of thieves nailed to poles had become hives of maggots, a warning to the hill bandits troubling the farms. *How long ago was that?* Three millennia before this sweltering night of noisy buses and cars spewing noxious fumes.

That had been the season of myths. Standing in the shadows at the gates of the market, listening to cries of babies, the farmers hawking their produce, he had watched the athletes, glossy with oil, emerging from the gymnasium, crossing the courtyard of the palaestra to the contest field, not even noticing the piked heads, so intent were they on their own prowess.

Until that day, he could have competed with any of them. But he felt it then, for the first time—the stiffness of his hips, the ache in his knees. He had been touched by time. His body had begun to die. He heard the warning of the severed heads.

So long ago . . . Since that far-gone time, all his magic had only delayed the inevitable. Even walking had become strenuous, especially in this humid summer heat. He paused in the air-conditioned sanctuary of an electronics shop, regarding the latest computerized trinkets from Asia. A clerk approached, saw his leprous face, and stood back while Nox fidgeted with a handheld electric fan. The whirling yellow fins of soft plastic stopped harmlessly at a touch, and he smiled, revealing his tiny seed-corn teeth. With a whisper, he announced to the mesmerized clerk that he would take this toy. He departed, training the fan on the sweaty iguana creases of his neck, while behind him the imaginary sale was rung up.

For a while he strolled with his face upturned, cooling his hollow cheeks and gazing through the halogen murk of the night at the darkness burning with a few rare stars. He was determined to live to see those stars burn out. He would live long enough to walk off Earth to other worlds, other suns. He would live forever. And though he had entertained doubts of this ambition after time had begun to wither him, recently the possibility of eternal life seemed plausible again.

In a trance he had seen the beastman trekking through the north woods. He possessed the power Nox needed to rejuvenate himself. He had to be summoned. That was delicate work. Nox knew that the beastman—Dogbrick, his companion had called him—had the magic of another order of creation. He could reshape reality as powerfully as Duppy Hob, the magician who had come to this planet before the beastmarked man. But this new arrival lacked the awareness of a magician and so was more readily accessible—and far more dangerous.

Laughter ferried him into a sidestreet, toward the Eternal Ones of the Dance. *Ah!* They wore different faces, but they were the same ones he had met before on the mud banks of the Euphrates, in the festival plazas of Nineveh, around the ritual fires of Dionysus at Thebes, in the alleys of Rome, on a sidestreet in the Alhambra, in the heat waves of seven thousand summers. A young princess of the Gypsies and her consorts danced a rhumba to a bongo drum; the old jazz baron, king of song, sat on the stone steps, clapping his hands and stamping his feet; the blare of a trumpet in a third-storey window called down to earth the spirits of small paradise, haunt of dead lovers and lost children, and the hot air curled with honeysuckle and reefer smoke.

They recognized him, too, when he sashayed into their dance, his caftan jumping with his happy steps as he moved to the drum. Dancing, he shared his magic with the Eternal Ones and their latest disguises, frenzied, reckless with something crazed, something darker, waking in them something hungry for the light and lighter on their feet, lifting them with hollow bones, spry as spirits, into splendor and the holy madness of the dance.

Grinning hideously, the drummer played faster, and the princess and her shirtless consorts danced quicker and more lively than in any of their lives, their wide, bright grins blurs in the neon shine. And the turbaned man pranced among them, light and nimble, singing in a high eerie voice how love would never die, how love would dance forever and carry them all from life to life. And from high overhead, the trumpet rode the crest of their frantic rhythms with a scream like a soul spilling into the night.

Nox left his battery-powered miniature fan with the old man on the steps and ambled with satisfaction toward Columbus Avenue. The dance had enlivened and emboldened him. He would speak with the dead. He would consult with those who had gone before. To master Dogbrick, he needed information. If he miscalculated with these beings of a hotter reality, all that he had carefully built for himself over the millennia would be lost. Yet if he successfully manipulated this creature, he could master not only his own life but the world entire.

Alas! The dead were bound to nothingness, and to speak with them required blood heat. *Who will it be?* He looked into each face that he passed on the street of intermittent trees, each tree in its iron cage. One of the apartment buildings on Central Park West belonged to a coven member, and he briefly thought of using her. That was the ritual end that awaited each of them eventually: When they had served their lives out and had begun to dodder, he took them into the park and splashed their blood heat to attract the dead. That way, he had a chance to converse with friends of elder times, and no covener was remanded to an arbitrary death in a nursing home. But the member he had in mind was not doddering yet, and finding a suitable replacement in time for the next meeting in Octoberland would be far more difficult than choosing a victim.

Nox took no relish in this necessary work. He had marked out no place in his heart for murder. He preferred a swift and clean ritual act. It was the dead that he wanted, not the killing.

On the steps of the Museum of Natural History, he spied an old woman feeding birds. Something in his chest told him that this was the one. The startled look of surprise on her worn face lasted only an instant when he stood before her, bowing to bring his skull-shrunk face close to hers. Then he whispered her name, and she rose, almost weightless.

Together, they walked through the webs of light toward the park and its fields of darkness. The birds followed them as if they were saints.

I HIDE IN THE SKY

THE BLOOD HEAT DREW THE GHOSTS, AND NOX WAVED THEM OFF with muttered curses. Drug addicts and suicides came first, as usual. After them wavered the bewildered dead, the accident victims and stroke-struck taken swiftly in mid-stride of their busy lives. Grumbling unhappily, he dismissed them all. Those that lingered, he jolted with cold fire so that they flitted away wailing—a whistle of the wind.

"Duppy!" he called among the ectoplasmic shadows smeared on the darkness. "Duppy Hob!"

"He is not among us." A calm voice spoke from out of the panting wind.

"Who are you?" The sound of that voice, so distinct and reverberant among the thin mewlings of the dead, announced a presence of a stronger reality. "What is your name?"

"I am Caval—a wizard from Irth."

"What age of Earth?" Nox inquired, baffled that such a strong being could have arisen on this cold planet.

"Not this world. I am from Irth among the Bright Worlds— Irth of the Seven Dominions."

"Yes, yes!" Nox's bones shook like sticks, he trembled so violently with excitement. "I know of your world. Duppy Hob fell to Earth from your world—long ago."

"Duppy Hob is dead, slain in Gabagalus. His forlorn ghost wanders the ocean bottom, held fast at night by the Charm of the sunken continent and held fast at daybreak by the radiance of the Abiding Star. You will never see Duppy Hob again."

"How do you know this, Caval? And why are you here, so far from your world at the beginning of time?"

"Like you, I am a sorcerer. I trained here on the Dark Shore as a youth. It was Duppy Hob summoned me here then, though I knew it not at the time. I know it now. As a ghost, I know a great deal now."

"Show yourself to me, Caval, sorcerer of Irth." Nox squinted to discern the voice's source. "Let me see your countenance."

"I am here, Nox of Jarmo, Nox from the foothills of the Zagros Mountains."

Nox looked left and right, saw nothing, then turned and

confronted a tall, robust man, who wore his bright red hair cropped close to his chiseled head, his orange whiskers precisely trimmed to outline the sharp angle of his long jaw and the stern contours of his hard mouth. Garbed in bright tinsel and blue gauze windings, he appeared to Nox like a fierce mummer out of a carnival parade.

A small shout escaped the coven master, for he had never beheld a phantom so fully realized, so humanly whole. He reached out a scaly hand, and the apparition sifted under his touch like bright dust, not forming again where he had touched its tingling, magnetic texture. "By the gods themselves! You *are* a being of the first light! How came you here and I did not see you climb down our sky?"

"I have told you. Duppy Hob summoned me. And he kept me well hidden for a terrible purpose—a monstrous hope of mastering the author of the worlds herself."

"The Queen of Heaven, Dumuzi-abzu, the Quickener of Life in the Deep—" Nox felt dizzy and backed away a step from the vivid wraith, frightened by the hard stare of its cold eyes. "How can that be? Can the wizards of the first light master the gods themselves? Is that possible? Speak the truth, dead one!"

Caval smiled thinly. "You have not summoned me to hear how Duppy Hob hoped to master the author of worlds and failed. Why am I here before you, Nox, who learned his magic in Eridu from the steppe wanderers, the wayfarers on the plains beneath the star houses?"

"How do you know so much of me, of my origins?"

"When first I came to the Dark Shore, I built a laboratory for myself in the sky. There, I gathered the very rare and most powerful Charm peculiar to this side of the Gulf so that I would have greater strength in my own world. Before I left, I sprinkled enough of that Charm behind me to find my way back should I ever lose my body among the Bright Worlds and be cast into the Gulf. When that fate finally did befall me, I simply allowed my soul to follow the crumbs of Charm to my old haunt on the Dark Shore. Now, I hide in the sky. From there, I see everything—everything that is and all that was."

"Then you know of Dogbrick?"

The ghost nodded, a light of revelation brightening in its eyes. "So that is my use to you, Nox of Octoberland. You wish to harness the power that Dogbrick carries unwittingly from the Bright Worlds—to heal your time-ravaged body."

"Will you help me?" Nox asked eagerly.

"I am but a ghost. My power is too dim to change anything."

"Not you, wizard. Dogbrick. Will you help me to win his magic?"

Caval gestured to the dead woman lying faceup on the grass, her breastbone split and her viscera glistening purple in the dull light. "I was reared among the Sisterhood of Witches and sworn to break evil and discipline madness. Look at what you have done, Nox, and then tell me if you are worthy of my help."

"She was an old, decrepit woman!" Nox protested shrilly. "Death had her in his jaws before I found her."

"If she was worthy of destruction, are you not even further jammed in death's jaws and thus all the more ready for doom?" Caval pressed closer, his angry stare hardening to a scowl. "I am your enemy, Nox. I am the enemy of everyone like you. And if I have my chance, I will destroy you!"

Nox swiped his hands through the face of the ghost, clawing away the wrathful expression until only a headless phantom remained. Then, he hurled cold fire at what remained and burned it to charred shadows and the stink of burned vomit.

Panting, he backed out of the glade and left the hungry ghosts to feed on the dimming heat of the corpse, the old woman's ghost herself in the midst of them, jostled, startled to find herself among the ravenous wraiths, her familiar face staring sightlessly up at her above her cleaved torso.

Striding with angry vigor, Nox returned to the brilliant pools of light around the museum. Ghosts followed him like gnats.

He shooed them off and paced along the walkway to the planetarium, muttering to himself.

Caval was a ghost and could be mastered like any ghost. The coven would give Nox the power. He considered how soon he could begin to gather more cold fire and if the phase of the moon was ripe enough for massing the strength he would need.

He stopped abruptly. A slithery sound rustled the hedges at the bottom slope of the footpath. A long shadow stretched across the reach of the lamplight there, and the old woman shoved through the shrubbery, her blue bowels in her hands.

A passerby screamed; two others shouted. Nox stood and stared and stared. He discerned the astral shimmer around her as she staggered onto the path: The shine that the wizard Caval's power was animating her corpse; and her face was a rubber mask, her eyes clouded.

One hand lifted, ropes of viscera dangling, and pointed toward him. Her mouth sagged open as if to speak before she collapsed in a lifeless heap as Caval's strength dimmed.

Nox turned and walked off without glancing back. At his heels, in the stifling heat of the summer night, a cold wind spun.

IN THE FOREST EVIL

BY DAY'S END, DOGBRICK AND MARY FELIX HAD CROSSED THE highland meadows of wildflowers, the carpeted acres of purple gentian and blue morning glory, and stood in scarlet light before a primeval forest. No track entered the perpetual gloom of the trees, yet a singing sifted from far within the dark interior, a droning song broken close to silence by the wind. It came and went like surf.

"Do you hear that?" Dogbrick asked.

Mary stood staring up at the cold voids hanging among the early stars. The absence of arthritis pain for the first time in years left her feeling airy as the sky. In the violet depths she watched the galaxy venting its glowing vastness across the void. Her renewed youth drank deeply of this vitality, the vaporous shine from billions of suns folding like milk to the horizon. "What?"

Dogbrick listened and heard only the droning of bees from some hive in the high branches. The stink of bear wafted dully from scat hours old. "Come." He turned his back on the agate evening, and he shoved through undergrowth of soft-barbed thorns and entered the forest.

Among draperies of hanging ivy and a fallen tree flanged with mushrooms, he wove the cold fire to a dreamy sunlight. An owl called. He straddled the log, and Mary sat cross-legged on the leaf mulch. Her young face shone with expectation, her luxuriantly jumbled masses of chestnut hair aglint with sequins of caught light.

"No one will find us here tonight," he said, glancing around at the high storeys and their burdens of darkness. "We have a chance now to know what has happened to us."

"You have the magic, Dogbrick." She held out her young hands and turned them in the saffron light. "Look at how you've changed me. I was a seventy-nine-year-old woman. I'm nineteen again!"

"But I don't know how I did it." The orange eyes in his bestial face gleamed with a worried sapience. "I feel that this strength is using me."

A giddy fright swarmed in Mary. She stared at the hulking figure astride the dead tree like some ensorcelled animal king of a fairy tale, and she asked with hushed temerity, "Then why are we here? It's night in the wilderness—I'm young again! And you—you look like a regal beast. This feels like a medieval story to me, as if we are in the forest evil."

"You sense it, too?"

"Sense what?" she asked nervously, her fright thickening to a cold syrup in her bones.

"Evil." His tufted ears lifted and moved independently, sampling the forest sounds. "That's what you said—evil."

"Maybe we should go," she offered gently. "Come with me and meet my friends, my colleagues. I know you don't want to—but you have so much to offer us! And what can we hope to find out here? I'm a scientist, and I can take you to our world's best minds. They will help you."

Dogbrick shook his head adamantly. "The others—the Sasquatch—they knew to stay away from your kind. I trust them. I don't belong in your world. You go. Don't think about it. Just take the strength I've given you and go. Leave me here."

"I want to know more first—about you." She rose to her knees and reached for the cold fire that he had shaped earlier and left nodding beside him like a large glass flower, a candescent polyp breathing the night air. "There must be a way to use this magic on you—to help you remember who you are, where you come from."

Dogbrick heard it again—a surf of singing voices, droning in the distance. "What is that?"

She listened and sensed the wind writhing in the sedge, scudding among the boughs. "I don't hear anything." The cold fire tickled her wrists. Wonder widened through her, and she discovered that she could shape the blue plasma. She fashioned gloves for her hands and held them up to her magical companion. "Look."

He showed his fangs in a vague smile and gave her more strength, until the fire that sheathed her hands shone a frosty green, almost white. When she stood up and came to him, he did not object and did not move as she laid her radiant hands upon his brow. Her hands felt cool, and their chill rang through his brain.

A dream-bright vision opened in Mary, and she saw herself standing on a brown curb on a narrow, high street of old cobblestones and paving bricks. Lean, high houses of glistening blue-black rock with round windows ranged up and down the steep lane, strange barnacle houses affixed to a cliff-side lane. Between the houses, she glimpsed factory flues and luminous fumes crawling through the alleys, bright as moon smoke. And overhead, in the narrow track of sky, planetary orbs glowed among cometary veils of fiery translucence.

"Saxar—" she breathed softly.

Dogbrick jolted. "Saxar—the sea-cliff city of my dreams!" He stared sharply at the young, dreamy face. "What else do you see?"

Mary removed her shining hands from Dogbrick's brow and placed them against her own forehead. The vision sharpened. She staggered backward, shoved by an inrush of memories, names, images—all the world of Irth now a single stream of thought abruptly crammed into her consciousness. It was as if God was thinking about Dogbrick and Saxar, and the divine attention had joined with her own small mind, a speck of dust flung into a huge world: *Worlds!* Nemora and its icy caves, volcanic Hellsgate, World's End so close to the charmful brilliance of the Abiding Star. . . .

She collapsed, her mind overflowing with alien knowledge, stuffed with a lifetime of remembrance, a drawer that would not close.

Dogbrick crouched over her, trembling with worry. He gave her strength, and she shuddered but did not rise. The power drove her deeper into her vision of worlds beyond the Gulf. A strange, yet familiar destiny had seized her and escorted her to a central place within her being where all reality touched. The more power that Dogbrick fed to her, the more strongly she bonded with this unitary center, this oneness that underlay both the Bright Worlds and the Dark Shore.

And there, she felt her own small life like a flimsy web, mostly emptiness, glistening with impressions gathered from her lifetime on Earth. And at the very center, at the core absence of herself, she found them—the goblins. Small as dolls with large, round, hairless heads and droopy eyes of cracked crystal, the dear ones watched her. She could feel their telepathic allure. They wanted hex-gems. They had depleted the Charm in the cache they held, and they needed more to continue their mastery of the trolls and ogres. Their little eyes gleamed like hex-gems, mesmerizing her with their need. . . .

Dogbrick shook Mary, but she remained inert. He felt her throat for the knock of her pulse, though he already knew it was there. He could feel her life, feel the seething warmth of her body's cellular kinesis. Yet the more strength he gave her the deeper she seemed to sink into dreaming.

He reached into her with his mind and stood before solid emptiness.

He pulled out with a howl that made the forest quiet.

Through the silence, he heard the far off singing he had sensed before. Quickly, he lifted Mary in his arms and carried her body among the looming trees toward the voices. They grew more distinct, and he heard the dolefulness of their chanting, warbling something about the night's remorse for the day's vanity.

Their cries melted toward silence, then crisped louder. He felt with the hairs of his soul that they were coming and going from this world, yet he did not turn to flee from them. The woman who had tried to help him had fallen into jeopardy because of him, and he had to see if these ghostly presences could save her. He was not afraid of them.

With horrified clarity, he understood that the evil he had sensed in the forest was himself.

SINISTER ANGELS

IN A MOON-BRIGHT CLEARING, HE FOUND THEM—A CIRCLE OF twelve sinister angels. They were ectoplasmic shapes, men and women white as packed snow with blurred wings of thermally wrinkled air. Their eyes shone green as star-bright flecks of twilight, and their alabaster faces sneered with the malevolence of bats. At their center a gristly skeleton danced, a ghost shape of a naked man withered to his bones, light leaking through flesh waxy as a lampshade.

"Come, Dogbrick, come!" The ghost skeleton beckoned. He laughed, his face like a whiskery fish—scoop cheeked, the silvered brow dented at the sides where the ears had shriveled to holes. The cod between his legs dangled like dripped tar. "Come into Octoberland!"

"Who are you?" Dogbrick called from the mossy ledge of an uplifted root. "What manner of beings are you? Ghosts? How do you know my name?"

The circle of malefic angels stopped singing and opened to a line of alternating men and women. Their nakedness looked as beautiful as their faces were wicked. Even the eldest among them had firm torsos and elegant limbs, all shining with moon fire. Only the central figure appeared malformed, aged to a caricature of death itself. He smiled, showing tiny discolored teeth. "We are not ghosts. We are the living. Our bodies of light have been projected into these woods to reach you—to help you."

"I heard you in the field and saw something before that in the deep woods." The apparition he had encountered in the daylight had displayed color and more substance. "Who are you?"

"We are Octoberland." The thin, fluorescent-tube arms waved him closer. "We have been watching you since you arrived in our world, Dogbrick. We have been trying to contact you. But we are far away, and it is difficult to project our bodies of light. Come. Join us in our dance and let us share our magic and our knowledge with you."

Dogbrick hesitated, alarmed by the cruelty of their stares. "You frighten me. You look . . . evil."

"Have you looked at yourself recently?" The skeleton laughed with zestful mirth. "Like yourself, we are warriors against evil. But, as we say in this world, one must fight fire with fire. And so we wear the ferocity of our enemies, the wicked ones who deceive their victims with cruel beauty. Look at me!" The revenant turned to reveal the knobby length of his spine, the palings of his ribs, and the flat razors of his pelvic bones. "I have worn myself to the brink of death fighting the wicked of this dark world. I have given everything I have to break evil and discipline madness. Now I am at the brink of death—but I do not despair. My life has been well spent."

"You are wizards?" Dogbrick asked hopefully.

"Yes, yes, wizards!" The bone ghost gusted forward as if borne on a forceful wind. "I am the wizard Nox. And this is Octoberland, my coven. We draw power from the sky, from the auroras, the magnetic field of the planet." Nox lifted a smoky hand and pointed a splintery finger at Mary. "And who is this? She seems to be a woman of our world. Is she ill? Perhaps our magic can heal her."

"Can you?" Dogbrick stepped down from the mossy ledge and approached Nox. "She has tried to help me remember who I am—and she fell into a trance."

"You have no recollection of yourself?" Nox asked, intrigued.

"None." He lifted the tranced body of Mary Felix toward the phantom. "Can you wake her?"

"Come—come into the circle." Nox waved toward where the coven wraiths had taken their places again. "We will use our magic to wake her."

Dogbrick carried Mary toward the effluvial gathering of Octoberland, but before he reached the circle, a voice called from behind. "Dogbrick—stop! You are in danger!"

Within a shaft of tarnished moonlight between the trees, a narrow figure emerged: a stern man with a trim beard wearing bright, tinsel raiment. Dogbrick did not recognize him and called out, "Who are you?"

"I am the ghost of the wizard Caval," he announced in a bold voice as he advanced. His body vanished in the dark spaces and reappeared wherever thin shafts of moonlight lanced the glade. "I was slain in the Dark Lord's Palace of Abominations and my soul drifted into the Gulf to this cold world on the Dark Shore. Heed me, Dogbrick, and stand back from those evil ones."

"*He* is the evil one!" Nox shouted. "Do not be deceived, Dogbrick! This is a spirit that has destroyed many a gullible soul. Beware!"

Caval glared angrily at Nox. "Look at him! And regard me. Whom do you trust, Dogbrick?"

"Appearances deceive," Nox growled, dashing to the protective center of the coven circle. "He is a master of deception. Use your power against him, Dogbrick! Smash him with your strength and protect yourself—protect the woman in your arms. Protect us!"

"Dogbrick—" Caval turned a firm but benign aspect upon the beastmarked man. "I never met you among the dominions. But as a ghost, I saw you in the garden of the Dark Lord's palace— with Tywi. I fought beside your staunch friend Ripcat. I served the margravine Jyoti Odawl and her brother, Poch. I fought the lord of the cacodemons, Hu'dre Vra! Trust me! Come away from these vile creatures and spare yourself and the woman you carry."

Dogbrick shook his maned head. "You confuse me with these names—Tywi, Ripcat, Jyoti, Poch. . . ."

"You recognize them—you must!" The ghost came forward in stripes of moon glow, tinsel-bound arms grasping. "Open your mind to memory. . . ."

"Don't let him touch you!" Nox shouted. "You will die!"

Dogbrick dropped to his knees and rolled Mary onto the forest floor. With both hands, he heaved cold fire at the ghost, and it splashed over the striding figure in sticky flames.

For a moment, Caval writhed in agony, then dissolved into

sparkling motes that flurried like blown pollen and thinned away on the wind.

"You've saved us!" Nox stepped through the circle, his skullish face jubilant. "Well done, Dogbrick! Well done!"

Dogbrick lifted Mary again in his arms. "Will you heal her now?"

"Of course!" Nox ushered the couple into the circle. "Octoberland receives you into our care. Lay the woman at the center and stand back, Dogbrick. Stand back."

Dogbrick did as instructed, gently placing Mary Felix among the enclosing wraiths. He stepped back from the circle and watched as the slow walking dance and droning singing commenced again. In moments, a fog rose up from the bottom of his cranium, and his knees wobbled.

"Sit down," Nox advised, stepping from the circle to his side. "We are using your power to undo what you have done to this poor woman. You are feeling groggy. But that is not to be feared. Sit down. That's good. Sit and rest." Fingers of smoke touched Dogbrick between the eyes, and sounds became cottony. "Your power is joining ours to heal this good woman. Yes. Close your eyes. That is good. Close your eyes and sleep. When you awaken, all will be well."

HOW THE WITCHES LIVE

REECE WATCHED FROM THE GONDOLA WINDOW AS THE RAINBOW Forests of Bryse drifted below. The prismatic trees gleamed with jeweled daylight. At night, under the incandescent sky, the woods shimmered like the sea. He kept apart and refused the food the witch Esre offered him from the dirigible's galley. When he slept, he strapped himself into one of the cushioned seats to keep his charmless body from floating about the cabin, adrift on the nocturnal tide that hoisted all charmless things into the Gulf.

He dreamt of a large cat, a lynx or a bobcat. It was jerked an inch off the ground by a harness, its claws scratching frantically for purchase. A leering charmwright held the harness, while a veiled witch slid famous manuscripts under the flying claws, shredding folios and scrolls beneath the panicked talons of the snagged beast—*The Talismanic Odes* ripped to confetti, the Gibbet Scrolls tattered. . . .

He woke with a start. Mount Szo, the glassy capital of Bryse, loomed on the horizon. Its heraldic, stained-glass towers and crystal spires flashed with dawn light at the summit of a mountain flanked by gorges of spectral trees and morning vapors.

The dirigible glided into the trestle moorings of the city's sky bund, and when Esre opened the hatch a wisp of a witch garbed entirely in black veils entered. The scarred woman curtsied deeply and stood aside with the solemn announcement, "Von, witch queen of the Sisterhood."

The diminutive witch parted her black veils, showing a youthful almost perfectly round face, and smiled benignly at Reece. "Magus, thank you for heeding the summons of our Sisterhood."

"Heeding?" Reece stood up angrily, but the weight of his dream held down his ire. He understood that the frantic cat was himself, Ripcat, harnessed by his need for Charm to stay alive in the Bright Worlds. He had to calm himself, for the dream warned him that the witches would offer much of value, which his rage could destroy. "I was taken by force, Lady Von. And many others were sacrificed so that I could be brought here."

"The goblins force our hand, magus." The witch queen nodded to Esre. "Each of us in the Sisterhood has a gift from the Goddess that we give to life. There are healers, teachers, and mechanics in our service. I myself was a veil dancer. Esre comes from the Brood of Assassins, and her assessment of danger and her skills at survival are exquisitely developed. If she sacrificed others, they died for a greater good, I assure you. She is a witch, and her first priority is life."

Reece held in mind his dream and its vibrant warning and simply nodded.

"Come, magus." The witch queen took his hand and led him through the hatchway. "You are hungry and without Charm. I will feed and clothe you, and we will discuss the latest evil to beset the dominions."

On the scaffold walkway of the sky bund, Reece winced against the glare of the brilliant morning reflected in the many facets of the glass city. He searched the crisscrossed levels of catwalks and platforms and saw the usual stevedores in their orange, padded bodysuits guiding giant crates and bales with the aid of hover charms—but no guards, security officers, or soldiers. The unimposing figure of Esre offered the only protection. "The trolls have not attacked here yet?"

"Not so long as I am here." Von waved a black scarf at a skyline of amber domes, belfries of peach glass, and pyramids of mirror gold. "This is a beautiful city, isn't it? That is why I am here and not in my sanctuary at Andezé Crag. The goblins know better than to attack witches and warlocks. Goblins are telepathic creatures, and we have the skills to baffle and hurt them. But there are too few of us to protect all of Irth, too few, indeed, after the slaughter of the Dark Lord's Conquest. That is why we need your help, magus."

Esre opened the grilled gate, and they entered the cage of a drop-lift.

"Lady Von—" Reece peered into the queen's round face, veiled again behind jet gauze. "I am no longer a magus. I lost my magic—"

"I know." She patted his arm consolingly as barred shadows blurred through the cage as they descended. "You lost your magic on the Dark Shore. The devil worshipper Duppy Hob used you as he used Caval before you. And now Duppy Hob is dead and your magic is gone. Yet, you are still a magus—a man trained to climb between worlds, to converse with the invisibles, to catch the dead. That is what brought you here among us, isn't it?"

"I can't do those things anymore." He placed both of his hands on his naked chest. "I am just what you see. A man."

"A man of the Dark Shore—here among the Bright Worlds." The drop-lift stopped softly at ground level, and Esre opened the gate on a brick street fronted by corrugated storehouses. "You are a unique man on Irth, and one who has encountered evil before and triumphed. You were central to the downfall of both Hu'dre Vra and Duppy Hob. That counts for much against the monstrosities we face now. The goblins fear you, and you are worthy of their fear."

They emerged among the sadder regions of the radiant city, the impoverished purlieus in the shadow of the sky bund, where the near-charmless scavenged a dire existence from the castoffs of the wealthy importers. People grown old without Charm labored in a refuse lot, rummaging for kindling among damp, discarded crates. Others spooled the spider skeins of wrapping nets. Families in their loose rags filed past with sleepy children, inspecting the gutters for whatever edible produce had toppled off the morning delivery trucks. In the warehouse alleys, squatters watched Esre and Reece with worn eyes, then lolled their heads when no charity was offered.

A tent of faded awnings and weather-bleached canvas occupied a desolate lot between ramshackle storage sheds, long ago abandoned by the importers and now used as hovels by the street people. The witch queen invited him into the tent. "My residence on Mount Szo."

"You live *here*?" Reece gawked at the crude cane chairs and upended fruit crates that served as seats. Several rope hammocks had been secured to the interior tent walls like macramé hangings to make room for a splintered trestle table. On the table lay some mold-peppered boxes of herbs and plant cuttings, a hide box, a cast-iron jar, a purse of bones, several handblown bottles of oily ungents, a small alcohol burner, and pins and cloth strips—the crude tools for crafting witch amulets, talismans of humble Charm sufficient to keep the charmless from drifting away on the nocturnal tide.

Reece glanced at the black newt's eyes in the iron jar and the white star pearls in the hide box, the cheapest hex-gems. "You are the witch queen. How can you live like this?"

"Some of my predecessors preferred more opulent surroundings, it is true." Von sat on a melon crate and offered a cane chair to Reece. "But I have chosen to live as most of the Sisterhood lives. Each witch is a wife of darkness. We are married to what most requires the light of the Abiding Star. That is our purpose, to tend the needs of the charmless."

"A noble calling, Lady Von." Reece allowed a hint of ill humor in his voice. "But don't you think your energy would be best spent trying to convert wealthy Peers to the campaign of stamping out poverty?"

"Oh, magus, you misunderstand our purpose." The witch queen parted her veils to show a concerned frown. "We do not hope to overcome poverty. Poverty will heal itself when darkness no longer shrouds the human heart. We live to bring light to the darkness. That is why we called you here."

THE RETURN OF RIPCAT

THE TENT FLAP OPENED, AND SEVERAL WITCHES ENTERED WITH BURL bowls of steaming porridge, small loaves of berry bread, and a basket of fruits. "Please, eat." The witch queen accepted a clay flask from one of her attendants and unstoppered it. "Sparkling Szo water, the finest in the dominion. Please, drink."

"Though I would like to help you, Lady Von, I cannot." He sipped from the flask to wet his dry throat, the better to explain himself. "My friend Dogbrick is stranded on the Dark Shore, and I must go back for him. If you will help me get him back, I will do all that I can—"

Reece stopped in mid-sentence. A chill widened through him and a melancholy, as if he were inside a great sadness, inside chance where all will had been forfeit.

"Remain calm." Lady Von swept to his side and put her warm hands on his icy face. "The Szo water has been charged with wort of Gabagalus. Not much. Not enough to induce telepathy, only receptivity."

Reece grabbed the witch queen's wrists, wanting to push her away. Before he could act, she pressed her veiled forehead to his brow. An image fluttered over his sight like a windy scrim: Flames strobed from the windows and rooftops of a tiered jungle city.

"New Arwar—" Reece groaned, transfixed as the sudden vision zoomed along mazy, cobbled streets frantic with trolls. People lay eviscerated and dying in the gutters—and among that gory crowd he glimpsed Jyoti's brindled topknot, her face lacquered with blood, her torn body a rag doll stabbed by the claws of a monster. He struggled to push to his feet.

"Calm yourself, magus." The witch queen's breath smelled resinous as a split pine, and he knew that some magical plant was working in her. "What you see has not yet happened. But it will. The Sisterhood and Brotherhood have both seen this, and it is certain. Unless—"

Reece stared with fevered eyes at her face. "Unless what? What do you want of me?"

"Not you, Reece Morgan." She moved back from him and drew the gauzy jet veils again over her face. "We need Ripcat."

He tried to rub the frostiness from his face and told her with glum truthfulness, "I don't have the magic anymore. I have lost my beastmarks."

"The Sisterhood will provide the magic—if you will once more wear those beastmarks."

He shook his head. "I'm just one man. What can I do that all your witches and wizards cannot?"

"You can save your lover, Jyoti Odawl," Esre said gruffly, "and New Arwar, and all the cities in all the dominions of Irth."

Lady Von placed a restraining hand on the maimed witch, and through a slit in her sheer mask her dark eyes fixed on Reece. "The goblins are telepathic, but they cannot reach into your mind when you are Ripcat—a man from the Dark Shore shielded by beastmarks."

Esre nodded. "No one else on Irth can track them down and kill them before they use the trolls, the ogres, the basilisks, and everything else they can inflame to kill us. Only you."

"What about the Goblin Wars of the past?" He shot her a harsh, sidelong glance. "You defeated them then."

"We didn't *kill* them, magus," Lady Von answered. "We drove them into exile. It took thousands of days and many thousands more in lives, whole dominions driven mad." She laid a hand upon his shoulder, and he felt her placid strength. "The dominions are far weaker now than we were then. Hu'dre Vra has slain too many of the best among us. We can't win against the goblins this time. And they know it. That's why they've come back."

"What about Dogbrick?" Reece asked, weakly. "I can't leave him marooned on the Dark Shore."

"Do you want to bring him back to an Irth ravaged by goblins?" Esre whittled her voice to a sharp whisper, not wanting to panic the people outside the tent. "Do you want to come back and find New Arwar a heap of ash and your Jyoti gutted by trolls?"

Reece's shoulders sagged, and he spoke with cold resignation. "Give me your magic, witch. I will wear the beastmarks—and we will kill goblins."

Esre grinned. "When we are done with the goblins, Reece Morgan, I will accompany you to the Dark Shore, to bring back your friend."

Reece nodded sullenly and accepted the small, dark emerald that Lady Von produced from the folds of her robes.

"Grasp this hard," she instructed. "The Charm in the hex-gem will provoke your beastmarks."

For Jyoti's sake, he took the emerald and closed his fist around it. A fiery strength blazed up behind his eyes. Sounds poured into him more brightly: Distinctly he heard his heart slamming, the witches whispering, chanting behind their veils, and the drop-lifts several blocks away, winching bales of goods from the trade dirigibles to the waiting trucks in their berths.

Colors sharpened. He saw the tiny, tight weave of the witch queen's gossamer mask and behind it the shadowy details of her staring eyes, wide, alert, watching the changes coming over him.

He glanced down at his hands and chest. Blue fur hazed over his flesh like a mist he could swipe away. But when he brushed at it, the fumes tightened to a pelt with a nap dense as velvet. His furred fingers pulsed, and black claws curled from their tips. He retracted them at once and fisted his hands, shaking them at the witch with a curling howl.

The witch queen did not budge, other than to reach to the table, upend the plate of loaves, and hold the silvered disk toward him. The oval mirror at its center reflected a round head with cub ears and slant brow under a mantle of short blue fur. Oblique green eyes blinked, and snarling black lips exposed two braces of fangs.

Anger lurched him to his feet. His tinsel-seamed trousers bulged, stretched by his packed muscles, and the leather of his ankle-length boots swelled. Animal fury whelmed up in him, filling the vacancy that his own magic had once occupied. He raged at his losses and what seemed to him a trap that the witch queen had sprung on him.

Aghast, Ripcat remembered his last dream as Reece and realized it had foretold that the charmwrights would harness him in this feline form for the witches. He howled again, and his fist came down on the table, smashing it to spinning splinters.

His claws flashed open, and he lifted them, trembling with violence, before the witch.

Esre jumped to intercede, but Lady Von motioned her aside. The witch queen threw off her cowl of veils, exposing her round face with its shorn brown hair. "If you must kill me to fulfill your rage, I will not resist and none of the Sisterhood will avenge me. Strike if you must."

Again, his dream haunted him. She had placed herself beneath his furious claws like a precious manuscript, the masterwork of her Sisterhood, Irth's greatest humanitarian hope. Ire wrenched in him, held in check. His claws retracted. *"Aaarrh!"* He spun away and burst out of the tent.

Esre caught up with him as he stalked across the vacant lot, startling squatters in their cardboard huts and making children scream with fright. "Where are you going?"

Ripcat glared at her and showed his fangs.

Esre swept back her veils and shoved herself in front of him, confronting him with her patchwork face and a hard stare from her one eye. "Where are you going, Ripcat?"

"Get out of my way, witch." He slashed one hand before her, an inch from her good eye and yet too fast to see, its wind gusting the veils from her shoulders. "Don't try to throw me around again, Esre. I'm five times stronger than I was."

"Steady, Ripcat. Your wrath is a side effect of the transformation. It's irrational. Control it!" She dared place her hands on his furred shoulders and felt his bunched muscles. "We need you to stop the goblins. Help us."

The plea in her voice cut through his animal ferocity, and he remembered who he was, remembered Jyoti and Dogbrick.

"Where are they?" He glared at the scarred witch. "These goblins, where are they?"

Esre paced beside him as he strode high hackled through the weeds. "Calm yourself first. Calm." She pointed to the wild-eyed children with lean gray faces who watched him in terror from behind a desolate yard tree. "Think about the margravine and what she would want of you."

Ripcat stopped beside the old stone footings of a lost warehouse. At the mention of Jyoti, he slung his head forward, fangs gleaming. "Where are the goblins?"

A lopsided smile graced Esre's scarred face, and her hand tightened with heart-strong vigor on his shoulder. "We will have to track them down, Ripcat. They are small and wickedly clever. But they stay together. They must cleave to one another for the telepathic strength they need to possess the trolls and other beasts. The Sisterhood will guide us."

"Us?" The puma-stripes bracketing his hollow cheeks flexed to a grimace. "You want to continue to use me?"

"We are all used, Ripcat—some by what is noble, others by what is base."

"I do this for love—for Jyoti."

"Love is not enough." Esre stared directly into the bestial dark of his vertical pupils. "It's never enough against evil. That is why we must help one another. We are witches, and we believe what the Gibbet Scrolls teach—'Love, and you will have many helpers.'"

OVERY SCARN

PRIMROSE STILTS, THE MOST ELEGANT TEMPLE GROUNDS IN Arwar—Odawl—many would say on Irth, where the Peerage traditionally held its coronations since pretalismanic times—had been restored in New Arwar by the magus with great precision. The temple consisted of "stilts," seventy-seven pillars of gray stone set with obsidian inclusions and smoky strikes like marble. Upon each of these tall columns, thick rose vines twined, with numerous splashes of pink and yellow blossoms. From the lofty gallery supported by the stilts, lanterns, wrought in black silver and green copper, hung by thick chains above a labyrinth of topiary hedges, dwarf trees, and numerous gardens circumscribed by granite walks, some with pools and floating lily leaves, others with musical fountains, raked sands of divers colors, or mossy rock enclaves. These were the fabled walled gardens featured in much of dominion poetry and lore.

Atop the gallery supported by the stilts, a tessellated range stood open to the sky. Time dials, which measured the Abiding Star's shadow cast by an agate gnomon upon a limestone disk, stood at each of the four corners. A small observatory of red-veined blackstone occupied one end, and an elegantly simple rostrum of pale chalcedony adorned the other. The wide expanse between stood empty, the mosaic surface swept by cloud shadows. But the magus had altered the random pattern of variegated tiles so that the range displayed the names of everyone in Arwar Odawl who had been slain when the cacodemons dashed the floating city into the jungle.

Poch stood before the name of his father, Keon Odawl, as the bond agent from Dig Dog Ltd. addressed him. "You agree, of course, that your sister, the margravine, must never hear of our meeting?" The agent smiled knowingly, a portly woman with meadowsweet flowers in her curly brown hair and an amulet-frock of power wands and clustered rat-star gems hidden almost entirely by gauzes, ribbons, and colored silks. "She is— you will excuse me—a fanatic, as I suppose margravines must be. She is zealous about guarding her rights of ownership to this city."

"She and the magus did rebuild it from ruins," Poch said without removing his eyes from the name before his white kid boots. "There would be no New Arwar this day if not for my sister and her consort."

"True. That is why Dig Dog prefers to keep her brood in

place to manage the city. Though, naturally, if another brood were to come along with the resources to pay off the debt, they could claim rights of rulership."

"Not likely in this war-stricken time," Poch said almost distractedly.

The agent noticed the name that Poch had fixated upon. "Your father would surely have wanted to keep the lineage of this city intact. You and your sister are the last of your brood. It is just and good that you fulfill the titular role of margrave when Dig Dog assumes proprietorship of the city."

Poch looked worriedly at the agent. "Jyoti will not happily relinquish her station."

"But she cannot legally challenge us." The agent turned so that her green velvet slipper covered the name of Keon Odawl, forcing Poch to look at her. "Though your sister rebuilt the city, she financed all the goods and services necessary to bring the city to life with us. Dig Dog paid for locating and transporting the infrastructure workers. We also installed lumber mills and carpentry shops that are the mainstay of the city's economy, such as it is. Without us, all that we would have here in the midst of the jungle would be an elaborate monument to the dead. We gave this heap of stones life." She swept a wide-sleeved arm at the surrounding hillside streets and the undulations of tiled roofs and chimney pots. "It's unfortunate that the dominions are once more threatened by goblins and the margravine cannot make her payments. But we must protect our investment. That is my job, my sworn responsibility as Dig Dog's bond agent."

"Dogbrick would write off the debt entirely."

"Yes, he probably would. He structured Dig Dog to retain that authority for himself." Her thick eyebrows bent with feigned sorrow. "But Dogbrick is not on Irth, is he? He might not even be alive, for all we know. Dig Dog Ltd.'s investment return is now my responsibility." The pudgy fingers of both her hands pressed against her chest. "I must answer to our investors. I, Overy Scarn. No one else, because I am the accounts manager as well as bond agent. And, frankly, the goblins are hurting me, too." She shook her head with stricken anguish, and a meadowsweet blossom fell from her curls. "Many of my investments in other dominions are unrecoverable—completely lost—because of rampaging trolls. What am I to do? How am I to answer those who have entrusted me with their money?" Her eyes glistened, verging on tears. "New Arwar has not yet been struck. Dig Dog's investments are still intact here. That's why I have to foreclose. I need to cover my other losses. You see what I'm saying?"

Poch gave her a crisp stare and a cold smile. "Why do you need me at all? Evict the Odawls and take the city for yourself. Then you can call it Arwar Dog."

"Don't be sharp with me, Poch." Overy Scarn's wet eyes hardened. "You know that only a Peer can rule a dominion. No matter how much money Dig Dog invested, we cannot *take* this city for our own. We can declare rights of proprietorship, but only if the ruler consents. Your sister would certainly choose to declare bankruptcy. In that case, Dig Dog will lose everything we invested. And this dominion will have to scrape by on its own, without further investment capital."

"In this perilous time, with goblins using trolls to tear everything apart, what has Jyoti to lose?" Poch passed an impatient hand through his hair. He knew that this penurious agent had a strategy, and he wanted her to simply state it and stop circling around. "I'm surprised she hasn't declared bankruptcy already."

"She expects the magus to find Dogbrick on the Dark Shore, and he will forgive her debts. Then, she can continue to finance her ambitious rebuilding program." Overy Scarn leaned conspiratorially closer. "But I don't think Dogbrick is coming back. Not from the Dark Shore. And when the margravine realizes that, my opportunities in this city will be lost. Unless you are margrave."

Poch looked askance at her. "But I am not margrave."

"Assume the debt," the agent answered flatly. "If you can make the payments, then regency law declares that you have the right, as the only survivor of the Odawl Brood, to replace your sister as dominion ruler."

He offered her a hapless shrug. "I don't have the funds to make any payments at all."

Overy Scarn reached out and set right several skewed amulets on Poch's vest, then stood back and searched his face carefully before she said, "I will see that you get those funds. I will have them secretly transferred to a private account we will open for you here in the city. You tell whoever asks that these are funds you earned from adventuring in the Reef Isles of Nhat while you were docent at Blight Fen. In these frenetic times who will challenge you? Say that you found treasure hidden by Hu'dre Vra. Dominion law states that the finder keeps such plunder. It will be legitimately yours. Use it to pay the debt and to take your place as margrave."

"Titular margrave, of course." His gaze thinned knowingly. "You will, in fact, own New Arwar and run the commercial concerns of the city, compounding your initial investment manyfold."

"You understand perfectly." Dimples small as puncture holes deepened in her cheeks. "Do we have an agreement?"

Poch glanced at his hearken fetish and saw that the quartz pendant remained cloudy, indicating that no one was eavesdropping. "My sister has tried to manage my life since I was a child. When our parents died, she became unbearable. I'm unhappy around her. I wouldn't even be here now if my consort had not been too timid to stay at Blight Fen." He lifted his chin proudly. "When the money is in place, I will confront Jyoti and take the title of rulership for myself."

Overy Scarn's small, cherubic lips curled to a gracious smile.

"I anticipated your acceptance. The funds are already in the city's bank under your name, margrave."

MENTAL

JYOTI SAT AT AN ONYX-WOOD DESK IN THE NICHE OF AN ORIEL window that looked down from her manor on blue- and red-tile roofs and flamboyant flame trees under the white sublimities of a tall cumulus. She reviewed reports of troll attacks from every dominion. Chaos reigned. The goblins had used their insidious telepathic prowess to direct basilisks and ogres against every major city.

"Why are we spared?" the margravine asked her weapons master.

Nette stood at the vaulted room's center, leaning over a viewing orb, a crystal sphere Charmed to scan the surrounding jungle. She saw roisterous corridors of monkeys and bright birds carousing among spiny palms and pea vines. Flowering trees and shrubs sprang up on every side, but nowhere were trolls or ogres visible within their shadowy nooks. She spun the rotating platform of the pearl-inlaid table so that the viewing orb's scene soared out of the fierce greens of the jungle and the terraced city of New Arwar came into view. Briefly, she scanned over the rooftops of gingerstone buildings until she came to the corbeled window behind which sat the margravine. "I see no threat, my lady."

Jyoti slapped the reports onto the onyx tabletop. "Why? Why are we spared?"

"Our jungle troops are well armed," Nette offered. "The high-way patrols also."

"Ux and Sharna-Bambara are even better armed, and yet they are plagued by raids." Jyoti shoved back from the table and swiveled around. "The goblins are sparing us. Why?"

Nette straightened and clasped her hands behind her back. "Perhaps they believe the magus is still with us. He is of the Dark Shore. Perhaps they cannot sense he has departed."

Jyoti accepted this with a clenched expression and shake of her head. "Our search for him has gone beyond Moödrun. Too many people know he is lost." She sighed. "And where *has* he gone?"

The assassin drifted closer. "I did not want to tell you this until I had confirmation, but there are sightings from Bryse of a beastmarked man that fit the description of Ripcat."

The margravine stood up. "Could Reece have changed again?"

"These are unverified reports." Nette looked down at the sheaf of battle notices on the desk. "This is a tumultuous time. I would not leap to conclusions."

A knock sounded at the paneled door, and Nette glanced at the eye charm on her cuff. "Your brother, my lady."

Jyoti nodded for him to be admitted, and Nette waved the key amulet that unlatched the door.

Poch stood at the threshold and stared uneasily at the assassin. "May I speak with you alone, Jyo?"

"Come in, Poch." She gestured him to a window bench in a bay of the room bright with silver light from a sky window. "You can speak freely in front of Nette."

"I'd rather not." He walked slowly toward the tall windows. "This is something that concerns just you and me."

"Whatever it is, you'll have to say it in front of her, Poch." Jyoti crossed to the cushioned bench and sat down. "She's my weapons master. I can't have any secrets from her, no matter how personal. You understand how it is. I'm margravine."

"Not anymore." From a sleeve pocket, he unfurled a slip of bank-ochre paper dense with cipher notations. "I have personally assumed our dominion's debt to Dig Dog Ltd. I'm margrave now."

Jyoti canted her head with disbelief.

"You're surprised?" Poch dropped a soundless laugh. "I don't blame you, Jyo. Not one bit. How could a failure like me retire such a huge debt?"

"Let me see that." Jyoti stood and took the cipher note from his hand.

"It's legitimate, Jyo." He sat himself where she had been sitting and crossed on leg over the other, both arms stretched out across the bolsters. "Regency law states—"

"I know about regency law." Jyoti spoke softly, still scrutinizing the note. "Where did you get this kind of capital?"

"I found treasure the cacodemons hid on a reef isle." His eyebrows shrugged. "Work as a docent at Blight Fen proved more lucrative than you guessed, hasn't it?"

"That's a lie, Poch." She tossed the cipher note into his lap. "You didn't find any treasure."

Poch's square face hardened. "Don't tell me what I did. Not anymore, Jyo. I'm margrave now. I'll tell you what happened. And if you don't want to believe me, you can leave New Arwar. I believe there's an opening at Blight Fen."

"Where did you find this treasure?" Jyoti challenged quietly. "How did you recover it? Who appraised it?"

Poch rocked his head side to side. "I don't have to answer any of that. All that matters is I've got the money to pay Dig Dog—and you don't."

"I will put a trace on where this money came from—"

"No, you won't." He thrust his chin at her defiantly. "A money trace requires authorization of the ruling Peer. In New Arwar, that's me now. I'm margrave. You're just my sister."

Jyoti shook her head. "There has to be a review of venue before the ruling title changes."

"Nope." He smiled, and crinkled lines of merriment radiated from his eyes, because he had anticipated this. "I thought you said you knew regency law? Well, I guess you know less than you thought. I looked into it, and there is no review of venue within the same brood so long as there is no challenge from any other Peer in the brood. It's just you and me in our brood, Jyo. Just you and me. And there won't be a review."

Jyoti sat down beside him. "Poch, why are you doing this?"

"Because I can." A somber expression shadowed his face. "Why shouldn't I be margrave? Don't you trust me to do as Father would have done? You can't treat me anymore as if I have some mental incapacity. I'm a man now." His eyes glittered merrily. "And I'm going to be married and have heirs—and a whole new dynasty will begin with me."

Octoberland

Life shapes itself on the anvil of dreams
—and the hammer is death.
—GIBBET SCROLLS: 21

STREET EXILES

"YOU DON'T HAVE TO STAY WITH ME," JYOTI FLATLY INFORMED THE assassin Nette. "I am no longer margravine, and you may now serve my brother as weapons master."

They were alone in the conference chamber behind the audience hall, where Jyoti had announced to her personal staff the new order. Her brother had chosen to select his own people to run the government, and with the last of her powers as margravine, Jyoti had granted potentially lucrative bonds in the city's timber and agricultural concessions to all the members of her staff, from economic advisers to cooks. For every one of them, she had taken pains to find new positions in the corporate lodges that privately conducted commercial en-

terprises in the surrounding jungle. Only Nette remained
without station.

"Forgive me for speaking so candidly, Lady Odawl," Nette
said with firm yet quiet deference, "but your brother is unstable.
If his amulet-vest were removed, he would collapse into a gib-
bering idiot, I'm certain. I cannot serve him. And you should
not have conceded readily. Why would you not allow me to
conduct a thorough investigation of his funding source?"

"Because I already know his source is bogus." Jyoti's hushed
voice reverberated in the chamber, a domed compartment fur-
nished only with a long table of petrified wood, archaic pedestal
chairs around it, and a holoform projector at its center, generat-
ing in midair a luminously detailed image of the city. "If we
challenge Poch, he will make a lot of noise to cover the illegiti-
macy of his claim. He will stir up all the avaricious factions
that see me as an obstacle to exploiting our position. All those
who have been demanding a sky bund and industrial tracts in
the jungle will rally to him. There would be insurrection."

"We would quash it quickly." Nette stood behind one of the
chairs and set its bucket seat spinning with a decisive twist of
her wrist. "You are still popular. We have the allegiance of the
jungle troops and the highway patrols."

Jyoti leaned back against the table. "Whoever is orchestrating
Poch's ascension does not care about popularity. Only power.
Terrorist bombings, rioting mobs, assassinations—anything to
wreak havoc. People will die. And I will not have New Arwar
become a place of slaughter."

"So you have given your brother the city you rebuilt. And
now he will work it hard and not for the good of the people.
Your ancestral city will serve his masters." Nette arched one
pale eyebrow. "Is that what you want?"

Jyoti hung her head, her chin touching her chest. "I have no
choice—for now." She looked back up at the assassin. "Do you
believe it is chance alone that has spared our city from the
goblins?"

"Indeed, they have attacked every dominion, every major city, and most of the hamlets and thorpes." Nette stepped around the chair and stood before the deposed margravine. "Are you implying that the goblins have spared New Arwar because they are backing your brother?"

"I don't know." She straightened and glanced at the tinted windows, looked at the oblate disk of the Abiding Star filtered by the dark glass of the recessed casement. She could hardly believe that she was no longer the dominion's ruler, and she gritted her teeth, making herself feel the muscular reality of the moment and the truth of what had happened.

Again she faced the compact woman in front of her, the assassin's eyes watching her with a cool intensity. "Goblins?" Jyoti relaxed the fists she had clenched at her sides. "Now that is Poch's problem, not ours. We can retreat and see what develops. In time, Reece will return with Dogbrick. The old debts will be forgiven and the illegal source of Poch's funds can be safely exposed. By then, perhaps, we will know more about the goblins and their opportunistic war."

"And how do you propose we retreat, my lady?" Nette asked, her mouth barely moving, her attention fixed on the younger woman. "Where will we go?"

"First, you must stop calling me 'lady.' I am not the margravine anymore. I am just Jyoti." She clapped a hand on the stout woman's shoulder. "And again I say you are not obliged to stay with me."

"The wizarduke, Lord Drev of Ux, commissioned me to serve as your weapons master. I believe that you will need me even more in exile than you did in office—Jyoti." She placed her square hand over the hand on her shoulder. "To where will we retreat? The jungle? Or shall we go to Dorzen and inform Lord Drev directly of what has transpired?"

"We're not going anywhere. We're staying here." Jyoti removed her hand to point at the three-dimensional map of light. "The city will be our sanctuary. It's a big place with numerous districts. And I know every corner of this town, every one of the lanes and alleys. We will become street exiles and hide in the outlying warrens, where we can watch my brother."

Nette looked skeptical. "You will be recognized."

"You think so?" Jyoti asked, still regarding the map, playing her gaze over the maze of convoluted byways and wynds, tree-clustered parks and tiered precincts. "All these residents are new—immigrants from across Irth come to New Arwar to begin untried lives. They don't really know me the way the original residents did." She put a hand to the gold cinch that held her hair at the crown of her head. "Without my topknot and with a change of garments, I'm just another anonymous woman come to the city looking for work. I'll call myself Jyo. And you— you're my sister, Nette."

"But it will be dangerous to stay here." The weapons master stepped close behind the taller woman and spoke in a near whisper, full of dire portent. "If the goblins are in any way involved in your brother's promotion, they will use their telepathy to seek you out and destroy you. And even if it's not the goblins, whoever backs Poch will want you dead. You pose too great a threat alive. The assassins will come."

"Then it's good I have an assassin to watch over me." Jyoti offered a kindly warmth that showed her gratitude for the vigilant woman who wore soft body armor and stealth togs. "We will leave the manor at once. We'll depart in a convoy for Moödrun and once out of sight we'll circle back on foot. If we come in through the timber camps, the jungle troops won't even notice us among the ranks of workers."

Jyoti packed all her clothing trunks and amulet scabbards aboard a convoy's passenger trailer and departed New Arwar with Nette at her side. Poch and Shai Malia watched from an oriel window of the manor, and Overy Scarn observed directly from the platform of the freighter berth, wanting to make certain that her investment had indeed purchased the exile of the former margravine.

As the convoy rolled along the city viaduct onto the jungle-cloistered highway, Jyoti cut her hair into feathery locks that fell just over her ears. Then she selected the amulets she would need and addressed the remainder to a witch hostel in Moödrun. When the convoy glided to a stop within an atrocity memorial park, she affixed a do-not-disturb sign to the door of her private berth, and she and Nette slipped away unseen through a noisy group of blue-haired ælves fleeing the jungles of Elvre for the rocketpads at Moödrun and the safety of the outer worlds.

OUTCASTS OF THE LIGHT

"She's gone!" Poch spun away from the oriel window with a giddy step. "I'm margrave! And I don't have to answer to her anymore—ever again!"

Shai Malia removed her cowl of veils and tossed it on the bronze-embossed footboard of the round bed. "You have done well, Poch. Very well."

"Well enough for you to marry me, Shai?" Poch took her by both shoulders, his wide, freckled face grinning, his merry eyes searching her through the long strands of henna-colored hair that fell across his brow. "We will rule New Arwar and Elvre together. You will have equal status with the conjurer Rica, who once mocked you for a ne'er-do-well. You will be co-ruler and a margravine!"

"Yes, we will be married." Her dusky face tilted toward him, her glistening black curls spilling over her shoulders, her almond eyes lidded heavily. "But I will take no title. I will be happy simply to be your wife. You will rule solely—the one master of the dominion."

"Well, at least in title." He lifted his eyebrows resignedly. "Dig Dog is master. Without their money . . ."

"Money!" She laughed and climbed into his arms, twining her petite body about his and whispering huskily into his ear, "There are powers greater than money."

"Charm," he agreed. "Charm and love."

"Yes, Charm." She nibbled at his earlobe. "Charm spins the worlds on their axes. But love—ha!" She slid away from him. "What do the Gibbet Scrolls say of love? 'Love is a question.' We wonder, will love fly? Will it carry us above ourselves? Or will it abandon us?"

"You do love me, don't you, Shai Malia?" Worry stamped Poch's petulant features, and he reached for her.

She let herself be caught and twirled against him. "The Screed of Love says that 'Love is the fullness of lack.' What would I be without love?"

Poch laughed. "The conjurer Rica's spoiled brat."

"Sadly true." She frowned, then tweaked his snub nose. "And what would you be, my anxious fool? What would you be without love?"

"Docent of Blight Fen, exiled in the swamps among the Reef Isles of Nhat." He hugged her closer and breathed the cinnamon fragrance of her sable hair. "Your love drove me to this. You made me margrave. But there is no love between us and Dig Dog. They put up the money, and Overy Scarn will be here shortly to instruct us how she wants our first edicts drafted to serve her enterprises."

"Yes—Overy Scarn . . ." Her voice trailed off, and she began again, sidling closer, pressing her back snugly against him. "Dear, dear Poch. What do you think the screed means when it informs us that 'Lovers await the tread of the Huntsman from whose hand they will feed?' Do you have any notion?"

"I am the son of a margrave as well, you know." He pulled her to the bed and sat down with her in his lap. "I may be your fool, but I am not uneducated." He bounced her playfully in his lap. "The Huntsman whose title is capitalized must be death. And lovers feed from his hand, for they are his trackers, who lead him to his prey. And death's prey—well, that is what comes of love—the babies, the children—for all that is born sooner or later must die."

She pushed him down on the bed and squatted over him. "Yes, you understand the screed perfectly."

"You—you're not proposing we murder Overy Scarn?" Poch propped himself up on his elbows, horrified.

"My, what a wicked mind you have." She laughed and pushed him back down on the bed. "No. I'm not suggesting you murder anyone. You are margrave. Others murder for you. All I am saying is that there are greater powers than money. Charm, love, death."

A knock thudded at the door.

"She's here!" Poch tossed Shai Malia off him and leaped to his feet, brushing the wrinkles from his trousers and shaking the disarray from his amulets. "Enter!"

A brawny guardsman in the heraldic crimson-and-gold uniform of a manor sentinel stood before a wood cask with dark brass hoops and dented studs. "Mistress Malia asked that this be delivered as soon as it arrived."

"Bring it in," Shai Malia commanded from where she sprawled on the bed. "Set it in the middle of the room and leave."

The guard complied, and when the door closed behind him, she bounded off the bed. Poch held her back and pointed to the port of origin stenciled on the gray, moldered slats of wood: *Nhat.*

"It's probably from your aunt—the conjurer." He shook his head dubiously. "We should have the charmwrights open it. Perhaps she's sent an enscorcellment."

Shai Malia pushed him aside with a roll of her eyes. "You see evil everywhere, Poch. Your time in the Palace of Abominations really demented you." She removed a hex-ruby from her amulet belt and smashed it across the top of the cask. "There, you see? There's nothing to be frightened of here. I personally packed this shipping barrel and had it sent to arrive in time for our wedding. These are friends—the dear ones."

The brass hoops snapped apart, and the cask slats fell away exposing a cluster of filthy dolls—five in number—small and bald as babies. A rancid stink gushed out and gagged the scream in Poch's throat: "Goblins!"

"Must you use such a vulgar name?" Shai Malia scowled at him. "These are our dear ones."

The babies squirmed and rose on misshapen legs, alien and unreal, distorted figures from a dream. Their tiny, warped arms reached for him, their dirty arms and naked, swell-bellied bodies, smudged with dirt, and stinking of clotted decay, reached for him. Their eyes looked wrong. Bruised lids drooped unevenly over irises like cracked glass. And their tiny mouths opened and closed soundlessly, a trace of smile upon them, gleeful and wicked.

Shai Malia knelt before them and took their soft bodies in her arms, and their small hands clutched at her. Their bulbous heads were too large for them to hold upright long, and they lolled against the woman's breasts and lay in a loose jumble in her lap. "Come, Poch. Come and hold these dear ones with me."

Poch staggered backward, horrified, the cheesy air curdling in his lungs. He wanted to reach the door and fling himself into the corridor. But the door had retreated from him. He saw it far away across a wider space than he had strength to cross. With a mournful cry, he sagged to his knees.

"Don't look so troubled, Poch." Shai Malia emitted a sparkling laugh. "It's the dear ones. They'll help us. They have a power stronger than money. That's what I was trying to tell you."

Poch shook his whole body, trying to extricate himself from what held him in the feculent room. The puckered mouths of the dolls hooked to sharp little smiles, thin filaments of black spittle drooling from the corners. Their opaque orange eyelids twitched. Suddenly, he felt himself inside their bulbous heads in a darkness disdainful of time and space, a darkness of such amplitude it enclosed worlds and all the outcasts of light.

OCTOBERLAND

SUMMER THUNDERHEADS TOWERED ABOVE THE MANHATTAN SKY-line. In the purpling light, the skyscrapers stood like the gods of a monolithic time, an older order of ritual realized more perfectly in the modern era.

Steamy heat rose from the pavements. Thermal shivers accrued to watery reflections at the bleared ends of the avenues. And from the rooftops, a haze hung over the hot and smoking city.

A different world waited within the water tower with the shagbark exterior. Once the ram's-head knocker sounded three times and the curved door opened, autumn poured out. Yellow and mauve leaves swirled on a gust of wood smoke, a breeze freighted with mountain coolness and a redolence of trees gone barren.

Octoberland enclosed its members in an eternal season of leaf falling. A languorous chill hung from the rafters where large boughs bunched with dead leaves rustled. A frosty downdraft wagged the hanging totems of carven apples shriveled to wrinkled visages. Corn-silk poppets in gaudy rags dangled as elvish merrymakers among cobwebs and spiders like tiny black marionettes. Within the smoky air mingled heathery scents from bines of twisted herbs and eldern grasses, and tendrils of small dried flowers embroided the walls like tattered motley.

The coven squatted in ceremonial tunics on the crimson perimeter of a circle that enclosed a large pentagram. In Octoberland, they carried the names of the zodiac, each member selected for the attributes of the sign they represented. Aries of the glowering brow and fleecy silver hair sat at the eastern point, a prominent minister, leader of his flock. To his left hunkered Pisces, a pale woman with sable hair, renowned marine biologist and board member of the city aquarium. And to Aries's right, Taurus, a banker with brown, bovine eyes and strong shoulders. She glared unhappily at Nox, who stood in his black robes at the mossy pentagonal altar of obsidian.

"I sensed you the other night, master," Taurus grumbled, her African features compressed to a frown. "I sensed you coming for me—as though my time were done and all that remained of me to serve you was my blood heat. Is that so?"

Loomed fabric of midnight blue and lunar phases lay under Nox's spidery hands as he leaned far forward across the altar to return the big-shouldered woman's stare with his adder's eyes. "This is so. I needed blood heat to summon the dead, to learn more of the magical one from the Bright Worlds—Dogbrick."

"The understanding, master, is that we are not to be culled until we are doddering." Taurus thumped a fist against her chest. "I'm still strong. You frightened me when I felt your mind turn toward sacrificing me. You frightened me. And that wasn't necessary."

The others in the circle murmured agreement, and Nox took in hand the stave of cracked and resinous wood, knobby with galls, and knocked it so hard against the planked floor that its fins of scalloped fungus trembled. "Hush, all of you! Remember we are in meeting. Only one may speak at a time." He nodded toward the woman who still held her clenched fist to her chest. "You are correct, Taurus. Your blood heat was not needed. I found another. But you are wrong to assume I cannot cull you as I please."

Another disquieted muttering passed around the circle, until Nox thumped the stave again.

"I have not done so before, because there was no need to break our circle. But this is a unique time. And the magic I will show you now, you have not seen before." Nox released the stave to lean against the altar and reached into the sordid urn that sat atop a dish of hammered brown metal. His hand came out gripping a finger-long needle, black with a tarry drool. "I need blood heat." He pivoted on his heels and pointed the dripping needle around the circle. "I need enough power to draw Dogbrick to me. Who will give me their blood heat?"

"Do not break the circle, master," Scorpio pleaded. "Let us dance up a devil and use that heat for your spell."

"No." Nox laid the black needle on the altar between two fat black candles. "No dance can muster a devil potent enough to draw Dogbrick. He is a being from a hotter reality. I need blood heat itself if there is any hope of manipulating this beast-man. Who will give to me for all that I have given to you? Who?"

No one budged. But Taurus whimpered, for the master gazed directly at her.

"I am too young," she protested. "I have served you but twenty years. I can serve you another twenty; I know it."

Nox's skullish face smiled, showing his tiny, multicolored teeth. "Twenty years of perfect health. Of every whim fulfilled. What have you been denied? And why do you now deny me?"

"There are others who have served you longer!" Taurus's eyes stared wide. "Take one of them! Take Gemini! Take Leo! They have enjoyed your gifts for thirty and forty years!"

"But they have not questioned my right to their blood heat." In his right hand, he lifted from the altar the poison needle. "I have been generous with all of you. Money. Status. Health. Freedom from loss for yourselves and those closest to you. How else could you possess all this except by me?"

"Master—I apologize." Taurus pressed her brow to the wood floor, and when she rose, beads of sweat and tears glinted on her cheeks. "You have been generous. But I am too young. Take one of the elders. Not me!"

"I may take any of you whom I choose, whenever I choose!" The smile curdled on Nox's decayed face to a scowl of wrath. "None of you has been forced to the circle. All serve with the understanding that your blood heat is mine. Does anyone disagree?"

The circle sat silent.

"Good." Nox pointed the sharp death at Taurus, and her mouth opened woefully around a noiseless cry. Then, his wrist snapped, and the needle flew over his shoulder and pierced the unsuspecting eye of Virgo. The youngest member of the coven, a flaxen-haired woman of twenty years, fell backward; her limbs jerked twice, then stiffened and went still. "Ah, that was swift, mercifully swift, wasn't it?" He swung an urgent look around the circle. "Now we must be swift, before the blood heat escapes. We need it to summon the companion of Dogbrick— who will take her place in our circle."

Leo and Libra stared aghast at the dead woman between them.

"Feel no anguish for her," Nox advised, striding to the dead woman and kneeling beside her with the brown metal dish. "In the four years she has served me, she has possessed the power to heal all whom she touched—and she touched many hundreds and brought them back from suffering and certain death. I am certain she does not begrudge me her blood heat."

Nox withdrew the needle from the punctured eye, and with it came an effluvial thread of incandescent blood heat. He wound the thread about the needle, then deposited the shimmery ectoplasm in the metal dish before dipping the needle again into the stabbed eye and drawing more luminous life force, smiling a mummy's grin as he worked busily.

NAILING HEAVEN AND EARTH

DOGBRICK WOKE, AND HIS OWN FACE FELT STRANGE. HE SAT UP among feathery grass that moved so fluently in the wind it seemed for a moment like another language, a different kind of speech.

He saw Mary Felix standing against the cotton of the sky. She possessed a youthful beauty, and he watched her with a passionless intensity, noting her masses of chestnut hair, her pale skin ruddier on her arms where the sleeves of her plaid shirt had been rolled up. The sun had tinged her brow and cheeks so that her freckled face appeared bright as the weight of a flame.

"I fell asleep." Dogbrick groaned as he pulled himself upright. "What happened to us? I don't remember."

Mary faced him squarely, her dark eyes glittering with tears. "I know who you are."

Dogbrick slouched toward her. "Who—who am I?"

"You are a beastmarked man from Irth." She bit her lower lip and shook her head softly. "You don't remember anything, do you?"

He shook his head in time with hers.

"Irth—it's where you're from. It's a planet at the edge of the Gulf. Don't these names mean anything to you?" She watched him closely for some sign of remembrance, but his orange eyes gazed from bone pits shadowed with befuddlement. "The Gulf is the abyss that separates the Bright Worlds from this Dark Shore, where we are now." She frowned to see that he did not remember. "I know it all now. Your magic put all your memories into me."

"My magic." Dogbrick looked at his heavy hands with their black palms and tawny-furred backs. "What is my magic?"

"You come from—" She took his big hands in hers. "You come from a long, long time ago. From the beginning of everything. Your world is not made of this cold stuff but of light. When you fell here, with the others—with Ripcat and Jyoti . . ." She kept searching for flickers of recall but saw none. "You fell into the shadow of the worlds of light where you belong. You have the power to reshape our shadows—our world."

Dogbrick squinted, trying to comprehend. "Why can't I make myself remember?"

"It's easier for you to shape shadows than your own light." Holding his hands, *knowing* who he was, Mary felt a wind in her veins, as if she were about to blow away before all that had already happened—and all that was yet to happen. In her former life, she had become so accustomed to making rational inquiries, to thinking scientifically, that what had befallen her seemed more than just unreal. It was a violation of her identity.

She had been prepared to prove the existence of Sasquatch, but what she had discovered instead had cancelled all her previous beliefs about existence itself. She still wanted to understand what had made her young, what had filled her with knowledge of other worlds—yet, the knowing within assured her she could never know. She felt its depth extending far beyond the wan light of her mind, a history wider than her brain. "Your friends are gone, returned to Irth," she continued. "While they were here, a devil worshipper, Duppy Hob, mastered them and prevented them from using their magic. But he's gone, too—taken back to Irth and slain on Gabagalus."

"How do you know this?" Dogbrick squeezed her hands, trying to draw knowledge from her. "Was I with them before they left?"

"No—these are not your memories." She tilted her head and regarded the flood of sunlight among the spruce before facing him again. "Your presence has attracted the attention of a magician here on the Dark Shore—Nox. He is very old, and he wants you to make him young, the way you made me young."

Dogbrick's squint tightened. "This magician—Nox—he came to you?"

"While you were asleep, he came to me, as a phantom." She sighed and released his hands. "He has put a spell on me. He cannot control you. You are too powerful. But even now as we speak, he fashions a hideous spell to draw me to him. I won't be able to resist. And if you try to use your magic to stop him, I will die."

"Then we will go to him together." Dogbrick shook off his confusion. "I will make him young. Where is he?"

"Dogbrick, this will not be so easy. There is more." She threw her arms up helplessly. "There are goblins."

The beastmarked man bent forward and peered into her bright eyes, seeing the film of tears. "Why are you crying?"

"Because if we go to Nox, he will use you." She kicked at the tufted grass, flustered. "And if he uses you, the goblins on Irth will have a way into this world."

"Goblins are bad, aren't they?"

"Very bad." She clutched at his arm. "They are the most gruesome creatures I've ever seen. They have powerful, evil minds, and if they come to the Dark Shore, they will enslave all the world." She held so firmly to him that she nearly pulled herself off her feet. "I've decided. I'm going to die."

"What?"

"I'm going to kill myself so that Nox can't bring you to him." Her wet eyes held his stare firmly. "Without you as an anchor, the goblins are too weak, too small to cross the Gulf."

"Are you sure about all this?" Dogbrick put his palm against her bereaved face. "There's been a lot of magic tossed around. Maybe you're confused."

"No. I'm not confused." She released him and wiped the tears from her eyes with the backs of her wrists. "I saw the goblins. I saw Nox. And I remember Irth and your life there."

"Then, it's me that has to die—not you." He cast a dolorous look at the dark woods that appeared lamplit from within, where sunlight shone off a starry creek, and he wished he had stayed among the others, the Sasquatch, and been happy with his anonymity.

Mary grabbed his arm. "You don't have to die. You have to leave here. You have to go back to Irth. Then the goblins and Nox can't use you."

"How?" He looked up hopelessly at the sky, as if he had to climb the clouds. "How do I go back across the Gulf?"

"There are charmways—corridors that connect the Dark Shore to the Bright World. The devil worshipper Duppy Hob created them while he was here." Her tear-dazzled eyes looked hopeful. "If we can find one before Nox finds us, you'll be free."

"And you?" Dogbrick tossed the wind-scattered mane from his eyes. "You can't stay here now that Nox has put a spell on you."

Her gaze dimmed, and she stepped back from him. "I would go with you, but I can't. His spell would kill me. But you *must* go—or this whole world is in peril."

Dogbrick declined and Mary insisted, so they argued as they strolled over the meadows. When the day waned, Mary opened her rucksack and took out bags of dried fruit and nuts. "Don't you have any meat?" the bestial man complained, frustrated by what he could not remember and all that his magic was hopeless to change.

With his cold fire, he struck a hare senseless in the grass verges and gutted and skinned it with his talons. The ruby signet of the sun hung in the trees as he roasted the skewered animal over a twig fire. "We've discussed this back and forth for hours," he groused. "I'm tired of words."

"There is nothing more to say," Mary agreed, gnawing nervously on a dried apricot. "The rational decision would be to go to Manhattan to find Duppy Hob's charmways. Nox is calling us there anyway with his magic. I'll feel the power of it by morning, I know."

"And does he know about the goblins?" Dogbrick asked. "Are they part of his evil plan—or is he entirely unaware of them? Perhaps we can reason with him."

"Perhaps." Mary shivered, and a green flare of twilight spilled upon the vastness, nailing heaven and earth. "But I think that if Nox could see the goblins, he would want nothing to do with your magic."

THE PALACE OF SKULLS

RAIN DRAGGED THROUGH THE PRISMATIC TREES OF BRYSE AND FELL in rivulets off the boughs, flooding the depressions between the root buttresses of the forest floor. Rainbow leaves like colorful reflections floated in mats upon the boggy puddles, and several times Esre stepped on what she thought was solid ground and found herself waist deep in water. Ripcat, who adroitly moved on the narrow root ledges, jumping from the base of one tree to the next, lifted her out of the mire with one arm while clinging to a dangling branch with the other.

"Where are we going?" he asked, wiping raindrops from his tufted brows and glaring irately at the witch. "How will we find the goblins?"

"South," Esre replied laconically, watching her footing in the forest.

"Are you sure you know what you're doing?" Ripcat griped. "I don't want to wear beastmarks if I don't have to."

"South," Esre repeated, "to the Mere of Goblins. That is where the creatures were exiled at the end of the Goblin Wars. No one has seen them since, and I think they are still there. Also, the attacks first began in the south, near the mere."

"Isn't that where dragons go to die?" Bedraggled Ripcat led the witch toward a tussock. "If the goblins were there, dragon-bone hunters would have reported them long ago."

"The mere is a labyrinth of pools, tarns, and lakes." Esre's conjure-silk cowl repelled the rain and even her sheathed feet appeared dry. "Most dragon-bone hunters never return from the mere—that's why their wares are so precious. Common knowledge says they are lost to the quicksands—and the giant centipedes and firesnakes. But rumor has always warned of goblins."

"I still don't see why we couldn't ride a dirigible south," Ripcat ventured, gesturing at the rain pouring through the canopy in long rills like silver harp strings. "I'm drenched to my marrow."

"No one must see you." Esre clambered beside him to the crest of the tussock from where they could observe the tops of other hummocky mounds floating in the forest haze. "The goblins are telepathic. They can't sense you as long as you are Ripcat. But if others see you— Well, I am carrying a lapse-gap agate that will wipe selective memories, but we can't use that on more than one mind at a time. You must stay hidden. No amulets or talismans, either. The goblins could well sense disembodied Charm moving through the dominions and know it was you. Then we will have the entire troll horde after us."

Ripcat accepted his wet misery silently after that, though his thoughts were a welter of frustration, confusion, and concern for Jyoti and Dogbrick. As Ripcat, travel on the Dark Shore would be more difficult and finding his friend all the more perilous. And if the witches did not transform him back to his human form, what would become of him and Jyoti? The only possible resolution lay in a future beyond the goblins, beyond doubts, and he concentrated on the immediate tasks at hand.

The rain abated during the night, and the following day they ascended through a rocky pass among flowering rainbow trees whose pollen flurried in the wind like fiery motes. Dark gorges gleamed ruddy orange with boulders covered in luminescent moss, wild grottoes of cloven rocks that shone like lava streams. The forest glittered under the rays of the Abiding Star, the rain-washed trees an iridescent mesh of refracted light and splintered spectra.

By noon, they came upon a brilliant glade where over ten thousand human, ælf, and ogre skulls had been stacked in a monstrous array that resembled columns atop a broad stairway. "A palace of skulls," Esre breathed in horrified awe. She searched her niello eye charms and saw no dangerous creatures nearby.

"Troll spoor." Ripcat pointed to the claw prints in the rain-softened ground. "The trolls did this."

"No." Esre nudged aside the gray veil across her eyes to better view the abomination. "Trolls are brute carnivores. They have not the imagination for this. What we see here is the terrible genius of the goblins. They directed the trolls to construct this—this shrine of terror."

Ripcat gaped at the gruesome ossuary. "They must have ravaged every hamlet south of Mount Szo to gather this many skulls."

"That confirms the reports I've been picking up on my aviso." Esre stepped back toward the shining forest. "Let's get away from this horrible place."

"Wait." He stepped closer, slowly, like a man in a trance. "I want to see what they put inside their shrine." Up the four steps of cranium cobbles he mounted and peered through the colonnade of stacked skulls. In the bent light, all was dim and hazy with bone dust. A single shaft of daylight illuminated a mound of skeletons caulked with grave dirt, and at its center sprouted a single flower. Its velvet blue petals burned like a flame in the dark. Lit by one thread of radiance, it shone with an alien, unreal intensity, a blossom foraged from a dream.

Staring up at the surrounding pillars of eyeless dead, he realized that the heaped skulls had been arranged precisely to block out all illumination save this one filament of bright Charm. Through the circuit of the day, the string of light entered from different angles yet always touched the blue flower. "Why?"

"The goblins are of another order," Esre answered from behind him. "They are not of Irth. Who of our worlds is to guess their reasoning?"

"What order spawned them?" Ripcat edged away from the blossom until he stood again atop the bone steps in the comforting brightness of day. "From where have these goblins come?"

Esre took his arm and guided him after her down the steps, back toward the spectral forest. "Beyond World's End, higher than our sky, is another level of reality."

"The Nameless Ones dwell there," Ripcat added. "The author of these worlds is one of them."

"Few know about the author of the worlds—that all of our reality is a dream of a hotter being." A mosaic of rainbows illuminated the translucence of her witch veils as they entered among the bright trees. "Reality exists in levels. Each level higher than ours is closer to the Abiding Star, to the Beginning of All—and hotter, with more Charm, more light. Some say there is no end to the levels. And each level has its worlds, who are gods to the colder levels below them."

"And the goblins—they've come to Irth from the hotter realm of the Nameless Ones?"

"The lore says that they are pixies among the Nameless Ones." Esre parted a trumpet vine, reading her eye charms to find the safest route through the forest. "When the author of the worlds first dreamed our reality, some pixies, who were unhappy with their lot as merelings in their domain, climbed down into these colder worlds, thinking they would be as gods. But the dream was vaster and stronger than they, and they could not control it as fully as they had desired—nor could they depart it. Ever since, they have wickedly struggled to suppress all other creatures who strive for dominance. Only their small number has kept them from overwhelming the endeavors of humans, ælves, and gnomes. Or so say the legends."

Cloud shadows darkened the grove around them. "Why don't they climb back, then?"

"Legend says they cannot." The threat of more rain turned like a rumor on the wind. "Charmways do not climb to higher realities. Not usually. On the Dark Shore, it took the devil worshipper Duppy Hob two hundred thousand days to open charmways back to Irth. The goblins are pixies, not wizards."

"Pixies." Ripcat grunted a dark laugh. "That sounds so harmless. Little mischievous sprites, imps of the forest."

"If they are pixies, the legends make sense of the sacred flower in the palace of skulls." Esre had to speak louder to be heard above the birds frenzying in the canopy as the cloud shadows passed. "The goblins revere life. It's sentience that they hate. The minds of others are a mockery to them of the awareness that led them here, that exiled them from the world where they belong."

FAERÏE CHAMBERS

POCH FELT THERE WAS A FOREST INSIDE HIMSELF AND HE WAS LOST among its wild avenues. He kept circling back to the same clearing, where the little dear ones sat in a shaft of daylight contemplating a single blue flower.

Where once he found them repulsive, now fully entranced by their magic, he ached with inconsolable yearning when he looked at them. They were so full of mortal beauty, so fragrant of minty grasses that he cried with happiness in their presence.

They possessed a loveliness that the world could not bear. That was why they hid here in the forest inside himself, where no one would find them except himself and Shai Malia. The world misunderstood them and called them goblins. The world wanted to destroy them. But here, they were safe. They knew he would bring them the hex-gems they needed to continue their war of survival and righteousness.

Looking at their small bodies, their gentle faces translucent with withheld light, he understood this was a dream that would never end, that would never leave him—a dream he could die of. He wanted to stay in the light-struck clearing with the little dear ones, embraced by their precious smiles, their eyes clear as pieces of the day sky. But they needed him to find his way out of the forest, to return to the world of shadows and assassins and fear. He had to find his way out, to gather more hex-gems so that they could continue safe in the dream of loveliness and peace, in the faerïe chambers of serenity that they were growing like a flower.

Through the skeletal silence of tree shadows, he walked. To keep from circling back again, he avoided the light and steered himself toward the darker lanes of the woods where the flowers remained closed and the tree boles appeared moon colored. He walked a long time with only the wind's utterance to complete his loneliness before he saw her in her witch veils. He ran toward her through the gray, lapidary light. The towering trees bore grim shadows, dull as bones. She stood among them, wrapped in her veils. At her feet, a flower burned blue in a thread of light.

He reached out for her, and even as his hands touched her veils, he sensed that this was not his beloved Shai Malia. She was too large, too big in the shoulders. The veils gusted open, and a face sewn together with scars glared at him.

An electrical scream jolted through him and broke to a gasp in his throat when he saw what stood beside her. Before a tower of skulls reared a ferocious man with beastmarks of blue fur, lynx eyes, and a snouted mouth heavy with fangs.

Fearing they would crush the blue flower and with it the prosperous dream that belonged to the dear ones, Poch flung himself toward the monsters—and trembled awake.

Shai Malia took him in her arms. They were in the plush anteroom outside the main audience hall. Many times as a boy, he had waited here for his father, Lord Keon, to complete some ceremonial function or other. Poch's eyes wheeled in their sockets, taking in the red velvet walls framed in bluewood molding, the heavy, dark chairs, their plump cushions embroidered with the family's armorial crest. "Why are we here?"

"The dear ones are in your sister's old suite—our bedroom," she reminded him with a gentle whisper. She nodded to the brawny sentinel in the manor's heraldic crimson-and-gold uniform, and he backed away through a side portal that led to the scribes' intricate alcoves, where he used to play hide-and-seek as a child. "I had him carry you down here so that we could meet the agent from Dig Dog in the audience hall. We don't want her disturbing the dear ones, do we?"

He rubbed his face with both hands, returning feeling to his numb flesh. "They are so—lovely."

"Yes, aren't they?" Her almond eyes glittered with happy intensity. "I knew you would adore them."

"But we must protect them." He clutched at her veils, and they sagged from her swart and smiling face. "They are so fragile. And I saw—I'm not sure what I saw. Something evil."

Concern narrowed her stare. "Tell me. What did you see?"

"The dear ones—so lovely, so very lovely, in a forest glade." His voice sounded washed out with dreaminess. "They need us, you and me, Shai! And not just for these five. I sensed others—hundreds of them, sleeping, lulled by the coldness of this world. They're used to the warmth inside the Abiding Star! That's why only five are awake now. And we have to bring them hex-gems so they can amplify their telepathy. They have to protect themselves! Others are coming for them! A witch—a horrid witch with one eye and a face of scars. And there's a beast-marked man, an evil thing—with blue fur . . ."

Shai Malia stroked the worry from his brow with both her thumbs. "There. Put that nightmare out of mind. The dear ones are safe here with us. That is why I brought them here. I knew you would care for them as deeply as I."

"Let's go back to them now," Poch said eagerly. "I want to bring them Charm and play with them in the faerïe chambers."

"Hush!" She touched the hearken pendent on his amulet-vest. Its quartz had gone clear. "Someone is listening. Hush now. We will talk more of this later."

Poch snapped the hearken pendent free and touched it to the niello eye charm at his shoulder. In the ebony interior of the eye charm he spied who listened: a court official with a long face and a tall hat beaded with hex-gems like a glistening fruitcake. Once he identified the listener, Poch fit the pendent to an amber power wand with a conjure-wire clasp and spun it once over their heads, dropping a shroud of silence about them. The quartz of the hearken pendent clouded. "He can't hear us now." His voice sounded muffled in the cottony enclosure of Charm. "It's an astrosopher."

"Of course." Shai Malia smiled at him impishly. "I summoned him to the hall to marry us. He's probably wondering where we are. I hope you don't mind."

"Mind?" Poch blinked with surprise and pulled her closer to him. "I've wanted this for so long. I can't believe that you initiated this yourself."

She pressed her cheek to his. "I said I'd marry you when you were margrave."

"But don't you want a grand ceremony?" He pulled away from her so that he could see the emotion in her eyes. "We can do better than an astrosopher. We'll have a wizard marry us. We'll get the master-wizard from the Calendar of Eyes to marry us!"

"No, no, Poch." She brushed his long, rufous hair from his face. "Think of the dear ones. They need our care now. A grand ceremony will only distract us. An astrosopher is good enough."

Poch nodded, a moue of perplexity replacing the dreaminess in his expression. "The dear ones—where are they from? How did you find them? What—what exactly can we do for them?"

"Protect them, Poch!" Startled at his question, she reared her head back. "They are so small, so delicate. They come from beyond World's End, you know. They are pixies from the Garden of the Nameless Ones."

"From beyond World's End, from inside the corona of the Abiding Star." Poch mouthed aloud his realization, quiet with awe. "They come from another range of time, another level of being. No wonder they touch us with such beauty. How did you find them?"

"By accident, my love." She shone with enthusiasm to share her discovery. "They had crawled into the Cloths of Heaven—"

Poch shuddered. "Ugh. That ugly place. They found their way from the garden to one of the most unhappy places on Irth. The wraiths there could have devoured them."

"And might have, but I heard them, in a dream, when I was with you at Blight Fen."

"Why didn't you tell me then?"

She cocked her head at the silliness of his question. "And what could you have done for them? You were just a docent. But now—now you are margrave. We have this manor, this city, and all of Elvre to protect them."

"Yes." He clasped her tighter, with shared determination. "These pixies have come to Irth to build their faerïe chambers at a dangerous time. They will need our protection and our sustenance. Shai, do you see? They are our children!"

THE ASSASSIN'S ART

AFTER THE MARRIAGE RITES, POCH SAT IN AUDIENCE WITH OVERY Scarn. The portly woman squatted beside the margrave's ornate chair on the hearing bench, a narrow wood settle made purposefully uncomfortable to keep petitioners from lingering too long. While they chatted, the capacious hall twirled with ribbon dancers and fire jugglers to amuse the galleries of trade brokers, lumber mill agents, merchants, and their families who perpetually loitered in the opulent hall and who had been surprise witnesses to the margrave's marriage.

Shai Malia had exited immediately after the rites, informing her husband that she intended to look in on the dear ones. He longed to accompany her, but Overy Scarn needed to make immediate arrangements for her investment company to begin swath harvesting timber at a scale the margravine never would have allowed. While they discussed details, Shai Malia retreated to a dark alcove lit by a solitary incense-filament lantern. A gaunt figure awaited her there—a cowled man with a hawkish profile and small, black eyes.

"N'drato, I assume." Shai Malia, staring through the gauze of her veils, saw the soft nod and the hard stare. "Confirm."

His raspy voice spoke the code promised by her contact in the Brood of Assassins: "To wipe away memory—I kiss your brow."

For payment, she had offered the Brood of Assassins one fifth interest for five thousand days in all of Elvre's timber concessions. This was a steep price even for the assassin's art, yet the necessity of this mission justified the expense. "I will authorize transfer of bonds once I have proof of your success."

"Do you have what I require?" N'drato extended a hand gloved in black silk so tight it appeared painted on his flesh.

"I believe this should be sufficient." Onto his palm, Shai Malia placed a round ceramic box no larger than a thumbnail. "I gathered them myself from her pillow."

N'drato backed into the liquid shadows cast by the smoky lantern and vanished silently. Moments later, when Shai Malia stepped forward to see where the assassin had gone, she found the round ceramic box sitting in a wall niche before a jade statue of the Goddess. The lid was off and the strands of hair within missing.

Those filaments of brindled hair had been deftly coiled into a seeker amulet. As the margrave's wife had suspected, the seeker revealed the presence of Jyoti Odawl within the city limits. N'drato slipped out of the margrave's manor by a narrow utility portal that returned him to the nettle ditch from where he had entered. One by one, he removed the foil dishes, the Charm reflectors, he had hung in the hedge to baffle the manor's sentry amulets and slung the tinsel straps over his shoulders.

With the foil dishes hung around him like a mantle, he strode down the manor hillcrest and melled with the enclosing dusk that flared full of planet shards and star clusters through the jungle fronds. He followed the icy directional cues within the gold housing of the amulet and ambled across the sloping parkland behind the manor. As he went, he folded the foil dishes, his silhouette dimming to a shimmer of gray, a wind blur on the lawns.

Avoiding the pale orange cones of lamplight, he moved into the thin dark trees on the sward above the manor footpaths. Soon, he passed the stele and obelisk of monument stones that bore the names of the margrave's lost brood, the dead in whose memory these streets and buildings had risen from ruin. He was fully aware that he had been hired to destroy one half of what remained of this once venerable family.

Along pavings shadowed by flame trees, he descended from the manor heights, crossing streets only when the black shroud of running clouds obscured the cratered moons in their webs of star smoke. Scores of people milled on the boulevards and chatted on the street corners, yet no one noted his transit.

The seeker amulet led him between buildings lifted against the night like ramparts disordered and aberrant. He had departed the elegant heights and begun the descent into the bleak perimeters of the city that lay below the treeline.

The cobbled paths ended, and narrow sandy lanes meandered past corrugated warehouses, sawmills, and storage barns. Lumberjacks and sawyers on their way to their shanty sheds or to the noisy mead hall slouched out of the jungle into the wan glow of pole-hung lanterns.

Alongside their parked timber haulers with giant muddy wheels, drivers sat with their boots propped on crate wood, guarding the day's cutting from poachers, while their partners fetched food and drink from the hall. None of these guards noticed the slinking shadow of N'drato. He passed behind and between them, a liquid black ripple at the edge of sight, come and gone.

The assassin found Jyoti behind the mead hall, under a window with tin panes and rusted frame. Dressed in buckskin trousers, boots, and a torn frock dangling straps and leather cords empty of amulets, she looked like a common laborer. Intent on gnawing her rusk of bread, her bowed head never saw him from where he sat on a stack of old dark brick.

N'drato timed his movements with the boisterous noises from the mead hall, gliding between rusted trash bins. The tight passage led him to her side, and he drew a black blade as he slipped closer. For one instant, he paused to identify where her guard was positioned.

He saw no one and felt a flash of doubt, a moment of spoken doom, because he knew the Brood of Assassins had assigned Nette to protect the last of the female Odawls. Before his doubt could stymie him, his hand reared back and spun fluidly, aiming the black blade for Jyoti's exposed throat.

From the trash bin, a gloved hand struck, snatching his arm and spoiling his throw. The knife clanged off the tin pane beside Jyoti's head, and she jumped up in time to see Nette surface from one trash bin and shove a shadowy figure against the other. The two grappled momentarily, and then the shadow wrenched away and vanished in the dark beyond the timber haulers.

Nette brushed off sticky tuber rinds from her black vest and stepped to Jyoti's side. "You did well," she said to her startled companion. "You drew him close enough for me to disarm him. I'm sorry that I couldn't kill him. He's very adroit—a master."

"You know him?" Jyoti slid her attention across the grots of darkness among the tall trees and shrubbery reflecting the yard lights, futilely searching for shadowy signs of him. "You predicted his attack perfectly."

Just moments before, they had been sitting on the brick pile, sharing a meal, when Nette had whispered for Jyoti to act as though nothing were happening.

"How did you know?" Jyoti asked. She inspected the eye charm under the fold of her torn frock but detected no nearby motion other than wind and nocturnal animals. "Who was this assassin?"

"N'drato. He is a master, with murderous skills beyond mine.

But I know him too well to be fooled by his tricks." Her eyebrows flicked with resignation. "He is my brother."

Jyoti straightened with a jolt of surprise. "And you would have killed him?"

Nette deflected the question. "We are assassins. My job is to protect you. I have failed."

"You saved my life."

"No. I put it in jeopardy." The assassin opened her gloved hand, showing a gold coin lensed with witch glass. "A seeker. I took it from him. It has your hair in it."

"My hair—how?"

"Only one realistic answer." Nette lowered her chin. "I did not purge the manor well enough before we departed. Your brother—"

"Poch would never hire an assassin!" Jyoti said adamantly. "Not against me. I know him as well as you know your brother."

Nette held her sharp stare for a moment, then slipped the seeker into an inner pocket of her vest. "Someone went to great expense to have you killed, Jyoti. Master assassins are not cheap."

"He's still out there." Jyoti continued to scan the ill-shapen dark of the jungle. "What are we going to do?"

"What else can we do?" Nette picked up the assassin's knife and handed it to the Peer. "We must hunt him down."

THE DEAD AWAKE

THE WORLD FELT SLOW WITH DESIRE WHENEVER MARY FELIX LOOKED south. Nox was calling her to Octoberland, to take her place in the circle of his coven. All other directions seemed gray, numb, hopeless. So she journeyed south with Dogbrick. They moved quickly along the logging roads, stepping into the woods whenever a vehicle growled past.

Along the way, she began to share with him all that she had learned from his magic about Irth and the Bright Worlds, describing with the scientific avidity of her training the mesh of cultures under the Abiding Star. "Gnomes, elves, and people, these comprise the three most anthropic cultures where you come from. Among the people, I'm including the salamandrines of Gabagalus, who are clearly human. But to me it's highly debatable whether ogres qualify as anthropic. They are undeniably sapient, but their intelligence is the least humane of—"

She broke off, seeing in his face a terrible aspect, a change that choked her words. "Your features—" She stopped, her heels digging deeper into the gravel as she leaned away, shocked. "You look—different."

Dogbrick reached for his face, and his fingers trembled in the vacancy where his snout had been.

"Your hands!"

The fur had thinned from his hands and his black palms had faded to ochre. He bent his fingers, searching for his claws—but they were gone. Among the bunched weeds at the roadside, he sat, stunned. Since yesterday, he had been feeling different, as though his face were not his own, as though his viscera were tightening and shifting inside him, but he had paid no heed to these strange sensations in his strange situation.

"You're losing your beastmarks!" Mary knelt beside him and touched his sturdy profile.

He sat perfectly still while she traced his human lineaments with her fingers. From within himself, he drew strength but had to reach deeper than before, and the power he found moved more thinly through his fingers. "And my magic—it's less."

Mary examined her own hands to see if she had begun to revert to her aged self. They appeared young.

"You haven't changed," Dogbrick reassured her. He touched his arms, noting that the shaggy fur had thinned to burly hair. "I think I've used up my magic."

She touched him and felt warm skin under his body hair. "Most remarkable. But I don't understand what's happening."

"What are we going to do?" He brushed his hands through his mane, and it felt less substantial. "How do I look?"

"Like a brute—but a man. A brute of a man." She stood up and experienced the spell that Nox was tightening upon her. "I have to keep moving or I'm going to be sick."

"I have some magic left." He pushed himself to his feet— bare feet, smaller and suddenly aching with weariness. "Maybe I can break the power that is holding you."

They left the road and entered among the dusty trees into a corner of burdock and nettles hidden from view. Between his hands, he gathered all the strength he could hold.

What to do with it?

He tossed it to her, and her heart paced faster, her inner knowledge brightened—yet the taut summons from Octoberland persisted. And when she stood back from him, he looked smaller than before and less hirsute.

"It's not working." She helped him stagger through the underbrush back onto the road. "Are you okay?"

Dizziness swarmed through him briefly, and he bent over and caught his breath. When he stood, he had to tighten the gray breechcloth about his waist. "I think my magic is gone." He regarded the brown flesh of his limbs and the blond glints of hair. "At least it gave me a language you understand—and a body that seems to belong in this world."

"Your coloring is a little off." She paced around him, taking in the massive musculature, the ponderous shoulders. "People with brown skin don't usually have blond hair—or orange eyes."

He opened his mouth and ran his tongue over his teeth. "My incisors—they're gone, too!"

"No more fangs." She put a fist over her stomach. "Come on. I've got to keep moving. Maybe we can catch a ride and get you some clothes in the next town. You'll open some eyes, but no one's going to think you're from another world."

They trudged along the unpaved road two more hours before a truck going their direction slowed to pick them up. Then, the driver got a good look at the loinclothed giant and sped past. Mary hopped angrily and shouted obscenities, and Dogbrick sat down at the edge of the road with his bare feet spread and plucked gravel and threads of weed.

"We best keep walking," Mary said, clutching her stomach. The spell twisted insistently.

"How far to anywhere are we?"

"I don't know. Twenty miles. Maybe thirty." Mary looked at the sky, to gauge the time of day, and noticed a man standing in the trees across the road from them. He was tall, with a long face, and the odd garments he wore seemed to shimmer in the tree dark. "Who is that?"

Dogbrick got up and crossed the road. The figure appeared familiar. He wore wrappings of silver and gold foil that dangled streamers of tinsel. In a dream, it seemed, they had met before. He recognized something about the ruddy complexion and the red beard trimmed to the strong outline of his jaw. "Who are you?" he asked, and before the words were out of his mouth, he noticed that he could see the tree trunks behind the stranger. He jumped backward.

"Don't be afraid." The ghost waved them closer. "I am dead, it is true. But your power has awakened me. I am from Irth, the same as you. My name is Caval."

"I've seen you before—"

"I tried to warn you about Nox—but his magic was stronger. I am, sadly, but a wraith. I hide in the sky." Caval's image bleared among the sun shafts. "Now your power is spent. And I am come to warn you—"

Mary sank to her knees in the roadway, nearly doubled over. "I can't go that way. Nox fills me with too much pain if I even think of it."

Caval moved back, and his body grew more substantial, augmenting itself out of the darker shadows. "Come, Dogbrick. Leave her be. Nox will not allow her to enter my presence."

Dogbrick followed Caval into the forest. "Are you a wizard?"

"Yes." Caval's figure shimmered as if about to dissolve into emptiness. "I lived a long life on Irth and collected enough Charm from the Abiding Star to survive my transit through the Gulf to this cold world. But the less I tell you of that, the better for you."

"I've lost my magic," Dogbrick admitted. "I don't understand."

"You lost your magic because you do understand." Caval wobbled closer, gleaming like water. "All your Charm is in your memories. When they were forgotten, you had ample Charm to throw around. But now—now you have given those memories to that woman. Your Charm is squandered. And worse yet— the more she tells you of Irth and your life there, the less you will become, until you are a ghost like me. Only, I have resources of wizardry that you do not. When you are a ghost, you will slip into the frenzy of rebirth, your Charm, your life force taken up entire into the animal shapes of this cold world."

Dogbrick gaped in horror at the phantom. "What can I do?"

Caval glared somberly. "You have become a mortal being of the Dark Shore. Whatever you do, you will have to do as a man."

ASTRAL VIOLET

THE MORE THE WIZARD TALKED, THE THINNER HE BECAME. Already Caval was narrow as a pencil, as if peering out at Dogbrick from the crevice of another world. If he said another word, he would be pulled to a string stretched from the stars to the center of the earth. He kept his silence, though Dogbrick flung questions at him whose answers he ached to tell him.

In Caval's eyes, the physical world shone transparently. Dogbrick, the trees, and the sunny tableaux of the roadway where the woman sat curled on herself faded against a dark blue sky, a moteless void of astral violet. Emptiness was swallowing him. But he was not afraid.

The wizard knew that the warning he had given Dogbrick served him as well. He had little Charm left, and unless he gathered more his identity would be stretched to a tight filament and snapped. The sprung ends of himself would scatter across this cold world and be absorbed into the kaleidoscopic resonances of life, into the shifting crystal patterns that lensed flowers and their bees, rabbits and their wolves, people and their fates. Caval would die, his Charm dispersed like mist in the void, reborn in loamy mushroom beds and in the hearts of trees.

He wanted that. He had lived too long confined by cerebral tissue. Even as a ghost, he projected the repetitive neural patterns, the behavioral arcs that had radiated from cerebral lobes, hippocampus, brainstem, all the neurofibrillary contours of his lost body, the old prison. The time had come to free himself from the past.

But before he let go, he chose to fulfill his religious obligations and end his life in the manner of his Brother Wizards and Sister Witches—by parsing himself among the Three Blind Gods. Throughout his training and the long life that followed, they had guided him. And all he truly knew of the mysterious future that awaited him on the Dark Shore was that they were already there and would guide him again, whether he knew it then or not.

Death had aleady taken his body and stood poised to take the rest. Chance, too, lingered close by, visible in the faded scrim of the physical world, swaying in the treetops with each gust of the wind, as demented and unpredictable as ever. But he could not give himself to them until he had completed his devotion to the third god—Justice.

That god demanded that the circle be closed. Duppy Hob

had brought him to the Dark Shore to help return the devil worshipper to Irth. But the blind god Chance had intervened, and the blind god Death had taken Duppy Hob to dance on the ocean bed at Gabagalus. That left Caval on the Dark Shore, to satisfy the blind god Justice and close the circle.

Close the circle—

Caval drifted away from Dogbrick. The wizard did not expect to undo all the talismanic work that Duppy Hob had accomplished—the cities, the electrical gridworks—a massive, planet-sized amulet that had opened charmways across the Gulf to the Bright Worlds. Caval had not the strength to even begin to dismantle that horror. He decided he would satisfy the blind god if he could at least return Dogbrick to where he belonged on Irth.

Up the transparent road he glided. Astral violet wobbled around him. The road vibrated and shook, blurring into a dozen roads. On some, the ambitious sunlight traveled the road alone with its shadows. On others, vehicles traveled, some up the road, others down, all trailing dust like the smoke of a lit fuse. The fuse ended where a Jeep or a pickup or a trailer braked to a stop before a naked brute of a man and a young woman in his arms—and there, the future exploded.

The wizard did not have the Charm to review all the possible vehicles that stopped and where they led. He had strength to choose one. And he honored the blind god Chance by directing his Charm randomly into one of the vehicles driving down the road—a van with a cracked windshield and wings of dried mud sprayed along its sides. He breathed ease, confidence, and good-will into the driver, an older man, a mechanic who had been seized with an irrational but urgent desire to return to town and complete the paint job on the backyard fence that he had put off too long.

As the van eased to a stop before Dogbrick and Mary Felix, the wizard thinned to a thread, a hair-thin wire stretched to a vibrant tension. He hummed with the resonance of the void, astral violet quaking in waves from him. The waves shredded the mirage of the physical world.

And yet, he did not die. Tenuous as a thread of starlight thrumming tautly in the void, the wizard Caval persisted. He clung to consciousness despite his exhaustion. From deep within the darkest blue of nothing, he watched Dogbrick carry Mary into the back of the van.

Dogbrick felt a cold whisk broom brush his shoulders as the door slammed and the van spewed gravel and rocked into motion. He heard a voice addressing him: "I say, what's wrong with the lady?"

"Something I ate," Mary Felix groaned and forced herself to sit up. Now that they were driving south, the claws of the spell relented, and she took a deep sustaining breath. "I'm feeling better already."

The older man's flinty eyes scrutinized them in the rearview mirror, compassion creasing his sunburned brow. "Who are you people, this deep in the backcountry?"

"Campers," Mary replied, staring gratefully at Dogbrick. "We lost everything in a boating accident. Even his clothes!" She attempted a laugh and was surprised how strong she felt. "You are a godsend. I guess we looked pretty bad. No one wanted to stop for us."

The driver launched into a monologue on civility, and Mary engaged him happily. Dogbrick listened only distantly. His alertness had dulled to a stubborn astonishment, and he kept examining his hands, his torso, his limbs, and his feet. Like a sand sculpture slowly sifting in a gentle wind, the shape of his body seemed to change, whittling gradually to human dimensions.

"I say, mister—what's your name?"

"Uhm . . . Brick."

"Well, Brick, you must feel pretty darn lucky to survive rapids strong enough to tear off your clothes."

"Darn lucky." His voice sounded odd to him.

Mary asked the driver about his family and freed Brick to touch his nails and poke at his wrist, studying the fate lines in his yellow palm. He sensed that somehow the wizard Caval had helped them get this ride. But had he helped them or hindered them? The gravel road climbed a rise, and out the mud-smeared windows he saw across hilltops of forest to the straight lines of other roads that cut through the woods. He was in the bloodstream of a human world, a reality that the first people who had tended him feared more than anything.

The Sasquatch had sensed evil in these creatures. He had seen it, too, when he first touched Mary Felix. He had entered a hive of evil. And the evil had entered him. He had become like they were. He turned his naked hands in his lap, cold in his heart to see how weak they looked. If the Sasquatch saw him, they would flee.

He reached for the strength in him. It was still there, in the interior dark, but very small. There was barely enough to hold in one hand, even these small hands. He left his strength inside his mortal darkness, small as a pearl, and he remembered the wizard's warning: *Your Charm is squandered.*

"You okay, Brick?" the driver called. "You look like you're about to be sick."

Monstrous Immortal

For the lost and the hunted,
time weighs a little more.
—GIBBET SCROLLS: 26

ETERNITY AND SPACE

THE NEAREST CHARMWAY IN SHARNA-BAMBARA WAS A SINKHOLE. Standing among the switching grasses and staring down into the unplumbed depths, Esre and Ripcat perceived bulky shadows shifting in the darkness. "The sisters warned of spiders," the witch said, stepping away from the tufty brink. "They said we should avoid the charmways and continue south on foot."

"It will take us days to reach the goblins in Nhat." Ripcat squatted. His night vision penetrated the gloomy hole, and he noted crevices where predators waited. "The longer we spend traveling, the more people the goblins will kill. And the longer my friend Dogbrick must linger on the Dark Shore."

"The Sisterhood was firm." The veiled woman turned away. "We are not to enter the charmways if they can be avoided."

"They cannot be avoided." He tossed a pebble into the maw of darkness, and it plummeted soundlessly. "Did they give you directions? Can we find our way to Nhat from here if we go in?"

"No directions."

Ripcat approached Esre where she stood in grass taller than their heads. "Give me the aviso. I will speak with them."

"And betray your presence here to the goblins?" Esre shook her head. "We must continue on foot. It will take longer, but it is more certain."

"Then why did the sisters tell you the location of this charmway when you asked?" Ripcat pranced in front of her and blocked her way. "They are leaving the decision to us."

"I spoke only briefly with them, to keep our profile as low as possible in the event the goblins or their minions somehow are monitoring our communications." She looked apprehensively over her shoulder. "I told them we've traced the goblins to Nhat. Witches and wizards have gone ahead of us to destroy those creatures, and we may not even be needed. The Sisterhood gave us the site of this charmway as a refuge in the event we must elude an immediate threat—such as a troll swarm."

"We *are* eluding a troll swarm—one that has overrun Irth." He searched the gray layers of her shrouded face for some response and, seeing none, stepped past her. "I will go alone. It's better that way. I can move faster without you and elude whatever spiders come for me."

Esre's face veil fluttered with a sigh of exasperation. "I can't send you down there alone. There are composite spiders."

"I know about the spiders—"

"Do you?" she asked doubtfully. "They're not like spiders where you're from. These are made of thousands of smaller arachnids joined by Charm to a ferocious size. They will overcome anyone, even you, without the protection of firecharms."

"I've been in charmways before." Ripcat strode to the sinkhole and paced the perimeter. "It's dark, and unless we know where we're going, we'll get lost. I say, I go in alone. I have the strength of my beastmarks to guide me. You continue on foot, and we'll meet up at the Cloths of Heaven in Nhat."

From under her raiment, Esre produced a headband of lux-diamonds. "We'll see well enough with this—though I doubt we'll like what we see."

"You don't trust me," Ripcat said, showing a fanged grin as he lowered himself into the hole. "You think I'll abandon you for the Dark Shore."

"Would you?" she asked, drawing aside the veils from her scar-patched face and strapping the lux-diamond headband across her brow. "I doubt it. You could have eluded me anytime in the rainbow forests. You gave your word, and you are true."

Ripcat's long green eyes shone from below in the lightless pit. "Yes, I gave my word."

"This is a frightful way to go, Ripcat. I do not like it." The lux-diamonds illuminated slick walls that descended in knobby steps toward numerous shafts and boreholes. "How will we find our way?"

"You have amulets." He moved adroitly down the natural steps and offered her a helping hand to guide her along the notched face of the precipice. "I thought the goblins track Charm."

"They do," Esre admitted as she consulted her eye charms, searching for the nearest spiders. "I've sensed the goblins watching me since we left the shrine of skulls. But they haven't seen you yet . . ."

Spiders lurked not far distant, appearing in the niello of her amulets as silhouettes still as boulders. Moving slowly down the skewed ledges of the sinkhole wall, she pointed out the niches that harbored the largest arachnids.

"Who built these charmways?" Ripcat inquired when the penetrating rays of the lux-diamonds had finally led them past the

most perilous shelves. "The Sisterhood must have some notion
of the history of these passageways among worlds."

"They're natural formations," she said—and he was gone.

Ripcat's night vision had sensed the grotto floor, and he disappeared ahead of her, plummeting into darkness and landing
spryly at the dusty bottom of the hole.

She jumped after him, and his strong arms caught her and
softened her landing. Even lit by the tiara of lux-diamonds, the
vast cavern was hard to see. Silently, they crossed an ashen
grotto and approached a titanic wall. The glistening rock was
riddled with apertures, some cavernous, others narrow slots and
asp holes.

The witch monitored her eye charms and saw the bouldery
shadows stir before their sounds echoed from the wall of holes.
"Spiders!" She clutched Ripcat's arm. "And they're coming!"

A clicking, rasping, chitinous noise mounted louder from the
perforated wall. Overlapping echoes frenzied to a din.

"We're trapped." Ripcat spun, searching for escape. "Which
of the holes in that wall is empty? Which way do we go?"

"They're all filled with spiders!" Esre drew her firecharm. "Stay
behind me."

Ripcat shielded his eyes with his hand when Esre aimed at
the ground-floor caves. A blue flash stabbed like lightning, and
an anguished screech resounded from the cavern. Simultaneously, hooked legs appeared in many of the openings, and a
horde of spiders emerged.

The witch fired as she ran, striking at the largest of the beasts,
and spiders big as cows exploded to burnt ash. Hoping to clear
a way out of the grotto and dissuade pursuit, she fired rapidly
into the caves. A stench of burning exoskeletons oozed from
the holes, the shrieks and chatterings of the spiders clamorous.

A deafening explosion shook the very rock beneath their feet.
Esre toppled, and Ripcat snatched her by the arm and pulled
her upright. Green flames gushed out of several chutes, and
Esre yelled, "Charmfire!"

Ripcat swept the witch into his arms and lunged into the passage before them even as the grotto was flooded with a swirling conflagration of green flame.

SPEAK OF HELL

"WHAT HAPPENED BACK THERE?" RIPCAT'S VOICE SHOOK AS HE RAN with Esre in his arms. The glare of the burning grotto threw their shadows before them, long, thin, and battered by fiery radiance.

"I hit it!" she shouted jubilantly. "I didn't think I would! One eye—no depth of vision. Didn't think I would!"

"Hit what?"

"Something—something with a lot of Charm." She clung to Ripcat, staring over his shoulder at the green cloud of fire billowing after them. "Faster!"

Ripcat dived into a side corridor, and a gust of virid plasma filled the tunnel they had just left. The heat from the blast tightened their flesh, inspiring them to move deeper into the side vent. When the noise dimmed and the air cooled, he asked, "What could have that much Charm?"

"A lode of hex-gems and conjure-ore." She glowered at the firecharm in her hand when Ripcat lowered her to her feet. "Drake's blood! I did it! I hit the trigger of the mother lode for sure!"

"What are you talking about?" He peered back the way they had come and saw glimmering shades of green energy pulsing along the rock walls. "You planned this?"

"Not the stampede of spiders." Esre's one eye wrinkled with merriment. "That surprised me. There were more in that wall than I expected. But they didn't stop me. Look!" She held out an eye charm whose interior shone like green coral, like the vascular system of a luminous plant. "You're looking at a schematic of the local charmways. The lode of hex-gems that I struck has ignited. The charmfire is spreading."

Ripcat's velvet brow wrinkled. "That does not sound good."

"It's very bad for anyone caught in the charmways," Esre confirmed and pointed to the rapidly widening web work of green radiance. "There are veins of charmrock and conjure-ore strewn throughout the planet. When the charmfire I ignited hits them, they—"

The walls shook violently, drizzling gravel and sand and spinning them on the balls of their feet. Ripcat braced himself against the shuddering wall and snatched Esre as she nearly collapsed. The tremor died down, and other explosions boomed from farther away.

"Why?" he asked, though he already knew. The Sisterhood was burning bridges.

"Charmwrights contributed the gems and ore, and wizards and witches planted the trove at a critical juncture in the charmways—a juncture closest to where the goblins are hidden." Esre took back her eye charm. "If we came this way, I was instructed to ignite the trove once I got you past. Now it's a wall of fire. The goblins won't be using the charmways to escape to the Dark Shore or anywhere else."

"What about us?" Ripcat sensed tremors through his feet. "Can we get out?"

"If you mean, can you get to the Dark Shore and back with your friend Dogbrick before this storm destroys the charmways across the Gulf?" She waved him after her and hurried into a dark corridor. "Only if we hurry."

Ripcat followed her, grousing, "What hope are you leaving me or Dogbrick?"

"Don't blame me, irascible Cat. I didn't want to come this way. I'm not that good a shot. But you insisted. And I had to obey my vow to the sisters that if we entered the charmways I would at least try to hit—"

Another explosion rocked the floor so vehemently they had to sit down to keep from falling.

"You could have told me . . ." His voice shuddered with the ground. When the trembling abated, he blew a sigh. "No, I guess you couldn't have told me. I wouldn't have agreed. It leaves too little hope for Dogbrick."

"Then don't speak of hope," Esre called above the rumbling vibrations as the quake subsided. "Speak of hell. If we fail to get out quickly, the charmfire will consume us."

The assassin-witch examined the eye charm closely, comparing it with another on her charmbelt and then concluded, "From here we can jump to a nest of goblins at the Cloths of Heaven. The static from the charmfire will hide the movement of my amulets, and we may actually surprise them. But we must hurry. If our timing is off, we'll leap into the holocaust."

"Then, go!" Ripcat shoved the witch ahead of him and followed her through the wending passage toward a chute of salt-crusted rim rock. They leaped into the chute together and tumbled onto the sandy field of a subterranean arena.

On all sides, bench rocks rose in widening tiers toward a gargantuan ceiling of fanged minerals. At one end of the arena, the numerous passageways glowed hotly with green light. A seething bellow from the conflagration quivered the grains of sand on the rock floor itself.

"A mother lode of conjure-ore is behind us, if I'm reading my eye charms right." Esre pointed to the darker end of the arena. "That's the way toward the Cloths of Heaven and the goblin nest."

"We're not going to make it." Ripcat stared in fright at clouds of green fire gusting from the honeycombed wall across the chamber.

Esre unholstered her firecharm. "I'm going to jam my weapon. When it explodes, the blast will collapse this whole cavern. The charmfire will be blocked."

Ripcat cocked his head querulously. "Do you know what you're doing?"

"We'll find out." She set the lock on her firecharm. "Once I pull the trigger, we'll have a very short time to get out of here."

"Do it already!" He glared at the far wall, buckling into a web of green fire.

Esre set the pin and yanked the trigger, then tossed the firecharm to the ground as Ripcat scooped her into his arms.

He charged toward the dark hallways at the far end of the arena, running hard over the dimpled sand. He did not dare look back at the charmfire blowing in gaseous streamers from the rock sieve of the far wall.

Esre's patched face appeared healed, smeared whole in the glare from the fire rushing behind him. The back of his legs and his shoulders suddenly seared hotter, and the roar churned so loud he felt the sound would consume him.

Esre clutched Ripcat tighter when the blast wave lifted them off the ground and propelled them forward with blurring speed. A hole in the riven wall tilted toward them, and, helpless as flung rags, they hurtled into darkness and another room of the world.

SECRET HONOR

POCH GRUMBLED AS HE STOOD IN THE CORRIDOR OUTSIDE OVERY Scarn's suite with his hands above his head while a Dig Dog Ltd. security agent waved a defender rod over him. "I'm the margrave!"

The double-paneled doors swung open, and the hefty figure of Overy Scarn emerged in ruffled robes of ocean blue, small red blossoms tucked among the tight curls of her brown hair. "Poch! You're so sweet to indulge me like this." She accepted the security agent's curt nod and dismissed her with a shift of her small eyes. "In a moment, you will understand why I must be so careful with anyone who approaches this suite."

"You're in *my* manor!" Poch watched angrily as the svelte security agent in her silver tunic turned her back on him and returned to her station at the head of the winding staircase. "You've taken the best chambers for yourself. You've brought in your own guards, these—these seductive glamour devils. *And* you have the audacity to summon *me*, the margrave, to you as if I were your abject servant. Scarn, you go too far."

"Wait, margrave." Overy Scarn smiled benignly at him. "Make no stern judgment of me until you see the necessity for all that I have done. None of this is meant to diminish your person— but rather to protect your station and offer you secret honor. Come."

Poch straightened his amulet-vest and entered the large suite with its array of tall windows. He squinted against the morning light pouring from the bay casements. Chandelier prisms in long loops dangled from the center of the raftered ceiling to the sea-nymph moldings of the corners, catching the daylight in radiant shards of rainbow. He reached to his vest for his cowl, to shroud his wincing eyes from the glare, and Overy Scarn stopped him with a gentle touch.

"Try these." She handed him a dark eye mask of a lightweight substance. "You wear it on your face. They're polarizing ocular lenses. Wraparound shades. Sunglasses."

Poch tried them on, and his face relaxed. "They're light-weight. What is this strange material they're made from?"

"A wonder indeed." Overy Scarn put on her own pair of wraparound shades. "It's called plastic."

"These charmwrights have outdone themselves," Poch marveled, craning his neck to take in the softer contours of the daylit chamber. "Who are these Charm masters? The wizards of Ux?"

"No, margrave. These shades, these sunglasses, they're from the Dark Shore." Her small lips curved to a smile at Poch's

surprise. "Yes—we have access to a world on the far side of the
Gulf. That is why I asked you to come here alone. Do you
understand the importance of this?"

Poch noticed the shrouds in the far corners of the chamber,
behind the dragon-hide divans and griffin-bone chairs. "Dig Dog
has a trade route to the Dark Shore? How?"

"Not exactly a trade route—and not Dig Dog." Overy Scarn
waddled to the shrouds and pulled them aside, exposing a row
of wooden crates, each stamped with unfamiliar glyphs. "Gabagalus has been sending airships through a charmway to the
Dark Shore. The devil worshipper Duppy Hob established the
charmway about eighteen thousand days ago. But he did it secretly from Gabagalus. . . ."

"Much is secret in Gabagalus."

"This is one of the bigger secrets." Overy Scarn leaned on
the crates. "These containers were filled with sample goods man-
ufactured on the Dark Shore and brought to Irth by Duppy
Hob's people in Gabagalus. The devil worshipper had very big
plans. He was going to conquer the entire universe. These samples were gathered simply as curios to amuse his people in
Gabagalus. But now Duppy Hob is dead—and the charmway is
still open."

"How did Dig Dog get these samples?" Poch stepped closer,
curious to see what the crates held.

"With Duppy Hob dead, the people he left in Gabagalus are
looking for some way to cut their losses." Overy Scarn smiled
smugly and sat on the edge of a crate. "During Dig Dog's inquiries in Gabagalus about Dogbrick, we learned of these goods
and made an offer. Now, we are the dominions' sole trading
agent with that mysterious continent on the far side of Irth."

"What did you learn of Dogbrick?" Poch asked eagerly. "He
is my friend. He helped me after the Conquest. He showed me
how to get strong again after the torments of Hu'dre Vra."

"Dogbrick?" Overy Scarn lowered her double chin to her

chest. "He's lost on the Dark Shore. I doubt he will ever be found."

"You mean, you doubt you will make any effort to find him." The margrave crossed his arms over his amulet-vest with a look of disdain. "You're far too comfortable as the head of Dig Dog to ever want to return the company to your old master."

"You have what you want, *margrave*. And I have what I want." She lifted her chin proudly. "But I am not the one who exiled Dogbrick on the Dark Shore. He did that to himself."

"But now that you have trade relations with the Dark Shore, you should be able to find him."

"Trade relations?" Overy Scarn's small mouth opened around a silent laugh. "Hardly. Duppy Hob insisted that the existence of Irth be kept from the denizens of the Dark Shore. To this day, his people in Gabagalus refuse to violate that secrecy. These samples were taken surreptitiously."

"You mean stolen?"

"Thanks to the advantages of Charm, our airships maneuver very quickly on the Dark Shore. We are so rarely seen that the people there have no idea who we are. And those few who have spotted our airships have no concept what they've witnessed. They call our vessels *unidentified* flying objects. We are anonymous."

"So, we could send a mission to find Dogbrick?"

"We could—but we won't." She stood up and rapped her knuckles against the crate. "Margrave, the contents of these containers will revolutionize life on Irth. Look at what we have." She lifted the top of one box and removed sturdy blue trousers. "Their textiles are durable and lightweight. These are called denims." She pulled out ankle-high boots with rippled soles. "These are sneakers. And not just for sneaking. For walking. You must try on a pair. You'll never wear those clunky sandals again." She tossed out armfuls of denims and sneakers and then hauled up a box with a bubble lens at one end. "This is truly amazing."

She set the box on the dragon-hide divan and attached the dangling wire at its back to a power wand fitted with a conjure-clip. The bubble lens lit up with a blizzard of sparkling motes. Into a slot in the housing below the lens, she inserted a cartridge. A moment later, images appeared: frenzied musicians thrashing loud music from their instruments. "Entertainment! In a box!"

Poch removed his wraparound shades and squinted with amazement at the view screen of music from another world. Then, he shook his head ruefully, remembering the dear ones and the danger that threatened them. "Scarn, you're forgetting something important. We're at war. Trolls could attack us at any time."

"Ah! Yes, trolls, ogres, and goblins." She bent deep into the crate and rummaged around. When she straightened, she held in her hand a firecharm, only smaller than a firecharm: Its bore-hole was no larger than a pencil. "This is our answer to the Goblin Wars. Projectile weapons. *Firearms!* This one is for you, margrave. A three-eighty caliber auto pistol. Don't look so baffled. Its mechanism is quite simple. Let me show you how it works."

THE TERRIBLE REALITY

NETTE, IN ASSASSIN BLACK, BOOSTED HERSELF TO THE TOP OF A wall of chipped bricks and reached down to grab the wrists of her companion and hoist her up. Together, they leaped to the other side.

When N'drato rushed into the alley, he saw their hands fly above their heads as they fell. He knew better than to charge after his sister. Instead, he climbed atop a dented trash bin, grabbed the wooden roof gutter of the hostel in front of which he had surprised them minutes earlier, and pulled himself onto the roof.

Against a night sky of spun star webs and planet shine, he mounted the steep pitch. Wooden shakes creaked and splintered under his weight. In moments, he attained the crown of the building. From among vapor pipes, chimney pots, and cables of conjure-wire, he stared down at sandy lanes and cobbled alleys that crisscrossed between the jumbled buildings of the tree cutters' cantonment. This was an excellent district in which to hide: It fringed the jungle, offering escape into the night forest; also, no two streets ran parallel, and so there were many courtyards, garden enclaves, weedy lots, and shadowy warrens offering sanctuary—but not from a master assassin.

N'drato spotted his quarry scampering along a wooden walkway behind a furniture depot and a carpenters' hall. He hurried down the high roof and used his momentum to launch himself across the lane onto the depot's brick parapet. Stealthily, he crept the length of the building and sidled along a drainage pipe into the alley toward his sister and Jyoti. As they came around the corner, his blade flashed.

Nette caught the weapon in a swift crosshand maneuver, seizing the cutting edge between the thick leather of her gloves and disarming him—exactly as he had anticipated. While her hands twisted his dagger away, he swept his leg behind hers, throwing her to the cobbles. Completing the fluid turn of his body, he grabbed Jyoti by the back of her buckskin trousers as she turned to flee and yanked her into his lap, close enough to sting her carotid with a poisoned needle.

Before the stinger plunged into her throat, he saw the strange profile—the flat nose and jutting jaw of a different woman. He hesitated, and Nette's gloved hand seized his wrist and twisted the needle from his grip. The strange woman swam to her feet with a desperate cry.

"Where is she?" N'drato yelled, deftly curling free of his sister's grip. The question lingered longer than the assassin. Into

the alley darkness he fled, suddenly one with the shadows cast
by planet light and star fire.

Nette sprang to her feet, smiling, and an array of newt's-eye
hex-gems appeared in her fingers as if plucked from the air.
"Here, woman. You ran well."

"You didn't say we was running from anyone!" the woman
whined and swiped the newt's-eyes from Nette's fingers. "He
tried to kill me!"

"Sorry," Nette called after the stranger as she fled in the
opposite direction from N'drato. "He really meant you no harm."
More softly, she added, "It's Jyoti he's after. And by now, she's
far away."

Jyoti had used Nette's ruse to elude N'drato and return to
the manor at the crest of New Arwar. Having rebuilt the city
with the help of Reece's magic, she knew the secret passages
into her childhood home, and she entered the manor through
a corridor that opened onto the stele and obelisk monuments
to her lost brood. No sentinels nor any of the sentry amulets
observed her entry, and she used her eye charms to elude guards
and find her way through the corridors to the chamber where
she found her brother.

Poch was alone in the capacious room, sitting on a griffin-
bone chair and staring at a box with a shining screen propped
on the upholstered cushions of a divan. The double-paneled
doors stood unlocked, and she slipped in and closed the latch
behind her, unnoticed by her brother. The raucous music blar-
ing from the box masked her sounds, and the images flickering
on the screen fixed his attention. He sprawled in the chair
dressed in odd garments—black ocular lenses on his face, his
amulet-vest worn casually over a shirt stenciled with the image
of a bare-chested man standing on a board in the foam of a
crashing ocean wave. His baggy blue pants and pattern-designed
footwear reminded her of garb she had seen during her brief
trespass on the Dark Shore.

"Jyo!" Poch leaped to his feet in surprise. He pointed the thin, rectangular object in his hand at the screen, and the images and boisterous music disappeared. "What are you doing here?"

"I came to talk with you." Her eye charms told her they were alone in the suite. "Are you expecting anyone?"

"No." He stood immobilized with astonishment to see her dressed in street rags—a gray, tattered frock, rope sandals, her hair shorn. "What's happened to you?"

"What do you think?" She walked around him, frowning quizzically at the inert box that had been emitting loud music and vivid, colorful images. "You booted me into the street. Surprised to find me alive?"

"The street?" Poch threw the remote control onto the divan. "I thought you had fled to Moödrun, to take sanctuary with Earl Jee. What are you doing here—and looking so scruffy?"

She locked her green eyes on his black eye mask. "You didn't send an assassin after me?"

"No!" He removed his shades and squinted at her. "What are you talking about?"

"N'drato from the Brood of Assassins—he nearly killed me." She strolled to the opened crates and regarded the heaps of clothing and scattered tape cassettes. "If it's not you, it's Shai Malia. You're margrave now. You look into it. You'll see."

Poch looked hurt. "Shai Malia is my wife now, Jyo."

"So—that makes her too good for murder?" She picked up a pullover with an embossed picture of a blue planet aswirl with feathery clouds. "The Brood of Assassins does not kill Peers for free. The terrible reality is, a lot of funds are going from here to the Assassins, and I'm certain it's Shai Malia who authorized the transfer. Did she also assume the debt that made you margrave?"

"No, Jyoti Odawl—that would be me." Overy Scarn's voice sounded through the paneled doors before they opened and the large woman stepped into the room holding a silver object in her hand—too small for a firecharm yet obviously a weapon, perhaps a dart shooter. She waved it at Jyoti. "Step away from your brother, please."

Jyoti moved toward Overy Scarn. "If Dig Dog put up the money, then you're telling me that the transfer of debt was illegal. I'm still margravine."

"Not anymore." Overy Scarn fired, and an asp tongue of flame spit from the gun muzzle with a sharp, loud bang.

The amulet-belt under Jyoti's frock exploded outward, sending splinters of hex-gems tinkling across the polished wood floor. The impact flung her backward and slammed her hard into the griffin-bone chair, smashing it beneath her.

BUILDING GOD

Nox sat alone in Octoberland. Naked, his knobby back pressed against a side of the five-sided obsidian altar, his stilt legs stretched out straight on the smooth planks, he appeared still and shriveled as a corpse. The wrinkled lids deep in his crusty sockets twitched, his eyeballs trembling, seeing the bright smoke that twisted from the smoldering flesh fire inside him that was his dwindling life. Solitary in his rib-slatted body, he felt like the shadow of someone else, emaciated, weak, and weary. Nightmare had drawn its circle around him.

What was to become of his life? He might live another century, maybe two. But the world itself was dying. The science that the devil worshipper Duppy Hob had brought with him from the Bright Worlds had poisoned the Earth with its toxins, stifled the sky with poisonous heat, polluted the rivers and seas, sickened the land, and torn away the forests. Hob had not cared. He had cherished dreams of returning to the Bright Worlds and ascending beyond to the Greater Reality within the glare of Creation. From there, he would have ruled all worlds, a monstrous immortal. But death had taken him.

Death.

Nox had become the apparition of the very god he feared. Skeletal, draped with mummy skin, his face a no face—nose charred to a dried twist, lips stretched black against discolored, worn-down teeth—he manifested the living personification of the reaper. He was Death. And yet he feared it.

He would never die, he had often chanted, though he knew that was not necessarily true. He could dance forever among the living only if magic made him younger—and the planet did not die.

Earth herself was changing, becoming hostile to the human life he had nurtured for seven thousand years. Soon, only sea worms at the volcanic vents on the ocean floor would thrive. Duppy Hob had cursed humanity and blessed the sea worms.

Nox's emaciated body rocked, trying to shrug free of the nightmare, and then fell still again. *Dogbrick,* he thought, calming himself with the presence in this world of an entity from a hotter order of being. *Dogbrick has the power to change it all.*

Dogbrick's ignorance made him different from Duppy Hob. The beastmarked man had no notion how to focus his power. But the talismans that Duppy Hob had created over the millennia remained in place: the global pattern of cities with their amulet-skyscrapers gathering the tenuous Charm from the void by their very geometries.

Nox was aware of them. With this knowledge and Dogbrick's magic, it would be possible to change the world. Not only could Death be thwarted for himself but also all humanity could benefit. A new era of global harmony would supplant the rapacious greed of history. He would be young again, forever, and humanity would devote its remarkable energies to building God on Earth instead of destroying itself.

Inspired by this hope, Nox gathered to himself the power of Octoberland. Seven thousand years of accrued magic widened around him. It gave him the strength to stand. He leaned heavily upon the obsidian altar while dizziness circled through him. When the momentary spell of vertigo passed, he reached for the stained urn that sat atop a dish of hammered brown metal. His hand came out with the black needle. Something thermal glistened around it, a chrism of body heat stolen from a dying woman.

The ghost of a young woman glimmered briefly in the air above the altar, a thermal shroud with the dolorous expression of the flaxen-haired Virgo, who had died under the needle on the planks of Octoberland. Nox waved the needle in the wraith smoke, absorbing her heat once more into the dented urn, and he whispered, "Virgo, you are dead, but by your sacrifice a new era becomes more plausible. Summon to Octoberland the Virgo who will take your place—Mary Felix, companion of Dogbrick."

The needle stirred in his grip and writhed with vibrant power.

The feel of it alive in his hands filled him with the same exaltation he had first experienced in the time when kings could read the meaning of stars. Seven thousand years of magic thrived in him. Earth magic, it was not strong enough to make him young, yet it had the power inside it of a shining wind that had crossed miles of fields amber with grain, filled with the golden smoke of pollen. Earth magic was strong as an underground river that reached up from its darkness into the loamy roots and striving stems of brave grass and into the grasping branches of trees, clutching for the sky and the light of a higher world.

Nox walked slowly about the altar, following the circuit of the painted circle, stopping at each of the five points touched by the pentagram to whisper to the sticky needle in his hands, "Mary Felix, you are Virgo, come take your place in Octoberland."

The thin wind inside the implement slipped out and left the sliver of metal dull in Nox's bony hands. An astral breeze swirled once around the ritual chamber, and when it streamed past the altar, the wicks of the two fat black candles ignited, and the flames wagged in silent jubilation.

Out through the shagbark walls, the magic wind flowed, out into the night sky over Manhattan. The city shone with a fury that dimmed the stars. The needle's breath rose above the city's brilliance into the upper air about the Moon. And the Moon's red hands took it and carried it across the sky. On the black surface of the sea, the moon's light looked like thrown-out bones. In the night-held forests, municipalities glowed like splashes of magma. Everything was other than itself. Everything was changed.

The needle magic carried Nox's insistence down the night to where Mary Felix sat with Brick on a bench in the halogen radiance of a fuel depot in the remote woodlands: a tarmac field with a diesel pump, a shed fitted for air and water, an outhouse, and a pay phone. They had traveled all day through the north woods to reach this humble station on a narrow timber road. From here, she had made a phone call with change given in charity by the driver who had deposited them here. Soon, her friends from the university would send someone for her and Brick.

Nox sensed all this through his magic. Seven thousand years of gathering cold fire to himself from the sky moved like a wind in the red hands of the Moon. It brushed through the long grass in the ditch behind the truck stop, whistled over the open mouth of empty half pints of Wild Rose, rustled Burger King wrappers, and dispelled diesel fumes with a pungent scent of crushed cinnamon, trampled leaves, pond mist, and flax straw at threshing time.

Mary Felix sat up taller. A cool air had penetrated the muggy night. A fragrance of oat stubble and rain scum from the crotch of willow trees swirled suddenly among the refueling trucks. Her nostrils widened, her eyes gleamed with alertness. Her feelings had turned inside out. The magic that Nox had sent to call her south to Manhattan had disengaged from within and filled the space around her.

She felt the grooves in her brain sparkling and knew that

something strange was about to happen. She looked about her, and when her gaze brushed the ground, her blood swerved with fright.

In an oil-spilled rainbow at her feet, a face began to form. It had skull-like features, adder eyes, and tiny teeth in a grin wider than illusion.

A BIOGRAPHY OF THE SKY

"BRICK!" MARY FELIX NUDGED THE SLEEPING MAN BESIDE HER. HER scientific mind assured her she was hallucinating—but she wanted to be sure. "What do you see in this oil smear?"

Brick roused himself from his stupor and glanced at the spectral colors on the concrete. "I don't see anything."

A horn honked a quick greeting, and a beige pickup truck swung onto the tarmac apron in front of them. On its door, a university seal announced this was the reply to Mary's telephone call.

The driver in faded jeans, plaid shirt, and mud-caked boots stepped out and offered a puzzled smile. Brick recognized him as the researcher who had accompanied Mary Felix on her search for Sasquatch. He looked no worse for having had his soul knocked free from his body. His bald, sunburned head gleamed under the station lights.

"Ryan!" Mary Felix leaped to her feet.

The researcher gawked, his lantern jaw loose. "Mary Felix?"

"Her granddaughter," Brick offered, standing up behind Mary.

"Yes—yes, I'm the one who called you." Mary shifted uneasily under Ryan's intense stare. "I talked to your machine. I'm glad you got my message. Like I said on the phone, my grandmother—she gave me your number in case I needed help." Her freckled cheeks burned at her lie. "We were in a boating accident—"

"My office assistant relayed your message. . . ." Ryan shook his head with disbelief. "Your voice—your face—my God, it's too weird—you sound and look just like your grandmother! Your name is Mary, too?"

"Yes. We were boating north of here—"

"Then, you don't know." Ryan exhaled sharply. "Your grandmother is missing." His pale eyes widened with concern. "I'm sorry. I'm really sorry. I lost her on a fauna count—a university expedition in the reserve. It was horrible. I don't really know how to begin."

Brick and Mary looked at each other.

"We've had helicopter flybys and team sweeps of the area where I lost her," Ryan continued in a faltering voice, "but we haven't found much of anything. And the worst of it is, I know what happened to her—yet no one believes me." He crossed one arm over his chest and with the other reached around to scratch the back of his head. "I don't even know if I should be telling you this."

"Grandmother said she believed she had seen Sasquatch in the outland woods. She told us that the fauna count was just an eco excuse to get funding from the university so that she could track Bigfoot. She found it, didn't she?"

Ryan's eyes flickered with surprise, then cast a nervous glance at Brick before turning excitedly to Mary. "We found Sasquatch, all right. We really did! And it knocked me out with one blow. I had to be sent back for medical observation. You can see the bruise." He turned his cheek and displayed his mottled jaw.

"You're okay?" Mary asked, touching his arm with concern.

"Yes, sure, I'm fine. But—I'm ashamed to say this, Mary—I left your grandmother out there. She convinced me to leave her where we made contact. And now, she's missing. I feel terrible. I never should have left her. That creature must have come back and taken her. And now she's gone."

"You mustn't feel bad, Ryan." She tightened her grip on his

arm. "It's not your fault. I know my grandmother very well, and she would not want you to blame yourself. . . ."

Brick leaned forward. "Look, I'm sorry to interrupt but I could use some clothes."

"Oh, of course." Ryan reached around to the back of the pickup and removed a duffel bag. "I brought a double set of everything. The message said you were big, but I didn't realize you were this big. These will be a little tight, I'm afraid."

Brick accepted the bag with a grateful nod, opened it, and began taking out the clothes.

"I also found your grandmother's emergency cache just where you said it would be." He handed Mary a Velcro-sealed pouch. "There's cash in there, which will help you get back home. I know you probably want to stay here and look for your grandmother. . . ."

"How can we help?" Mary asked the question she knew Ryan expected.

"You can't." Ryan shook his balding head grievously. "Your grandmother disappeared up-country. There's nothing you can do. It's best that you just go home. Where is that?"

"Manhattan." Mary fit the snaps of the pouch to her belt. "I feel bad leaving grandmother lost—"

"We'll call you soon as there's word," Ryan promised and opened the door to his truck. "Come on. You're a long way from nowhere out here. I'll drive you back to civilization. If we leave now, we can make it to a station by morning, and you can get a train."

On the ride through the night, while Ryan energetically voiced his guilt and Mary reassured him, the scent of autumn thickened in the truck. A chill of spruce resins filled the cab. Surprised by this, Ryan dangled his arm from the window to feel the warm night. He reminisced about Mary Felix, and Mary stopped listening. Dreams pressed close to her—a vision from an evil Marc Chagall: angels with bestial faces in a flurry of autumn leaves.

Brick worried when she fell asleep and he tried to wake her, but she would not be roused.

"Better let her rest," Ryan advised, breathing deeply the redolence of a leaf-clogged creek. "You've been through a lot."

Dawn stretched a green wire under a gray sky when Mary woke, her body soaked in an ether of north wind and deadwood. She asked them to pull over. The dreams of the animal angels flying in the night terrified her, and she felt certain that something wretched would happen to Ryan and Brick if she stayed with them. On the pretense of relieving herself in the shrubs, she slipped away.

When the air went hot and still, Brick realized that she had left them. Without alerting Ryan, he pursued, calling her name, and wandering into the woods of the brightening day. A sour smell of leaf drift and the rot of unburdened apple trees guided him.

Far away, Nox sat in trance beside the obsidian altar, the needle of black poison loose in his hands. From this distance, he could see into her as into a lucid pool that magnified the slime-muted shapes at its bottom. And there, he faced the goblins. His skin puckered at the sight of their filthy flesh, hairless heads swollen and dented, bone-hooded eyes.

He realized that these frightful little dolls were thinking about him and how to explain themselves. With an unsheltered sorrow, they decided to share with him a biography of the sky. They began with the clouds, the dragon breath that rose from the moist earth and chilled to rain. They climbed above the clouds to the ionosphere, the fringe of the atmosphere buffeted by the solar wind, where electrical powers circulated—the source of the cold fire in the planet's magnetic field, the origin of his terrestrial magic.

Entranced, Nox rode the thoughts of the goblins higher yet, into the Gulf, the fifteen-billion-year void in which hung all the galaxies and their shrouds of cosmic dust and gas. Mounting higher yet, he glimpsed the Bright Worlds, the chaff of matter aswirl in glowing eddies of Charm, billows of comet veils and star smoke—Irth, Nemora, Hellsgate, and hundreds of planets beyond, afloat like motes in the fiery fumes of the Abiding Star.

There, within the blinding brilliance at the beginning of time was the original home of the goblins. In that luminosity began the real worlds of which all the Bright Worlds in the aura of the Abiding Star and all the galaxies of the dark Gulf and the tiny Earth itself were but shadows hung in a void.

Nox cried out to see this, and his vision curdled to his own shrunken body, his heart knocking in its dark cave, his breath laboring with the heat of an August day in Manhattan.

THE ETERNAL GUARDIANS

Two MANOR SENTINELS IN HERALDIC CRIMSON-AND-GOLD UNI-forms burst into Overy Scarn's suite followed by Shai Malia, veiled in gray and black. She had searched for her husband with her eye charms and had summoned the guards when she heard the explosion from the bond agent's suite. "What has happened here?" she asked sharply, looking irately at the woman and then at Poch in his strange garb before noticing Jyoti on the floor.

"She shot my sister!" Poch cried and knelt over her. "Opals—quickly!"

"She broke into my suite," Overy Scarn asserted defensively. "Margrave, tell them. I was merely defending myself."

"You shot my sister!" Poch spat back, yanking theriacal opals from his vest and pressing them to Jyoti's body.

"Get that weapon away from her," Shai Malia commanded and went to Poch. "What was Jyoti doing here?"

"She's not dead!" Poch grabbed at his wife's robes, reaching for the opals beneath her veils as she crouched next to him. "The projectile struck her amulet-vest. We can heal her internal injuries with theriacal opals. Give me yours!"

Shai Malia obliged him and whispered, "I will take her to the dear ones. They will see that she is healed."

Poch faced her with a dismayed expression. "She says you hired an assassin to kill her. Is that true?"

"She speaks from her rage." With a nod, Shai Malia signaled a guard to take the body. "You shocked her when you usurped her power. She will say anything to cause you pain."

"She knows how we financed her overthrow." Poch threw an angry stare to where Overy Scarn stood in the custody of a sentinel. "Scarn told her."

Shai Malia stood and addressed the guard she had summoned. "Take the former margravine to the suite she once occupied and stay with her outside the door. But do not open the door. Do you understand?"

"I am going with her," Poch declared and followed the guard who carried his sister to the door.

Shai Malia took his arm. "Wait." With a wave, she dismissed the sentinel who stood behind Overy Scarn. When he had departed, she pointed to the open crates and the heaps of clothing. "What is the meaning of this, Scarn? Why is the margrave dressed in such ridiculous garb?"

Overy Scarn explained to the margrave's wife what she had earlier told Poch himself. "With Dig Dog's connections among Duppy Hob's remaining contacts in Gabagalus, we can bring many new and wonderful products to the dominions. The Brood of Odawl will achieve prominence once again."

"Hm, yes—and you will manage this monopoly for us, won't you?" Shai Malia sneered. "And the dragon's share of the profits as well, I'm sure."

Overy Scarn cocked one of her small eyebrows. "Would there be a margrave—or his wife—if not for Dig Dog's investment?"

"Why did you tell my sister the source of our funding?" Poch jabbed a finger at her. "It was you who hired the assassin—to protect your so-called investment. Admit it."

"I did no such thing. But—" she straightened her large shoulders and acknowledged with a cold look—"the margravine's death would assure your position as margrave. I took advantage of her illegal trespass of my quarters to shoot her. I did it for you."

"Do me no further favors, Scarn." Poch turned abruptly and left the room.

"We shall discuss this further at a later time." Shai Malia gestured to the open crates. "Box all these goods and be certain no one else learns of our access to the Dark Shore."

On the polished resin floor of the corridor outside the chamber that contained the goblins, Jyoti lay with Poch squatting beside her. He plucked from her torn frock the dull opals whose Charm had drained into her wounded body and then said to the guard nearby, "We must summon a healer."

"That won't be necessary," Shai Malia spoke from under the round pomegranate-stained glass at the head of the stairway. She sent the guard away and examined the amulet-sash under the margravine's torn frock. Every one of the hex-gems had been shattered and the amber power wands were ruptured lengthwise. "Scarn's projectile weapons are powerful. But the talismanic strength of the sash protected her. Not even her flesh is pierced."

"But she may have internal injuries." Poch's voice nearly broke to a wail. "She drained all the opals."

"Trust that the dear ones will heal her. Now open the door."

Numb-edged with fright for his sister, he touched his amulet-key to the latch, and the door swung open on a filthy cloud mass of clotted webs. Nauseous miasma oozed from creamy mounds of larval eggs that dangled like drool from rafters, wall beams, and furniture. The ichorous gossamer wove the chamber into a giant cocoon.

In the midst of this sickly hot convolution of webbed tissue,

the goblins clustered. Their fetal bodies twitched in the light
filtering through the gauze that matted the windows. They ate
the light. And from their orifices they exuded the gummy web-
bings and their white, throbbing roe. Dried, blackened spicules
of these excretions grimed their stubby hands and streaked their
bloated bellies.

To Poch and Shai Malia, the fetid air smelled sweetly floral
and inviting. They dragged Jyoti into the sweltering hive. "Oh,
dear ones—dear ones—eternal guardians of Irth! Can you save
my sister? Can you heal her?"

The goblins blinked their toadish, gold-speckled lids.

Poch drifted into a dream of sledding on the Kazu sand rivers
with his sister, breathless with laughter, intoxicated with the
redolence of sweat and heat-baked dunes as though this were
the incense of always. He sagged among the reeking webs,
smiling.

"Yes, dear ones, yes!" Shai Malia squatted over Jyoti's
sprawled body. "Let him sleep. His emotions for his sister cloud
his judgment. Let him sleep while you and I search deeply
in her."

A flush of fever shivered Shai Malia as she felt her way into
the unconscious woman. The dear ones gave her the strength
of their deep seeing so that she could possess this flesh that
had served as a lover to the one they hated, the one they
feared—the magus of the Dark Shore, Reece Morgan. His skin
had pressed against hers—and the psychic imprint remained of
their commingling. By this intimate link, her awareness reached
out across Irth, grasping one lover and searching for the other
half of their splendor.

A bestial man with a nap of blue fur marked by shoulder
rosettes and maroon face stripes appeared in the mental space
she shared with the dear ones.

"No wonder we could not find him!" Shai Malia jubilantly
thumped the body under her with both fists. "He is hidden
by beastmarks!"

She peered again into the psychic expanse of the trance and saw twin porphyry towers topped by winged sphinxes and beyond them ruins pierced by fronds and spiraling vines. "Ah! We have found him! We have found our enemy. He has tracked you five dear ones to where you had hidden yourselves before we brought you here! With wicked cunning he stalks you. But now, we have found him! He is at this moment among the Cloths of Heaven."

IN JUDGMENT OF GHOSTS

THE CHARMFIRE EXPLOSION SEARED THE FUR OF RIPCAT'S BACK AND tattered Esre's witch veils. In terrified embrace, they flew through the charmway, propelled by the shock wave, and tumbled among dusty, rocky detritus. The witch collapsed on her back, and the illumination from her lux-diamond headband vanished among heights of ruin. Storeys of skewed girders and sagging floors spiraled upward to the crown of a crushed dome, where daylight penetrated in numerous laser-thin rays.

Ripcat had been thrown against a cracked and jarred pillar, and he shook off the stupor of his pain to look around. A forest of staggered columns ranged ahead, disappearing into darkness. The charmway through which they had passed, a jagged crevice in a wall of faded glyphs and engraved dragon coils, smoked with dust. The passage had collapsed under the force of the blast.

Esre read the wild look in his feral face. "We're in the Cloths of Heaven—and there's no way back."

"Are you okay?" Ripcat stared uneasily at her distorted face where she lay among rock shards, but he saw no open wounds.

"My amulets protected me." She pushed to her feet, ignoring the aches of her bruises. "Only my veils are shredded."

Beneath her torn robes, she wore a sable undergarment that

fit her like a bodysuit and the empty holster of the firecharm that rested against her hip. Conjure-filaments outlined her muscular legs and thick torso in a gold circuitry that connected clusters of hex-gems at vital points on the suit. Against her thigh, a curved blade fit snugly in its strap.

"Are your eye charms working?" Ripcat craned his neck, searching for some way to access the higher storeys. "Can we find the goblins?"

"They're not here." She showed him the niello lozenge she had been carrying in her palm. "At least, they're not here anymore. See in this corner—the webs?"

He sunk his sight deeper into the black crystal in her palm and discerned a vault of tilted slabs draped with cobwebs. "Is it a spider's nest?"

"No, it's goblin spoor."

"Let's go there."

They followed the eye charm among rust-varnished rocks that had fallen from ceilings far above. Hollow voices called remotely from on high. "Wraiths," Esre said with brittle fright. "They are the phantoms of ancient wizards who survive in these ruins by thriving off the blood heat of the living—plants, toads . . . and humans if they can find them."

Among fallen entablatures and fractured pillars, they beheld the green ether of the ancient dead. Swirling in a feculent stench, weightless as smoke, smoldering shapes rose. Arms like tentacles reached for them, and grievous voices swollen with emptiness droned a hypnotic chant. Ripcat felt the chant tightening in his frightened muscles, paralyzing him so that the leprous shapes could gather around his blood heat and feed.

Esre smashed a theriacal opal among the rock shards, and the wraiths flew to it, ravenous to absorb its Charm. While they fed, she and Ripcat fled through the forest of tilted and fallen pillars. The witch smashed two more opals during their run to keep the wraiths occupied.

Beyond the shelled façade of an anonymous structure whose

pale stone piers upheld a hieroglyphic frieze, they found a broad stairway. The smashed stone steps ascended into a domed vault of rubble. Among these broken slabs of masonry, they located the abandoned hive, its stone walls thick with scurf.

Ripcat plucked at a woolly clump of web and found, snagged in its midst, an egg sac. "What is this stuff?" The fragile glazed sac broke in his grip and oozed a milky liquid. "They made this?"

"Secreted from their bodies." Esre scanned the dome for cracks and found a fissure hung with ganglia of jungle creepers and vines. "They absorb the Charm in the light of the Abiding Star. What you're holding are the toxins they eliminate—their feces."

Ripcat dropped the clotted web and stepped away. "Cripes, it looked like something alive."

"It was." She kicked at the sacs, and they collapsed in a hiss of dust. "The goblins are from a hotter reality. Even their waste partakes of their higher energy and lives. Not in any sentient way. Like amoebae, I suppose. But the goblins use their web works to focus their telepathy. The intricate geometries serve as antennae for broadcasting their will widely. And those who hear must obey, for we are like phantoms to them and they are powerful wizards in judgment of ghosts."

"Where did they go from here?"

Esre's twisted face constricted. "I don't know. It seems they left here sometime ago. We had better get out ourselves—before more wraiths descend on us."

They clambered over jumbled plates of stone. But as they mounted upward to where daylight revealed emerald glints of jungle, the long shadow of a man fell upon them. Ripcat lifted his head in time to see a flash of blade whirling at him, too close to evade. A violent collision knocked him sideways, and the flung knife pierced Esre's throat. The hilt lay flush against one side of her neck and the blue metal tip emerged from the other. Her eyes stared lifelessly at him from within her mask of scars.

When Ripcat looked up, the killer was gone. Stunned by the efficiency of the assassin's strike, he lowered Esre among the fallen slabs, his heart punching hard. He reached for the knife strapped to her thigh, and a metal whip sang from below and snagged painfully about his leg. The killer had dropped noiselessly to a ledge below him, so quickly that Ripcat feared for an irrational instant that he was a ghost. Then, the whip coil tightened and jerked him off balance.

N'drato had emerged from a crawl space between the rocks, leaning his full weight onto the metal lariat. The beastmarked man glared at him and actually roared. That made the assassin smile, which further infuriated the beastman. He grabbed for the metal coil snaring his leg, and when he pulled on it, N'drato let go.

Ripcat flew backward, skipping over the tilted and uneven stones, and fell just as the assassin had planned. He spun about in midair and saw the pool among the sharp rubble before he struck it. Helplessly, he splashed into it, his claws open, thrashing about the mineral-dense water. But before he could pull himself from the slurry pool, the blade that had killed Esre glinted for one instant in his sight, the sharp edge thwacking him hard between the eyes and cleaving his skull.

N'drato used the metal whip to dredge the corpse from the thick water. Briefly, he studied the dead beast. The knife had penetrated deep enough to pierce the brain, and the green eyes in the bestial face had crossed to see the blade that had skewered his skull. He yanked his weapon free and wiped it clean on the blue nap of fur across the dead man's chest. Then, he looped the metal coil about Ripcat's ankles and dragged him behind.

THE WORLD OF YOUR EYES

MARY MOVED QUICKLY SOUTH. THE GRIP OF OCTOBERLAND WAS strong, and she knew she could not elude it. But she was determined to protect Brick, the magical being who had lost his magic by restoring her youth. By mid-morning, she had slipped through the woods back to the road and caught a ride to the highway in a logger's truck.

Noon found her in her cool aura of autumn at a small train station where heat bleared the tracks and crinkled the air in the distance. A rural family huddled in the meager shade of the platform awning and stared askance at the young woman under the smiting sun with the lilting breeze stirring her masses of chestnut hair and yellow leaves dancing around her hiking boots.

In the air-conditioned passenger car, the chill nimbus surrounding Mary was less noticeable, but her perfume of heather and gray mist drew a smile from the conductor and the easy comfort of the riders seated near her. She bought a ticket for Toronto, where she would catch a flight for New York. Her mind continued to offer plausible hypotheses, scientific considerations of Dogbrick and the new reality that had abducted her.

All creation is energy, she thought to herself. *Einstein has shown that. The worlds of the Abiding Star are the energy in the first instants of the universe. They are hot and very small compared to us. Yet they are a lot like us. Or I guess it's us who are like them. We're the shadow worlds of their light. Obviously, it's not hot enough out here on the Dark Shore for dragons, gnomes, hippogriffs, and goblins—all those creatures of Charm. But our lives still shadow the basic contours of their reality.*

Speculative thoughts like these occupied her for the first hours of the long ride. Eventually, the shuttling sound of the wheels, the rocking of the car, and the green sameness of the landscape lulled her contemplations of reality and her worries about what she would do when she finally confronted Nox, and she drifted to sleep.

Stars shine most clear in the darkest night—and the darkest night of all opened within her dream: the Gulf. Pinpoint lights retreated in every direction among aisles of emptiness, the unconnected lines of madness, not going anywhere.

Not anywhere—until in her dream she lifted free of the galactic plane and saw how the seemingly unfocused scattering of

stars fit together into an immense pinwheel, darkness enclosing
a vast whirlpool of light.

She lifted farther away, into a wider darkness. Now the galaxy
and all the nearby pinwheels and globular clusters looked like
icy flakes, a random dusting of snow. She soared through her
dreaming, through thickening clusters of galaxies. Then darkness, motelessly empty, stupefied her, and she thought her
dream had ended—until another wave of galactic fog swept
around her.

Flung by her dream to the very height of the Gulf, she gazed
back at streamers of galaxies twisting like incense smoke,
braiding long stretches of darkness between them. The whole
universe lay beneath her—a pit fifteen billion light-years deep.

And when she turned, she faced into the incomparable radiance of the Abiding Star. Its silver light blinded her, and a
cathedral of time built itself out of the glare before she could
turn away. Archways of star smoke vaulted alcoves of darkness
glittering with planets.

Her dream zoomed her toward one feathery blue world.
Night's crescent covered the planet's oceanic hemisphere, where
she knew from Dogbrick's memories that the continent of Gabagalus had sunk once more into the sea. Facing the full brightness
of the Abiding Star, the dominions of Irth gleamed in a colorful
mosaic of geographies: from the Qaf's cankerous cinderlands
umber and black edged to the wild, demonic gleams of dragon
pools, tarns, and linns among the numerous Reef Isles of Nhat.

She fell to Irth. For a moment, she stood where Dogbrick
had once stood, on a street corner in the industrial cliff city of
Saxar. Broken gods stared from the broad-leafed ivy of a building, faces faded by erosion, eternal world dancers carved into
the stone edifice of an office tower that bore the gold plaque:
Dig Dog Ltd.

Curbstones verdant with moss brinked a blue brick street
where gilded trolleys powered by Charm clanged past, carrying
veiled witches, leather-harnessed charmwrights, and lyceum stu-

dents in purple frocks and saffron box hats. On the pitched streets below squatted factory tenements effaced with soot and vat-shaped refineries unrolling sulfurous clouds. The sea gleamed at the bottom of the terraced cliffs, obscured by a cumulus of pollution.

Her dreaming mind lofted away on the sea wind. Dogbrick's place on Irth retreated. She stood upon the arc of the world and watched the bodies of the dead drifting up on the nocturnal tide of the planet's twilight. They sailed away into the Gulf, unanchored by Charm. She sailed with them, on her way back through her trance to her own body at the far end of the universe. Astonished, she watched as one of the many corpses launched at day's end into the night sky and disappearing at the horizon of sight as specks of reflected light, tumbled toward her.

The carcass rolled close enough for her to see that this had been a woman—but a ghastly one, her face a quilt of livid scars. Puncture wounds gaped at the sides of her throat, and from these gouges her soul leaked. A pearly foam oozed out and evaporated quickly in the cold.

Caval—The soul whispered to her as it seeped from the corpse. *This world in your eyes was once his own. Find him on the Dark Shore. Use my life to find Caval—the wizard on the Dark Shore—*

The corpse collided with her, and the sticky mess of her soul splattered over Mary and gummed up her dream. A flash of a spinning blade whirled at her, and pain slammed her neck, spiking fire into her brain and jolting her awake. With a small cry, she sat up straight in her seat on the passenger train to Toronto.

MADNESS

BRICK KNEW HE HAD LOST MARY FELIX WHEN HE COULD NO longer smell autumn among the jeweled green light of the summer forest. He cursed the loss of his beastmarks and grasped his nose, trying to widen his nostrils, hoping to catch again the leaf-smoke taint of her. "You call this a nose?" he groused angrily. "It's a pathetic and useless lump of cartilage—a semblance of a nose!"

Ryan, who had been bent over, trying to read Mary's movements from impressions among the leaf litter and bent branches on the underbrush, stood up with a bewildered look. "What?"

"She's gone. We're not going to find her here." Brick twisted uncomfortably in his tight jeans and Bigfoot T-shirt stretched almost to ripping across his massive chest. "We have to get to New York. That's where she's headed."

"But I have to get back to the university." Ryan scratched his head and peered hopefully through the sun-shot foliage. "I've got summer school classes to teach."

"Show me how to drive the truck." Dogbrick shoved through the shrubs, striding back toward the pickup. "And point me toward New York. Is it far?"

"You can't take the truck. It belongs to the university." Ryan rubbed the back of his neck, thinking out loud: "Something's definitely fishy. First, her grandmother disappears and now her?"

"It's too complicated to explain, believe me, Ryan. But we know she's going to New York. I can't let her go without me." Brick opened the driver's door and gave a hopeless shake of his head at the sight of the three pedals and the dashboard dials. "Just show me how to use this thing. I'll get it back to you."

"Why did she run away from you?" Ryan asked from the far side of the truck, eyes hooded suspiciously. "Did you hurt her?"

Brick straightened. "I didn't hurt her. She's trying to protect *me*. But she's putting herself in danger."

"What are you talking about?"

"Look, you wouldn't understand. Just get me to New York."

Ryan shook his ruddy head. "No way. For one thing, I don't have enough gas to get you out of the province."

Brick huffed an exasperated sigh. "Maybe you could put me on a train. Mary talked about taking a train to New York."

"That's expensive, and you don't have any money. You know, I'm beginning to think you two aren't on the level."

Brick reached inside himself for power, wanting to widen his sense of smell to a fraction of its former acuity so that he could scent out which direction Mary had fled. But he felt nothing inside except his tight stomach. He was frustrated—and hungry.

"Listen, Ryan—" Brick ran both large hands through his straw-blond hair. "You feel responsible for losing Mary Felix in the woods after the Sasquatch?"

Ryan nodded slowly. "Yeah, though I hardly believe myself anymore. But I *know* it happened. The damn thing knocked me unconscious."

"Okay then, believe this: *I* knocked you unconscious." He tapped a husky finger against the stretched fabric of his T-shirt. "You had two pointy-eared, red dogs with you, remember? I threw sleep at them when they came at me. They collapsed, and you took a rifle and shot a dart at me. You hit me here." He slapped his thigh. "You stood over me with the rifle, and I struck you across the jaw."

"You?" Ryan angled his head with incredulity. "No, uh-uh. I saw something bigger than you—hairier, with a face you wouldn't believe."

"That's because I'm changed now—just like Mary is changed." Brick pushed his face urgently toward the researcher. "How else could I tell you what happened unless I was there?"

"Mary Felix told you somehow—when you found her in the woods. . . ."

"That *was* Mary Felix who ran away from us!" He thrust his big arm at the woods. "You heard her voice. You saw her face—her eyes, her nose, her mouth. Who else could that *be*, for God's sake? That *is* Mary Felix."

"No." Ryan shook his head insistently. "Mary is nearly eighty years old. Her granddaughter looks like eighteen at most."

"Mary doesn't have a granddaughter." Brick glared at Ryan.

"She doesn't have children. She and her husband were childless. You must know that."

"I thought so, too, but then I figured—maybe a child from another marriage . . . ?"

"Look at me, Ryan. Have you ever seen a human being that looks like me? My coloring—my size?"

Ryan studied him dubiously. "You've got a point, I guess." He backed off a step. "Maybe you should get in the truck and tell me the whole story. We're not going to find Mary out here. And I've got to get back to the research station."

Brick agreed eagerly. While they drove, he tried to tell Ryan everything that he could remember from the time he woke in the woods among the Sasquatch pack until he encountered Caval's ghost on the logging road. "I think we might see him again. He's trying to help us."

"This wizard—from these, uh, Bright Worlds—you knew him?" Ryan asked as they drove through a small town of weatherboarded buildings.

"Well, I don't think we actually met before, Caval and I. He helped my partner, Ripcat—a magus from the Dark Shore, where we are now. But, as I've said, I don't recall anything of the Bright Worlds. Mary told me. All my memories are with her."

"Right, of course." He slowly pulled onto a long rutted driveway beside a university extension sign and drove toward a cluster of cinder-block buildings. "So let me get this straight—all your Charm was used up when you made Mary young again. Then, when she tried to get you to use your power to revive your own memories, they flowed into her. But I'm not clear on why she had to run off. Tell me that part again."

"The sinister angels," Brick reminded him. "The coven in New York called Octoberland—"

"Right, right. Their warlock has a magical hold on Mary and is drawing her south—to get you there so that he can use your magic for himself." Ryan braked to a stop under the corrugated zinc canopy of a crude carport. "But this warlock—"

"Nox."

"Yeah, Nox—" Ryan got out of the pickup. "He doesn't know that you've already used up all your power."

"I don't think he knows that—or about the goblins." Brick stepped out among gravel and weeds. "That's what Mary hopes to show him—the evil of the goblins. If he sees that, he won't want anything to do with me."

"Of course not." Ryan crossed the carport, past a van and a Jeep, both beige and bearing the university seal on their doors. "And the charmways in Manhattan—the wormholes to the Bright Worlds that the devil worshipper Duppy Hob took six thousand years to create—that's an even better reason for Mary to get you to New York, so you can escape from the Dark Shore and not draw the goblins into our unsuspecting world."

"That's right." Brick followed Ryan among pigweeds as big, bent, and rusted looking as old machinery. "I think she wants to confront Nox alone—to try to protect me now that I've lost my power."

"Yeah, that must be it." Ryan approached a brick storage shed next to the tool shop and struggled with the rusted padlock. "Help me with this, will you?"

Brick wrenched open the lock, and Ryan slid aside the heavy metal door. The tired iron runners shrieked. He stepped in and flicked on the overhead light. The small space stood empty, waiting to be stocked with winter supplies.

"Would you give me a hand with this?" he asked, and as soon as Brick entered, he curled around him and slammed the metal door shut, slapping the padlock into place with a expression of immense relief.

"Hey!" Brick shouted with surprise—but heard no reply.

The City of Lost Light

For the holy and the damned,
time weighs a little less.
—GIBBET SCROLLS: 22

OUT OF THIS DARKNESS

NOX STEPPED FROM OCTOBERLAND ONTO THE HOT TAR PAPER OF an August afternoon. He reeled almost drunkenly among black vapor pipes and silver air-duct exhaust fans, weary from his long trance work. He wanted relief from the pewter shadows of the coven, the weak colors, the smudged odors of lost leaves, and he moved out of this darkness into the radiance of day. He doffed his ceremonial robe, left it like a puddled black shadow atop the zinc housing of an air-conditioning shed, and stood in his red briefs under the styptic gaze of the summer sun.

The ancient sorcerer looked as though he had stepped from a furnace: His crinkled flesh was charred, stretched like crepe over his angular bones, and the thin hair on his scorched skull

wisped like the torn veils of spiders. He sat atop a curve of
elbow pipe and lifted his sunken eyes toward the sun, glad for
its savage fire. He had grown weary of trance work and ghosts
and their effluvia. He stretched his withered arms up to the
creator light and beseeched the powers to fulfill his ambition
and make him young again. Mary Felix was on her way to
him, and the coven was in place to receive her. Once she
was installed in the circle, Dogbrick would follow, and the
beastmarked creature's Charm would heal seven thousand
years of time.

Out of the sun's glare, an image from the first temple formed:
a standing goat with angel wings—a deity from long ago, a god
of Sumer. Nox blinked. The summer heat drained from him in
a cold wash of fright. An entity in the sky with one end hooked
to the stars had connected its other end to his soul, to one of
the deepest memories at the bottom of his mind. *Who?*

A vibrant hum made the sunshine jiggle like sheets of sulfur
dust, and a voice resonated within him: *I am with you, Nox of
Jarmo, Nox from the foothills of the Zagros Mountains, Nox from the time
before the first cities.*

"Caval!"

*Yes, I am yet with you, Nox, who learned his magic in Eridu, Nox
who took knowledge from the steppe wanderers, Nox who has lived too long
by cunning from the wayfarers of the plains beneath the stars. I hide in
the sky, Nox, and I see everything. No good will come of drawing Irth's
Charm to you. The innocent Dogbrick cannot help you. . . .*

"Begone, dead thing!" Nox crisscrossed his arms with a scis-
soring swiftness, and the presence thinned almost to nothing.

*Wait! You have the power to dismiss me easily enough. I am weaker
now than ever. But I have come to you for a purpose.*

"To destroy me! Away with you, wizard of Irth."

*I—am—truly a wizard of Irth. Hold to me, Nox, and I will show
you the Bright Worlds themselves. Hold to me—*

Nox desisted from motioning his arms and instead crossed

them over his rib-grooved chest. "You are a thin thread of a being, Caval. I can snap you and break what little is left of your life to the heat simmer of gravel and street dust. Do not think to deceive me. I am too wary for tricks. Yet I will see what you have to show." He opened the burnt sticks of his arms and received the shine of day and within it the energy of the wizard.

In an instant, the harmonic force of Caval's wire-thin being matched the frequency of waveforms from the Bright Worlds, and the mind of Nox ranged across the Gulf, across fifteen billion light-years, to the brightness of the Abiding Star. The fierce radiance blinded Nox. Immediately, he pulled back, seeing nothing but silver luminosity.

As he fell away, his vision adjusted, and within the glare he perceived flame shapes, smoke turnings, vaporous neon shimmerings—the star fumes and comet vapors that enclosed the planets of the Bright Worlds.

From out of that foggy coastline, sparks sifted. Grains of light sublimed from the white aura of the Abiding Star and dissolved into the abyss of eternal night. *These are the dead of the Bright Worlds. Their bodies, unanchored by sleep and death, are blown on the charmwind of the Abiding Star—blown into the void.*

"Why are you showing me this, wizard?"

All souls come from the Abiding Star. Once, you too lived among the Bright Worlds, in another life, with other memories.

"Help me to harvest this Charm, wizard. Gather this Charm into my flesh and make me young again."

The Charm of these dead is too thin to change a dense being such as yourself.

Nox withdrew from the vista of sugary smoke wafting into the dark, the seeds of Charm that would grow other lives among darker worlds. He retreated toward his earthbound body, and as he floated back to himself, he noticed the few sparkles of charmlight that followed the same cold vector.

Distinctly, he saw their bodies rolling head over heels through the vacuum—and though they were shaped like people, they were not human.

Stymied by wonder, Nox hovered alertly in the emptiness, watching bodies with blue and green hair, tufted ears, and flesh as glossy purple as eggplant tumbling toward him.

Ælves—their corpses bound for the Dark Shore.

The colorful carcasses, dressed in garments of bark, moss, and vines, began to erode like mud shapes in a wash of rain. Diaphanous peelings of flesh and braids of hair spiraled like foam and faded to a bright haze that then dimmed to a tinsel glint in space. Soon, nothing remained of the ælves but flecks of light, a drizzle of Charm aloft above the blue orb and feathery clouds of Earth.

Down they sifted, fireflies, sparks guttered against the night, caught on the planetary wind and swept over oceans, where most fell. Some random chaff of these lives descended onto the continents and seeped down through the atmosphere to forests and grasslands.

A little of the bright grit accompanied Nox on his return toward his body. Below, the neon night shapes of Manhattan flung their luminous reflections in the twin rivers and stood recast in the water like submerged torches. The seemingly momentary journey had consumed the day. His body received him from where it had slumped against a standing elbow pipe, and he sat staring at the fiery geometry of the city.

Nox staggered to his feet in time to see sprinkling toward the street the flecks of Charm that had accompanied him on his journey across time and the Gulf. "What is happening to these lives? How will they be reborn down there in the gutters?"

The lives lost among the Bright Worlds are cast widely across the Dark Shore, Nox. Most drift endlessly through space. A few land among dead worlds. The rare souls who reach Earth on the winds of chance wind up on the floor of this world and are gradually taken into the mineral matrix of the planet, perhaps to find lives again among algae, plants, and eventually animals. When you die, that will be the fate of your soul.

THE THOUGHTS OF THE RAIN

"I AM NOT GOING TO DIE!" NOX SHOUTED DEFIANTLY. HE DANCED across the rooftop under the haze of city lights and a few hard stars. "I haven't lived this long to collapse to insensate minerals."

You will die, Nox—

With an abrupt slash of his arms, Nox broke the bond with Caval. The wizard's voice vanished among the distant sirens, diesel noise, and horn blasts of the streets. "No, Caval. You are dead. But I am yet alive. And I will live forever."

He retrieved his ceremonial robe from atop the air-conditioning shed where he had flung it. After donning it, he climbed the wooden steps to the shagbark door of the converted water tank and entered.

As ever, Octoberland bore a heady scent of leaf drift and mossy, mist-rubbed rocks. In the chill and lightless interior, he moved hurriedly to the five-faced altar of obsidian and drew the black needle from the stained pot that housed it. It moved with jerky quavers, like something getting stunned. Dancing and chanting, Nox pranced with the poison tip hugged to his chest, then bending his blackened lips to it, then stooping low and making it skim the floor, releasing it, watching it slide through the oily light to the spot where Virgo had died.

Nox knelt in the umbrous dark before the living needle and whispered to it, "Come to your place in the circle."

Six miles high and hundreds of miles away, Mary Felix heard him. She sat in the window seat of a plane that would bring her to Manhattan with dawn. Silver blushes of lightning pulsed in the dark clouds, and at first she thought she was hearing the thoughts of the rain: *Come to your place in the circle—* The rain,

risen from the baked earth into the thermal swell of the sky,
brushed against the frigid edge of space and turned back to the
night world below.

Mary had been flitting in and out of trance since abandoning
Brick. She had visited Irth and been instructed by the dead
there to find the wizard Caval on the Dark Shore. So new was
she to these powers of astral visitation that none of her attempts
to contact the mysterious wizard had been successful. Instead,
she had sat in the airport lounge watching summer twilight
stretch patiently through orange and red to indigo. She had
nodded to sleep. In the rest room, washing weariness from her
eyes, she had gawked at her young face and tried to make sense
of her new identity.

Her youthful features gazed back at her from the airplane
window backed by night. The engine noise droned with a fearsome din of barely audible voices, psychic mutterings from her
troubled soul and the memories that Dogbrick had poured
into her.

She felt bad for having left Brick behind with Ryan. She had
fled the magical being who had given her youth and knowledge
of the Bright Worlds. At the same time, she felt she had no
choice. The knowledge she possessed was their only weapon
against Nox.

Come to your place in the circle. She closed the shade of the
window at the sound of Nox's voice inside her. That he could
reach to her even up here, at the limits of the sky, frightened
her. She turned to the passenger in the seat beside, wanting to
ignore the telepathic summons. The woman sitting there was
flaxen haired and young, oddly dressed in a white robe, and
Mary realized she had noticed her before.

"Don't be frightened," the stranger said in a quiet voice. "I
was frightened at first myself. But once you feel the power,
there is nothing to fear."

Mary Felix stared at her with narrowed eyes. "Excuse me?"

"You don't have to pretend with me." The young woman placed an icy hand over hers. "I know what's happening to you."

"You do?"

"My name is Virgo—like the sign of the zodiac." She smiled serenely. "Octoberland sent me."

Mary withdrew her hand as from a flame.

Virgo shook her head with disapproval. "I'm not going to hurt you. I came to reassure you. There's nothing to fear. I can answer all your questions."

"Pardon me, please." Mary unbuckled her seat belt and stood up. She edged into the aisle and toward the back of the plane. When she glanced back, Virgo was gone.

Inside the lavatory, she washed her face—and Virgo stared back.

"You're going to take my place in the circle," the specter told her with a jubilant smile.

Mary crashed into the door in her frenzy to get out. Once in the aisle, she was afraid to return to her seat. She searched among the other passengers for the ghost and did not see her. Out the window, a splinter of dawn gleamed. They would be landing soon.

At the far end of the aisle, Virgo stepped out of a lavatory. Mary turned away and bumped into a stewardess.

"May I help you?"

"That woman is following me." Mary pointed down the empty aisle, where no one stood. "I'm sorry. She was there a moment ago." She scanned the faces of the passengers and did not find her.

Mary refused to return to her original seat and instead found a vacant one next to a sleeping businessman. The stewardess brought her an orange juice, and she sipped it while glancing around apprehensively.

Nox felt her fear six miles below in the approaching city. He laughed. "Very good, Virgo. Very good. Keep an eye on her, and you will soon be free of the black needle. This one will take your place, and you will be free. . . ."

His laughter sounded hollow to him. Contact with the wizard

Caval had polluted him with fear even more thick than what his prey felt on the incoming flight.

Death meant collapse to the mineral level of reality. He could not abide even the thought of that, and he got up and went to the altar. With a hissed cry, he ignited the fat black candles, and their flames jumped brightly, wagging shadows over the mossy walls and lifting into the visible the hanging chains of shriveled apple faces and bines of herbs.

Transparent to the shuddering shadows, the young, flaxen-haired woman stood. "Release me now, master."

"Not yet, Virgo. Not yet."

"My replacement is found. Release me. I'm cold, and I want to die."

Nox lifted his fungus-gilled staff from the altar and swung at the apparition, shattering her like glass. The luminous shards skittered across the floor and spun to dull, brown embers that unfolded bristly legs and scuttled away as cockroaches. "Are you satisfied now, Virgo?"

He shuddered and threw the staff to the ground. Death appalled him. Caval had whetted its fear. The wizard had forced him to see the insensate limits of extinction—and the eternal endlessness of being. He did not want to become dust. He wanted to live forever as himself, only younger, stronger.

Among the leaping shadows, he began to dance. His feet pounded the planks, wanting to feel the actuality of his bones, the liveliness of his muscles and ligaments. And as he danced, he sang, "I will never die. I will dance forever and forever—and I will never die!"

THE DARK VOICE

N'DRATO DRAGGED THE CORPSE OF RIPCAT THROUGH THE MURK of the Cloths of Heaven by the metal coil that bound the dead thing's legs. Glancing up at the dark keeps within the yawing well of collapsed storeys, he gauged his location within the dripping shadows of the ancient ruins—and he searched for blood-hungry wraiths. Gray clots of anonymous shapes moved at the higher levels, but nothing nearby approached.

He intended to bring Ripcat's carcass whole to Shai Malia, to be stuffed and displayed in the hedgerow gardens of Primrose Stilts. However, that ambition required his finding a charmway close by. The path through which she had dispatched him on this mission lay several storeys higher, and if he could not locate the adjacent passage down here that would lead him back to New Arwar, he would have to sever the beastmarked head for a trophy.

Eyes moving, constantly on the watch for blood feeders, N'drato grimaced and lugged the dead body over chunks of fallen masonry. He veered past pools that stirred with small bubbles of gas erupting in iridescent wisps. How Shai Malia knew so well these hideous ruins, the assassin feared to guess. Not even his own brood had dared map this doomful place with the precision that she had offered him. If she were a true witch, he would have accepted that the Sisterhood had imparted their comprehensive understanding—though, even then, he would have had difficulty believing her, for witches devoted their powers to serving the indigent, not the vampirical.

Shai Malia's description of the rifted byways in the forest of graven pillars proved entirely accurate. N'drato hauled the corpse through a nameless dross of fungal gray dust mixed with decayed stone, bat dung, and dead beetles. Pausing when the body foundered on a masonry pedestal smothered in the dread waste, he laid his hands on the carcass and lifted it over the obstruction. The lifeless stare, still locked cross-eyed on the wound that pierced its brain, had dilated to reveal a hollow interior. Meager light from the cavernous surroundings entered the vertical gash and incandesced in the empty skull.

N'drato thought little of this at first. A droning had begun in the disordered interior of the forsaken temple, and he moved quickly to reach the exit of the charmway. As an assassin, he had been trained to slay every form of living sentience, and even these wraiths voracious for blood were creatures that fell within the purview of his murderous skills. Vague entities that they were, they were not beings easy to destroy. Yet, they lived, and so they could be slain.

The difficulty was that these were not common mortals such as people, ælves, gnomes, or even ogres. They were wizards—enormously old wizards. Grown dim over the ages, they nonetheless had survived by their magic and their willingness to take for themselves the blood heat of whatever lived and trespassed the Cloths of Heaven—toads, bats, even the saprophytic growths that furred the fecal droppings of toads and bats. Killing them would prove challenging, and he preferred to avoid such a contest.

The subterranean metropolis contained many collapsed shrines and the pseudomorphic shapes of gods alien and improbable. Beneath the mandibles of a deity shaped of ebony and buried to its compound eyes in cinder and brick, he found the charmway where Shai Malia had promised it would be.

A burnt scent of scorched stone lilted from the skewed crevice, a sooty smell that penetrated the fusty atmosphere of the ruins. Curious stobs of marble in the grim dirt prevented him from dragging Ripcat through the low opening, and he had to take the corpse by the shoulders and lift it over the stone shapes of purposes long forgot.

Seizing the body, he noticed again the excavation of the cleft between the crossed eyes and this time, something more. The eyes themselves had crinkled and sunk like chitinous shells drained empty.

The murmurous chantings of the ravenous wraiths urged him to hug the dead man close and retreat bent over and backward into the charmway. The rock-scorched odor thickened around him, and he dared brighten several more lux-diamonds on his headband to better view the passage.

Thin fumes curled in the light. *Does New Arwar burn?* he wondered as he advanced, once more pulling the dead man after him. He knew the wraiths would not follow, for fear of losing their way among these lifeless corridors. Without Shai Malia's impeccable directions, the assassin himself would have become befuddled by the bronchial tubings that opened on all sides, none offering clues of destination.

A sizzling sound rasped from all the many corridors, growing louder as he advanced. Dimly, he began to suspect the nature of what tainted the air with stench and static. His heart paced faster at the thought. And when a green glimmer glossed the rock walls ahead, he knew he had read the signs correctly, and he departed the path that led to New Arwar and moved quickly toward the shining rocks, teeth gnashing, blood whipping loudly in his ears.

Around the next bend, a hot wind choked him with rock smoke. Amplifying the protective Charm from his power wands, he yanked the corpse after him toward where he saw the green fire pulsing. At the brink of a wide pit, he lay on his belly and gazed at a churning inferno. Gouts of flame filled all the passageways around the cavern, many of them flaring vengeful fiery talons into the open space.

N'drato pulled back and lay facing the corpse's snarled mask, panting. "Charmfire," he breathed hotly. "All the north and west corridors are filled with charmfire. It's burning its way across the planet!"

He sat up. The passageway to New Arwar had not yet ignited. He had to hurry, cross to New Arwar, deliver the body, and return to the Brood of Assassins to warn the others, if they did not already know.

He grabbed the body to shove it ahead of him and saw the green light of the fire passing into one ear and out the next, an emerald filament threading an empty head. With a startled grunt, he heaved the corpse upright and pierced its abdomen with his knife. He pulled back the furry skin and found the interior empty.

Shouting, he tossed the ponderous body to the ground and hacked at it with his blade. In moments, it lay cleaved in large pieces beneath him, a thick, heavy hide that had split open along the spine and released its human content back at the Cloths of Heaven. All that remained was the dead husk of the man, the beastmarks emptied of the life he had been hired to destroy.

N'drato stalked angrily through the charmway back the way he had come. He struck at the walls with his blade, scattering sparks, infuriated that he had deceived himself in his eagerness to escape the ghastly Cloths of Heaven. He had known that this had been no ordinary beastmarked man. This was a magus, who wore beastmarks as a guise, a protective shell. He should have beheaded him on the spot and confirmed his death.

Without pause, the assassin approached the entry to the ruins from where echoed the mournful, droning cries of the blood-mad wraiths. He burst out through the stooped crevice into the crumbled temple with a knife in each hand and a ferocious snarl on his gaunt face. Skidding down a tailing of rubble and broken brick, he slashed at the hungry wraiths that swarmed over him, shouting in the dark voice of his rage, "Reece Morgan!"

THINK OF A NEW GOD

REECE ROSE UP AND UP ALONG THE CONVOLUTED WALL OF HIS brain. Bright bubbles dazzled his sight, and underwater singing wobbled on all sides. Huge and pulsing pain occupied him. Adrift in fetal buoyancy, he rolled, rising, turning in his other-body, eyes open and seeing through the brilliant, silver paisleys of air smoke another reality.

The room had a warped look. Yet, it *was* a room that he saw, a chamber of white walls hewn from limestone, with coral shapes bulging from ceiling and floor. And scattered throughout this ghostly vault, babies. *No*—he thought, as thinking began again in him. These were not babies he saw but dolls, bald, warp-limbed dolls. Scurfy and clotted with blood-brown crust, hundreds of them lay sprawled among the coral bulges and knobs of the white room.

Goblins! He recognized them from what he had seen in an amulet Jyoti had shown him. But then there had been just a few of them. Here, in this vision, scores of naked, swollen-headed goblins cluttered a coraline gallery. They possessed no large motion, yet he sensed they lived. Speckled eyelids twitched, squat limbs budged. They slept, dream bound, basking in a mauve light that filtered through holes in the dome of the salt-caked ceiling. They were dreaming of him—willing him to think of a new god. . . .

His vision pulled sideways, retracting from the assembly of goblins, and he saw that the white room was a crater, a coral grotto capped by mineral leachings that had gathered in a chalk mass among tangled trees. All around, the viscera of fallen drag-ons trembled with squirming swarms of worms and minute car-rion eaters. Disemboweled dragon hulks reared upon the shoals, their upturned ribs resembling the palings of storm-broken ships. . . .

Reece broke the surface, and air burned its way into his lungs, inspiring hurtful awareness and forcing him to his senses. He thrashed in the murky water, spewing the briny syrup from mouth and nostrils.

He groped to a rock shelf and pulled himself naked from the pool that had received him from his shucked beastmarks. Hand to his forehead, he felt for the blade that had pierced him and felt no wound. Ripcat had absorbed the full force of the death-blow and had died for him.

Gasping for breath, he remembered yet another dying for

him—Esre shoving him aside and taking through her neck the assassin's dagger meant for him. He lurched about, looking for her body on the slope of upended rock slabs.

Black blood stained a ledge in the planet shine let down from the gaping hole above. Esre's body was gone, lifted into the night sky by the same tide that had hoisted him unconscious from the depths of the pool.

Rendered senseless by the blow that had broken his beast-marks, he had been sustained underwater by a caul of Charm. Sticky remnants of it peeled away in cool wisps fragrant of kelp and brine, and now the parasitical wraiths came flying toward its promise of body heat. Their lusting moans trembled around him, and he swayed upright and began climbing the heaped slabs.

Like hornet stings, the wraiths stabbed him with their sharp mouths. Their death odor shrouded him, and he fell to his knees, gagging. "Get off me!" He writhed, swatting the air with both arms. The clamor of their wailing hurt his ears, and he leaped to his bare feet and hurried upward. Blood trickling from a dozen puncture wounds, he scrambled to the crest of the rock pile, a brown aura of ghostly shapes surrounding him.

Into the night air, the wraiths dared not pursue him. The nocturnal tide was strong enough there to whisk their nearly insubstantial bodies to the Gulf. Reece himself felt lighter of foot at the crumbly brink of the collapsed wall that plunged behind him into drafty darkness. He bounded over mud and mats of creepers and vines.

Once the wraiths were wholly behind him, he slowed and proceeded warily. He did not want to fall into another sinkhole, and he strained all his senses to find his way out of the Cloths of Heaven. Odors of swamp decay relented to a tang of salt in one direction, and he moved that way, listening to the traffic of nocturnal creatures among the rock piles and the tumultuous encroachments of the jungle.

Ahead, a plaza descended in broad stone steps to where a

wide expanse of water and the sky shared a common body:
Bright air heavy with planets and comet fumes stood doubled
in the still water. A raft of logs had beached on a mud bank
where a traveler had abandoned it long enough for ivy to scrawl
its bow.

Reece did not hesitate to shove the raft free of the mud and
its ivy moorings and set himself adrift. The current drew him
away from the shore of overgrown spires and domes, and soon
the Cloths of Heaven disappeared completely among the scaffolds, nets, and tiers of the jungle.

For a while, he paddled with his hands, urging the raft farther
into the night—until he spied a slithering movement on the
slick water. Then, he pulled himself to the middle of the wet
raft, where water gurgled between the tied logs, and let the
current captain him.

At dawn, he passed the swamp angel. Its star-glint eyes glared
at him from a mud-gobbed face veiled in seaweed hair, and its
mossy wings luffed the air with the jungle's warm fetor. He
remembered the day that the charmwrights had created this
illusory figure to frighten plunderers away from the sunken Pyramid of Abominations, and he quailed to find himself naked and
bereft of magic all these days later.

His life had come to nothing but evil. His arrival on Irth had
ushered in Hu'dre Vra and the cacodemons. His return to the
Dark Shore had emboldened Duppy Hob to raid heaven itself.
And though both the Dark Lord and the devil worshipper were
destroyed, their savagery had made possible the rise of the goblins. Guilt wracked him for marooning Dobrick on the Dark
Shore and abandoning Jyoti in a city as dust-crowned as Troy.

Watching the day rise in steam from the swamp waters and
the ashen horizon run red, he remembered the vision he had
seen when the nocturnal tide lifted him from the cave pool. He
had confronted hundreds of sleeping goblins.

"Hundreds!" he said aloud to the bluing sky and its planetary

shards. He wondered if that sight had been hallucinatory—
or telepathic.

The Abiding Star rose, and its heat burned him. Seeking
shelter from its fierce rays, he dared reach into the water and
paddle himself toward the nearest reef isle. He drew close
enough to recognize the timber ramparts of Blight Fen and
slowed down. No one hailed him from the walls, and the frightful thought occurred to him that trolls had overrun the camp.

The front gate stood open, and the range of colorful tents
woven of theriacal fabric remained unmolested. The islet was
empty. In one of the prismatic tents, Reece found sealed carafes
of spring water from Mirdath and tins of dried fruits from
Sharna-Bambara. In another tent, he discovered the wardrobes
that Poch and Shai Malia had left behind when they deserted
the atrocity museum.

He dressed himself in gardener's togs—sturdy viper-skin trousers, ankle-wrap boots, and a loose-fitting brown chemise over
which he wore an amulet-harness fitted with power wands and
starbursts of hex-gems. Immediately, the Charm healed his
bruises and lacerations, and he strolled out onto the grounds,
strong enough to visit the blackstone exhibit hall and its epoxy
cacodemons, hoping for succor and maybe even guidance from
them in his battle with the heirs of their evil.

THIS DREAMING THING

SHAI MALIA AND POCH SAT WATCHING TV IN THE CHAMBER OF
Presence, where in days past the brood had gathered to worship
their forebears and celebrate the living glory of their most venerable dominion. Walls of black onyx with milk-white veins
stood three times an ogre's height; slender columns of red mar-
molite supported a vault roof of hammered gold with an ivory
frieze carved to depict the charmful asp-flowers, mucronate

leaves, and ice-mint herbs from which were fashioned the first amulets at the beginning of talismanic times.

To cut the glare from the balcony, a tall screen had been unfolded, its sable surface woven ornamentally with silver-thread depictions of planets in their auroras, comets of passage, and star clusters. Jet draperies had been hung over the chestnut-red double doors so that light from without would not wash out the image on the TV screen when servants came and went. At either side of the divan, where the couple sat with their sneakered feet propped on ottomans, a short tripod of bronze bore a shallow basin of pink carnelian filled with heat-exploded kernels of grain from the Dark Shore—what Overy Scarn called popcorn.

Shai Malia initially had scorned the odd garb her husband had accepted from across the Gulf. But after trying on a pair of red canvas espadrilles and finding them comfortable, she shed her witch veils for stonewashed narrow leg denims and a black mock turtlenecked shirt. A lavender cloth headband held back her glistening black curls and exposed her face and the rapture with which she watched the flittering images on the screen.

A mesh net of sapphire hex-gems snared the speaker consoles at the sides of the TV, translating the voices of the screen figures to Irth dialects. By turns laughing and staring in mesmeric silence, the couple remained immobile on the divan. Servants in heraldic attire replenished the carnelian bowls of popcorn along with carafes of effervescent brown sugar water and wafers of an equally brown confection called chocolate.

"Where are you going?" Shai Malia asked when her husband stood up. "She's about to find out if her lover is blackmailing her father. There's going to be trouble. . . ."

"I've got bladder-bursting fullness." He took the remote from the arm of the divan and paused the cassette tape. "We've been sitting here for hours watching this dreaming thing. Don't you think we should look in on the dear ones?"

"You just want to see your sister." Shai Malia reached for the remote. "Let's find out how she takes the news about the black-mail, then you can visit the latrine."

"What will the dear ones do with Jyoti?"

"Whatever they do will be less harsh than the murderous intentions of Overy Scarn." Shai Malia tugged at Poch's arm. "Come on, give me the remote. I want to see what's going to happen. We can replay it when you get back."

"Fine." He handed her the control unit and strode toward the jet draperies. "I'll be back in a minute. And I'll see if we have any more of that disc bread with the red berry sauce and melted white meat—"

"Pizza," she reminded and added without taking her eyes from the screen, "and don't disturb the dear ones. Your sister is all right. Soon, she will see their grace as we do. Oh, and don't forget the caramel corn."

On the way back through the jasper columns that fronted the manor's redstone baths, Poch stopped short, confronted by a hefty figure among the pillars.

"Margrave—I must speak with you." Overy Scarn produced a palm-sized packet in crinkly clear wrap with an image of a dromedary printed upon it. "Cigarette?"

Poch stood, arms akimbo. "You're not supposed to be on this level of the manor, Overy."

"I spent a hefty fee to buy this access, margrave—please, do not deny me a moment of your time." She shook a thin white tube from the packet. "Would you like to try a cigarette? Come on—you must have seen them on TV."

Poch took the paper tube and placed it between his lips as he had seen demonstrated in the movies. When Overy Scarn lit it for him, he breathed in an acrid lungful of heat and immediately jetted vehement smoke through his nose, withholding a cough. "It's hot as Hellsgate!"

"Don't draw so deeply." She lit a cigarette for herself and puffed placidly. "You'll find it most soothing if done properly. Take the pack. I'm sure your wife would enjoy the experience."

"Why did you bribe your way past the sentinels?" Poch attempted a more tentative inhalation from the cigarette. "What do you want that you don't already have? Isn't Dig Dog satisfied with its profits from our jungle industries?"

"Most satisfied, margrave." She exhaled a languid stream of smoke. "I'm not here to discuss money. I want to know about the goblins."

"We've been spared the goblins." A dizzy flush of nicotine obliged Poch to lower the smoking tobacco away from his squinting face. "I've seen all the reports from the other dominions. The troll and ogre attacks have overrun all the farming communities. There will be famine. And if they come out of the Qaf and take Saxar, the talismanic industry itself will be crippled. These are terrible times, Overy. We must get the projectile weapons shipped to the other broods and quickly."

Overy Scarn blew a ring of blue smoke. "Have you not wondered why New Arwar, isolated and entirely vulnerable in the midst of Elvre's jungles, has been spared? We have endured not one troll attack or ogre raid. Why?"

"The blind god Chance favors us—for now."

"Perhaps." The trade agent flicked ash to the shiny resin floor. "But remember this—Dig Dog's resources are deep. It bought you your title. It bought me your sentinels so that I could share this smoke with you. It has even bought the exclusive trade rights to the Dark Shore. And look at you—I see you are glad of the sartorial manner my funds have brought you." She gestured with the glowing tip of her cigarette at Poch's jeans and T-shirt.

"You have enormous funds, Overy," the young man acknowledged and breathed more smoke. "I *am* grateful for your help. But you tried to kill my sister. That was unnecessary. You must keep your distance now. I know you meant well, in your misguided way—but that was too much."

"If you are grateful, then make your wife aware that I *own* New Arwar." She dropped the butt of her cigarette and crushed it under her heel. "Make her realize that I will not be relegated to the servant's quarters to await her commands. I may not be a Peer, but I have the resources to act as one—and to reveal to the other Peers of Irth what I may learn of the goblins and why our beloved city has remained unscathed."

THE WATERS OF FIRE

"SCARN KNOWS ABOUT THE DEAR ONES," POCH MOANED TO HIS wife upon his return to the Chamber of Presence. "She calls them goblins!"

"Hm?" She waved him to his place on the divan beside her. "She *knew* her father was being blackmailed—it was *her* idea!"

"Scarn has no father. She's an orphan from Zul. . . ."

"Not Scarn! The TV." Shai Malia jutted her chin toward the colorful screen. "Look—she's going to run away with his second wife. They're lesbians and planned her father's downfall together."

Poch seized the remote and shut off the TV. "Shai—Overy Scarn accosted me outside the baths. She is aware that we are sheltering the dear ones."

She pulled her legs off the ottoman and sat up, rigid with indignation. "What is Scarn doing on this floor anyway? I told her she was to keep to her quarters."

"She made it clear that she will not take commands from us." Poch placed a sneakered foot on the divan and leaned over his knee, staring at his wife with wide-eyed alarm. "She says she owns New Arwar—and I do not dispute that at all. Dig Dog's funds have bought us everything. But she knows about our dear ones!"

"Do you think they've summoned her?"

"No, no, not at all—that's the problem!" Poch grimaced with worry. "I don't know how she did it, but she saw them and yet did not feel their grace. To her, our dear ones are goblins! I'm afraid for them, Shai."

"So long as she sees them as goblins, they *are* in jeopardy," Shai Malia agreed, clutching her husband's hand. "But our dear ones barely have enough strength to fight for a place in this world. Dare we ask them to use their magic to make Scarn see them for the exiled pixies that they really are? The illusions of this world are hard to break. They're straining now to make enough magic eggs to lift the spell of disgust from your sister. This could completely exhaust them!"

"If Overy reveals their presence here to the other Peers, they will be exposed!" Poch nearly wailed. "We must give them more hex-gems and ask them to clear Scarn's mind."

"It doesn't matter how many gems we give them, Poch, they can only use so much Charm at a time. We could hurt them if we ask more of them." Shai Malia stood up, outraged. "All because Scarn has intruded on us."

"Let's go to the pixies now and warn them." He took his wife's hand, and they hurriedly exited the chamber.

Within the goblin's suite, Jyoti lay among woven gossamers and creamy masses of throbbing larval eggs. Each egg was a packet of precise and complex chemical instructions exuded from the goblins' bodies. When the eggs matured, they ruptured, releasing mesmeric fumes that delivered their orders to whoever breathed them. The orders were always the same— fidelity to the dear ones, care for the pixies from the higher world, and an intense vivacity of love for the cheesy ordure of the little creatures, a passionate hypnosis that made the fulsome seepings smell like attar of roses.

Jyoti lay paralyzed by the goblin's telepathy. Bereft of her amulets, devoid of Charm's protection, she lay wholly under the spell of the powerful minds from a hotter order of being. The baby bodies crawled over her, hex-gems in their wee hands and from their glossy bodies fibrous excrement oozed in nacreous sheets that stuck to her hair, her face, her limbs. Wrapped in a chrysalis, she felt herself gradually lifted up as the filaments tightened under the slow-turning bodies of the goblins. They rolled around their stubby torsos the threads attached to her casing, and she inched upright.

A thick, white deposit of larval thoughts pulsed like living pearls in the web around her. Soon, they would burst. The chemicals in them would invade her brain and influence the cortical patterning of her neurons, physically persuading her to their passion.

Helpless, she stared out from her immoblized body. The putrid stench of the crawling bodies at her feet burned her sinuses and scalded her throat. She wanted to retch. Nausea swept through her in waves, but her body could not convulse to release the sickening sensation.

The door opened, and through the gauze that masked her face, Jyoti saw a silhouette approach. Fingers ripped away the strings that held her standing, and she collapsed into the soft mat of the goblin's furry white excrement. Lying there, she felt the telepathy of the evil creatures struggling with the interloper.

The goblins' minds strained, baffled by Charm, the condensed energy of the Abiding Star. The struggle would not last much longer: Their hot minds burned brighter even than Charm, and Jyoti sensed them incinerating the hex-gems that guarded the silhouette stooped over her.

The cool flat of a knife kissed her cheek and cut away the stinky fabric that covered her face. Nette's pugilistic features bent close, cobwebs stuck in her bristly, silver hair. "Can't save us both—" She groaned as she lifted Jyoti in her arms. "Get away from here."

Nette carried the margravine through drifts of sticky webs, the larval eggs hobbling her ankles.

The goblins cowered under the windowsill, their lobed brows glistening with mica flecks of sweat as they exerted their telepathic power against Nette's vest of amulets. One by one, the power wands cracked lengthwise, their amber translucency clouding instantly black.

The assassin wanted to slash at the goblins with her knife and cut open their small bodies. But the air around them was too dense with the vibrancy of their strength. If she had dared to approach them directly, all her power wands would have cracked and she would have fallen helplessly before them with the margravine in her arms.

Instead, Nette kicked at the window above them with her boot heel, and the latched frame burst open. She lurched forward as the last of her power wands split open spilling their Charm, and she lowered Jyoti out the window.

The margravine clutched at the wall ivy and brick grout, and the assassin gasped from above, "Beware N'drato—I'm lost to you—"

A sudden inrush of air slammed the latched frame shut when Nette's Charm exhausted itself and the telepathy of the goblins seized her and pulled her toward them. A smoky weaving of silver filaments clouded the cracked window panes, and Nette opened her mouth to cry out. But no sound emerged. The larval sacs at her feet had burst, and their fumes swirled up through her nostrils into her brain. The spinal fluid and cranial liquids of her brain quivered, the waters of fire that held the small lightnings of her thoughts, of her very being, shivered with the dendritic changes that altered her.

The door to the room swung open, and Poch and Shai Malia advanced gingerly among the torn webs. "Dear ones—why are you so frightened?" Shai Malia called out. "Why are you cringing?"

"Jyoti!" Poch cried out. He rushed to the kneeling figure by the window and pulled her head back by its short silver hair. "What have you done with my sister, assassin?"

"Out the window!" Nette cried. "By the gods themselves, I lost her to us! I lost her!"

Poch flung open the window and saw the path of ripped ivy

where Jyoti had climbed down the manor wall. Among the black flame cypress trees, there was no sign of her.

"What have I done?" Nette wailed. She gazed with tear-blurred eyes at the goblins—the pixies—her hands opened before her beseechingly. "Forgive me, dear ones. Forgive me."

Shai Malia knelt beside her and cradled the assassin's sobbing head. "Hush now. The dear ones love you—and there is time yet for you to show your love to them."

TERRIBLE LOVE

SHORTLY AFTER THE JETLINER LANDED AT NEWARK INTERNATIONAL Airport and before it completed its taxi to its gate, Mary Felix was on her feet and headed for the exit. She was glad when a stewardess stopped her, because the ghost of the flaxen-haired young woman that she had been seeing throughout the flight did not approach other people. During the descent, the pale woman had disappeared entirely, as did the chill autumnal energy that had surrounded Mary for most of her journey. Even so, Mary feared the phantom would reappear at any moment, and she was among the very first to deplane.

"Mary!" A short minister with fleecy silver hair waved at her, and a sunburst halo shone briefly around him. "Mary Felix!"

She watched him timidly, afraid that he, too, was a ghost.

"You've come to find Octoberland," the minister said earnestly as he stepped up to her. "I've been sent to escort you there. Please, dear, come along with me."

Mary backed up against a row of plastic seats, a vacuum in her chest. "How did you find me?"

"Find you?" The minister offered a merry smile. "We've been with you all along!" He offered his hand. "I am Aries—the first in the circle and so the first to meet you here and introduce you to the others. But you've already met Virgo, the woman whose place you are taking."

Understanding flexed in her mind like an alignment of forces, like something magnetic and physical. "The ghost—she is one of yours. . . ."

"*Was* one of ours." Aries swept his arm toward the sliding glass exit doors. "Come along, Mary, and I'll tell you everything you want to know."

Mary hesitated. She had journeyed this far to confront Nox, to see what she could do to save her savior, Dogbrick. But now that she had arrived, her fear seemed heavier. "This is all so new to me—magic, ghosts, even my own body! I'm not really this young, you know."

"We know." Aries smiled gently, and when he took her arm an electric warmth pulsed through her with a charge of well-being. "We helped revive you in the forest not long ago. Don't you remember?"

"I was groggy." She allowed herself to be led out of the airport to an off-duty taxicab waiting for them in the lot. Though morning had not yet delivered the sun into the sky, the air outside the terminal felt close and sticky. In the east, above the controller's tower, Venus blazed as a morning star, a candlewick held against the last blue shadows of night. "Where are you taking me?"

"Why, to Octoberland, of course." Aries ushered Mary into the backseat of the cab and sat next to her. "Our driver is another coven member. Her name is Taurus."

The driver, a big-shouldered black woman with large, bovine eyes and a ready smile pulled the cab away from the curb before the minister slammed the door. "You look frightened, sweetie." She swung a smile over her shoulder. "You mustn't be. Octoberland is about life and joy."

"Virgo didn't look very happy—or alive," Mary dared to say and was surprised at the laughter of the minister and the driver.

"Everyone has to die." Taurus winked at her in the rearview

mirror. "Except the Master. He is going to live and dance for-ever and forever."

"Nox," Mary said.

"Oh, we never call him by that name, dear." Aries reached over and squeezed her hand firmly. "He is the Master *because* he is never going to die."

"Even Jesus died," Mary ventured and cocked an eyebrow at Aries. "You're a minister. How can you call anyone but Christ your master?"

More glittering laughter filled the cab. "I'm a banker," Taurus offered, "but I don't worship money. Aries is a minister. He tends to the sick and the desolate, but it's not Jesus that gives him the power to heal illness and change lives. It's the Mas-ter's magic."

"Surely, you understand," Aries picked up. "Look at yourself. You're a teenager. Was it a miracle that transformed you from the crone you were? Not at all. It is a science we only dimly perceive, yet a science nonetheless. By that science, the Master will never die."

"And you?" Mary inquired coldly. "And Virgo? Why is there only enough *science* to keep the Master alive forever?"

"She's a feisty one!" Taurus laughed. "You are going to have a high old time with the Master. A high old time!"

On the busy viaduct above the tule grass and green pools of chemical waste from the surrounding factories, the minister asked, "And what is your faith, Mary Felix? How do you recon-cile what has happened to you with what you know of God?"

"I'm a scientist," Mary answered, though she felt increasingly unsure about any part of her past identity. "I believe God wants us to think for ourselves."

"And in your thinking, Mary, have you left any room for faith?"

Mary suppressed a shiver, a tremor of fear at finding herself alone in a car with these strangers, on her way to a place of evil. She fixed her mind on a neon eagle spreading its wings

over a brewery. "I have faith that when there's no room left for
thinking, God will take care of the rest."

"Good answer," Taurus interjected. "Leave mystery where it
belongs. Our responsibility in this life is to deal with what we
already know. If we would just do that, the world would be a
much finer place."

"But surely you must have some idea of the Supreme Being,"
the minister pressed.

"My husband did," Mary said, watching a police motorcycle
pull alongside. "He used to say that God was Nature itself, that
we're already in heaven and in hell—and living was learning to
tell the two apart."

Aries leaned over Mary and waved to the motorcycle officer.
"That is Gemini. He has agreed to escort us. And there is Cancer in the cab ahead of him, with Sagittarius driving."

Mary peered out the window and indeed saw an old Asian
woman in the back of a cab driven by a smiling Amerindian in
a cowboy hat. A Mercedes glided past in the lane to their right,
and an elegantly dressed couple nodded and waved, the driver's
full blond hair coiffed like a lion's mane, the long-throated
woman sitting tall, her honey hair poised atop her head.

"Leo and Libra," Taurus introduced. "We are surrounded by
friends. They have all come out to see that you are safely
brought to Octoberland."

"Are you afraid I might try to escape?" Anxiety tormented
her with the certainty that she had made a terrible mistake in
leaving Dogbrick.

"Escape?" Taurus threw her head back with a bright laugh.
"Where could you go? This whole world belongs to the Master."

For the remainder of the ride into the city, Taurus and Aries
reminded her how happy she was going to be in their circle,
devoted to a long life of magic. Her attention drifted to the
cardboard hovels on the wrought-iron stoops of old brick buildings, and she heard the minister commenting about them.

"Jesus knew, God loves them more—the homeless, the infirm,

the diseased. Do you know why, Mary?" His hazel eyes watched her with a cold intensity. "Remember, Jesus said to love your enemies, because *God* loved them! God made the rain and the sunshine to fall upon the wicked no less than upon the righteous. Remember that? And in Isaiah, Jesus's favorite prophet, the voice of God declares, 'I make good *and* evil, I the Lord do this!' Do you understand?" He smiled without mirth. "God loves us. But it is a terrible love."

EARTH, BE A ROAD

BRICK POUNDED ON THE HEAVY METAL DOOR OF THE STORAGE shed. "Hey, Ryan! Let me out of here!"

No reply came, and Brick sat down in the middle of the empty space, certain that Ryan had fled to report him to the other staff members of the university research station. This infuriated him. He had been sincere with Mary's colleague, believing that the truth would be plausible to a man who had actually seen him as Dogbrick. He groaned and kicked at the door.

A long time passed while he sat fuming, and eventually he grew tired of picking at straws. He lay down and drifted to sleep. He dreamt of wading through shallows, where sea horses shed bright peels of color through the crystal-lit water and periwinkles swirled up in his wake. He arrived at a pier and climbed a ladder notched into one of the tar-painted pilings and mounted to a lantern-hung den at the end of a pier. There, sail menders and talisman braiders ate together at an open grill. He sat on a wobbly bench at a cracked table of lashed driftwood under a sharkskin lantern. Through the open sides of the den, a sea wind brisked, and he stared across a sparkling bay at industrial fumes shredding from the sides of a cliff to reveal in broad daylight oxide-seared streets and roasted buildings carved into the rock face of the palisades. Cancerous colors blistered the cliff slopes, which had been riddled to a charred labyrinth. Then, a feathery thrashing from a draped cage beside the grill caught his attention. He removed the magenta shade of dried kelp with a flourish and confronted a small figure of marbly nakedness shielding itself with its crimson and green wings. Greasy hair covered its face until he asked, "Tell me true, sibyl, am I man or am I dog?" An alabaster visage lifted toward him, its faunish features watching him with oblique jade eyes. From a perfectly round mouth, a tongue of blue flame spit, *"How you die decides that!"*

Brick woke with a start. He knew he had dreamt of Irth, of his life there as Dogbrick, yet he did not know if this was a memory or a fantasy. The lucidity of the dream assured him that what he had experienced had been seen before. He strained his mind, trying to remember more of his former life on Irth, hoping that perhaps his memories were beginning to return. Nothing more emerged, and soon he began to dwell on what the sibyl had said. He wondered if the dream were premonitory of his death, now that he had become a man.

Brick pounded at the door again, then angrily paced the small room. He jumped at the walls, smacking them with his soles and palms and pushing off, infuriated. Then, he seized the door handle and tugged with all his might and whirled away when the latch did not budge. Furious, he grabbed at the light switch and yanked mightily, ripping the wire from the switch box.

A jolt of sudden current ripped through his hand and up his arm. The lightbulb overhead dimmed to a gray shape of itself, the red filament throbbing. Brick's knees buckled, and he jerked to release the naked wire. But the electricity sluiced hotter, holding him with a fiery tenacity.

In the pulsing shadows, he saw his electrocuted hand and arm swelling. Tawny fur stood fluffed with static energy, and sparks jumped from his brown talons and spun like blue spirochetes in the air. His body expanded with a sound of rent fabric, his flesh shuddering violently on the sturdy scaffold of his bones.

The electric power draining into him carried with it the Charm that Earth's vast amulets had accrued: the power line grid works, the mammoth hydroelectric dams, the cities with their geometries of talismans. All the millennial handiwork of Duppy Hob that had made of the planet a giant Charm collector poured its force into Dogbrick. With the return of his magic, he abruptly understood this; in that split second, it all became clear to him again.

The overhead light blacked out, and the electricity in the ripped wire cut off. Dogbrick's night vision detected the minute threads of light slipping through the jamb, and he put one hand on the metal door and tore it from its frame with a rasping cry of dislodged bricks. The door clanged to the ground, and he emerged into a night of faultless beauty.

No artificial lights marred the celestial radiance of the Milky Way pouring its star flow across the sky. He reached within himself for strength and loped into the night, gravel crunching loudly under his heels.

Later, a flashlight's beam would wag along the pebbly drive as Ryan emerged from the darkened research building. He would find the wrenched metal door, the shreds of clothing, the split-open boots, and the inhumanly large footprints marking the long stride of a giant runner. And he would know with a cold shudder and a dizzy brain that every mad detail of what Brick had told him was true.

For the moment, though, Dogbrick fled into the dark forest with no one aware that he was loose upon the face of Earth. He ran with indefatigable vigor. The charge of electricity pouring into his body had underscored what Mary Felix had told him about Duppy Hob's labors over six thousand years to create the civilization of this planet as an array of amulets. And now he knew that all the highways, all the power lines and cables, all the jewel-like cities existed to gather Charm for him.

He moved south through the woods, and as he ran, effortlessly, in a blur of liquid speed akin to the wind itself, he contemplated his dream. *Failure is heroic*, he understood from the sibyl's message. It mattered not whether he was a man or a beast, only that he was mortal. That thought made him speed faster through the starlit corridors of the forest, branches rattling and leaves spinning in his wake.

He remembered almost nothing of his past. Yet he knew the great truths that would guide him to his fate: Darkness hid meaning; light revealed; fire burned; hope dwindled. These truths stirred deeper feelings not yet memories—and he had the sensation that thinking hard was what he had done often in his former life, thinking hard for everyone, trying to grasp the meaning of meaning. And it became clear, as he hurtled toward Octoberland and the sinister angels who had stolen Mary Felix from him, that at the end of this journey there would be a new meaning to his life—but for good or evil, he could not tell.

COLD STARS WATCH US

OCTOBERLAND BEGAN TO APPEAR LESS FOREBODING TO MARY FELIX during her taxicab ride through Manhattan, so completely did she now feel under its sway. Even though the coven members had plucked her out of the airport and whisked her into the city with the alacrity of an abduction, they themselves bore no aspect of evil. Even their zodiacal names, which she supposed should have troubled her with their anonymity, lent them a playful air and made her want to guess at their true names and identities. Silver-haired Aries in his clerical attire had the genial features and watery eyes of a pastor with allergies, and she felt comfortable enough with him to ask if his name was Walter, the same as a softhearted uncle of hers.

"No, my dear. Theodore." He squeezed her hand warmly.

"But you must call me Aries. And you are Virgo. We have roles to play, you see. We have our places in the timeless circle."

The cab pulled over to the curb, and a stocky woman with a Peruvian facial cast got in on Mary's side, wedging her against the minister. "And this is Scorpio," Taurus introduced and slid the cab back into the flow of traffic.

"Hello, Virgo." Scorpio handed her a box. Inside was a white ceremonial gown identical to what the flaxen-haired ghost had worn.

"Now, you are Virgo," Aries told her. "And when we arrive at Octoberland, you will meet Capricorn, Aquarius, Pisces, all the others. They are preparing the ritual that will admit you to our circle."

Mary knew she should be afraid, but the smell of leaf drift from the flowers assured her that she had found her way to where she was going.

Scorpio lifted the white robe out of its box and held it up to display its ecru embroidery of harvest sheafs and vintage grapes. Her Incan face peered around it with a smile. "When you wear this, you will not be Mary Felix any longer. You will be one of us."

"What happened to the last Virgo?" asked Mary, curious more than fearful.

"What happens to any of us?" Aries rejoined. "We are all mortal beings. Only the Master will live forever."

"He wants Dogbrick," Mary asserted. "That's why I'm here, to lure Dogbrick to Nox."

"The beastman has magic." Scorpio nodded and folded the white robe in her dark hands. "Will he help us, the way he helped you? Will he make the Master young again?"

"How do you know he helped me?" Mary cast a watchful look around the cab and out the windows at the coven members in the Mercedes on one side, a taxi on the other, and the motorcycle officer behind. "What do you know about me?"

Taurus tossed a bemused grin over her shoulder. "In the circle, we know everything we want to know."

"The Master is a sky magician," Scorpio said in a tone soft with awe. "He learned from the first sky magicians, the ones who built Stonehenge and the other ritual rock circles of the North. He knows how to collect the cold fire from the sky."

"That's why we bear zodiacal names," Aries added, as if by explanation. "We are like a magnifying lens that focuses very tightly the energies of the sky—the power we see in lightning and among the auroras. The potential difference between the ionosphere and the Earth is vast."

"Oh, don't badger her with your scientific prattle, Aries." Taurus glared at him in the rearview mirror. "Listen, sweetie, the beastman comes from a world higher than the sky. His magic is many times stronger than anything we have ever known. The Master wants to use it for the good of us all."

"You're lucky you're the one who found Dogbrick." Scorpio gleefully nudged Mary with her elbow. "Look how young you are now!"

"There's something you should know." Mary pitched her voice to carry apprehension. "There are goblins. I think they come from a world even higher than Dogbrick's. Do you understand what I'm saying? Their magic is stronger than anyone's—and they are evil."

"Evil!" Aries launched a laugh that caromed through the interior of the cab. "Good, very good! The Master will love that. Evil!"

Bewilderment squeezed Mary's young face. "How can you laugh? These goblins will devour you—and our whole world!"

Taurus's eyes appeared merry in the mirror, and Scorpio held a hand to her mouth to keep from laughing outright. Aries patted Mary's knee consolingly. "Weren't you listening to what I said earlier? The very God of the Bible creates good *and* evil. Don't you see, young lady? Everything born must die. We are already devoured."

"That is why we call our coven Octoberland." Scorpio nodded knowingly. "As Virgo you must understand this, for autumn is your season, the time of harvest."

"We are as grass under the scythe," Taurus spoke.

"Our strength—our *power* as a coven—is that we know this," Aries went on. "And we use it. We use our mortality to dare what others fear. We know we are doomed. We are all doomed. Every amoeba and every sequoia. All doomed. Cold stars watch us come into this world and leave it. But we know we are doomed, and so we dare to use good *and* evil to fulfill ourselves before God."

"If you saw these goblins . . ."

"Oh, Mary," Scorpio said in a hush of intimacy. "We have seen our own deaths. No goblins can frighten us."

The cab pulled to a stop before a massive apartment tower, whose mustard-yellow bricks climbed higher into the sky than any of the other nearby buildings on the avenue. Mary briefly entertained the hope of escaping this mad troupe of death worshippers for whom evil offered as much fortune as good. But when she exited the cab, the coveners from the second cab and the Mercedes, as well as the motorcycle officer, formed a cordon and steered her into the building.

On the ride up the elevator, the group crowded around her, and Scorpio began to undress Mary. "You must put on the ceremonial robe for your induction." Mary pushed her hands away, but the stern expressions of the others informed her there would be no reprieve from this command. She compromised by leaving on her clothes and slipping the ceremonial robe over them.

No one said anything. In the reverential quiet, Mary heard her heart pacing, and she began to feel foolish again for having abandoned Brick in the Canadian woods. The certainty of convincing these people of the danger of their ambitions had evaporated during the cab ride, and she was left feeling small and vulnerable. Their magic was more powerful than she had anticipated, leaving her with no hope of fighting them or protecting Dogbrick.

August heat visibly crinkled the air above the rooftop tar paper. As if in a procession, the coven members escorted Mary to a large wooden water tank on an iron scaffolding. Varnished steps led to a door with a ram's-head knocker that Aries pounded three times. The curved door swung outward with a chill breeze scented with autumn woods soaked in twilight.

Mary entered trepidatiously, slow as though lugging a sack of stones. Coming from the sun-bright summer day, her eyes saw little but shadows, though she sensed she had entered another reality: she inhaled briar smoke, the murmurous chant of the others displaced the already receding traffic noise, and where the sunlight from the open door wedged, she noticed a floor of polished planks painted with a crimson circle incised by a pentagram. Then, the door shut, and the gloom hardened.

The coven members took their zodiacal stations on the circle, and the passengers from the Mercedes—the blond-maned Leo and honey-haired Libra—each took one of Mary's elbows and guided her to her place on the circle between them. Her eyes had adjusted sufficiently to discern all the details of the shagbark-walled room—the hanging bines of herbs, the totem of apple faces, the big black block of an altar with its mossy shroud, fat black candles, and the four tools of the magician: galled stave; hammered plate of black silver; dented, tar-crusted urn; and knife, with its silvered edge and sharp smile.

WHITE COLD BLOOD

STARLIGHT BROKE DOGBRICK'S HEART. IT REMINDED HIM OF THE great barrier between himself and Irth, the world of his origin. Mary Felix had called that barrier the Gulf; and she had said it was billions of light-years deep and held in its abyss all the galaxies of the universe. She had told him so much, he ached to think he had let her escape from him, running away with all his knowledge in her head.

As he lunged through the night forest, he remembered what she had told him about the Abiding Star—the source of Creation, from which the entire cosmos had emerged at the beginning of time. All the stars scattered in the void had begun there. And this planet of the Dark Shore had been there, too, just as he had been. The fires of the Beginning had cooled to atoms, and all matter was actually light in its last disguise.

Dogbrick felt glad when the sun rose. In the dark, his mind ranged among endless thoughts. With colors fitting themselves back into the world, he had other things to occupy his attention. He observed the delicious flow of things carried away by motion. The blur of trees flying past in undulating waves, sunlight sparkling like ocean spray on leaves as he rushed headlong out of the woods onto the smooth, black arm of the dream that was a highway.

Fatigue did not touch him, yet he feared being seen and hunted. When a trailer truck appeared ahead, he sprinted to it and leaped upon the metal step at its back, then crawled beneath the undercarriage. The road streamed beneath him, inches from his suspended body. When the truck rolled into a town, he slid away between the big wheels. Men in billed hats and flannel shirts gawked and pointed, and he threw sleep at them. They collapsed next to their rigs, and he bounded away unseen over the sun-baked tarmac, an amber shadow streaking past the diesel tanks of a truck stop.

He ran across wild country, bursting through bramble and leaving a trail of shredded leaves and burst branches. Dogs howled to hear him coming, then whimpered, wondering where he had gone. Cows felt their rose-pink nostrils tighten at the scent of his passage, then relaxed back to their grazing. He paced the sun, the yellow barge drifting on the ocean of the sky.

Contoured fields of farmlands and static villages floated past in the distance. He leaped hedges, and his magic lifted him off the ground. The earth quilted below him, a patchwork of fields embroidered with roads, rail tracks, and the brown seam of a river. He did not fly, he walked into the sky as into a big blue kitchen. Clouds fogged around him, and he stepped above them. Along the hazy horizon, he watched jetliners crawling.

The power he experienced striding above the planet tempted him to turn his magic upon himself and pull forth more memories of Irth and the city called Saxar where Mary said he once lived. Yet he sensed in an irrational part of himself that was too dangerous, and he put aside that urgency to find himself so that he would not lose the strength to find Mary. The ease with which he strode over the cirrus marblings assured him that once he was united with her again, he would have the strength to draw his own memories out of her head and place them firmly back inside his own.

He walked along the river of day, searching the terrain for New York City. Frustration tangled with anxiety in him as he struggled to identify the numerous splotches of concrete that flourished like mosaic viruses on the green earth, and he just knew that if he had been trained as a wizard he could more aptly direct his power.

Ice clouds glinted in the stratosphere like cold gods, like the dead dreaming of the living. He swiped at them with his magic, hurling at them his memory of Mary Felix, and they flurried their tiny, glittering rainbows to semblances of her.

"Go to her!" he commanded, and they rained away in sheets of hail. "Go to Mary Felix!"

Holding firmly in his mind the memory of his friend, he stepped down the sky on steps of hail and rain. Lightning forked. Thunder spilled around him. The way down was longer than he had realized, and the sun bled into the horizon leaving behind sponges of pink and green light.

He did not let the day's sooty sediment distract him but kept thinking of Mary Felix and all she had told him about himself and the Bright Worlds.

All matter is light, he was thinking as he stepped through the feverish clouds of sunset and descended toward a glittery city on a narrow island. He knew this was Manhattan. His memory of Mary Felix twanged more tautly in him as he approached the massive twin towers at the southern end of the island. In the waters shining with twilight, he saw a giant green statue of a robed woman holding a torch high over her spike-crowned head. Boats floated around her like sparks in the gathering dark.

"All matter is light," he said aloud, intrigued by what Mary had told him of the origins of the Dark Shore. "Light lost in matter." He descended boldly into the City of Lost Light, following the tight thread of energy that he sensed connected him to the woman who held his memories.

He stepped over rooftops cluttered with ducts, pipes, and water tanks and came down before a large, cone-roofed edifice with a ram's-head knocker holding the last ray of the fallen day. Mary was inside. Through the static of traffic noise, he heard her singing a dark song accompanied by the voices of the sinister angels.

"Mary!" he called in his booming voice. "Mary Felix!"

The curved door opened outward, and Nox emerged, gauntly shrunken to the bone, the cowl of his black ceremonial robe drawn back from a long, blackened skull. "Welcome to Octoberland, Dogbrick!" He waved a tall, knobby stave in greeting. "Come in and join the circle."

Dogbrick threw sleep at him, and Nox caught it with his fungus-frilled stave and threw it back at him. Like a balmy wind, weariness doused the beastmarked man, and his legs sagged under him. Abruptly, he found himself lying on his back upon the tar paper roof, staring up at stars that glinted like tears.

Nox loomed over him and thumped him once with the blunt end of his stave between the eyes, hard. The blow sprayed bright dust across Dogbrick's brain, and his limbs stiffened numbly. "Ah, you have journeyed a long distance to be here," the skull face said. "Rest now. Your journey is done."

Dogbrick struggled to move, and a shudder passed through him and twisted his joints with an aching pain.

"Lie still, Dogbrick." The adder eyes narrowed, and Nox showed his tiny teeth in a grimace. "I want to do this cleanly." A black knife appeared in his spidery hand. "This will hurt, I'm afraid—but hurt less if you stay still."

The point of the blade pierced Dogbrick in the pit of his throat where his collarbones joined and cut to the beastbone. Incising vigorously, Nox sliced from throat to groin, and a muffled cry leaked from Dogbrick's paralyzed throat. In moments, Nox had flayed the skin, and the fur peeled away from the torso with a wet sound.

The dark singing from Octoberland continued, floating above the seething sounds of traffic. The black knife worked busily, and Nox's seed-corn teeth gleamed and gleamed.

The Underlife

The Goddess provides. Life sucks.
—THE GIBBET SCROLLS: 15

AS DOES THE TROLL

N'DRATO TRACKED REECE THROUGH THE CLOTHS OF HEAVEN TO the edge of the inky, root-stained water. Under the twin columns, each crowned by a winged sphinx, he stared out at the mirroring swamp, saw the braided vapors of star fumes reflected in the depths, and found no foothold in his brain from which to pull hope out of his heart. His quarry was lost.

The assassin turned and looked at the Cloths of Heaven, cruel in its ruin. The skeletons of creatures drained of their lives by the blood-mad wraiths hung among the looping vines and niches of eroded stone, glowing softly in the dark. He contemplated returning to the temple depths and locating the charmway back to New Arwar. Could he find his way with the charmways on fire?

From his black leather harness, he removed an aviso and sent a coded warning to the Brood of Assassins, alerting them to the charmfire spreading through Irth. Their response came immediately: *Complete your mission.*

With a sigh, N'drato sat on the cracked stone stairs and drew the knife he had used to hack apart Ripcat. He removed wiry blue hairs that, gummed with blood, had caught on the edge, and he inserted them in a seeker amulet. The thin cold sensation within the crystal lens of the amulet pointed across the inverted sky of black water.

Before he began gathering the logs and vines to fashion a raft, he opened his aviso again and sent a coded signal to his sister: *Must talk.*

No reply came. This alarmed him. All their professional lives they had kept this channel open, even when working on rival assignments. N'drato considered Nette a disciple, and she had always been attentive to his instructions. His guidance had been key to her swift advancement in their brood. That she did not reply meant only one thing.

No knowledge avails against the final end, he quoted *The Talismanic Odes* to soothe the sudden pang of heartache within him.

The remorseless training that had shaped him asserted itself, and he compacted the mourning anguish that swirled in him and put aside that packet of pain, to be picked up at a more appropriate time. For the moment, he had to complete his mission, and to that end he began foraging in the maze of the night jungle for rafting material.

Dawn smoke lit the sky, and the planets glittered in the ether levels of the evaporating night when his aviso touched him with the silent hum of an incoming call. The frequency informed him at once that his sister was contacting him. "Nette! Why didn't you reply sooner?"

Her voice came to him with a greater stillness than he had ever heard in her before, a soft voice as if wise from sleep. "Priority silence. Even now, I cannot talk long."

"You didn't return the priority silence code," he accused, using an edge to his voice to cut through her thick tranquillity. "What happened?"

"I cannot tell you now."

"Have you informed the brood?" he asked and stepped onto the mosswood float he had created. "Do they know what you're doing?"

"I am completing my mission—protecting the margravine."

"You sound—different." He sat on the float and examined the directional cipher lights that formed pinprick patterns along the inner shell casing of the aviso. "You're calling from New Arwar—from the manor. What are you doing in there? Has Poch taken his sister back?"

"I can't talk now. I see you are in the Cloths of Heaven. Have you tracked down Ripcat?"

"Yes. I made my report. The brood will fill you in. When you call, ask about the charmways. You'll see what I mean. And be careful in that city of ghosts. My patron has resources."

" 'No death in honor.' "

With that grim quote, she broke their aviso link. For a long moment, N'drato sat still, pondering why she had chosen to end their conversation with the maxim of their brood—an adage usually reserved for those who lost their lives on assignment. The serene, almost rapturous, tone of her voice belied the possibility that she was sacrificing herself. Yet, she *was* inside the manor of her enemy. No code phrases had been used to indicate jeopardy or subterfuge; so he concluded that she knew precisely what she was doing.

Only later, as he skimmed over the slick water, catching the wind in a frond sail he had stretched over the antlers of a branched bough, did he suspect otherwise. He called in to the brood, ostensibly to report massive troll movements among the Reef Isles, but he wanted information about Nette. He learned then, she had not reported to them since declaring her intent to enter the manor and retrieve the margravine.

Shaded by a leaf canopy, with the sail's guy ropes in his hands, N'drato wished he had not asked the brood for direction but had simply gone back through the charmway to New Arwar. Now he would have to complete his mission before he could find out what had really happened to his sister.

Movements on the island shores distracted him from his concern for Nette, and he again trained ocular lenses into the green tumult ashore. Among stilts of swamp groves and on the broad boughs of mammoth trees that stood up to their knees in algal water, he spotted more trolls.

They were moving in the same direction as he, and at first he thought they were stalking him. Only as he leaned over to bank his float around the percolating black waters where the swamp angel stood guard did he notice that the trolls were not only swarming across the Reef Isles, they were also in the water. The metallic sheen of their bodies glinted sharply in the murky depths. If they had been after him, they would have boarded his float long before.

"You run in my shadow," he said aloud to the fanged faces and bolt eyes skimming beside him. "You are tracking the magus, too, aren't you? I am running him down with a seeker amulet. How are you sensing him? Or are you? If I no longer move as does the troll, will you know how to find him?"

To test his theory, N'drato steered away from the direction of his seeker and found himself running toward a Reef Isle with a palisade of timbers—Blight Fen. The trolls changed direction with him. "You evil things! You're using me to find the magus. But how? How do you know I am running him down— except . . ." A chill braced his ribs. "Except the telepathy of the goblins informs you?"

The thought that somehow the goblins had penetrated his mind disturbed him, and he decided he would try to break their psychic hold. He beached his float at Blight Fen and ran through the open gate to prismatic tents of theriacal canvas. Brood reports had told him this isle was abandoned when Poch and Shai Malia departed from it, and he also knew there was much charmware left behind. He gathered all he could find—healing opals, amulet-harnesses, hex-gem vests, and stacked them atop the crates of power wands that Poch had left behind in his haste to flee for the sanctuary of New Arwar. The assassin set a timer-rigged blastcap among the trove and retreated the way he had come.

At his float, he found trolls emerging from the swamp, shawled in water and kelp. A few short volleys from his fire-charm shattered the nearest of them to floating bags of viscera and limbs writhing in the sand.

He shoved off and sailed around Blight Fen, leading the horde of trolls into the vicinity of the Reef Isle. When the timer exploded the blastcap, all Blight Fen ignited in a storm of charmfire. The shock wave bleached everything to a sky-white scream and sent the float hurtling over the swamp water into a rain of bone and blood.

FALSE STAR

THE FIRES OF THE DESTRUCTION OF BLIGHT FEN BURNED ALONG the ragged horizon of the swamp like a false star. Reece Morgan saw it from leagues away, far to the north, where he had drifted on his raft into the Mere of Goblins. He stood up on the gravel bar where his charmpowered vessel had grounded, and he marveled at the brilliant green light that burned behind the trees. He wondered if it was a charmway that had blown out from the fire that Esre had inadvertently touched off under-ground.

"Is the whole Irth going to explode?" he asked his shadow. "Have I brought doom to the entire planet?"

The star dimmed away, and he turned morosely toward a raucous vista of gloomy corries and hills of rotted vegetation saddling dark fens, a concourse of fearsome heath, steaming in the brown daylight. Dragon bones littered the landscape. Gulls flurried among the palings of great ribs. Firesnakes skimmed brightly over the muddy shoals where mire and dragon's blood mixed.

The amulet boots he had stepped into at Blight Fen kept away the vipers and centipedes, and he marched with the strength of his power wands into this phantasmal scene. The stench of putrefaction did not faze him, for his amulet harness generated a nimbus of clear air around him.

Protected by hex-gems, he made easy progress through the mere along trails of root ledges and dragon vertebrae like big stepping-stones in the muck. Draperies hung on all sides: vast sheets of moss, tangled vines, and dragon skin flayed from wings twisted free of their sockets among the treetops. In this umber darkness, he wandered, searching he knew not for what—yet searching.

Bees droned in their canopy hives; dragonflies darted, constantly swerving to adjust their errancy; and waterbirds stood one-legged like pink-and-white lanterns in the dismal forest enclaves. He felt a kinship with these creatures. They, too, were seeking, and it was always the same, something to eat. For him, the quest was not for food. He would have remained on the Dark Shore with the creatures of his own world if eating were his sole concern. He had come to Irth seeking salvation for what he had lost on Earth: food for his hungering spirit.

That same spirit drove him now deeper into the Mere of Goblins. As he had risen from death in the mineral pool under the Cloths of Heaven, he had glimpsed a trove of goblins hidden among these necrotic pools. Their revival in this world was his doing. He had blindly sought magic and power with Caval, and they had thus unwittingly served the devil worshipper Duppy Hob, who had unleashed Hu'dre Vra upon the Irth. The

Dark Lord's devastation had weakened the dominions sufficiently for the goblins to attack. He was responsible for that.
But what did these goblins want? Why did they use their telepathy to destroy what Charm had built?

Bounding among the root mats and dragon bones, he remembered the blue flower in the palace of skulls. The goblins had
gone to some trouble to create that shrine—to what? To the
hotter reality they had lost? To the beauty of this world that
they wanted wholly for themselves?

These thoughts pestered Reece through that day and the following night of his wandering. He thought of Dogbrick, amne-
siac on the Dark Shore, and Jyoti, left alone to defend her city
without his help. He had owed both of them so much and yet,
slogging through the swamp, had nothing to offer them but
his perseverance.

Through the bioluminescent tiers of the jungle, dawn light
filtered like scattered rubies. By that red light, he came upon
the salt dome he had seen in Ripcat's death vision—white as
the chalk house of Earth's Moon. What he sought was there,
he knew at once, and he moved quickly through the loops of
a dragon's leathery bowels hung from where they had snagged
as the great beast collapsed into the forest.

He circled along moss rocks that surrounded the salt dome.
Frequently, he stopped and pressed against the crystal surface
to peer through its webbing of cracks. He saw nothing. After
completing a circuit, he climbed up the rough surface, his
boots crunching on the glassy nodules. A crevice large
enough to squeeze through presented itself, and he entered
feet first.

The air was putrid, and even the amulets of his harness could
not filter out all of that ghastly stench. Both cool and burning,
the atmosphere of the interior enwrapped him in an other-
worldly sensation. He emerged on a spiral shelf cut into the
crusty rock and squatted above the capacious amphitheater of

his vision. Below, basking in the lilac morning light, hundreds of goblins lay sleeping. Their small, naked, doll bodies lay scattered haphazardly among knobs of salt and glossy mineral accretions.

The weirdly chilled and singeing air seemed to bear the burden of their souls. He could feel their dreaming twisting inside him. A fine snow fell through his mind, icing his muscles. He leaned back, pressing his shoulders against the nuggety wall, hoping to keep himself from pitching forward and falling down among them.

Pink crevices in the dome let down dawn fire and illuminated the greasy bodies, the shiny, bulbous heads and warped limbs. They smoldered pink, streaked black with filth, embers softly glowing through soot. The heat of their dreaming lifted his psyche up through the dome roof of his cranium, up past the dome roof of the salt cave, up past the dome roof of the sky, into the glare of the Abiding Star.

The goblins were dreaming of their lost lives as pixies. Under blue mountains, the smell of something wonderful burning ran with them into jade shadows. They crouched under fronds and lacy ferns, gazing into a cobbled garden that spun with golden leaves. In the garden's marble pool, a young woman with long tresses of cinnamon hair bathed her swollen belly. Her bright ringlets spread like flames in the ice-green water under temple column and a sky of mauve dusk.

Reece tried to pull himself awake. He knew this young woman. She was the author of worlds. . . . The pixies watched her weave her magic. Her purpose, they knew, was to generate a Charmful experience of light and dark, good and evil by which to teach her child when it was born. But the pixies had another use for her power: They would climb down into her magical dream and live there not as mere pixies but as gods.

Forcing his eyes open, Reece looked down at the goblins sleeping in their grime. They had succeeded. They had infiltrated this colder world, and with their hotter minds they were exterminating the only ones who could deny them their god-hood. They were not evil. They were dear ones looking for a world of their own, where they could run free in their naked happy bodies.

THAT JOY IN DEATH

Smutchy with goblin ordure, Jyoti staggered across the manor grounds, her face lifted to the strong rays of the Abiding Star. Residual telepathy from her time with the goblins filled her head with a mist of noises: the thoughts of everything around her. She heard the cypress trees, each with its ten or twelve hearts throbbing in the underground dark, thinking about the rising day, talking with chemical noise to one another on various subjects—the loom shafts of daylight, the acids seeping from the rocks and diffusing with last night's rain, the rumor of sapsucker insects from trees on the other side of the wind.

She heard the agitation of the gnats and flies as they sacked the land for food and sex, the utterances of the grass under the weight of her feet, the grief of a squirrel who had lost her young to an owl, and the joyful noises of the owl as it ate. For an instant, she experienced that joy in death that had been life's most primal justification from the first, and it appalled her.

Holding her head in her hands, she wended her way among the trees toward the glider field that Overy Scarn had cleared from the nut groves on the crest adjacent to the manor. When she heard people with her mind, she slipped into the shadows of the trees or ducked into coverts under the shrubs.

Still panting from her strenuous descent down the ivy wall of the manor, she lay in green darkness, her head filled with the smell of loam and lichen of the thicket—and a strange vision, an inward bond with the goblins themselves, opened in her. She saw them in their hundreds possessed by a wild pa-

tience thick as sleep, waiting within an albino cavern of limestone and salt, their tiny bodies spasmodic with dreams of the
world beyond World's End.

They remembered their former life as pixies, eternal babies
of the forest, children smiled upon by cloud shadows and the
mineral faces in rock shelves, their small, powerful bodies
clothed in milkweed and mallow, decorated with bits and shards
of wasp's nest and chips from ancient lamp saucers. They re-
called sneaking into the lady's garden and hiding under the
arbor, beneath an aspiring helix of clematis and hanging roses
white and yellow and afreight with golden bees intoxicated
by attar. . . .

Jyoti rubbed her face with dead leaves until the sour resins
broke the goblin's spell. At first on hands and knees and then
crouched over, she shambled through the bushes, scratching her
face and hands and glad for the pain that fit her back into
her body.

As the goblin vision faded, she knew she had to get away
from New Arwar before the vile creatures used their enthralling
power on her again. They were hungry for hex-gems, famished
for Charm to extend the reach of their telepathy, and they
called for help. Her mind raced for escape, yet thinking had
grown difficult.

The mob in her heart sounded louder than she had ever
heard them before. These were her own thoughts, the telepathy
of her personal unconscious spilling voices in the waves of her
pulse and heartbeat. A crushing rhapsody of fears, doubts, and
rage polluted her, distracting her with their insistence. She
needed Charm to silence them. Her breath turned to groans as
she limped out of the underbrush and approached a hangar still
under construction.

*You are a weakling and a sniveling coward. Look at how quickly you
submitted to Poch's false claim, how eagerly you surrendered your rightful
station and with such craven alacrity.*

No workers occupied the hangar when she arrived. She could

hear them and several sentinels in the distance, eating lunch among the stacked lumber and the behemoth, orange grading machines. Their thoughts pattered like a rainy drizzle, not nearly as loud as her own psychic voices.

Because of your lack of leadership, everyone suffers. Nette has given herself to the goblins so that you can crawl away through the bushes. Your weakness in the face of challenge has brought doom to your entire city!

Jyoti tried to ignore the swarming recriminations and forced herself to act despite her fear. She strode across the concrete flight apron with its wooden braces still holding the wet stone in place and entered the hangar. Past an airfoil, a flying machine with blue canvas wings, brace wires, struts, fins, a bubble canopy, and a Charm-injected engine, she walked. Her telepathy guided her behind crates of unassembled airfoils to where she heard two sentinels conversing.

There are two of them! You can't take both. They're armed with firelocks, cudgels, and charmor. You don't even have a single power wand and no weapon at all. Stop now—sneak back into the bushes while you can. . . .

Jyoti did not want to attack her own guards, but she knew she had no choice. They served Poch, who served the goblins— the dear ones to him as they had almost been to her as well, before Nette freed her from their influence. For Nette's sake, for whatever hope there was of stopping the goblins, she moved to attack.

Stepping out from behind the crates, she heard alarm in the skullbound brains of the guards, heard their hearts leap, and saw the surprise in their broad faces harden almost instantly to aggressive grimaces. The flicker of a moment where they took in the scurfy woman befouled in goblin grease and then shockingly recognized her as the margravine permitted her to advance within striking distance. She caught the arm of the nearest guard as he reached for his firelock, twisted his wrist, and sharply slapped his larynx.

The other guard drew his weapon, and Jyoti used the falling momentum of the first guard to pull her head and shoulders toward the ground and scissor-kick upward with her legs. One boot knocked the firelock from the shooter's grip, the second caught him under his sternum.

The guard who had braced her kick hit his brow on the concrete and lay dazed under her as she unholstered his gun. She rolled to her feet, setting the charge pin to fire stun bolts, but that was not necessary. Both sentinels lay curled around their pain, and she stripped them of their charmor vests and amulet harnesses with no resistance.

You were lucky. They were caught by surprise—but others must have heard the scuffle. . . .

The telepathic voices ended abruptly when she slipped into an amulet harness and slung the other over her shoulder with the two heavy charmor vests. As she had feared, the other sentinels had heard the noise of her attack, and they came running across the flight apron with the workers. Not breaking her stride, she fired stun bolts, striking two of the three guards in their legs.

The third dropped to a firing stance, and she twisted to one side as if to leap away then abruptly spun back and fired, hitting him in the side of his head as he turned to fire at where she should have been. The workers turned and fled.

Jyoti climbed into the flight pod of the waiting airfoil and locked the bubble canopy in place. Engine thunder shook the airframe, and the props whirled to a shadowy blear. She rolled the machine onto the apron, careful to avoid the stunned sentinels. As soon as she reached the flight field, she pulled back on the yoke and lifted the airfoil into a vertical ascent, rocketing into the sky.

BEAUTY AND THE BALANCE

THE ABIDING STAR SHONE LIKE WHITE ACETYLENE IN THE ABUNdant blue of the sky. Jyoti basked in its radiance, her stunned body healing under the influence of the hex-gems within the harness she had strapped on. Soon, the scratches on her hands and face had healed and the vertiginous fear that the telepathy had inspired vanished. She bestowed herself to silence briefly, glad that the accusatory voices in her head had departed.

Once she regained confidence in her wholeness, she allowed herself to dwell on Nette and the others who were in jeopardy: Poch, Reece, New Arwar, and all of Irth. She could not go back for Nette. The goblins were too powerful. Nevertheless, she was determined that Nette's sacrifice would not be empty.

She remembered the vision she had suffered under the manor's shrubs. Somewhere among the dominions, hundreds of goblins lay dreaming of their former lives as pixies before the dark father enticed them to invade Irth. They were the greater threat by dint of their numbers, and she decided to find and destroy them. With a smear of the gummy web strands that clung to her buckskin trousers and boots, she loaded the lens of a seeker amulet that she found in her harness.

The directional coolness of the amulet pointed her back toward New Arwar and the goblins who had entrapped her. She pulled the airfoil higher into the sky and swung out farther over the verdant horizons of Elvre. As she banked south, the chill thread of sensation within the amulet pointed away from the city—toward the Mere of Goblins.

Flying high into lashes of cirrus cloud, Jyoti followed the seeker amulet across the rumpled green ranges of jungle and then above the sea's sparkling facets. She arrived over the blotched marshland and pock-hole pools of the Mere of Goblins late in the afternoon.

Amber slants of light cut banks of storm clouds to ethereal stairways, and treetops glowed like flame-soaked wicks in the waxy dark of the bog forest. Hung among the branches, she spied dragon carcasses fat as burst weed pods. A salt dome shone in the morass, white as a giant's skull.

She circled it once, then set the airfoil down on a nearby

gravel bank. With the firelocks she had taken from the sentinels at New Arwar, she would blow up the temple of evil, and she holstered them with the harness straps at her back and shouldered the extra harness to help fuel the charmfire she intended to set ablaze. Then, she deplaned and stood in the purpling light, steeling herself to enter the monstrous enclave.

On her flyby, she had spotted a sizable crevice in the dome, and she climbed up the salt face to that rift and squeezed through. She stepped onto a crusty shelf and teetered precariously above a large gorge of glutinous baby shapes. The fetid air stung her nostrils until she activated all her power wands. Even then, the ugly stink nauseated her, and she scanned the depth of the chamber with a sneer of disgust.

By the light raying through the cracks and holes of the dome, she saw goblins in their hundreds just as they had appeared in her vision. And among their plumply small and oily bodies a single glow of storm shine stood, purple human light, a man in amulet vest and gem-studded boots—Reece!

Her heart banged hard at the sight of him, excited to find him alive, amazed to find him here. But she was afraid to call his name, afraid to wake the dreaming goblins. She caught his attention by waving a headband of lux-diamonds.

"Jyoti!" Reece shouted, and his voice boomed resonantly in the vaulted chamber. "Come down! Come walk among the dear ones!"

Jyoti edged along the shelf, working her way slowly along the spiral curve that descended to the cluttered floor of the dome. As she proceeded, the heat of the goblins saturated her with their stink and their dreaming.

Again, she found herself remembering her vision of these invaders as pixies in their own arboreal world. She saw them prancing in goldenrod, dressed in rough-headed blooms, armed with thistle knives, sneaking their way into the garden of the nameless lady. . . .

No! Jyoti insisted. She had seen this vision. She knew where it led, and she would not go there again.

Focusing on the prisms of storm haze let down from the cracked dome and littering the slimy bodies, she broke the spell. When she reached the dirt-streaked dolls with their enlarged heads, thunder banged sharply overhead and rain sifted like powder through the cracked dome.

She waded gingerly among the twitching goblins, nudging them gently with her boots to make space to step.

Reece knelt over the dear ones, cupping his hands to gather moisture and daubing their smudged brows. "Look at them, Jyoti, so lovely in their smallness."

With the extra harness that she had lugged, she draped Reece and activated all the power wands. The surge of Charm loosened him from the goblin's spell, and his face winced with alertness.

He blinked, at first not recognizing her with her hair sheared and her face smirched. "Jyo?"

He stood and seized her, gaping about at the sprawled goblins, appalled by their slick, dirt-streaked bodies and the miasma that oozed from them. "Jyo! How did you find me?"

Jyoti's mind reeled to actually hold him in her arms, and at last she could admit to herself that he was not an illusion, not some telepathic simulacrum of the goblins. She pressed her face against the side of his neck and nuzzled him, defying for the moment her fear of where they were.

"I came to destroy them," she said when she lifted her face, her eyes glinting with tears, "and you were here." She pulled him away from the sleeping goblins, guiding him with well-placed steps toward the wall.

He followed gladly, clinging to her, drinking in her voice.

"My weapons master, Nette, told me that Ripcat had been seen in Bryse. That's the last I'd heard of you."

Reece began to tell her about Esre and his abduction in Moödrun, and Jyoti stopped him. She pointed with her chin to one side, and when he turned he saw a gaunt figure with a face sharp as an ax and small, black eyes. "You!"

Jyoti reached for a firelock, and the grim man in ebony robes shook his hairless head. "There is no need for a weapon. If I had come to slay you, you would never have seen me."

THE STRANGE CREATURES CAME

"YOU KILLED ESRE!" REECE POINTED AN ACCUSATORY FINGER AT N'drato. "And you almost killed me."

Impassively, the assassin looked about at the stained, little bodies strewn at their feet, stinking like some reeking issue of death itself. "I was wrong. Margravine—magus, the Brood of Assassins withdraws blood claims on both of you. For the witch's sake, I will make retribution to the Sisterhood."

"What has moved you to turn your knife, N'drato?" Jyoti inquired suspiciously.

The narrow man reached under his robe and amplified the outflow of Charm from his power wands, countering the wicked stench and the faint shadow of voices whispering in his head, plaintively chanting songs of the pixie, effervescent voices heating his blood so that fate felt like wine and he grew drowsy. "Assassins are not mindless killers. I suspected that the one who hired me was not the one I should obey. I noticed that trolls were following me to find the magus. The goblins want you dead, Reece Morgan—but the Brood of Assassins does not serve goblins."

"Shai Malia hired you," Jyoti knew and vainly looked for a glint of acknowledgment in the assassin's hatchet face. "She is a puppet of the goblins. And so is my brother. And so now is your sister."

N'drato's nostrils winced, betraying his surprise. "Nette is with these monsters? I don't believe it."

"She sacrificed herself to save me." Jyoti stepped closer to the clouded crystal wall and pulled Reece along, away from the ebony-robed man with the small black eyes. "I'm here now because she took my place. This gummy, white ichor that stains me, it's goblin scat. Your sister is mired in it right now."

N'drato hung his head to hide his horror. Nothing in his training or experience had prepared him for this. "I must return to New Arwar at once—but the charmways are burning."

"The Sisterhood is gutting those bridges to contain the goblins." Reece glanced up at rain threading through the cracked dome in shafts of storm-blue light and wondered about Dogbrick and the passage to Earth. "We have to get out of here before the trolls find us."

"Fear not. I forestalled the advance of the trolls for the moment." N'drato sidled closer. "Come with me. The Brood of Assassins has mapped most of the charmways among the dominions, and there is a passage near here to New Arwar that may yet be open. Take me to my sister."

"No." Jyoti motioned to the grotto of dreaming goblins. "I came here to destroy this horde."

N'drato shook his head. "I cannot destroy these creatures of another world without permission from my brood. And if I ask, they will learn of Nette's plight and perhaps deny me the chance to retrieve her. I cannot take that risk. Leave these goblins for now and come with me to New Arwar."

"Why should we trust you?" Reece watched him with obvious fright. "You were sent to kill us."

"Look about you." The assassin glanced at the slumbering goblins. "You fear me more than you fear them?"

Jyoti lifted her chin adamantly. "You go if you must. But we're not leaving until these things are dead."

The assassin's small, black eyes tightened. "If I stay, I must answer to my brood. I will answer for Nette but not for goblins."

He moved closer, a glint of metal in one hand. "As you will
not take me to Nette, then give me enough of the goblin's scat
to charge my seeker amulet, and I will find her myself."

Jyoti obliged, and N'drato scraped the sticky, cottony puru-
lence from the thigh of her buckskin trousers and packed the
lens of his seeker.

He felt the margravine surreptitiously snip threads from his
robe as he bent over her. He knew she was intent on charging
her seeker to follow him to the charmway hidden in the Mere
of Goblins, but he behaved as though oblivious of this. When
he had what he needed, he pressed an ivory coin into Jyoti's
palm. "This will guide you to the nearest charmway."

The assassin departed without farewell, his ebony robes fluttering about him as he climbed the salt shelves to the crack in
the dome where he had entered, nimble as a flung shadow.

Outside, the stormy night bore uncountable shapes among
the tossing trees, the stabs of lightning, and the wind-blustered
curtains of rain. N'drato rushed along unfazed. His amulets protected him, and his training guided him unerringly around
flashing pools of firesnakes and whip shadows of giant, frantic
centipedes—to the margravine's airfoil.

Under sizzling lashes of lightning and blares of thunder,
N'drato started the engine and turned the vessel into the wind.
Neither Jyoti nor Reece heard him take off.

He flew through the deformed darkness of the tempest, while
below the strange creatures came, blind, larval hulks, tentacled
chimeras, unreckonable beings stirred up from the putrid depths
of the swamp. Their roars rivaled the thunder, their fibrillar
heads silhouetted by the strobing sky above the shuddering
treetops. He winced before these furies into whose path he had
committed the margravine and her consort.

Then, the storm claimed his full attention for the rest of the
flight. Deep in the night, he brought the battered airfoil down

in a swatch of cleared forest outside New Arwar. Soon, he made his way by lightning glare to the great, jointed sewer pipes that emptied the city's bowels. These he followed like a spider, crawling upside down above the sluicing wastewater.

He crawled into vents that by blind turnings brought him to the utility ducts serving the manor. Chimes of timeless dripping accompanied him, and presently he barged through an insulation filter panel into a catacomb of exhaust fans and vent holes. From there, the seeker amulet's cool indicator pointed him to the air shafts that climbed the stone walls to the chamber of the goblins.

Nette hung upside down in a cocoon of webs. N'drato saw her through the grille of a floor vent gauzed over with gossamer. He forced the grille and slinked into the mephitic chamber. The power wands under his robe began to crack immediately, splitting lengthwise as the Charm drained out of them, and the rancid stench pierced his sinuses.

Bald, bloated, pale babies watched him, four, five of them huddled in one corner, each with one of their blood-smoked eyes staring intently, pupils blown wide, and the other droop-lidded, concussed, speckled flesh twitching. Their tiny mouths bent in sad, evil smiles.

N'drato drew his firelock and aimed it at the cowering goblins. He crawled through their creamy sludge, Charm draining from him. His body felt heavy, his arm too ponderous to move, his fingers too thick to draw back the charge pin and pull the trigger. Fear swung through him. And was gone.

Like a dawn sky of processional pink clouds, joy rose in him. He released the firelock and squatted in the rich and fragrant silk of the dear ones. He laughed at the empty fullness of his own being, his own perfect self.

His small, black eyes glinted merrily, and he laughed among the clouds of the cherubs, laughed at all the horrors he had learned to inflict on others so that he could love himself. All that was over now. He was no longer an assassin. He was not even a man anymore. He was just here, with the dear ones, free of all he had ever been.

ANGEL FATE

THE GOBLINS WOVE THEIR HAPPY THREADS AROUND N'DRATO AND hoisted him to the ceiling. This took a long time, for they moved slowly in this cold reality far from their home inside the Abiding Star. They moved slower yet for their melancholy, their loneliness laid bare. They missed their home in the wildwood and their former lives as pixies. The dark father had deceived them into climbing down into his wife's dream. He had said they would be as gods—but he had not made clear to them that they would be as gods among demons.

That was how the goblins perceived people. They were demons who fought and killed one another for land and Charm, who hoarded these possessions for themselves while others of their own kind starved, even to death. No pixie would do that to another creature, let alone to one of its own kind.

The dark father had tricked them, and now there was no way back. They were too cold to climb up and out of the dream. They were so cold it was easier to sleep, to weave their own dream of happier days among the leaf tops when they were so full of joy they did not even realize they were happy.

Why had the dark father done this to them? They had pondered this from the time they had arrived so long ago and found themselves in a world among demons. *Why?*

Because the dark father could. That was why. The nameless lady who had authored these worlds believed she was preparing a caul of knowledge for the birth of her child. She thought that the baby would be better for being born in the light, the mother's light that had poured into the void and filled the cold darkness with its warmth and energy.

The dark father wanted to rear their child in the deep of night, where darkness took on an urgency like the great turtle of time, shouldering its own shadow with a perseverance that engulfed every epoch with oblivion, every age a candle snuffed. There, the child would have to learn to make its own light. The young soul would have to learn to create its own hope, its own new face of time, its own bright mirrors of stars, its own road map of heaven. That was the difficult way, the way of uncertainty that led to strength—the way of the dark father.

Knowing this offered no comfort to the goblins. They mewled with sorrow and smiled at one another sadly, fools aware that they had been duped. There was nothing else to do but accept their lot and strive with all their strength and cunning against the wickedness that possessed this world. That was the angel fate of goblins, to struggle mightily against the monster fate of demons.

To that end, they strung up the demon N'drato. Clotted with the sleep glitter that had oozed from their bodies, his stenchy skin shining, he hung like a moon weight, a sac of fibrous moonbeams spun together, another dream no one wanted.

Purging egg masses from the orifices between their legs, the goblins prepared to commune with this demon. It was grotesque work that none of them relished, yet it had to be done to continue their fight. The slick egg cases oozed from their bodies like ectoplasmic bulbs, throbbing with the telepathic chemicals that churned within them.

The goblins hugged each other with dread and waited. Their hearts skittered like small animals. They clutched each other, being brave, each for the others. Since arriving on Irth, they had learned that love was not the birdsongs they had once believed it was. Love was strong-jawed as death itself.

With a popping hiss, a string of eggs released their hormonal burdens. The demon the goblins had most recently captured convulsed briefly as the fumes invaded his skull and twisted new loops in his cruel brain.

Fear gouged the goblins. They saw in N'drato his intrusion into the chalk house of their sleeping brethren, and they wailed. Their cries rang like a bell wandering across the glades, traveling across the forest and the leagues of sea beyond the forest to their sleeping kin.

Wake! the goblins cried, for they saw the magus and his consort, Jyoti, in their grotto temple. *Wake! Wake and defend yourselves! Demons are among you!*

The goblins grabbed at each other and pulled themselves into their nurturing aromas, strengthening their telepathic power. With this power, they reached across the world to the mindless beasts whose hollow minds held their commands most snugly. *Trolls!* they shouted as one. *Trolls to the House of Goblins! Go!*

Rain dragged its nets across the Mere of Goblins, snaring the tree coves and smoky floors of the swamp with the psychic insistence of the goblins. From out of the tussocks and bogs, the trolls—bolt-eyed humanoids with metallic skin and fanged faces—emerged.

Lightning swung its lantern. The silver light fluttered, went out, and was lit again elsewhere in the swamp. By that crazed illumination, the trolls gathered, slouching through the rain toward the salt dome that housed the rousing goblins.

And within that dome, the sleeping ones stirred. The dreams of haystack clouds and rambling fields of feathery grass dissolved. The speckled eyelids flickered and opened, wincing in the flickering glare of lightning that rayed through the cracked dome and shivering in the cold.

Other lights bobbed among them, and the goblins flustered with fear to see in their midst two demons.

Their minds reached out as one, terrified of the invaders stalking among them, waving their lux-diamonds, planting in the ground around them their horrible crystals of trapped Charm, rocks of exiled light. And with one mind, the goblins screamed.

LIGHT IN THE HEAD

ALL HER LIFE OVERY SCARN HAD BEEN TOO POOR TO AFFORD THE Charm that could have made her beautiful, and now that she had all the resources of Dig Dog Ltd. *and* New Arwar at her disposal, she was far too busy to undergo the laborious glamour-bloodstone treatments that could melt away her fat.

She did, however, have fashioned the spellbinder girdle that endowed her with irresistible sexual allure. The ecstasy-topazes and rapture-garnets alone had cost her dearly, because she required thrice as many for her girth than more svelte wearers. And the expense for the necessary conjure-wire to adequately encompass her folds of flesh had nearly convinced her to forgo the girdle altogether and take the time instead for the fat melting.

But time now was more precious than lux-diamonds. Reports from every dominion announced destruction and defeat under the relentless waves of troll and ogre attacks. Agriculture had been devastated, and all mining operations across Irth had shut down. In the coming days, famine and a poverty of Charm would effectively end the Talismanic Era. People would be forced to live as they had a million days ago, foraging for food, strapping themselves into trees and caves at night to keep from drifting away on the nocturnal tide as they slept. And those who did possess the remaining hex-gems would rule with a might greater than Peers.

All of Overy Scarn's time was consumed with her frantic efforts to direct Dig Dog into acquiring as many hex-gems as were currently available. With its headquarters in the industrial capital of Saxar, Dig Dog had already bought up the present stocks of talismanic goods from the manufacturers themselves. And with their ownership of New Arwar, the only city unmolested by the Goblin Wars, she had ample natural resources at her disposal for barter.

The only limiting factor was time. The destruction of the dominions was proceeding too rapidly, with a frenzy that threatened to plunge Irth into utter anarchy within fifty days or less. She needed more time to stockpile hex-gems and to conclude negotiations for mining concessions from their desperate owners. Yet how did one retard the fury of goblins?

Dressed in a kirtle of flowing orange satin overlaid with networks of blue lace and fastened about her ample waist by beads of levity-pearls that lent a buoyancy to her step, Overy Scarn paced before the gallery windows of her suite. Silver clouds, spun to spidery streaks, shone above the manor's champaigne with news of an incoming storm. Patterned to diamonds by the mullioned panes, morning light poured before her yellow slippers and glared off polished blond parquet.

She stepped to the open wardrobe with its frosted glass panels and dark wood frame carved with dancing satyrs and fauns and stood behind the spellbinder girdle that hung there. In the window light, its citrine starburst patterns of ecstasy-topazes and spiral trim of rapture-garnets glittered with aureate splendor. "You know what you must do, Scarn."

She stepped back from the sparkling girdle and addressed it as though the garment were herself. "I will know if you tell me, Overy. Don't expect me to do all your thinking for you."

The levity-pearls about her waist allowed her to prance gracefully behind the girdle again. "You're acting coy, because you think you do all the work, Scarn. But were it not for me, we would have no useful information at all. I'm the one who must give so much of herself to find out the truth of things. And soon now the knock will come and I must give again."

"I don't want to argue with you, Overy," she told herself, moving around to face the bejeweled girdle. "Yes, you have used yourself to our advantage. But remember, before we were wealthy enough to afford this spell-binder that gives you allure, I alone moved us from a charmwright's mail clerk to factory manager and then to an executive station at Dig Dog. That was all done by me, with my wits and my indefatigable industry, for who would find allure in the obese creature that we are?"

"That *you* are, Scarn. Not me," she replied, holding the girdle before her defensively. "So long as I wear this, I am Overy the lovely, Overy the irresistible. And as Overy have we not come to understand why New Arwar endures no blight from the goblins?"

She let go the girdle and paced thoughtfully. "Yes, Overy, we know from your intelligence won by lewd maneuverings that Poch and his shrewish wife are goblin puppets. Yet, I have two objections to the hopes you place in this intelligence. First, how can we be sure that what you have learned no others will learn in turn? If the other dominions suspect that we harbor goblins, New Arwar will be smashed to rubble in a torrent of charmfire."

With the resplendent girdle lifted to her chin, she answered herself, "This girdle is a *spellbinder*, foolish Scarn. My source will not even inform himself, let alone others."

A knock tapped a soft rhythm at the door.

"Ah! Now, Scarn, you shall have the opportunity to witness once more the effectiveness of this spellbinder."

She released the girdle and stood back. "Wait, Overy. Before you put on your precious hexware, tell me—why must I always be the one to confront the margrave and his wife? You are so proud of your spellbinding, why don't you manipulate them?"

"Surprise, Scarn. Surprise. The most powerful weapon in war." She wrapped the girdle about her waist and struggled a moment with her pudgy fingers to hook the conjure-wire clasps. "And do not doubt we are going to win this war with the goblins, Scarn. We must—or everything we have worked so hard to attain is lost. The dominions must be broken, yes, but not obliterated. At the correct moment, we shall use our ample Charm to crush the goblins and claim Irth for ourselves. And we shall rule as queen over all."

She motioned for the door to open, and a burly sentinel in heraldic crimson and gold entered. He dropped to one knee on the parquet, and she bid him rise and enter her waiting embrace. Once enclosed in her arms, the Charm that enraptured him shuddered him to the bones with ecstasy. "Tell me, Roidan, tell me all that you have seen."

The thick-necked Roidan tugged at his blazer, frantic to remove his clothes. The charmflow from the spellbinder so flushed him that he could barely breathe, and he spoke, panting, "Beloved Overy—beloved!" He nuzzled his face in her creased neck, his voice muffled. "The goblins suspect nothing. Nothing. Nothing at all." He lifted his fervid face toward hers. "From the attic above their suite, conjure-fibers capture all sight and sound from below, so subtly that they suspect nothing. Nothing at all!"

She helped him squirm out of his trousers. "You installed the conjure-fibers most expertly, my dear Roidan. Not for nothing are you a charmwright's son. The knowledge was in your secret mind all along and needed only my coaxing to bring it forth. But now tell me, what have you seen since last we embraced?"

Roidan's tufty orange hair tickled her chin as he smothered himself in her breasts. "Jyoti Odawl has fled—freed by her weapons master, Nette—who hangs now in the goblins' web with another assassin—a man that came to rescue her and was captured by—"

"Hush!" Overy's mind reeled. "Why did you not tell me of all this sooner?"

"Sooner?" Roidan lifted a thick face drowsy with rapture. "You told me to forget until your summons. I forgot."

With an annoyed hiss, she shoved his stupefied face back into the comfort of her breasts.

AND

A<small>ND WHEN SHE HAD TAKEN THE PLEASURE THAT SHE WANTED FROM</small> Roidan and had dismissed him with the command to once more forget their liaison, she removed the spellbinder girdle with trembling fingers. Much as she craved the carnal joy that the spellbinder allowed her, she had not enjoyed herself this day. Two assassins were strung up in the goblins' chamber, and that meant that soon the Brood of Assassins would send others to investigate. This unfortunate turn of events obliged her to accelerate her plan.

From her wardrobe, she removed a small satchel of red nylon and exited her suite. She moved quickly along the corridors, her yellow slippers just grazing the polished floor. At the double doors of the margrave's chambers, she nodded once to the sentinel. A share in the timber trade had bought from the sentinels access to every corner of the manor, and she entered without knocking.

Wearing bright parachute silk pants and batik pullovers, Poch and Shai Malia sat on a chamois divan, their sneakers propped on soft leather ottomans. Carnelian bowls on tripods stood at either side, filled with pretzels and potato chips. On the low rattan table before them, a half-eaten pizza and tinsel chocolate wrappers sprawled between two tourmaline ashtrays filled with ash and cigarette butts. The margrave wore mirror shades in the rusty nest of his hair, and his wife hid her smoke-burned eyes with wraparound sunglasses. Only the tremulous glow of television light illuminated the heavily draped chamber until the chandelier spilled its crystalline radiance.

Shai Malia stood up, indignant at the abrupt arrival of Overy Scarn. But Poch remained seated, his slack gaze fixed upon the nattering TV.

"Sit down, Lady Shai." Overy Scarn motioned for her to be seated and clicked off the TV. "I've not come to challenge you. Your titles are secure, your income from our various enterprises steady. I bring you no troubles whatsoever. Rather, I am here to share with you a new and most wonderful gift from the Dark Shore."

Shai Malia did not sit. "We have enough of your gifts, Scarn. Now we demand your respect."

"Ah, Lady Shai, please, sit down." Overy Scarn shoved an upholstered chair embroidered with griffins to the side of the TV table and sat. "I am a businesswoman. Whatever you get from me, you must earn."

"You think you own us." Shai Malia blew a stream of smoke from the corner of her mouth and jabbed the butt of her cigarette into an ashtray. "You think you're so powerful. I want you to come with us, upstairs. There is something I want to show you there that will earn your respect."

"I'm not going upstairs," Overy stated with finality and placed the small satchel of red nylon on the rattan table beside the cold pizza.

"Last time you berated my husband, you implied that you knew something of the goblins and why New Arwar has remained unscathed by their attacks." Shai Malia's black, eyeless gaze watched her ominously. "What do you know?"

"All I know is that the goblins have spared this city," she replied, seeing her twin reflections small and meek in the dark curved plastic. "There is something about the jungles of Elvre that intimidate them. And if I inform the Peers of this, they will come to seek the cause, and what autonomy you enjoy will be lost."

Shai Malia exchanged a slow look with her husband.

"Right now, the Peers are too busy defending their own dominions," Overy continued. "But as Dig Dog's chief executive, I will be heard by them if I speak up. So, it is wise that you do not act too imperiously with me. We are lucky to have escaped the notice of the goblins thus far. If the Peers pay our city heed, perhaps then their enemies, the goblins, will, as well."

Shai Malia sat down, signaling a sullen satisfaction with Scarn's answer. "I still think you should come with us upstairs and see what we have there."

"And what would that be?" Overy Scarn asked, innocently fingering her brown curls.

"My wife refers to the assassin we have captured," Poch intervened before Shai Malia could respond. "The weapons master, Nette, has returned and allowed my sister to escape. Jyoti has commandeered an airfoil and fled the city."

"And you scolded me for attempting to kill her when she trespassed the manor!" Overy Scarn wagged a finger at Poch. "I was trying to protect you. She knows that Dig Dog has underwritten your claim to the title. What we did is illegal, and if she brings her claim before the regency you will lose all you now possess."

"And so will you," Shai Malia reminded her. From the side of the divan's cushion, she drew a chrome-plated handgun and pointed it at the trade executive. "I think it's time we take you upstairs."

"And shut me in with Nette?" Overy Scarn hid her fright behind a sneering laugh. "You need me alive and free more so now than ever. The Brood of Assassins will surely want to know what has become of their Nette—and I have the resources to buy off their meddlesome inquiries. Besides, if you shoot me or hide me away, Dig Dog will necessarily review my accounts and the fact of my sponsorship of Poch's title will be revealed. So long as I am accounts executive and bond agent, we can use our wealth to counter even Jyoti's claim to the title."

Poch reached out and took the gun from his wife. "She's right, Shai. Her interests and ours are the same."

Shai Malia reluctantly released the weapon to Poch. "We want your respect, Scarn. We have earned it by hearing you out and letting you live. Do you understand?"

Poch shoved the gun under the cushion of the divan and smiled apologetically at Overy Scarn. "We must respect one another, don't you think?"

"Most certainly." Overy lowered her head deferentially, then looked up with a mischievous smile on her small lips. "And do not forget that I am your trade representative to the Dark Shore. The Goblin Wars will not last forever. When they are over, we will have all these goods to import to the dominions. We will usher in a new era on Irth. Meanwhile, you can enjoy these benefits for yourselves." She unzipped the nylon satchel. "Now, look what I have brought for you today from the Dark Shore."

She cleared a space among the crushed cans of cola and laid upon the rattan table a glass pipe, a butane lighter, and several yellowish molars, rough-cut pebbles of ivory, or perhaps crumbs of an aged cheese. "This is more rare than tobacco. It is the extract of a mountain plant called coca, specially prepared so that it may be smoked thus."

Into the glass pipe she placed a morsel of the coca extract and heated the bulb of the pipe with the lighter's tongue of flame. The morsel melted to bubbling tar, and she sucked its milky vapors into the pipe stem, sipping enough to demonstrate to the suspicious Shai Malia that this was not a poison. She exhaled it with a satisfied sigh and handed the glass implement to Poch.

After both the margrave and his wife had inhaled the fumes and sat back, swaying and feeling light in the head, Overy Scarn turned on the TV. "On the Dark Shore, they say that everything goes better with coke. I will leave you two alone to enjoy my gift." She stepped lightly to the door, paused, and turned to say, "Remember, if you find this smoke enjoyable, I will make arrangements for you to have more. I will do that for you."

SHADOW WITH A SHADOW

AN APPLE-FALL SCENT AND A RITUAL INCANTATION SEEPED ON A chill breeze from the open door of the water tank. Inside, the amber haloes of two fat, black candles lit the circular room with the peachy glow of a hearth. The roots of a tree hung from the rafters, a forest in itself, dangling minty sprigs, dried flower chains, wreaths of waxy leaves, shriveled fruit with crone faces, garbled vines and creepers withered like tangled wires.

Octoberland!

That was the name of this fragrant, autumnal niche in the hot August night on a rooftop in the blaze of Manhattan. Brick understood this—and so much more.

His flesh flayed from him, he glistened raw crimson, the packed meat of his muscles naked, shining with blood, their white ligaments striating the wet and oozy contours of his skinned body. Pain clothed him. Otherwise, he stood naked. Lifted by the magic of Nox, Brick stood, his thick body torn free of his beastmarks, stripped to the crinkled cellophane of his fascia. The gory sheaths of his sinews twitched with hurt, and his lipless mouth twisted around a silent scream even as his staring eyeballs in their gummy sockets gazed wide with terror.

Now, Octoberland would perform the ceremony that would make Nox young. Brick knew this with a telepathic certainty endowed him by the evil magician. The twelve were gathered— and among them, Mary Felix! They, too, would contribute their magic, the power of their lives, to transform their Master from a geriatric husk to a youth.

Nox danced around him. Shawled in the furry hide of Dog-brick, he pranced about with lively steps, the tawny mane jump-

ing on his back, the snarled fangs bright against the charred
black of his face. Like an African shaman, he crouched under
the pelt and paced with the feral rhythms of a beast. "Come!"
he shouted, and the pain brightened in Brick's exposed muscles.
Leaving bright-red footsteps, the flayed man agonizingly
stepped over the tar-paper roof and mounted the varnished
wooden steps to Octoberland.

Mary Felix nearly collapsed when she saw him. She waited
in the circle with the other eleven of the coven, standing in
the position of Virgo. And when Nox entered wearing Dogbrick's pelage, walking hunched over like some huge canine,
and Brick followed, dazzling crimson, shucked of his flesh, bald
as a skull, his face skinned to the cartilage and the integuments
that strapped his jaw, she shrieked.

Her cry dwindled above her as if she were falling. But she
did not fall. Her shadow held her up. Each of the twelve stood
before a shadow with a shadow beneath it. These standing shadows were the astral bodies of themselves, the sinister angels she
had first seen in the north woods. Now she had a sinister angel
of her own, and it held her up by the shoulders when Nox and
Brick entered.

These angels were Nox's magic enwrapped in the life force
of each coven member. Mary peeked over her shoulder and
confronted her own face demonically elongated, eyes tapered,
points sharpened, yet faded to shadow, like an old photo or an
ancient religious image. She whimpered and looked away, at
shaggy Nox and glossy Brick, ichor red and slick as a seal.

Brick spotted Mary and turned away from the horror in her
face. He recognized that same mix of disgust and fright in the
faces of all the others. They had never performed a ceremony
like this before. Only the shadows behind them grinned. He
knew as well, those shadows were the same sinister angels he
had met in the forest. But then they had been white as packed
snow. Here, they appeared sooty, tinted gray, shadowy as
clouds freighting rain. Their sleek eyes still shone green as flecks

of twilight, and their long faces sneered with the malevolence of bats.

At Mary's cry, the coveners, who had been chanting, fell silent. Their white ceremonial robes fluttered softly in a slim breeze of cold air that flowed from the obsidian altar, spilling out of the squalid urn with its tar-gobbed brim.

"Octoberland is the harvest," Nox droned, striding outside the circle.

The coven moaned, "Falling leaves, rising spirits."

"Octoberland is the harvest."

"What is full shall be emptied."

"Octoberland—Octoberland!"

"All that lives must die."

Nox entered the circle beside Mary Felix and tossed off the mantle of beastmarks. The large hide with its floppy arms and legs spun into the air above the altar and burst into flame—green fire—exploded Charm. The heatless conflagration widened to a radiant ring above the coven and faded, giving its power to the shadows that stood behind the twelve people.

The shadows brightened, glowing white as packed snow, and the people in front of them fell forward onto their faces, struck down by the force of magic that poured into their astral counterparts.

Bathed in the flash of white light, Mary felt herself shoved forward, the colors of her sight bleached away. Her young body trembled, the planks beneath her eyes downy as mist, spongy with emptiness: This was the haze of atoms that made up the floor. The glare of the sinister angels had pushed her beyond the limits of her human world. She had fallen into the atomic surf that crashed upon the void and shaped the physical world from its foam.

The other eleven were there with her, slowly emptying themselves, like she was, into the sinister angels that stood upon their backs. The angels were draining the lives of their surprised hosts. She and the others were thinning away, becoming emptiness, fading into nothing, eroding like mist, their energy harvested by the living shadows that Nox had set upon them. She wanted to cry out and knew the others wanted to cry also. But there was no energy left. They had already outlived their lives.

Brick stood over Mary Felix, powerless to help her. Pain owned him. And Nox owned the pain. When the magician waved him into the circle, Brick stepped past Mary and with aching steps approached the pentagonal altar. Within the dented metal urn, a black needle stood. Nox removed the sharp object and began chanting in a language so ancient it fit only his voice among the living.

From between the spiked haloes of the fat, black candles, the poison needle stared at Brick from Nox's hand. On all sides, the sinister angels drew closer, walking upon the fallen bodies of their hosts. And with them came his memories.

Already half a ghost, his life flashed before him, a kaleidoscopic inrush. He remembered Irth. He saw again the steep avenues, stairway lanes, curved rooftops, and smoky factories of the sea-cliff city, Saxar. Recollections of his days as a thief stretched back to his childhood in the sumac warrens of the industrial district, and he saw again how he had lived wild behind the factories, catching his food in the weed lots and the slag yards, sometimes stealing it from windowsills or bird feeders of homes on the bluffs where the factory workers lived. All his life, he had been running the angular alleys and hobbled stairs of dripping stone that plumbed this vertical city. And further back than his life, he remembered his prelife. . . .

THE MOON HAS A BOOK

On Nemora, among the Bright Worlds, gnomish magic fused the gametes of animals and mortals; thus, came beastmarks. Somewhere in the past, long before Dogbrick's orphaned childhood, the gnomes of Nemora had joined dog and mortal and made his forebears. His blood remembered that. And from that remembrance in the cryptarch of Brick's flesh, Nox withdrew all of the flayed man's Charm.

Brick convulsed, reduced to a mortal. Such a separation of mortal and beast would have been impossible among the hotter reality of the Bright Worlds. But Nox's magic belonged to the Dark Shore, and its cold suasion, accrued over seven millennia, possessed the dexterity to take from this body the animal Charm of its beastmarks and leave behind the mortal chaff.

Nox wanted the animal Charm, for that he could control. If he had taken Brick's mortal Charm as well, he would have tainted himself with his victim's humanity—and he wanted none of that.

The black needle began to glow with the animal Charm it withdrew from Brick. Around the altar Nox marched majestically, the shining needle upheld. When he came to Virgo, he grinned and showed his discolored seed-corn teeth to the sinister angel atop her. Then, he turned to Libra, and the glowing needle lashed out with a hot hiss and drew into its brightness the effluvial smoke of the sinister angel. Libra's body flopped like a beached carp, and her ceremonial robe sagged flat as her body caked to ash.

Nox stood taller, stronger with the assimilated life force. Next, he approached Scorpio. The needle struck, and the angel vanished, inhaled into the brightening aura about Nox. Scorpio's prone body banged against the planks, then flattened to a cinereous shape of itself. This time, black dust drizzled from Nox's face and hands, and he left a graphite trail as he walked to where Sagittarius lay, her angel shape reaching for Nox, eager to be absorbed by him and made a part of his magical glory.

The poison needle struck, the angel smoked into the luminosity around Nox, and as the outstretched body crumbled to cinders, flesh tones scabbed Nox's brow and stubble sprouted from his bald pate. With each of the coven members whose life force he pulled into himself through the magic needle, he grew younger and stronger. The old, necrotic flesh peeled off, and a youthful body gradually emerged. By the time he sucked into himself Leo's strength and stood again before Virgo, he faced her sinister angel with a proud visage of nutmeg complexion and long jet hair swept back to his broad shoulders.

"You will not die," he announced with a smile of perfect white teeth. "For with you, Mary Felix, I will begin Mayland, the coven of my new life's springtime." His almond eyes, brown and clear, gazed serenely into the astral shadow's wicked countenance. "Go down and bring her up so that Mayland will rise with her."

The sinister angel obeyed. Its spectral form seeped into Mary's prostrate body, and she shuddered awake. Like a sleepwalker, she rose straight up to her feet, and the angel stepped back from her, its wings beating in the air like thermal wrinkles.

Groggily, Mary blinked alert. The handsome man before her was Nox made young. She knew this not only by the black needle that he held but also by the brisk command with which he led her angel away. The two stepped to the altar, and the wraith looked back at her with her own face, cruelly sharper. The shade took the candle flames in her hands and exploded like bright sun's dust, pollen blown glittering to a momentary sphere that enclosed the circle of ash.

A balmy meadowsweet breeze blew away the cinders, leaving eleven body-long robes stained with soot.

"Octoberland is finished," Nox announced in a melodious voice and threw the needle onto Brick's bloody body. At the needle's touch, Brick flapped into blue flames, a tantrum of twisting gases and spurting sparks. The body lay unmoving, untouched by the fire itself as the residue of its magic burned away in an incendiary flare.

Darkness clapped and snuffed all light in the windowless coven hall. The blue night stood suddenly in the doorway as

Nox exited. And darkness slammed back into place as he shut the door.

Mary breathed the dewy redolence of coolness and freshness thrown off by a mossy brook intoxicated with spring water. No spark of light shone, and the only sound was the whirr of the flue that squatted darkly at the crest of the cone roof. She edged forward, feeling for the altar. Her hand touched sticky flesh and sparked a sharp cry from Brick.

Mary's touch broke the spell of Nox's trance, and Brick buckled around a howl of agony. He woke to complete pain, every severed inch of his skin shrieking. So vehement were his yells that Mary leaped backward and fell to the ground stunned.

Outside, the young Nox stretched his arms to their joint-popping limit, to embrace the screaming, the birth noise of his new life. The pain would not kill Brick immediately. This man had come from the Bright Worlds, and death did not easily fit him on the Dark Shore. It would take time for him to die. But with his eventual death after long suffering, Nox would come into sole possession of Brick's Charm. Enough Charm would swell in him to drive his youthful strength for centuries.

The mad cries dimmed. Nox relaxed his arms, shook them like a fighter limbering for the next round. He stood in the moonlight and halogen glaze of the city, shaking the meat on his bones, touching himself, flexing his limbs, and leaping. He bayed the curling howl of a wolf.

"The Moon has a book," he sang the poem his mother had chanted to him in Jarmo as a boy in a mud village. "The Moon has a book, and on each page are written the names of dogs."

He laughed across seven thousand years and heard the echo coming back to him from the blue haze of the Zagros Mountains.

"Enter my name in that book, Mother!" he shouted in the dialect of his boyhood. "I am the nomad of centuries. I am eternity's dog!"

He dashed in a whipped scurry among the vapor pipes and

air-conditioning sheds, yipping vigorously. Then he knelt and
bayed again at the celestial waters that reflected backward the
letters of the law.

The meek inherit the earth—the strong take the heavens.

He stood and began to move in a stately gait around the
perimeter of the roof. With regal bearing, he regarded the city.
To him, it looked like Babel lifting its random patterns of light
to write big under the heavens. His walk accelerated to a striding prance, remembering the pages of sand that covered the
mangled libraries and the ruins that once ran with the waters of
paradise. And he laughed at the corruption of time, the prophets
themselves so much dust in the desert.

From inside the water tank, Brick yelped like a nomad berat-
ing a camel; then came whimpering and silence. Death danced
in the darkness of the coven room, leading Brick into the un-
derlife, the caverns of hell, where the temple cities of empires
stood as monuments of dung. And Nox danced on the rooftop,
danced, laughed, and danced to an internal music he heard all
around him, the stars themselves his most triumphant chords.

He stopped at the roof's parapet and gazed jubilantly at the
smoldering lights of the city. This was the cold fire of Gehenna,
the heatless radiance at the place of sacrifice. Like the auroras
that curtained the void over the planet's altar, like the north
taiga and tundra where life laid down in obeisance to stone, so
here the stone rose up in servitude to mind. His life had joined
the extremes. He had brought the very old to the very new,
and now the world was his to command.

Rider of the Dream

Wisdom is not always wise.
—THE GIBBET SCROLLS: 18

THE BURDEN OF THE DREAM

JYOTI AND REECE HAD CLIMBED OUT OF THE CHALK GROTTO OF the goblins, anxious to see that the assassin N'drato had in fact departed.

"I don't see him anymore," Jyoti said, peering by revelations of lightning into a niello eye charm. From her high perch, she viewed the storm-lashed forest as if flying, and not even an assassin could hide from her gaze. "He's not lurking nearby. I think he spoke the truth. We are not his targets anymore."

Reece pressed his back against the crusty wall under the rifted cupola and watched the rain run off Jyoti's face, the smudges on her cheeks and brow washing away in gray tracks. He felt his heart pushing at him, aching against his ribs. Only now did he realize that they had been apart too long. Now that his attempt to rescue Dogbrick had ended in complete failure, their separation seemed so unnecessary. His abduction in Moödrun, the arduous journey south pursued by trolls, ogres, and giant spiders, the escape from the incendiary charmfire, and the death of Ripcat in the Cloths of Heaven—none of these had made him feel as vividly alive as looking at her profile painted by lightning.

"I can't find our airfoil." She squinted to better read the dark landscape. "Drake's blood! I think that son of a troll stole it!" She glared into the tempest. "That's why he gave me the charmway seeker—so we can find our way out of here."

"Through burning charmways." Reece thought of Dogbrick and questioned what hope remained of getting him back from the Dark Shore. "We have to hurry."

"The goblins—" Jyoti returned her attention to the squalid cavern. There were so many of those horrid imps below, she tried to quickly assess how best to destroy them all. She did not want even one of those abominations to escape.

Reece watched her staring intently into the grotto, and the sight of her served as an amulet to drive off his anxiety. Dogbrick could well be stranded on Earth forever, the beasts of the marsh might soon devour them, or charmfire burn them to ashes, but none of that seemed as dire now that he was united with this woman again.

"I don't think this can be done quickly." Jyoti noticed Reece staring at her and returned the niello eye charm to its place on her amulet harness. "What are you looking at?"

"You were right all along, Jyo. Let's not separate again—ever." Thunder spoke, and he fell silent.

She put a hand to his stubbled cheek. "I feel the same. If you'd been with me, I would have been stronger—I would have said no to Poch and made him challenge me for my title before the regent if necessary. I'm less without you, Reece."

"Then, we're decided?" he asked and wiped droplets of rain from her eyebrows. "We will stay together?"

"Always."

They embraced, and the air shook around them with the storm's din. Arms about each other's waists, they turned and gazed down into the lightning-wiped grotto. "Are they moving?" Jyoti asked, tilting forward.

Reece pulled her back. "No. It's the storm shadows. The goblins are asleep. I saw that in my vision, in the Cloths of Heaven."

"Tell me about that vision," she asked, craving assurance. "Talk to me as we go back down there. Tell me everything that happened to you."

Reece let her go so that they could feel their way carefully along the broken spiral ledge that curled toward the floor of the domed structure. But he held to her with his voice, recounting all that had befallen him since he had left her in New Arwar. By the time the salty floor crunched underfoot, he had described the strange sensation of waking alive in the mineral pool after Ripcat's death.

Jyoti listened intently, glad for the sound of his voice. "You've suffered enough. The sooner we're done here the better."

Reece upheld a wristband of lux-diamonds and scanned the large chamber of huddled, tiny figures. "How will we destroy them all?"

"I don't think we should shoot them." Jyoti unholstered two firelocks. "If they wake before we destroy all of them, their telepathy will overwhelm us."

"And that fractured dome up there might come down on us." He swept the light of the lux-diamonds along the knobby walls. "What do we do?"

Jyoti held out the extra harness of amulets she carried. "Here's how. We plant the firelocks at opposite sides of the chamber and place amulets from the harness on the floor in between. Then, we jam the charge pins on the firelocks and climb out of here fast as we can. When the firelocks explode, they'll ignite the amulets, and this whole vault will burst into an inferno."

"Can we get out fast enough?" Reece asked, looking askance at the uneven stone ledges that roughly spiraled the chamber. "I think it's better if we drop a jammed firelock from up there."

"That's good. But we'll have to use more amulets to make sure the initial explosion ignites them." She began unbuckling her harness. "Take off your vest. We'll use those amulets too."

"But how will we get through the swamp to the charmway without amulets to protect us?"

"Outside I have two charmor vests loaded with amulets. They were too heavy to drag down here, but they'll serve us well in the mere—" Her voice broke off, and she reached a startled hand for Reece. "They're moving—look!"

He saw a ripple of shared movement pass over the wide arena of small, twisted bodies. "It's a telepathic dream," he ventured. "They're dreaming the same thing and moving in unison."

"Maybe it's the storm that's troubling them." Jyoti began removing amulets from her harness and placing them among the small beings. "We better move fast."

Reece imitated her, stepping cautiously among the stirring doll shapes, dropping hex-gems onto the ground. Lightning flapped and briefly washed out the rays of his lux-diamonds, blearing the goblins to heaps of huddled babies.

In a niello eye charm that he tucked between curled bodies, he glimpsed an azure afternoon, a drift of summer-castle clouds risen above persimmon trees and shady clumps of evergreen splashed with bright spangles of mimosa—a parkland of the world above worlds. And there, in the wind-tossed grass were the sleeping goblins, pixies now, childlike creatures in flower necklaces and moss skirts, dancing with the splotched cloud light, leaving him standing there, holding the burden of the dream. . . .

"Reece!" Jyoti hissed.

He snapped free of the reverie he had glimpsed in the niello eye charm, yet for a lingering moment the resinous scent of evergreen and the perfume of mimosa superseded the rancid stink of the cavern. "Don't look into the amulets," he warned. "You'll see their dreams."

"I've seen their dreams," she answered. "And in them, we are the demons."

DEMONS

JYOTI BENT TO PLACE A HEX-GEM IN A NARROW GAP AMONG A CLUS-ter of goblins, and one of the vile creatures sat up. Its half-lidded eyes stared with tightening pupils, its pudgy, dirt-streaked face sneering angrily.

With the butt of a firelock, she struck the thing's bulging brow and knocked it senseless. A white milk oozed from the bruise on its smashed forehead.

She shook with violent fear, remembering the cheesy stench of the goblins invading her sinuses, souring her brain till she could not think, could not move. "They're waking up!"

Reece straightened, and the stabs of light from the lux-diamond revealed heads smooth as gourds stirring, rising.

Demons!

The word buzzed in the air, and Jyoti and Reece crouched under its impact.

Jyoti snapped the charge pin of a firelock to stun and fired a red bolt at a swollen head rising among the sleepers. The bright Charm slapped the goblin prone again—but a vast tremor passed among the entire horde.

"Don't fire!" Reece called. "The Charm is feeding them."

"Then let them eat this!" Jyoti pulled the charge pin to maxi-mum and fired rapid bursts of blue-white heat into the throng. Gouts of goblin flesh spurted into the air, spinning flames. A shrill scream as from one mighty being pierced the moment, then stopped abruptly. The harsh echoes faded to the crackle of burnt orange embers rustling in the ash where the bolts had struck among the goblins.

Reece jumped to Jyoti's side and seized her shoulders. "Stop it!"

She lifted the pink-glowing muzzle of the firelock and pushed backward against him, needing to feel his physical nearness to counter her fright. "They're still," she whispered through clenched teeth.

The entire chamber of goblins in their hundreds lay inert, their sleep piled like hay in the dark—a mounded stillness.

"We have to get out of here," Reece said, wanting Jyoti to move.

But she stood still. "Listen!"

Rain sizzled through the cracked dome. Thunder walked about in the distance. And from nearby came a scratching, a sugary crunching.

"It's from outside," Reece observed. "Something is climbing the wall."

"Not something—many things." She cocked her head and heard them from all sides: gouging, scraping noises encircling the entire chalk house of the goblins. "What is it? What's happening?"

Reece shook his head and followed the flurry of scratching noise up to the dark cope of the mineral ceiling.

In the clefts of the dome, lightning illuminated a swarm of bolt-eyed figures whose metallic skin reflected the flaring storm.

"Dammit! Trolls!" Reece spun on his heels. "They've surrounded us!"

Jyoti pointed her firelock at their fanged snouts and then lowered her weapon, fearful of shattering the dome and dropping massive chunks of rock upon herself and Reece.

"Our amulets," said Reece, flustered, reaching for the niello eye charm at his shoulder. "Search for a charmway. These goblins got in here somehow."

In the eye charms, enormous plateaus of summer clouds floated upon evergreen crests and mimosa meadows in pixieland.

"The goblins are blocking our eye charms with their dream." Jyoti watched the first of the trolls stepping onto the salt ledges, and she fired several yellow bolts of charmfire.

The trolls shattered against the white rock, leaving stains of black blood. Clawed limbs rained down and flopped among the still goblins. The talons dug into the crusty ground and began crawling toward the couple.

With a sweep of charmfire, Jyoti incinerated the severed claws. *Demons!*

The telepathic shout of the goblins staggered Jyoti and Reece and nearly dropped them to their knees.

As one, the goblins sat up.

Jyoti handed a firelock to Reece. "We have to burn them— as many as we can!"

"Wait." Reece pushed aside her weapon. In the hundreds of glinting eyes, he felt as though he were staring again into the amulet of their sleeping and he were a rider of the dream, gliding out of this haunted chamber to another world, a high heavenly forest of evergreen shrubs and persimmon trees. "There are too many to burn."

Jyoti threw a frightened look at him. "Don't stare into their eyes. They'll trance you."

"Try to communicate with them." Reece knelt down, so that he faced the goblin throng at eye level. Looking into their fat, dirty faces, seeing in their weary-lidded eyes their vision of a dawn forest where mist sleeved the trees, he felt lonely before such beauty.

"It's your amulet harness that is protecting you from their spell," Jyoti warned him. "When they exhaust our Charm, they'll possess us. They'll feed us to the trolls."

Reece would not budge. He had seen past the bloated bodies streaked with filth to paradise and the fabled folk of the earliest creation.

Jyoti aimed at the trolls creeping down the spiral shelves and blasted several more to blood smears on the salt walls. She burned the lopped limbs as they thrashed toward her.

The whining sound of the firelock's discharges shook Reece, but he kept his mind fixed on the blue-eyed grass and leaf light where the pixies squatted, garbed in chokecherry blossoms. "Do not fear us," he said. "Call off your trolls. Let us talk. Let us reason."

A creeping troll hand reached for Reece's ankle, and Jyoti kicked it away and seared it with a green bolt of charmfire.

"You have come from a world of beauty," Reece went on. "Why do you bring destruction to us?"

The pixies watched him from all sides of day, from the glowing nests of dawn and dusk and the gold branch of noon. In their leaf caps and bark boots, they appeared harmless and childlike. But the look in their large eyes shone with terror. And in those mirrors, he saw himself as the pixies viewed him: He held a firelock. The pixies knew that his breed had invented firelocks, weapons designed to kill not only other creatures but their own kind. And they knew he had come here to slay them.

Demons! the goblins yelled.

And their cry pierced him with its truth. He jolted alert and pushed to his feet.

"The trolls!" Jyoti shouted at him. "I can't get them all. There are too many. Help me!"

Shaken by what he had seen, Reece stood unmoving, watching the metal-sheened creatures climbing down the rock shelves to save the exiled pixies from demons.

DEATH'S NIGHTMARE

DEMONS! THE GOBLINS SHOUTED WITH FEAR—BUT THEIR TELE-pathic strength had dimmed. The trolls they had summoned reverted to the mindless carnivores that they were without the goblin's guidance and began to scatter in fright before the painful attacks of the humans. All across Irth, trolls fled back into the wilderness, seeking the sanctuary of rock coverts, forest canopies, swamp morasses.

Back in New Arwar, the goblins responsible for focusing the psychic power of their breed needed more hex-gems. The jewels they had dangled in their web works had emptied of Charm and dulled. Frantically, they called for the demons they had expended so much energy taming: *Shai Malia! Poch! The dear ones need you! Come to us again! Come at once! Poch! Shai Malia!*

But neither the margrave nor his wife heard the telepathic summons. With glazed eyes, they sat in their suite watching TV, a blackened glass pipe on the rattan table before them. Their drugged minds floated adrift in their skulls, so dark that the phosphor glow from the screen seemed bright as the Abiding Star itself, and they stared at it through dark glasses.

Daylight glittered its prisms in the webs that suspended the two assassins. Slowly and with stupendous effort, the goblins lowered one of the bodies. The cold of this world had taken its toll on the small creatures, and they did not want to reach again into the mind of another monstrous demon. They did not want to feel its cunning self, its capacity for deception, violence, and murder.

But they had no choice. Without hex-gems, they could not project their telepathy to the trolls and ogres. And without those beasts as defenders, the demons would eventually track them down and inflict on them death's nightmare: prolonged life under the scalpel and the exploratory needles.

They had seen this in the brains of every demon they had dared touch with their minds—the need to know at all costs, to dissect and analyze, no matter the suffering of their subjects. Cruelty emanated from these beings, for they were truly demons.

News of the weakening goblins spread rapidly. That afternoon, Overy Scarn received reports that the troll attacks in every dominion had lifted. This both mystified and alarmed her.

Strolling among the maze hedges and espaliered flower trees of Primrose Stilts, she contemplated what had gone wrong with the goblins.

"Use the ceiling camera to capture an image of the goblin chamber," she instructed her sentinel chief, Roidan, when they met among the topiary shrubs. "Bring the image to me in an eye charm. I would see what changes have befallen our guests."

She waited for him to return beside one of the temple's seventy-seven pillars of smoky marble and climbing rose vines, her large body occupying a wood bench. Its slats creaked under her weight, for she had neglected to wear her brace of levity-pearls.

Trepidation so occupied her that she noticed nothing of the fruited dwarf trees that shaded the floating lilies on the moss-rock pool. Beauty could not reach her, for anxiety had displaced all other feelings. Though her eyes gazed upon a wrought lantern of black silver and green copper hung by a thick chain from the high rafters, she saw instead her severed head. That would be the penalty in wartime for usurping a margravine if the Peers defeated the goblins and subsequently learned how she had misappropriated Dig Dog funds to take New Arwar and all its resources for herself.

When Roidan returned, she leaped from the bench and snatched the eye charm from his grasp. She saw within the dark lozenge a lucid image of the goblin chamber. The gauzy interior shone with silver webs and cottony fluff that obscured much of the room—yet there were the goblins themselves, their bulbous heads agleam like melons, their smutty, deformed bodies huddled together.

"There is only one assassin in this picture," she observed and looked up sharply at Roidan. She caught the hints of disgust in his stocky face—the wrinkles beside his bent nose, the curled lip, the dismay in his deep-set eyes—as he regarded not the goblins but her. She had neglected to wear her spellbinder girdle and determined to return to her bedchamber for it before she lost complete control over her muscular minion. But first, she had to know. "Where is the second assassin?"

"I know not." Roidan's block brow furrowed. "They were both there when I looked this morning."

"Go at once and look again," she ordered. "And bring another eye charm to my chamber. I must see for myself that they are both still there."

Overy Scarn returned to her suite and immediately opened her wardrobe, seeking her spellbinder girdle. "Ah, Overy, I need you now. Did you see the look on his face?"

"Roidan is a dolt, Scarn," she answered herself, running her thick fingers over the starburst of ecstasy-topazes and the spiral of rapture-garnets. "The spellbinder will keep him in line. After he—"

Her thought fractured when she noticed that her wardrobe drawer had been forced open: a curl on the head of a dancing satyr carved into a wooden drawer panel had been chipped. She opened the drawer and gasped. Her theriacal opals, sleep-emeralds, and serenity-sapphires were missing. "Who would dare?"

She crossed the room and stood before a TV monitor and tape cassette player she had attached to a video camera mounted within a three-hundred-and-sixty-degree dome lens on the crossbeam of her ceiling. No one in the dominions was aware of this technology from the Dark Shore, and so none had yet thought to elude it. She fast-played the day's recording and found the intruder—a slinky shadow who moved across the room like liquid darkness, his ebony robes gummy with goblin webs.

TORN AND MOST WHOLE

"THE GOBLINS NEED HEX-GEMS, SCARN," OVERY SCARN TOLD herself. "That was what Poch and his lovely wife were providing them—until they became too dizzy with coca smoke to obey their masters anymore."

She removed her spellbinder girdle and returned it to the wardrobe closet. "I won't let them have my hex-gems, Overy. The assassin N'drato was fool enough to leave behind the jewel case that had held those gems for so long. It will be expensive to have a charmwright place the case in a net of conjure-wire and use resonance with my stolen hex-gems to draw the Charm out of them. It will be expensive, more costly than the gems are worth by four or five times, but in this way we will deprive the goblins. N'drato was a fool not to take the entire case.

"Assassins are never fools, Scarn," she countered herself, holding the bejeweled girdle to her bosom. "He left the jewel case behind intentionally. It is a statement from the goblins themselves. They wish us to know that they are in command, not us. They defy us to take the Charm from them. If we do—they will kill us. They have in their power *two* assassins.

"Bah!" She stepped back angrily from the hanging girdle. "I do not fear those dirty little imps. It is the Peerage I fear. Let the goblins have their Charm—until they have destroyed the Peers and cleared the dominions of all opposition to our reign."

She held the glittering girdle again to her body and shook her round, curly head. "No, no, Scarn, that won't do. We must assert control over these dirty little imps immediately—or they may get notions that we are weak and they can command us. They may even seize the opportunity to turn the Peers against us.

"That we cannot have!" She slammed the wardrobe shut. "Overy, you have convinced me. A lesson is in order."

When Roidan knocked, she opened the door a crack and snatched the eye charm from his grasp, shouting, "Send a charmwright to me, at once!"

To the charmwright, she delivered the jewel case with information that the hex-gems within had been stolen and their Charm was to be drained by resonance. She then summoned the manor's maintenance manager and showed her the video cameras that had come from the Dark Shore.

Overy had originally intended to use the security cameras to guard her warehouses. But she instructed the manager to install the mirror-dome panoramic view cameras in the corridors and air ducts surrounding the bond agent's suite. And she specified that each camera was to be hidden behind sentry amulets.

After this work was done, Overy Scarn sat in an overstuffed chair of crushed hippogriff leather with an array of small TV monitors stacked on a low table before her and waited. At her side, hanging from a wooden clothes rack, she kept the spell-binder girdle, occasionally reaching for its sparkling fabric to converse with herself.

That night, with the windows behind her shining with star smoke and planetary orbs, she sat watching her monitors until she spotted the assassin outside her bedchamber. He wore foil discs to reflect the watchful Charm of the sentry amulets, which saw him not at all. Only the video cameras recorded his stealthy approach to her door. With a swipe of a keycharm, the lock snicked and the door opened.

Overy Scarn waited until he had closed the door behind him before turning on the soft, corner lights. "Come in, assassin. I have been waiting for you."

The assassin spun and reached for the door latch. Before he could exit, the jamb beside his cowled head burst into splinters.

"My next shot will blow out your brains." Overy wagged her chrome-plated SIG-Saur 9mm outfitted with a long black silencer at the assassin. "You've never seen the likes of this weapon—and you have no protection against it. Turn around and tell me your name."

"N'drato." The assassin folded back his cowl, his bald head and lean face holding shadows in sinister angles. "The dear ones have sent me to take your life."

"The dear ones, is it?" Overy Scarn kept the gun trained on the assassin as she addressed the jewel-studded girdle on the rack beside her. "Do you hear that, Overy? If they can make an assassin love them, none of us are safe from their powers.

"Watch him closely, Scarn," she warned herself as her hand drew the dazzling garment over her shoulder. "He has been trained since before birth to be dangerous."

N'drato's small, black eyes narrowed slightly. "Who are you talking to?"

"Why, to myself, of course." She emitted a bubbly laugh, giddy to have an assassin under her power. "On the Dark Shore there is a compilation of sacred texts called the Bible, and in chapter four, verse nine of the holy book of Ecclesiastes it is written. 'Two are better than one . . . for if they fall, one will lift up her companion.' So, you see, N'drato, I am two and stronger for it."

"You're mad." In his hand, the black curve of a razor knife appeared as if from nowhere. "I intended to make your demise appear accidental, to keep attention averted from the dear ones. But you force me to deliver you to a more bloody death."

"N'drato, you underestimate this weapon." Her mouth held a dark smile. "You'll be dead before you hit the ground."

"This is so—but only if your next shot hits me." The razor knife moved like a living thing in his hand. "If not . . ."

"Are the *dear ones* listening to what I say?" she asked coolly. "Is their telepathy strong enough to see me through you, or have the hex-gems that I emptied of Charm depleted their powers?"

"The pixies see and hear you through me." He seemed to float forward. "You have deprived them of their power to direct trolls at a distance, but they have the strength to guide me."

"Stop where you are." Overy Scarn pointed the gun at his face. "Don't make me kill you until your dear ones have heard what I have to tell them."

N'drato paused, the razor knife smiling in his hand. "Speak."

"Dear ones, pixies—*goblins*—I offer you an understanding." Overy Scarn spoke to the black bits of the assassin's eyes. "I shall give you all the hex-gems you require, and you shall remain unmolested here in New Arwar. No one will know of your presence except myself and the people you now have in thrall."

She pulled the spellbinder girdle over her shoulder and continued, "Scarn will provide this for you, and in exchange you will continue your war against the dominions. You will destroy the Peers. And when you are done, I, Overy, shall see that you have a dominion entirely to yourself. No people will trouble you there. You shall be free to live as—dear ones. That is what you want, isn't it?"

"The dear ones do not trust demons," N'drato muttered.

"They can learn to trust me—or they can die now." Overy Scarn waved her gun casually. "I can have their chamber gassed. Or torched. Or I can simply deprive them of hex-gems and keep them my prisoners. You see? I am in command here. Obey me and, as Overy, I can be generous and loving. You will have your own dominion and life everlasting. Or—Scarn will deal with you. What will it be?"

"Give me the hex-gems." N'drato offered an empty hand while the razor knife turned slowly in the other. "The dear ones will do as you say."

"Yes, I thought they would." She released the spellbinder girdle and sat forward. "Overy's terms are most generous. But, dear goblins, you must understand that Scarn will hold you to your promise." She fired the SIG-Saur from her lap, and the bullet struck N'drato under his jaw and penetrated his brain.

JOURNEY TO NO END

BRICK OBSERVED HIS DEAD BODY, SPRAWLED ON THE ALTAR, AND beside it, immured in darkness yet visible to his phantom sight, Mary Felix. She wept as though his spirit were numbered with the damned. He wanted to comfort her in the deepening drift of darkness—but his light had begun to fade.

His whole life, every event and deed, floated in nothing as a mote, each a little world, a fleck of dust in a universe of dust.

All his memories, all he knew of beauty and fear, of wounded love, hope, and mad prayer had spilled out and revealed themselves for what they were—nothing. Alive on Irth, he had believed himself a philosopher, groping for knowledge. And now he realized that, in truth, all knowledge was a journey to no end.

Formless and featureless, he drifted away. In the empty space of being, the water tank dwindled. He floated through the shagbark wall and across the cluttered rooftop, again unborn.

A handsome young man stood beside vapor pipes, naked but for a loin wrap, his dusky flesh glossed with city light, his shiny black hair swept back and cut bluntly at the shoulders like a pharaoh's cowl, framing a smiling, cleft-chinned face. The youth stood tall as the legend of himself—and Brick realized that this was Nox made young.

"Farewell, ghost!" Nox waved. "Farewell as you sink into the ancient well of night."

Brick watched the waving figure fade. The water tank and the city skyline diffused, sugar shapes melting away. Clear diamond glints of atoms remained, hovering in the void. . . .

"Don't be afraid."

The voice came from a thin ray that stretched among the diamond sparks.

Facing the glycerine emptiness—not dark, not light, just empty—he understood that the filament of light suspended in this nothingness was alive. That entity had caught him on the harp string of its being, stretched taut in the vast space between atoms.

"It is I—Caval."

"Wizard!" Brick shouted with surprise, and all of creation shook. The teeming atoms around them vibrated together like shaking sand grains resolving to an image of a dazzling city night and Nox stood before the water tank, his youthful body caught in mid-stride, arms outflung in a celebratory dance.

"Hush, Brick . . ." Caval's voice soothed him with simple indifference. "I am holding your waveform with what little is left of my Charm. If you become agitated, you may snap me like an overtight string. Then, we will both dissolve into a tenuous rippling of heat in the city's vaporous smog. Just stay still."

The image of the blazing city misted again into a colorless fog.

"How?" Brick dared ask, mustering the smallest of whispers.

"I am a wizard—a wizard who once gathered Charm here on the Dark Shore," Caval's voice answered quietly. "I prepared a place for myself here, in this sky. But I have so little Charm left that I am stretched to the breaking point. If you want to stay alive, you must remain still—still and silent."

"Let me die, wizard." Brick spoke through a sigh. "I have seen my whole life and it is done. I am a man now. Let me die as a man."

"And leave the spoils of this planet to the likes of Nox?" Caval's voice trembled with indignation. "Not on your life."

INVISIBLE LIGHT

"He is dead." The door to the water tank opened, and night's blue sliced the interior darkness to the bloody core of the altar.

Mary Felix knelt there, sobbing.

"Quiet your tears, woman." Nox stepped into the ceremonial room and breathed the meaty stink of decay. "This creature is dead."

Mary knew that this was true but did not move.

"I saw his ghost depart the ritual chamber," Nox announced in his vigorous voice. "He has faded to nothing. And by his death, I am made young."

"I should be dead," Mary whispered. "I was old. He gave me his Charm and made me young. But why should I be young? I should be dead."

"In time, your wish will come true." Nox coughed a cynical laugh and took her arm. "You are still mortal. Enjoy what life you have taken from this creature of another world."

She pulled her arm free. "You didn't have to kill him. You took his Charm. You could have left him his life."

"That was too dangerous. And I have lived too long to cherish danger." He seized her arm again and pulled her to her feet. "Come with me, away from this place of death."

"Leave me here. Go away." She tried to twist her arm from his grip, but he was too strong. "Just leave me. You have what you want."

"You can't stay here." He forced her toward the door. "Octoberland is finished. This is a place of death now. You don't belong here."

"What about Brick?"

"He is dead."

"You can't leave him here."

"He has already departed. He is now no more than a few photons expanding through the vacuum of outer space at the speed of light. Forget him." Nox shoved Mary through the door, and she nearly collapsed down the varnished steps. "You are alive and will live so long as you obey me."

Her boots clomped heavily under her as she staggered onto the roof. When she spun about, her pale face glowed in the dark, bent with anger. "I will not obey you. You can kill me now, you monster!"

Nox flung a laugh at her. "You think death is an escape. It is not. It is a diminishment. It collapses the tower of our lives to its mineral blocks and scatters the precious light that dwells within. Is that what you want?"

Mary stared at him with rigid defiance.

"Be patient. I will not deny you." His almond eyes gleamed with passion. "But first I need you, my young one."

"I am not your young one." She reared back from him in disgust. "I'm not even young. It's an illusion."

"Not an illusion, my dear, but Charm. Charm has restored your youth and given you importance in the ritual circle." His white smile gleamed like a blade in the nocturnal light. "You are my Virgo, and with you I will summon another eleven—a new coven to begin a new era in the grotto of Mayland."

"What about Brick?" She pointed to the water tank and the ram's-head knocker shining with city light. "You can't leave him there."

"Why not?" Nox tossed his head back to cool his shoulders from under the weight of his lush hair. "He is the final fruit of Octoberland. Let him rot there, emblem of my past, symbol of all the kings and their empires that have rotted in my time. In this heat, he will putrefy quickly, and soon his bones will decorate that forsaken altar."

"He will be found." Mary stepped away from the youth whose swarthy skin shimmered with sweat. "The police will come. You can't kill a dozen people without someone finding out."

"I can do whatever I please." His smile strengthened. "But I take your point. Pride goes before the fall. Know then, I will take precautions. The brass knocker shall be removed. The door sealed permanently. I own this building, and I will never return here after tonight. A simple spell will keep intruders away. Who would want to break into a water tank anyway?"

As he spoke, he advanced on Mary, and she retreated before him.

"The eleven who died—and the Virgo who was sacrificed before you—they are already forgotten." He reached for her, and tiny sparks whorled upon the tips of his fingers. "No one knows they were here. Their bodies now are ash. Nothing remains of them in this world. They have simply disappeared from this planet, and all inquiries will lead nowhere. Octoberland is finished. Nothing of it remains."

Mary backed against an air-conditioning shed, and the sparkling fingers of the ritual killer hovered before her, swaying with mesmeric cadence, his luminous hand like a flower at his wrist. Her frightened eyes tightening with the will to fight, she asked, "What do you think you're going to do with me?"

"Think?" He clapped his hands together, and the air between them exploded into ether flames—green and blue swathes of fire that emitted no heat. "You are mine, Mary Felix. And what I'm going to do with you, you do not want to know."

Mary lunged sideways to avoid the cold fire.

Nox kicked one leg forward and tripped her. As she fell, the refulgence blanketed her, and her thick hair fluffed, swept up in a static rush, each individual strand tipped with a pinprick of sharp light. Sleep wafted over her, and fear slimmed away.

"Good," Nox breathed next to her ear. "Now you are ready to hear what must be done."

He stood and motioned with his hands for her body of light to rise with him. A sinister angel stood upon her unconscious body. It resembled her in a wicked way, for it was in fact her life force but transfigured by his will.

"You will be my witch wife." He offered his hand, and when the ethereal figure took it, the aqueous fire that composed the phantom brightened. "You will weave compliance into this physical form. You will weave desire. I am young again, and the sap of life rises in me."

The sinister angel licked a toad tongue in the air.

"Good, good!" Nox burst with laughter. "You will fill this woman body with desire for me, her master. And I will guide her to the new ritual ground—the subterranean place where spring begins."

Gaseous strands of burning hair radiated from the angular face of the apparition, and she leered.

"That's right, Mary Felix. Your body of light obeys me, and you will obey me in turn. Together, we will go down from this high place to the depths where the sex of all things begins. Together, we will create Mayland."

EMISSARIES OF UNKNOWING

A LARGE CROWD HAD GATHERED AT THE MAIN HALL, OCCUPYING the four storeys of balconies and viewing arcades among the giant buttresses and tall, recessed windows. In the higher galleries, beneath the great crossbeams of the vaulted ceiling, a motley gathering of mill workers, lumber agents, building contractors, and laborers of every city guild sat on wooden bleachers with their families.

The upholstered settles of the pilaster boxes held the merchants, traders, and investors, who observed the amulet-festooned dais with oculars in one hand and stock reports in the other.

The city's elite sat in cushioned chairs within the colonnaded, open studios that encircled the dais: charmwrights with their glittering vests, master wizards greaved and mailed with conjure-metals, and Dig Dog executives elegant in silk tunics and firepoints of gems—yet absent from among them, their chief officer, Overy Scarn.

She stood in the plush anteroom outside the main hall, resplendent in her pale-blue raiment and spellbinder girdle, tiny whitethroat blossoms gracing her brown curls. With her round cheeks aquiver and her eyes slanted with ire, she faced the margrave and his wife. "You will go out there, both of you, and greet the city. The emissaries have completed their report, and you must officially accept it so that we can send them happily on their way."

In a heavy, dark chair, Shai Malia sat glowering, eyebrows arched above wraparound shades, black-denimed legs crossed, arms folded over an orange halter top. Her blue-painted nails dug into her upper arms. "I'm not going out there—not until I get more smoke."

"And I'm telling you no more smoke until you go out there and satisfy the emissaries and the crowd." Overy Scarn could not believe that her spellbinder girdle was useless in the face of coca smoke. The drug was more powerful than she had estimated, more powerful than rapture-garnets and ecstasy-topazes! She turned to Poch, who glided about the anteroom on Rollerblades, running his hands along the red velvet walls and bluewood molding. "Come here, you."

Her angry face swam closer, reflected in Poch's mirror sunglasses. He offered a lopsided grin around a smoking cigarette and zipped past her, his yellow parachute-silk pants rippling as he careened along the wall, weaving past armorial chairs. "We came down here for a private meeting with the emissaries," he said. "Send them in here and we'll accept their report. I'm not going to perform for the galleries."

"The galleries are your subjects," Overy Scarn reminded him in a sardonic tone. "This is your city, *margrave*."

Poch brushed cigarette ash from his red pajama top. "This isn't my city, Scarn. It's yours." He spun a lazy circle around his sulking wife. "And those aren't my subjects—they're parasites. Every one of them is here to suck off the city as it eats into the jungle. This isn't a community. It's a cancer."

"You know why those emissaries are here, don't you?" Overy Scarn leaned over the back of an armorial crested chair. "The trolls have stopped attacking the dominions. There's been a lull in the Goblin Wars. And the Peers have had time to look up from their desperate battles and their ravaged cities, and what have they seen?" She slapped at the armorial crest in the uphol-

stery. "New Arwar without a single troll sighting, let alone murderous raids and a gutted populace. Not a single sighting.
Why?" She swung an arm toward the bluewood door with its
oval one-way window that looked out upon the dais. "That's
why the emissaries are here. That's why they're reading their
damage reports from their provinces to the galleries, informing
everyone of the terrors they've endured. And when they're done,
they're going to ask, why has New Arwar been spared?".

Poch removed a band of theriacal opals and dropped it into
his wife's lap. "Here, Shai. Press this to your brow. It will clear
the ugly hunger for more coca smoke."

Shai Malia clutched the opals to her forehead and shivered
as her addiction drained. "The jungle protects us."

"The jungle offers no protection at all." Overy Scarn stepped
heavily toward the seated woman. "It's the goblins in your bedroom that have spared this city."

"What do you know of our bedchamber?" Shai Malia asked
irately.

And simultaneously, Poch declared, "There are no *goblins* in
New Arwar."

"Oh, that's right." Overy snatched the cigarette from Poch's
lips as he floated past, and she threw it fiercely to the floor.
"You don't call them goblins. To you, they're dear ones." She
fixed Shai Malia with a wrothful stare. "I believe that the assassin
N'drato called them pixies. Is that what you think they are?"

"What are you talking about?" Shai Malia rose, and Overy
Scarn shoved her back into her seat.

"You and the margrave are under their spell—as was N'drato,
the assassin you hired. As is Nette, Jyoti's weapons master—
hanging now in sticky white webs from the rafters of your
bedroom."

"You've been in the bedchamber?" Poch asked, his voice
hushed.

Overy turned on him, grabbed his arm, yanked him to a
chair, and sat him down. "Listen to me, you two fools. The

dear ones *are* goblins. They've poisoned your brains into believing they're adorable little creatures. They're not. They're monsters—and you are in their sway."

"No!" Shai Malia stamped her boots defiantly. "You're trying to deceive us. That's why you drugged us—to keep us away from them."

"What have you done to the dear ones?" Poch leaped up, alarmed. "Have you hurt them?"

Overy gathered him into her arms and pressed him against her ample flesh and its girdle of spellbinder amulets. "No, no— I would not dream of harming your 'dear ones.' "

"Let me go!" Poch squirmed, but in his Rollerblades he could not gain purchase to pull away from the large woman.

"Shush!" She hugged him firmly and breathed hot, moist words into his ears. "The coca smoke was meant for your pleasure, as were all my gifts. I had no notion it would interfere with the goblin's telepathic hold on you. But I have since learned that it does—and I have learned a great deal more about our pixies. A great deal more."

Shai Malia stood and pounded her fists against the broad back of the woman who held her husband. Overy Scarn locked Poch in one arm and with the other swept his wife into her embrace.

"The dear ones and I have come to an understanding." She clasped the couple tightly, her face jammed between theirs. "I will protect them and provide for them, just as you have done in the past. They are safe with me. Your beloved dear ones have nothing to fear in my care. But you must help me."

She released them, and they staggered backward and sagged into their chairs, suddenly graced with warm feelings for the bond agent from Dig Dog Ltd. "Do you really think our dear ones are goblins?" Shai Malia asked, bewildered.

"The emissaries would think so," Overy warned. "They would try to harm the pixies. But with your help, we can save the dear ones from this danger and turn their enemies into emissaries of unknowing."

WEAPONS FROM THE DARK SHORE

THE MARGRAVE SKATED FLUIDLY ACROSS THE DAIS, INTO THE MIDST of the emissaries, both arms raised in greeting to the stunned galleries. He gestured to the ramp that led from the anteroom, motioning for his wife to join him. Shai Malia skipped to her husband's side and waved to the murmuring crowd.

The seven emissaries, in their diplomatic scarlet robes and amulet waistbands, rose from their high-backed chairs, and the margrave motioned for them to sit. Each had already delivered a detailed report of devastation and horror. The chief of the delegation remained standing. Spare as a dragonfly, mostly eyes and gaunt frame, the speaker for the dominions glared at them from under hoary eaves. "What is the significance of this strange garb?" His hollow voice, amplified by the amulets that festooned the dais, echoed through the hall, and the crowd grew silent to hear the reply.

"Our garb illuminates our reply to your impassioned reports." Poch drifted across the dais and back, arms outspread to display his colorful clothes. "This is what is worn by the denizens of the Dark Shore."

Excited mutterings swept through the galleries.

"That's right—New Arwar has opened a route of passage to the Dark Shore!" He spun around to face the emissaries. "Until now, we have kept this route a Peer-class secret, for fear that general knowledge of it would expose our discovery to the goblin threat."

Shai Malia took the lanky chief emissary by his arm and guided him back to his chair. "Our discovery was made while we served as docents at Blight Fen in the Reef Isles of Nhat. It is the reason we returned to New Arwar and asked Jyoti to relinquish her leadership of the city."

"With the financial assistance of Dig Dog Ltd.," Poch went on, "we exploited our discovery to open a trade channel through the Gulf to the Dark Shore."

"And what has this to do with the Goblin Wars?" the chief emissary asked. "Have you discovered their sanctuary on the Dark Shore?"

"No one knows their sanctuary," Shai Malia declared hurriedly.

Poch nodded to Roidan, who stood in his heraldic crimson-and-gold uniform at the base of the dais. He in turn passed a hand signal to the sentinels posted under the colonnades, and they disappeared into the niches that led to the stairways.

"Though we don't know where the goblins are hidden," the margrave continued, "we know how to fight them. That's why our city has remained unmolested during these cruel days. We have brought back from the Dark Shore surveillance devices, very like our sentry amulets, only cheaper to produce and so capable of being distributed in greater numbers throughout our dominion. With them, we have scanned the surrounding jungles. When trolls approached, we dispatched them."

"But your security forces have remained within the city," the chief emissary noted. "All your firecharm squads are posted to protect the mills. We saw that for ourselves when we arrived."

"Ah, but we don't fight trolls with firecharms," Poch told the galleries with a coy voice. "The trolls absorb Charm, and that is what enables their severed limbs to continue attacking. We have a more efficient way to stop them—and it imparts no Charm at all."

"Only master sword fighters can get close enough to a troll to kill with a blade," one of the emissaries voiced an assumption.

From under his red pajama shirt, Poch withdrew a .38 auto pistol. "Not a sword—yet charmless metal, nonetheless. This weapon projects pieces of lead at high velocity. Behold!"

He aimed the pistol at one of the tall, recessed windows and fired. Glass exploded outward with a glittering noise.

The emissaries leaped to their feet with the crowd, and Shai Malia urged them back into their seats.

"A bullet in the head kills the trolls and provides no Charm to animate their vile corpses," Poch said, soothing the throng. He paused until everyone had settled, then added, "With these weapons we have protected our city. But we could not offer them to the other dominions until we were certain of their effectiveness."

Shai Malia stepped forward. "As a further demonstration, know that among you are seated five uninvited guests from the Brood of Assassins. They were sent here to infiltrate our manor and eventually work their way close enough to my husband and myself to interrogate us, to learn what has befallen others of their brood who spied on us and would have taken these weapons for their own use."

"This is the fate of those who defy the good of all the dominions." Poch raised his auto pistol in signal, and shots rang out from the galleries.

Screams and shouts burst from the arcades where five bodies seated among the upper balcony onlookers collapsed, shot by sentinels armed with 9mm pistols. Under the frocks of the corpses, the guards found the black strangling cords of assassins.

Overy Scarn, who watched the proceedings through the oval one-way window of the anteroom nodded with approval. "You see, dear ones, New Arwar is under my protection—impenetrable even to the Brood of Assassins."

Nette, her black robe laced with the goblins' white web works, her silver, buzz-cut hair glistening with ichor, appeared at a side door to the anteroom. The pixies had released her to retrieve more hex-gems from Overy Scarn, and she had stood silently in the alcove, watching with cold fascination as the members of her brood were slain. "How did you know who were the assassins in the crowd?"

"Cameras, dear ones, video cameras." Overy turned around, a tight smile on her small lips. "I have been very busy installing surveillance lenses throughout the manor. The Brood of Assassins knows nothing of this equipment, and so they are vulnerable to it. I assure you, the pixies are entirely safe from their murderous minions."

"Do you have the hex-gems that you promised the dear ones?" Nette asked.

"Most certainly." From beneath her spellbinder girdle, Overy Scarn removed a chamois pouch and tossed it with a clinking sound to the assassin. "These are sufficient hex-gems to resume the troll attacks. Do you hear me, pixies?" She reached with her stare into the cold, inset eyes watching her impassively. "We have given the Peers a reasonable answer to their inquiries into why our city is unscathed. That will keep them away for the time being, and thus you shall remain undiscovered in my care. But now you have to act quickly. The Peerage must be brought down, or soon enough they will see through our ruse and return with murderous intent. They must be destroyed at once. Not all of Irth, mind you! Don't be monsters. Just kill the Peers and accept someone with sympathy for you to rule the dominions in their place. Someone like myself, who will see that you pixies have your own land, free from all of us wicked demons."

Nette tucked away the gems but did not move to retreat. "You did not have to slay my brother," she muttered bitterly as if she had not heard a word the large woman had uttered.

Overy Scarn forced herself not to withdraw her SIG-Saur pistol from where her hand gripped it under her robe, for she knew if she did, her fear would make her use it and she did not want to lose this assassin just yet. "Would the dear ones have been as inclined to understand the extent of my control over them if I had not killed N'drato? I think not."

"It was murder for cruelty's sake," Nette said and stepped out the side door, fluid as a shadow, her voice lingering behind, "I will not forget."

MOTHERS OF MAGIC

OVERY SCARN TOOK NETTE'S THREAT SERIOUSLY. THE ASSASSIN would have to die—but not until she was no longer needed. Her destructive skills could yet prove useful, Overy believed, because the source of imports from the Dark Shore was not secured. A great deal of Dig Dog's funds had been invested in Gabagalus to purchase the goods in hand from an agent who once worked for Duppy Hob. That agent was unreliable. *Surely, he will want more money now that I have sampled his wares and found them enticing,* she reasoned as she made her way down the service passages into the basement of the manor. *The threat of a visit from an assassin may well keep prices in line.*

She found her way by globe lanterns adjusted to their dimmest illumination so that the empty stone corridor shone like thick dusk. Ever cautious, she kept one hand on her SIG-Saur 9mm, in the event that the assassin decided to make good on her threat. But no one occupied the corridor except herself.

Soon, she stood in the large chamber that housed the Charm-driven air cyclers—bulky metal cylinders, caged exhaust fans, and elbows of pipes jammed along the ceiling and walls. The last of her video cameras nested in the crook of an unlit corner, and she smiled up at the black lens that was invisible to all but herself; she alone knew it was there. Eventually, she would have enough cameras to watch over this entire route to the charmway, but for now the narrow stairwell that descended by switchbacks into the darkness remained beyond the range of her surveillance—and she proceeded with her gun drawn.

Her belt of levity-pearls eased the strain of the long climb down, and when she finally emerged in the black cavern, she

was not even breathing hard. Though the air was stifling and
rank with the sulfur reek of sewage, her amulets laved her in
cool sweetness, and she did not break a sweat. A disc of lux-
diamonds revealed the leather shrouds of bats on the hanging
spires. By this light, she made her way past stone scallopings
to a skewed tunnel of drafty blackness.

Once she entered the charmway, she holstered her gun beneath the green panels of her brown robes and proceeded con-
fidently. She knew well the mazy turns of the raw rock tunnels
that would lead her to Gabagalus and the office of the trade
agent who had worked for the deceased devil worshipper,
Duppy Hob. Only briefly did she pause at a forked passage to
peer into a corridor that angled toward some mysterious destination. Green beyond the limits of green, strange shadows fluttered down there, and she moved on hurriedly, not liking the
look of that quivering light.

The charmway delivered Overy Scarn to a small portal that
she herself had paid to build; it connected to the charmway
corridors so that she would not have to travel by airship halfway
around the world. The portal opened upon a spacious sea-view
chamber, a bubble dome attached to a cliff ledge on the underside of Gabagalus. Streamers of kelp on the rock walls wriggled
in the sea current, and yellow and blue clouds of fish darted
through them. She stepped onto a blue-carpeted deck before
an oval swimming pool that webbed the spare interior with
trembling green shadows. The transparent bottom of the pool
lensed more kelp tangles and spurts of bright fish.

In a wire chair sat a wisp of a witch garbed entirely in
black veils.

"Who are you?" Overy Scarn inquired, baffled to find a witch
where always before she had been greeted by the grinning
clerks and boisterous trading agents who had used this pool
room to lounge. "Where are the brokers?"

"They are gone," the witch answered quietly. "Come in,
Overy Scarn. Sit down."

Overy reached beneath the panels of her robes for her gun and sat opposite the witch in a wire chair barely large enough to contain her girth. Anxiety and anger competed in her, and she urgently wanted to know what had become of the festive men and women who had once frolicked here and who had been so eager to sell her products from the Dark Shore, so eager to take her payments of hex-gems. "Who are you?"

The diminutive witch parted black veils from a youthful, almost perfectly round visage, the unsmiling face of a person compelled to take unhappy action. "I am Lady Von . . ."

"The witch queen!" Overy Scarn nearly toppled backward with her jolt of recognition. The presence of this great personage boded ill for her, she knew. The queen represented the entire world of witches, and there would be no defying them whose history was older than talismans. Her hand released the gun, and she sagged with resignation, wondering how the witch queen had known she was coming. But she knew it was quite hopeless to question anything about these mothers of magic.

"You have reason to look glum, Overy Scarn." Lady Von's large eyes watched her coldly. "You have usurped the rightful ruler of New Arwar, and you have used weapons of the Dark Shore to murder agents from the Brood of Assassins."

The tight muscles around Overy Scarn's worried eyes relaxed when the witch queen said nothing of the goblins. *She does not know of my alliance with the dear ones!* She frowned to hide her elation before the large, watchful eyes. "I saw my opportunity for advancement, and I took it." Her coldly controlled voice made her feel proud. "Thus have dominions been won throughout the history of Irth."

"There will be no more weapons from the Dark Shore," the witch queen declared sternly. "There will be no more of anything from the Dark Shore."

I must show defiance now to keep her from looking deeper. "What has become of Duppy Hob's brokers? Where are the agents that I deal with?"

"Duppy Hob is dead." Lady Von pressed her fingertips together before her round, staring face, pale as a soul. "For the good of the dominions, the Sisterhood has laid claim to all his possessions in Gabagalus. His minions have been taken into our service. The women now wear the veil and tend to the gutter children and the charmless poor of the sprawling cities. The men work for the wizards in the mines, digging for conjure-metals and hex-gems. If these benighted men and women serve with their hearts, time will redeem them. As for you—"

"I am no minion of the devil worshipper!" Overy sat bolt upright. "You have no claim on me!"

"If you take the veil now, Overy Scarn, the Sisterhood will intervene on your behalf with the Brood of Assassins."

"I do not fear assassins!" She jumped to her feet, and the wire chair clattered backward. "I have slain only those who were sent to slay me. And I have weapons enough to protect me from all others that the Brood of Assassins may send."

"Sooner or later, your weapons will be exhausted. . . ."

"Never!" Overy Scarn backed away. "What I possess will act as prototypes. I will manufacture all that I need. I will not succumb. And eventually I will find my way back to the Dark Shore."

"I think not." The witch queen lowered the black veils over her face. "The charmways are burning. Surely, you saw the green fire on your way here. Soon enough, all the charmways to the Dark Shore and all the charmways on Irth will be destroyed."

Overy Scarn waited to hear no more but fled in a rush of anger and fear and dared not look back as she passed through the portal to the charmways.

AND STILLNESS, OUR DANCING

"NONE OF THE EMISSARIES SURVIVED THEIR RETURN JOURNEYS TO their dominions," Shai Malia read the report from the sheaf of printed messages that the manor heralds had deposited atop the onyx wood table of their suite. She had removed her wrap-around shades, and her eye makeup had smeared from the band of opals she had pressed to them, to clear her swarming chills and pulsing headache.

Poch, with mirror sunglasses and headphones on, lay stretched on the divan, watching a music video, and he did not hear her. The glass pipe, black from use, sat on the rattan table among crushed cans of soda.

Shai Malia walked over to him and dropped the sheaf of reports on his face. He sat up with an irate look, and she pulled the headphones from his ears. "The trolls are attacking again. More fiercely than ever. The emissaries never got back to their dominions. Only their aviso reports got through. There won't be any more visits from the other Peers."

"So?" Poch passed her an annoyed look, apparent even from behind his reflecting glasses, and pulled a cigarette from the pack in the pocket of his red pajama top.

"So I think it's time we speak with the dear ones again." She took the cigarette from his lips. "They won't like this smell on you."

"Why do we have to talk with them?" He reached for the glass pipe and the plastic bag of white crumbs. "They have Nette to fetch for them now."

Shai Malia put her hand on the glass pipe, but he held it firmly. "Don't smoke any more. Clear your head with the theria-cal opals, and let's go sit with the dear ones. I want to hear what they have to say."

"About what? Overy Scarn?" He pulled the pipe free from her grip and placed a morsel of the smokable crystal in the small, black-glazed bowl. "She'll watch us, and then we'll have to answer to her. Let's just sit and smoke."

"You're margrave." Shai put her hand over the butane lighter as he reached for it. "Maybe the dear ones will have some thoughts about how to defy Scarn and take the power that is rightfully yours."

"Don't hobble me with your fantasies." He pried the lighter from under her hand.

"Fantasies?" She picked up the plastic bag of crumbs and waved it at him. "The truth is, you are margrave. And look at how we're living."

"The truth is, I took the title illegally." He removed the plastic bag from her hand and tucked it into his shirt pocket. "And the truth is, the dear ones are goblins."

"That's the coca smoke making you say that."

"They're goblins and you know it's true." He lit the lighter and held the flame to the glass bowl while he sucked on the stem. "They're destroying the dominions—and Overy Scarn will pick up the pieces."

"I want to hear it from them." She sat next to him. "Please, Poch. If you love me, come with me. Let them tell us the truth."

"We already know the truth." Smoke jetted from his nostrils. "Whether it's coca smoke or the goblins' mist, it's just trading one chemical for another. So what does it matter? Let's just sit here and float. It feels too good now for us to change anything."

Shai Malia removed the pipe from his hand, and from the pocket of her black denims took out the band of theriacal opals. "Clear your head of this smoke first and tell me that again."

Poch knocked the band of opals from her hand, and it clattered among the empty soda cans. "I don't care what the goblins have to say. Or Scarn. Or you."

Shai Malia sat back, hurt.

"Don't look at me like that." He kicked over the rattan table, and the soda cans jumped across the parquet floor and bounced off the TV. "I've given you everything you wanted. I kicked out my sister. I gave her to the damn goblins. And I'm margrave. So don't look at me like that."

"When is the last time you wanted me?" She moped. "I haven't wanted you, either. Not since I've had the pipe. Don't you see? It's Scarn's way of controlling us."

"And the goblins weren't controlling us before?" He reached over perfunctorily and pulled the pipe from her hand. "Why do you think you made us leave Blight Fen and come here? Why did you make me become margrave?" His voice dropped to a pitch of flat weariness. "The goblins wanted it. You're not married to me. You're married to the goblins."

She pushed to her feet, a look of disgust on her face. "You stay here and fog your brains. I'm going back to the dear ones."

"Go ahead," he called after her as she strode toward the door. "Crawl with the goblins in their muck. Let Overy Scarn watch you pay obeisance to your masters."

"At least my masters are living," she shot back from the door. "You worship dead things—the ghost you suck out of that pipe, the phantoms in the tape cassettes of that dreambox."

"And the goblins make you feel real, Shai?" He pulled off the mask of his mirror glasses and stared hard at her with his red, hurt eyes. "Are they more real than you and me?"

Her tense shoulders sagged. "Poch—they're the dear ones. Have you forgotten?"

"Maybe I have forgotten them." He tapped the black glass pipe against his heart. "This smoke made it easy to forget them. But no matter how much I smoke, I could never forget you."

She stepped toward him. "We can't go on like this."

"Like what?" He shrugged at the disshelved room, littered with cans and strewn garments. "We're having fun. This whole city is having fun. Everyone is here to escape the war and make themselves rich. Even the goblins. They want to carve a place for themselves on Irth. What are we supposed to do? Kill the dear ones? They're pixies. They just want to be safe. Scarn is fixing it for them. Are we supposed to kill her? You saw what she did to the assassins. If *they* can't stop her, what are we supposed to do?"

"What is all this talk of killing?"

"That's the only alternative, Shai." He pulled a chrome-plated handgun from under the divan's cushion and clinked the glass pipe against it. "It's either the gun or the pipe."

"I don't want to kill—I . . . I want to live."

Poch returned the gun to its place under the cushion. "Then smoke with me, Shai. The goblins have Nette. And Scarn has the goblins. At least we have each other."

Shai Malia sat down again beside him. "We *are* together when we smoke," she asserted. "And it feels good—almost as good as when we used to . . ."

"Forget all that groping and sweating. Just smoke." He loaded the pipe. "With the smoke, it's enough just to be together. Silence becomes our words and stillness our dancing."

She nodded softly and took the pipe from him with both hands.

Voices Calling from Empty Space

Every sacred act is felt first in hell.
—THE GIBBET SCROLLS: 6

HUNTED BY THUNDER

JYOTI AND REECE STOPPED FIRING AT THE TROLLS THAT WERE CLIMB-ing down the crusty ledges of the goblin's chalk house in the mere. The carnivorous creatures had begun to flee. They scrambled into the crevices of the salt dome, their frantic silhouettes scurrying against the lightning glare. And in moments, the thunder swept away the last of their screeching cries.

Jyoti turned her firelock on the goblins, and Reece held out a hand to restrain her. The entire chamber had gone dormant. The goblins in their hundreds lay curled on the quartz-studded ground, their greasy, cherubic bodies twitching fitfully. "They're sleeping again," Reece surmised.

"No—they're stunned." Jyoti quickly began to tear hex-gems

from her amulet harnesses. "Maybe the pain of the trolls shocked them."

Neither of them could guess that Overy Scarn had deprived the wakeful goblins in New Arwar of the concentrated Charm they needed to project their telepathy. With that contact lost, the horde of goblins had not the strength to resist the somniferous cold of Irth. Numbed by the night chill and the seeping rain, they sagged helpless, paralyzed, yet alert. The amulets that the two demons cast among them offered the feeble warmth of embers, enough to foster awareness of their horrifying plight.

What are the demons doing? the swarm cried among themselves. *Why do they strew Charm among us?*

"We must hurry," Jyoti urged her partner. "Our reprieve might end at any moment. We have to get out of here before the trolls return."

Reece agreed, spurred on by the cobra darkness he had glimpsed in the bolt eyes of the trolls. He ripped hex-gems from his amulet harness and flung them over the drowsy bodies. With each handful that he tossed, the Charm enclosing him diminished, and the fetid stink of the goblin flesh gouged his sinuses. He broke off the last of his power wands and flipped them end over end across the wide vault, then lurched gasping to the wall, face squeezed shut against the stench.

Jyoti helped him sling his firelock on his shoulder and find purchase for his first halting steps up and out of the putrid depths. Slowly, without Charm to steady them, they picked their way along the rock wall, using the mineral knobs and stone ledges that offered themselves.

Below, the goblins writhed, trying to gather Charm from the hex-gems in their midst, trying to utilize that warmth to focus their awareness and summon again the trolls to help them against the demons. But there were too many pixies and too much cold. Holding five awake in New Arwar was all that they could manage in this frigid world. They lay paralyzed in the rainy night.

Lightning flapped, and those lying on their backs with their eyes glazed open watched the demons climbing higher on the curved white wall. Sorrow choked them with the knowledge that these evil beings had somehow won, though the terrible truth of their victory was not yet revealed. In their teeming solitude, they squirmed, losing their way inside their fear like children in the woods.

"I'm going to jam the clip of my firelock," Jyoti said when they had reached the gap in the salt dome through which they would exit. She pulled the side clip to its maximum and slammed the cartridge hard into the housing so that the trigger jumped forward. Then, she hurled her firelock into the grotto.

Reece followed her example, and when he rammed the bottom of the cartridge against the rock wall and felt the firelock begin to vibrate in his hand, he flung it wide of himself, into the dark house of the goblins.

Jyoti grabbed his arm, and they slipped through the large crack in the dome. Lightning crossed enormous distances, illuminating storm towers and thunderheads, a vast gray metropolis afloat in the heavens. With the rain, they slid down the rough outer wall into the dark tumult of the swamp.

The spongy ground shook underfoot. Through the crevices of the dome, charmfire rayed like a new sun hatching. The explosive aftershock followed, a din of concussive force that shoved aside chunks of the cupola and released tendrils of spinning green flames.

The goblins experienced a momentary warmth within the conflagration, their souls awake and perched on the world as if on a melon in a bright garden. They sat up together in the abrupt heat, sharing the attendant pain, yet grateful in their one moment of clarity for the looping blood in their veins that had felt life. Then, the flames ate more hotly than their flesh, unskilled at suffering, could bear. And they disappeared in the fire.

Black, oily smoke churned from the pyre and tangled its darkness with the night. Immense faces leered from the lightning-painted clouds, then lapsed again into nothingness. Reece and Jyoti looked back no more, for the night swamp threatened swift annihilation to the charmless.

They thrashed for a blind eternity about the perimeter of the burning salt house with only the brief flares of thunderbolts and gusts of green flame for illumination. Boulders hunched like crocodilians, and lianas lashed like vipers. At last, Jyoti lay hold of the charmor vests she had left in the underbrush.

When they pulled the sodden garments free, laughter replaced their desperate cries, and they lay panting with relief against each other.

Thus bolstered by the inherent Charm of the protective vests, they slogged through the Mere of Goblins. The only amulet that Jyoti had spared from her incendiary attack was the seeker that N'drato had pressed into her hand. The directional chill that it emitted guided them under the tuneless whistle of the storm, through a maze of root buttresses and canebrakes.

Not a dozen words passed between them as they walked. The charmor vests gave them the strength to shove through the waist-deep water and clamber over fallen trees and gravel banks blocking their way, and the seeker provided guidance. For protection against the giant centipedes and firesnakes, there was only their shared experiences of wandering the wild places of Irth.

As much as they could, they kept to the high ground, creeping along broad boughs, leaping from one root ledge to the next, until the seeker delivered them to a shallow cave beneath a limestone outcropping. It yawed above a lightning-polished pool, viscid as quicksilver, and appeared to lead nowhere safe— but it was welcome sanctuary under the lightning clouds hunched like beasts and hunted by thunder.

EATING THE WIND

THE CHARMWAYS GLIMMERED WITH GREEN SHADOWS AND A parched stench of scorched rock. "They're still burning." Reece stood at a fork in the passages, watching the pulsing radiance at the end of both corridors. "I think the fire has spread." He looked back the way they had come, then glanced again at the jumping shadows in the branched corridors ahead. "Which way do we go?"

Jyoti arbitrarily chose one of the two bright corridors. The heat beat against them as they advanced, and the sharp air burned their throats. Arms raised to shield their eyes, they turned a bend and found another fork. One blazed hot enough to brand their eyes with retinal blood flowers, and the other bored darkly to an unknown destination. They ducked into cool darkness and walked slowly hand in hand through the lightless passage.

"So long as we're together, I don't care where this leads," Jyoti said and pressed close to him.

Reece squeezed her hand. "The goblins are dead. We did it, Jyo! And we did it together. You were right—we should never be apart again."

"The blind god Chance alone spared us back there when the trolls were coming for us." Jyoti's voice floated in the darkness.

"I know it's odd but if we had died then, I would have given myself to those foul goblins almost happily," Reece confessed. "I saw them as—well, as beautiful. And we were the monsters."

"They called us demons," Jyoti remembered. "That was the trance they spun over us. What are they doing in New Arwar to Poch?"

An aqueous blue light shimmered ahead. They walked more quickly and soon emerged through a small portal into a spacious sea-view chamber that Reece remembered. "This is Duppy Hob's swimming pool on the underside of Gabagalus!"

They stepped cautiously onto a carpeted deck beside an oval swimming pool cobbled with light. A petite woman in black veils awaited them at the far side of the pool and greeted them heartily. "Margravine, welcome. Magus Reece—our circle is joined." She approached with small, quick steps. "I would have sent my sisters to lead you here when first I saw you in the charmways, but they are in other dominions, every one of them saving what lives they can. I am alone here—in Gabagalus, the nest of the nightmare."

"Lady Von!" Jyoti bowed before the witch queen.

"The charmfires led you to me." She lowered her veils before them, and her moon-round visage shone with sad benevolence. "Most of the passages have been consumed. Charmfire is burning the entire labyrinth of links on the other side of Irth, and soon it will reach here. When I saw that you had no choice but to come to me, I simply waited for you." She embraced Jyoti, then turned to Reece. "Magus, you fulfilled our mission— you and the margravine found the goblin horde and destroyed it. I have seen it in trance. Your presence broke the blinding spell that had always before hid them from our strong eye. Your body from the Dark Shore has been the focus of our trances since you departed my presence at Mount Szo."

Reece took the witch's news with weighty sadness, for now all hope of rescuing his friend Dogbrick was lost with the charmways. He swallowed, composed himself, and began, "Then, you know of Esre—"

"She died protecting you."

"She shouldn't have had to die at all. You should never have ordered her to abduct me."

The witch regarded him silently, then said, "The strong eye has shown us otherwise, magus." She put her hands on his wrists, and the Charm she shared lifted him like an old dog out of a cold stream. "Deprived of the magic that carried you here from the Dark Shore, have you also lost your percipience of magic?"

"You should have used that magic more effectively," he whispered gruffly, though he surged momentarily with the sunshine that flared inside him at her touch. "You should have given everything."

"Trust that we did." She let his wrists go, and he felt his soul swerve south, to the dark-facing side of himself. "Without you

in the Reef Isles, N'drato would not have followed. Blight Fen
would not have culled so many trolls from the marsh to burn
when the assassin destroyed it. No one would have been able
to get within a league of the goblin horde's sanctuary. It has
been there for ages, you know. The opportunity to pierce it
required the correct propitiation of the three blind gods—"

"Chance and Death were both satisfied," Reece responded
darkly, "but Justice?"

Jyoti pressed against him. "What future we the living build,
that will justify or condemn what we have done. Our mission
is not yet complete. There are other goblins in New Arwar."

Reece relented with a heavy nod. Fugitive as the last blue
hue of day, he accepted his smallness. What kind of savior did
he think he was, protesting the witch queen's actions? He had
no magic anymore, only an arrogant memory of its fabled
strength. Whom had he ever been able to save? Not Lara, the
soul who had first led him to the Bright Worlds; nor his mentor,
Caval; nor his friend Dogbrick; nor even Ripcat, the last mask
of his magic. He nodded heavily. "We must go to New Arwar
at once."

"You need Charm." Lady Von motioned for them to follow
her around the pool to where its gelid shadows fluttered upon
a hatchway. "I have prepared talismanic garments and weapons
for both of you. Come."

"Lady Von—" Jyoti strode to her side. "You said that the
green fire is destroying all the charmways of Irth. What will
happen to our planet?"

"Fear not, margravine." The witch queen took Jyoti's arm so-
licitously. "This is a controlled burn."

"But why?" Reece asked. "The charmways were the most powerful way to unite the dominions of Irth."

"Far too powerful." Lady Von stopped before the hatchway,
and her gaze touched each of them with cold severity. "You
have spoken of Justice. These charmways were the work of the
devil worshipper Duppy Hob. His evil magic created passages

that connect the Dark Shore with the land of his origin, Gaba-galus. This is the scaffolding by which he intended to raid heaven. It must not stand."

She led them through the hatchway to a metal platform above a colossal pylon of scaffolds and ramp ways that spanned two knobs of coral-like mountains. This was an air pier, replete with mooring trestles and berthing stanchions. At each end of the pier, a tunnel penetrated the pocked crags. Gummy green mucilage stained the perforated rocks and crevices of the tunnels, and a dim echo of their virid glow shone within those dark depths.

"The fire of Justice burns ever closer to these charmways," Lady Von announced somberly. "One last charmway will take you to the Dark Shore, to bring back Dogbrick. The other leads to New Arwar, where the last of the goblins must be destroyed. The glare of the fire blinds the strong eye. From here, the future is uncertain. You must choose which way you will follow."

TIME BEFORE TIME

CAVAL HAD LIVED A LONG LIFE, OVER 45,000 DAYS ON IRTH, THE equivalent of over 120 years on the Dark Shore. Death was an event he had been preparing for since his early days in the Brood of Assassins. Later, as a wizard, he had learned all its mysteries, and he knew exactly what would happen to him when the taut string of Charm that remained to him was broken. Consciousness of himself as Caval the wizard would end, and his Charm would scatter across the mineral floor of this planet.

But death had not yet snapped his charmstring, and he spent his time exploring all the possibilities of what remained of his life. Trained as a wizard, he knew well how to focus Charm.

He knew it so well that he had succeeded at focusing the Charm of his own life force even after his physical body had been destroyed on Irth.

In the hold of Octoberland, Caval told his story to Brick, hoping to keep the dead man's soul calm and still. Memories of Dogbrick's flaying and the agony of his demise had traumatized this soul, and Caval feared that the echoes of the pain would be too loud for Brick to bear, even with Caval's help.

"Why are you holding me here, wizard?" Brick asked. *Here* was a vacuous space, empty and colorless as air. "Let me die."

"Be silent!" Caval admonished. "Does not my history intrigue you? It is the story of how you came to be here on the Dark Shore."

"History is done with me. I am dead."

"Nonsense. Your physical body is dead. Your soul yet lives and will endure so long as you remain calm and do not disrupt what little is left of my Charm."

"Why?" Brick cried out in an anguished voice. "Just tell me why you hold me here in this void."

"We are not in a void," Caval declared in a quiet voice. "We are in the sky, the atmosphere of Earth. I had my refinery here once. It is safe from wizards and devil worshippers, and that's why I'm holding you with me. From here, one can see everything. Look, I will show you something you had never imagined. My Charm is stretched thin as a thread. One end is tied to Earth—and the other—" He laughed gently. "The other, dear Brick, is connected to the Abiding Star. Behold!"

Brick had no desire to see anything more. He craved only oblivion, a surcease to the suffering that resonated in him from his torturous death. But he had no training in the internal arts that would have granted him the power to focus his Charm the way the wizard did, and so his awareness moved at Caval's command.

Brick's soul rose up the thin, drawn filament of Caval's Charm and in an instant crossed the Gulf, the Bright Worlds, and the upper air. Within the Abiding Star, he felt as though the charmlight wove dream cloths around him, dressing him like an angel. In that bright raiment full of ruffles, windings, and streamers, his enormous grief got lost. He could not find what had pained him. They were sun-fallen shadows obliterated in his light.

He looked around. Time's hallucinations danced on all sides, and when he glanced left and right, he glimpsed past and future: A fractured vista of the past revealed him in Saxar as Dogbrick, a beastmarked boy prowling for food among the market stalls, sleeping in alley barrels, squatting under a sizzling grill on a pier listening to the instructions of his first and only real teacher, Wise Fish. . . .

In the other direction, he saw Brick, a brawny, blond-haired man with dark skin once again on the step-notched avenues of Saxar and, at his side, under the curved eaves, in the shadows of the cliff city's winches and pulleys, a young, freckle-faced woman with masses of chestnut hair—Mary Felix.

This vision baffled him, and he turned his attention downward, through levels of light and mystifying sheets of stellar winds. Down to Earth, his attention plummeted. In a moment, he was in Manhattan again. Dawn gleamed thin and watery at the vacant ends of the streets; above the East River, the gray sky was tainted vaguely red as fish blood.

CONJURING IN HELL

"Only a hand lighter than power can raise Mayland," Nox informed Mary Felix as they exited the building whose summit carried Octoberland. "That is why I need you."

Barefoot and wearing only a breechcloth, the lithe, muscular magician led the frightened woman across a street that shone orange and blue at early dawn. A jogger at one side of the street and two dog walkers at the other stared openly at the nearly naked man with the unhappy woman at his side. Then, the couple disappeared down the steps of a subway entrance.

"Into the earth we go, Mary," Nox sang with joy, a bold grin on his handsome face. "Down in these depths, the generative energies coil. We shall harness them and grow a new coven."

Reluctantly, Mary descended the stone steps, looking about for someone to help her. The platform stood empty. She flung a desperate gesture at the woman in the token booth, but with one glance, Nox turned her attention away.

"Don't resist me, Mary." Nox pressed her against an I-beam column, his Persian eyes kindling a mesmeric sparkle. "There are others who will eagerly take your place." He looked to where the twin white beams of an incoming train shone, reflecting slickly off the painted metal pillars of the dirty brick tunnel. "Would you rather be a corpse?"

"You're going to kill me eventually anyway." She pushed herself away from him. "Go ahead. Throw me in front of the train."

"Very good." Nox seized her arm and shoved her off the platform. He leaped after her, agile as a panther, and lifted her by her belt before she landed facedown across the tracks. The din of the arriving train quaked the air, and she only vaguely heard his shout, "We are going deeper!"

With voluptuous strength, he stood her on her feet, took her weight under one arm, and led her down the tracks ahead of the hurtling train, his legs consuming distance in wide, gliding steps. The train's horn blared behind them, and their shadows leaped ahead. At the last instant, Nox pulled her aside, and they stood watching the aluminum sides of the express gleam past inches away.

The stained white tiles of the nook that held them curved smoothly about a narrow opening through which Nox pushed Mary. She entered an alcove of electric cable frames, their gray dusty bulks limned in reflected light from the tunnel. Rats scurried between her feet. Nox lifted a ponderous stone plug using finger holes and his tremendous strength. "Down you go."

A dry, choking odor of dust and ash rose from the black well, yet Mary did not disobey. She descended into the dark on uneven steps hewn from the bedrock. Chimes echoed from far away, the incessant drip of water. When her boots found no more steps, her arms reached out and touched emptiness.

Stiles of blue light rayed down the stairwell. Nox followed, sheathed in an acetylene brightness, and she gaped at him. "Don't spread your awe before me." His shining arms motioned at the cavern around them. "Mayland is more worthy of your wonder."

Mary turned and faced a large cave with a groined ceiling supported by a proscenium arch of pocked stone. Alchemic figures bleared the eroded span with worn images of metallurgic sigils, winged beasts, and an eyeball circled by a tail-biting serpent.

Nox danced past her, and as he whirled, the blue flames spun from his body and ignited tiny flames among the faults and ledges. Soon, the cavern walls glimmered with a thousand votive candles fluttering to the clocked rhythms of treacly water leaks.

"Our temple," he announced. "Once it served Duppy Hob, more than a century ago. But now he is dead and our dream lives! From here, our magic will build a new world."

Beyond the tocking of leakage, the subway trains rumbled like a storm wind. Mary hugged herself and trepidatiously gazed about at the sparks of cold fire fluttering in their niches.

Nox's shadows standing upon the fiery walls blended as he danced. Waves of flickering phosphoresence ran through the cavern.

With a shout, Nox stopped his dance, and a fragrance as from a rain-soaked forest suffused the chamber, supplanting the taint of ozone and fust. Laughing, the magician turned to Mary and said, "Think what we will accomplish when our coven is gathered in full!"

Mary entered the cave, her step crunching gravel. Nasturtiums peeked from crevices in the arch of carved alchemic symbols. Trellised flowers gleamed in the dark.

"Water!" Nox cried. "What hope of spring without water?"

Again, he danced—and a soft stone echo announced the arrival of water. A rush of honeysuckle air breathed over them. Scrabbling blindly among the stones in the dark, a rivulet felt its way over stones to the boot tips of Mary Felix.

"I'm conjuring paradise!" Nox exulted and splashed through the rill.

"You're conjuring in hell!" Mary shouted. The smear of spring in the electric air emboldened her, and with all her strength she shrugged off the fear that had stifled her since Brick had died. She lugged a rock from the ground and heaved it at him.

Nox brushed it aside and called after the running woman, "This is your new home! Don't you like how I've decorated it for you?"

Mary reached the hewn stairs before a shadow fell upon her and she froze. Though she instructed her legs to keep running, her body would not move. Her hair tossed across her startled face like creepers, her tresses tangled to vines of waxy leaves. Staring at her hands, she saw her fingertips like exploded firecrackers, burst into blown flowers. Her wrists stiffened like her legs, taking on the rigidity of bark.

"You can't leave here, Mary." Nox crossed the shimmering creek. "You belong here with all the other emblems of springtime."

In her mind, she knew what was happening should be impossible. Nightmare jolts twisted through her but could not budge her rooted feet. All she could see from where she stood immobilized were leaves fluttering where her hair had fallen forward over her eyes. And the more she thought, the more syrupy her thoughts became, thickening, slowing to a sap of mute awareness.

Nox approached the small, spellbound tree, her boughs spun

in helix creepers, her tan bark smooth as flesh. He smiled and put an ear to her wooden heart.

ASSAIL INFINITY

"HOW MUCH TIME BEFORE THE GREEN FIRES DESTROY THE CHARM-ways to the Dark Shore?" Reece asked Lady Von, standing together with Jyoti in the brisk wind at the heights of Gabagalus. Several black dirigibles hovered above the green, coraline crags, conducting trade with the wort farms and the distant, crystalline cities that glittered like fallen stars, wholly indifferent to the threat of goblins.

"Is there time for us to return to New Arwar and destroy the last of the goblins?" Jyoti clutched the witch queen's robed arm. "Can we do that and still bring Dogbrick back to Irth?"

Lady Von took each of their hands. "The glare of the charm-fires obscures the Sisterhood's view of the future."

Reece cocked his head skeptically. "You've withheld information from me before."

"Esre's death must not burden you at this critical moment." Lady Von pressed closer to Reece. "I did not withhold fateful knowledge from you. You know that. So, trust me now. I cannot tell you when the charmway to the Dark Shore will collapse. There may not be time for you to go and return even now."

Reece anguished for his friend Dogbrick. *Is he still alive?* he had to ask himself to defeat the urgency he felt to return at once to Earth. The goblins in New Arwar *were* alive. That he knew, and this dark knowledge was sufficient for him to decide.

"It's clear we must go to New Arwar at once and destroy the goblins," Reece said.

Jyoti asked, "Can you not contact the Brood of Assassins and send them in?"

"I will do so at once. But there is little time." The witch

queen released their hands and stepped toward a metal door set among the bolted seams at the side of a massive berthing post for dirigibles. "The goblins in New Arwar have surely sensed the destruction of their comrades. The longer we wait, the greater the possibility they will elude us."

She opened the door and removed two amulet-shawls and a firelock. She passed them the shawls and hefted the blunt-nosed rifle, running her hand over the chrome barrel's heat tarnish. "This is the only weapon I could find at so short notice. In fact, it is the only weapon I have ever handled."

Jyoti and Reece dropped their heavy charmor vests and donned the shawls. Charm relieved their feverish exhaustion, and they stood taller and more alert. The margravine took the firelock from Lady Von, checked the gold-jacket Charm cartridge fitted into the black housing, and nodded to see that it was fully charged.

"Go get Dogbrick." Jyoti set the charge pin to maximum and backed toward the charmway that led to New Arwar. "I'll take care of the goblins."

"No." Reece strode after her. "We're staying together from now on. Remember?"

Jyoti stopped under the weight of a heartbroken frown. "I want us to be together, you know that. But I can't ask you to abandon your friend. The last charmways are burning."

"I don't even know if he's alive," Reece countered. "But we know there are more goblins. Thousands of lives are in jeopardy."

"Yes!" Lady Von waved them off urgently. "Go to New Arwar. I will find your friend Dogbrick upon the Dark Shore. I owe you at least that for what you have done to protect the dominions." She drew the black veils over her face. "Go quickly now. The goblins are alerted. You must catch them before they flee."

Jyoti and Reece ran together across the platform of the air pier and into the tunnel that the Sisterhood of Witches had connected by charmway to Elvre. They crossed through a corridor of raw rock, where green rumors of light seeped from the slick side passages with blowsy drifts of heat and a stench of charred rock. Presently, they entered a lightless cavern. The lux-diamonds of their shawls released eye sparks from a covey of bats among the stalactites.

They charged up a long series of switchbacking steps that brought them to a large chamber of massive, gray-metal cylinders radiating pipes coded by color. "We're in the manor's basement, with the air cycler," Jyoti recognized. "We'll take the lift to the goblin's floor."

"Better not," Reece warned. He pointed to a black lens hidden among the shadows of elbowing pipes. "We're being watched. That's a video camera. I didn't know you had that technology on Irth."

"We don't." Jyoti adjusted her charge pin and fired a red bolt that smashed the camera to crumpled metal. "It's Overy Scarn. She's taken New Arwar for herself." She checked her niello eye charms before shouldering open a service door beneath a lintel of brightly painted pipes. "You're right about the lifts. They're traps. We'll take these back stairs."

At the head of the stairs, the sentinel chief, Roidan waited with five guards, their .38 auto pistols drawn and pointing at the doorway the couple would pass through to access the goblins' floor. Overy Scarn had alerted them to the intruders she had seen in her surveillance cameras, and she watched the interceptors on a monitor screen in her suite.

Rapid bursts of yellow charmfire struck the guards from behind, throwing them against the door in a bloody huddle. Roidan spun about in a crouch, and a hot bolt struck his pistol and exploded it in his hands. The flying metal shards of the ripped weapon shredded his crimson-and-gold armorial uniform and tore the face from his skull.

Instantly, Overy Scarn leaped from the chair where she had been fingering her spellbinder girdle and stared aghast at the torn corpses of her sentinels. Jyoti's face appeared on the monitor, and she offered the camera a hard stare and thumbed the niello eye charm on her amulet-shawl that had warned her of the ambush. "You're next," she mouthed and pointed her firelock at the lens.

Static burst across the monitor, and Overy Scarn leaped back, shocked at how simply the margravine had eluded her trap by leaving the stairwell where she had last seen them and following an amulet to an unguarded flight of stairs.

"She relied too heavily on her Dark Shore weapons," Jyoti muttered angrily, stalking toward the door that led to what had once been her bedchamber. "She forgot about Charm."

Reece was not listening. He already stood before the goblins' door. He could feel them within, pulling at the Charm in his shawl, urging him to open the door. His blue-white knuckles glowed with pain in the hand that held the doorknob—pain that coursed from within, from the anguish of the five that remained—the last of the goblins.

A cry of mourning began to assail infinity, keening the loss of the hundreds, reaching in despair higher than time to the desolate emptiness outside pain, beyond suffering, to where the greasy smoke of the consuming charmfire had launched the souls of their dead.

Jyoti shoved Reece aside and kicked open the bedchamber door. In a gauzy nimbus of white webs, the room glared with light from the starry windows. An ammoniacal stink gushed out, and with it came Nette, a razor knife slashing. Jyoti blocked it with her weapon, and the knife and the firelock clattered to the floor as the two women collided. Nette rolled on top, her gummy hands reaching for Jyoti's throat, her grimacing face greased in goblin yolk.

THE DOOM OF NEW ARWAR

From behind, Reece tackled Nette, knocking her away from Jyoti and tumbling with her across the corridor. Immediately, he found himself on his back, his arms paralyzed by two nerve jabs so swift he never felt them. The assassin's left hand jerked his head back by the hair, exposing his larynx, and the right heel of her hand cocked for a death blow. But before she could strike, the margravine rolled to where the firelock lay, seized it, and fired, slamming Nette with a bolt of red energy.

The door to the bedchamber slammed shut. On her back, Jyoti rammed the door with her heels and knocked it loose from one hinge. She hurriedly crawled into the radiant room, the firelock thrust in front of her.

Five goblins bunched together in a corner, crying. Webs of planet light draped them from the night-shining windows, silhouetting their bone-warped arms and bowed legs. A curd of furry white gel sacs dangled like spider's eggs from the walls and window frame behind them.

Their cries wailed with an almost musical despair, and their craze-lidded eyes stared white and sharp with pain. Flexing their little hands, they reached for the demon that crawled into their chamber—not warding off their destroyer but beseeching her, plaintively summoning her—

Jyoti had no mind for mercy. She remembered what they had done to her when last she occupied this room, and was frightened that their gel sacs might rupture and mesmerize her again. She fired several frenzied rounds of blue-white energy at their cringing bodies. They splattered into burning gouts of flesh and writhing eels of sizzling viscera that shriveled almost instantly to a bubbling tar. The heat of the bolts ignited the goblins' web work, and the gossamer draperies billowed into vigorous sheets of flame.

Arms upraised against the violent heat, Jyoti jumped backward and collided with Nette. She whirled about, flames buffeting against the protective aura of her amulet-shawl, and brought her firelock to bear on the assassin.

"Don't!" Nette lifted her hands to show she offered no threat. "You stunned me free of the goblins' spell!" She grabbed Jyoti's shawl and fell backward to the floor, tossing the margravine over her and out the door. Jyoti crashed into Reece, and they both sprawled into the corridor.

In a moment, the assassin tumbled over them, her silver, bristle-cut hair was singed black by the conflagration that blazed in the doorway behind her. "It's going to explode!" She took the dazed couple by their elbows and stood them up. "Scarn stores her weapons and ammunition from the Dark Shore in the attic room above the bedchamber. We must get off this floor!"

"Where is Poch?" Jyoti cried.

Nette scrambled toward the main stairway, and Reece and Jyoti followed. A squad of sentinels met them on the first landing, and as they raised their auto pistols, the stored weapons in the attic detonated.

A fireball bloomed from the upper storey, and Jyoti charged ahead of it, screaming and shooting short bursts of star-white energy from her firelock, cutting her way through the startled sentinels. The assassin locked arms with Reece and leaped over the banister.

In the suite below, Poch and Shai Malia felt the blast despite their headphones and glanced listlessly at each other where they lay on the divan. As Poch reached for the black glass pipe, the double doors to the suite burst inward. Three steaming and charred figures staggered toward them, a wall of flames seething in the corridor behind.

Poch yanked the headphones from his head, heard screams from the inferno beyond, and groped among the divan's cushions for his gun.

"Poch!" Jyoti shouted. "It's me!"

Squinting against the spark-spinning smoke that slouched into the suite like a great beast, he recognized the smudge-faced woman with the cropped hair as his sister. He moved to rise, but his legs gave out, flopping him back down. "Jyo—"

"The manor's burning!" Nette yelled and beckoned them from their dream-bound lounge.

"Fire is gutting the charmways too!" Jyoti grabbed her brother under his shoulder and hoisted him upright. "We have to get out now."

Shai Malia found the chrome-plated handgun and pointed it at Jyoti's face. "This is a ruse! Where's Scarn?"

Nette kicked the gun from Shai Malia's hand. "It's not a ruse. The whole manor is ablaze!"

"They're doped," Reece said, staring amazed at thrashing musicians on the television, scattered cans of soda on the floor, and clothing from Earth strewn over the furniture.

A splintering crash shuddered the room, and the ceiling buckled, spewing plaster and fiery hail.

"Out!" Nette screamed and pulled Shai Malia by her elbow from around the divan.

Jyoti put her arm over her brother's shoulders and swept him away from the center of the room toward the door. "This floor is collapsing! Please, Poch—hurry!"

Reece lunged into the hallway, and only his amulets protected him from the column of flame that churned where the main stairwell had been. "We have to try for the back stairs!"

"Poch!" Shai Malia called to her husband. "The pipe! The coca crumbs!"

"Forget them!" he bawled, but she had already twisted away from Nette and scurried toward the divan. "Shai!"

Poch lurched free of his sister and ran after his wife. Jyoti moved to follow, and Nette grabbed her from behind. The assassin dragged her from the room as the buckled ceiling came pouring down in a deafening avalanche of flames and cinderous debris. "Poch!"

Dervish gusts of fire swirled up with scorching shrieks from the hole into which Poch and Shai Malia had plummeted under a torrent of incandescent ashes.

"They're gone!" Reece shouted, grabbing Jyoti's flailing arms. "And we're gone too if we don't move quickly."

Nette took the firelock from the margravine and activated all the power wands in Jyoti's amulet-shawl, easing her with Charm.

Pelted by searing cinders from the smoking ceiling, the three survivors dashed to the back stairs. Smoke hindered their descent, and they leaped down the steps with theriacal opals clasped to their nostrils. Behind them, explosions shook the walls. The charmwrights, wizards, trade executives, and guards who occupied the manor had fled onto the expansive lawns, and the back stairway carried no one else.

In the basement, among the mammoth air cyclers, Overy Scarn blocked the entrance to the charmway, her SIG-Saur 9mm clasped in both hands.

"The charmway is burning!" She waved her gun at Jyoti. "I can't find my way. But you know how to get out of here, and you're taking me with you."

Nette sidestepped in front of Jyoti and shot a blue bolt as Scarn opened fire. The assassin hurled backward and collapsed dead in Jyoti's arms, her face locked in a defiant grimace. Where Overy Scarn had stood, venomous flames curled from a char of ribs and boiling bowels, sputtering with the hex-gems of her spellbinder girdle. Hefty limbs lay scattered on either side of the dark portal, and her head had disappeared, cast into the charmway.

EVIL CREATIONS

BLACK VEILS FLOATING LIKE A SHADOW UPON HER, LADY VON strolled down Fifth Avenue, appalled by the fashions in the shop windows and grateful for the opal nose ring that filtered the city's toxic air. Morning sunlight slanted down the side-streets. Its bronze radiance fascinated her. It was so unlike the diamond clarity of the Abiding Star that it frightened her. She understood better now why these worlds were called the *Dark Shore.*

The Sisterhood needed their queen's authority to destroy the last remnants of Duppy Hob's evil creations: the cities of Earth. Should this dim planet be purged of all the devil worshipper's amulets? Should the populace be restored to their aboriginal societies, free from the perilous magic of science? The Sisterhood possessed the Charm to do this, but it would be gruesome work.

Lady Von had immediately quashed that plan and agreed with the Brotherhood of Wizards that the destruction of the charmways both on Irth and across the Gulf was sufficient to protect the Bright Worlds from Duppy Hob's wicked legacy. Staring at the weird costumes the people displayed in their most elegant storefronts and then scanning the slovenly crowds shoving through the dusty sunlight, she felt glad that soon this fetid place would be cut off forever from Irth.

A team of witches had prepared for this final tour of the Dark Shore, and they were angry with worry when Lady Von announced that she herself would go alone to shut down the charmways on Earth. They claimed—and rightly so—that it was too dangerous. The strong eye was blind to events on the Dark Shore. She agreed and turned the argument back on her sisters. "Better one should risk and fail that an entire team. What needs be done can easily be done by one. This is the decision of your queen."

That was why Lady Von had met the margravine and the magus in Gabagalus alone, with no aides. Her witchery was sufficient to direct the couple back to New Arwar, almost certainly to their deaths if the blind god Justice were to be fulfilled and the one man from the Dark Shore on Irth removed. Yet she had not acted maliciously. The amulet-shawls she had bestowed on them were the finest that charmwrights had ever crafted and offered the maxiumum protection from morbid forces.

What would happen to Jyoti and Reece had been cleanly

delivered into the hands of Chance. That blind god would decide their fates—but not Lady Von's. The Sisterhood of Witches and Brotherhood of Wizards had armed her with talismanic devices that wielded godly powers in this cold reality. Chance alone could not defeat her, for even if Death's blind hands took her, the wizards had rigged her amulets to release a white-hot ray of Charm focused to explode the Sun. One way or another, her mission to close the charmways would be fulfilled.

The transit from Gabagalus had been uneventful, and along her way through the rock corridors that led to Earth she had left behind a trail of conjure-metal. Those silver-green ingots would erupt into charmfire at her command. But before detonating them, she had several more tasks to accomplish.

Her stroll down Fifth Avenue, after she had arrived among the erratic boulders of Central Park, had assured her that no disciples of Duppy Hob remained. As she moved within the city-amulet that the devil worshipper had created, she listened to the intelligences it touched and heard only three resonant echoes of magical power on Earth: herself, Caval, and a denizen of the Dark Shore, no doubt a disciple of Duppy Hob.

She hailed a taxi. Without uttering a word, she pressed a seeker amulet to the clear plastic partition between her and the driver, and he turned off his meter and obediently drove her through the congested streets. When the seeker went cold in her hand, the taxi stopped at the curb before a tall building of mustard-colored brick. She exited the cab, and it glided away, the driver unaware of what had happened, already intent on finding his next fare.

The uniformed doorman stared at her with open amazement, until she waved aside his attention and pulled the door open for herself. In the elevator ride to the top floor, she felt for Caval again and almost did not find him this time—he had grown so thin, a filament of Charm stretched from the magnetic core of the planet up into the Gulf.

To the Abiding Star itself, Caval's voice whisked through her brain. *I am a slender ray from the star of creation.*

"The Brotherhood of Wizards said I would find you here," the witch queen whispered with awe, "but I did not believe them." She parted her veils, exposing the hex-gems she had pasted to her face to heighten her Charm. "You are more thin than any soul that has ever focused itself beyond the body!"

Duppy Hob's magic gave me this strength, and necessity the will to use it. Brick is here with me.

"You have Dogbrick with you?" she asked skeptically. "I sense only you."

He is dead. And he is not Dogbrick. He has lost his beastmarks to a local magician—

"The disciple of Duppy Hob's. I feel him, but not here."

More an admirer than a disciple. He calls himself Nox, and he has taken Brick's beastmarks and uses that Charm for his own magic. All that I have salvaged from this corpse is the Charm of a man.

Lady Von exited the elevator and followed Caval's presence across a carpeted corridor to a metal door and concrete stairs that climbed to the roof. Like a piece of windy night, she flew among the ducts and tar-papered sheds to the water tank with the ram's-head knocker on its door.

A weak spell sealed the door, and she snapped it with a tug that admitted her to a shrine of perdition. Death's incense stained the darkness, and on the altar lay a flayed corpse crusty with dried blood and flies.

The witch queen reached out with both hands and rubbed between her palms the thread of Charm from the Abiding Star that was the wizard Caval. The thread widened to a ray, and out of that transparent light seeped a strong autumnal scent of dried leaves.

RETURN TO OCTOBERLAND

VOICES OF THE VANISHED SEASON SWELLED FROM THE WIDENING ray of charmlight—the sizzle of pouring leaves in a forest wind.

The light tasted of wood smoke. Chilly gusts, speckled with
rain, scattered the flies from the decaying body. And the hanging poppets of carved gourds and sun-dried fruits rattled among
the herb bines and grass sheaves.

Caval flushed stronger with the Charm that the witch queen
poured into him. When the shaft of clear light had widened to
a trunk that enclosed the entire stone altar, Caval appeared as
he had looked in his prime—tall and robust, his bright red hair
cropped close and his orange whiskers precisely trimmed to
outline the sharp angle of his long jaw. Garbed in bright tinsel
and blue-gauze windings as if for a funeral ascension, he gripped
the edge of the altar and gazed at Lady Von with silence in
his face.

A brightness of understanding passed between them. "This is
a closing ritual," Lady Von stated softly. "I cannot bring you
back to Irth. Your soul is too thin for any living thing, and no
amulet smaller than this world itself can hold you."

"This is a closing ritual," Caval agreed, his voice riding a
heather breeze of echoes. "I am honored that the witch queen
herself is here to give me away to the blind god Death. I have
endured too long as a ghost balked about by emptiness: watchful of all that transpires under this wide sky yet helpless to
change it. Only for this moment have I endured."

Charmlight expanded to the circumference of the ritual circle,
and the rustling leaf wind that buffeted through the chamber
muttered with faraway chanting, voices calling from empty
space. Twelve shadows stirred in the ice-white radiance. The
coven's souls gathered form, swelling from mist, drawing upon
the witch queen's Charm until the sinister angels who had possessed the last worshippers of Octoberland stood ceremonially
robed in the frosty light.

"You are the latest ghosts of this atrocity," the witch queen
addressed them, staring into each of their tapered faces and
cruel eyes. "You are the last souls that your master Nox shaped
to his greedy will. Before you, in the seven thousand years of

his life, he corrupted many others, and all have faded into the void, as you too will fade in time. But now you must make a fateful choice. Let time whittle you away, as it did the others— or sieze the only freedom you have and use this Charm I have given you to drop yourself down into the earth and return your power to the mineral floor of creation. Begin again."

"Death always begins," Caval assented, and the twelve echoed his words vigorously, sharing avid glances of agreement—silver-fleeced Aries clasping hands with long-shouldered Taurus and she with lanky Gemini all around the circle, through flaxen-haired Virgo to Pisces with her dark, kelpy tresses.

Haloed by the thermal blur of their wings, the circle of hand-clasped angels gazed down past their naked feet. The charmlight shafted through the building. Its brilliance erased the opacities of the interior and spotlighted Nox.

The broad beam of blinding light erased Nox to a white shadow. Smeared features woefully gazed upward into the glare. The charmlight had caught him in midstep of his ritual dance. All around him bloomed wild, flowering walls of shrubs and vines: plantains and acacias, myrtles and spiny palms, all washed of color. Floral outlines dripped from the alchemic arch and vaults of the fanged ceiling, powdery as a charcoal sketch.

The wind of Octoberland descended with the gaze of the sinister angels—and Nox's magic ran to shadows like a mirage. Where a sinuous smooth-barked tree had stood before a small tiered waterfall, Mary Felix cringed at the foot of stone stairs. In the intense glare, she looked for Nox and saw him reduced to a skeletal shape, like a thing of wire. Only his head seemed substantial, his long skull bobbing with fright.

"Who are you?" Nox screamed.

"Do not be afraid." Caval appeared alongside the frightened magician and took the withered shape within the embrace of his tinsel and blue-gauze windings. "You are not alone. What you have feared all these thousands of years, we will face together."

Nox staggered away from the apparition of Caval and tried to hurry toward the raddled shadows outside the fierce illumination from above. "I'm going to live forever!" his tight throat croaked as he hobbled across the stone floor, his ligaments rasping. "I will never die!"

Caval rose before Nox, tinseled arms outspread. "We cannot flee, not either of us. Death is a god—and we are but men."

Nox saw the twin stars of certainty in the wizard's staring eyes, and he knew then that the eternity he had possessed only moments before had vanished. He had reached the end of an endless life. A great sob broke from his spindle-shanked body, and Caval's shining arms closed on him.

From above, the ring of sinister angels plunged with a banshee scream. The chamber flashed to stunned whiteness. Mary Felix's whole body winced, starting to twist away, too late. When sight throbbed back into her eyes, she gazed at embers of a human skeleton pulsing red and brown in the darkness where Nox had squatted in terror. By the sepia light of those smoldering bones, she felt her way up the stone steps and out of the grotto.

In the ritual room atop the roof, Lady Von waited for her. The charmlight had sunken into the earth with Caval, Nox, and the coven of Octoberland. A chill lingered in the air with hues of frost and cedar resins. But already that fragrance had begun to thin in the summer heat. The baked odors of the city widened through the room from the open door and its slant of morning light.

While she waited, the witch queen stroked the body on the altar with a power wand sheathed in a helix of theriacal opals. At the touch of these amulets, the flesh healed. Brown and black decay sloughed off the skinned body like scales of rust, and new flesh appeared through the orange haze of Charm—brown flesh, sleek and human.

Brick woke in the house of his eyes. He looked up at shriveled apple faces dangling in an amber wedge of sunlight. A round, pallid face bent over him, eyes large and luminous with reflections. At the black center, he saw himself, a square, brown face under a nest of blond hair.

He sat up and touched his naked skin, looking for the pain.

"Charm has made you whole—but human," the round-faced woman in black raiment told him. "You have lost your beast-marks and found a new life."

Her words mesmerized him, and he sat still in the absence of suffering, the warm weight of sunlight across his thighs. He closed his eyes to be sure he was awake. Behind his lids, dreams slipped by like a river of milk. And when he dared open his eyes again, Mary Felix stood in the summer doorway.

DIRTY REALITY

HEAT POUNDED THE CHARMWAYS. EVEN IN THEIR AMULET-SHAWLS, Jyoti and Reece could not stay in the smoky corridors long, and they ran a few paces and jumped out the nearest portal. They emerged on a high knoll in Elvre among snake temple ruins. This was a tourist destination for blue-haired ælves from Nemora, and several of them mingled in a shrine of serpent-coil pillars open to the sky. The surrounding alcoves, carved like fanged mouths, had been taken over by jungle creepers and monkeys. Scarlet birds flapped away heavily as the ælves rushed past those alcoves into the jungle, fleeing the soot-eyed couple.

Beyond the scaly rooftops of the temple village, Jyoti saw what had frightened the ælves, and she had to lean on Reece as her knees jellied. New Arwar filled the jungle horizon, a tiered mountain of ferny estates and tree-colonnaded streets that lifted above the forest in a majesty of haze. At its crest, flames stretched black banners into the sky—green flames. It took Reece a moment to see what Jyoti had known at once: Charm-fire was consuming the entire city from within.

Emerald sparks flashed from small fires among the lanes and terraces. The interior blaze had ignited charmwrights' shops and their warehouses, and whole tiers of buildings exploded. In moments, New Arwar had become a radiant torch heaving black clouds into the day sky.

Thunder from the explosions reached Jyoti and Reece, and they clutched each other tighter. A white star expanded to a silver sphere of moony brilliance when the conjure-metal girders of the infrastructure erupted. The conflagration imploded, and New Arwar collapsed into the jungle under a whirlwind of dazzling cinders.

The healing Charm of her amulet-shawl held Jyoti still and calm, even as she gazed into the black thunderheads where her capital had fallen.

"Let's get out of here, Reece," she murmured. "Let's go to the Dark Shore—and let's not come back."

Holding to each other, Jyoti and Reece turned back toward the steaming charmway under the ulcerous stones of the snake temple. "The goblins are dead," Reece spoke gently to her. "Irth will rebuild. We will find our place among the dominions."

She shook her head and turned to face him. "Before the charmways to the Dark Shore burn, let's go. And let's not come back. I mean it, Reece. I've lost everything of this world that mattered to me. Only you're left—and the future we'll build together. But not here. Not in a world that killed my brother, my parents—my entire brood. I don't ever want to come back here."

Reece saw the certainty in her face, like the cruelty in a knife. "We *are* meant to be together, Jyo. I feel as you do. I've seen enough of Irth. Other than the love we found together, I brought nothing but trouble to this planet. I want to go home."

Jyoti held his strong stare. "If we don't go now, we may never be able to cross the Gulf."

Together, they shouldered into the smoke-filled charmway. The lux-diamonds of their shawls penetrated the miasma, and they ran hard against the brutal heat. Green flames leaped from side passages and crevices in the rock walls. Reece feared that their amulet-shawls would explode if licked by those searing sparks, and he charged just ahead of Jyoti so that they could both run in the middle, away from the sudden jets of fire.

Ahead, the refulgent heat dimmed, and soon only the light from their amulets lit the way. No side passages offered themselves. This single tunnel led away from the holocaust. A cool waft of sea breeze pulled them around the next bend into daylight and an arched view of the green mucilaginous crags of Gabagalus.

Jyoti and Reece ran onto the air pier where they had left Lady Von and crossed the trestle platform to the tunnel at the opposite end—the charmway that descended through the Gulf to the Dark Shore. Not five paces in, they nearly collided with the witch queen. Two people were with her—a freckle-faced young woman with thick chestnut hair and a burly man in a breechcloth, his blond hair scattered and a lopsided smile on his strong face.

"Reece! You've lost your beastmarks too!" The large man slapped his naked chest with both hands. "It's me. Brick! Dogbrick!"

Reece squinted at him, and Jyoti searched her niello eye charm to see if he was wearing an illusion.

"Dark Shore magic changed me!" Brick exulted with a thick smile. He took Reece in his arms and then swung him to one side to take Jyoti into the embrace of his other arm. "The sibyl's prophecy is fulfilled! I died a man. And Caval and the witch queen have used their magic to bring me back as a man!"

Lady Von lowered the veils from her pale countenance and nodded, smiling. "The blind gods have been fulfilled on the Dark Shore. And now you two are here to complete our devotion in the Bright Worlds."

"You didn't think we'd survive New Arwar, did you?" Jyoti stepped away from Brick and looked hard into the witch queen's large, limpid eyes. "If Reece were consumed, the Sisterhood could rightly declare it had purged all remnants of the Dark Shore from the Bright Worlds." She recognized the glint of truth in those tranquil eyes, and she went on to say, "Your Sisterhood can still make that declaration, because Reece and I are leaving the Bright Worlds. No one will remain on Irth from the Dark Shore."

"But I'm from the Dark Shore," the young woman piped up from behind Brick. "And I've come to Irth to make my way with Brick."

"This is Mary Felix," the large man said, releasing Reece and taking her under his arm. "She was my champion on the Dark Shore—and she's decided to come back with me."

"There's nothing left for me on Earth," Mary admitted. "After a lifetime there, I'd outlived all that mattered to me. Now, Brick is giving me a chance for a new life—on Irth."

Lady Von lifted her black veils like wings. "The strong eye showed me none of this. Margravine—magus, believe me. You may well have died in New Arwar, and you both knew that when you went in to destroy the goblins. That the blind god Chance has saved you—that is an unforeseen blessing. Will you use it to serve the blind god Justice?"

"I've had it with your gods," Reece said. "I'm going back to Darwin with Jyoti."

Lady Von draped the black veils of one arm over Mary's shoulders and the veils of the other over the shoulders of Jyoti. "Before you take each other's place in your distant worlds, exchange Charm. In that way, Mary Felix will become a natural denizen of the Bright Worlds and Jyoti Odawl will herself belong on the Dark Shore."

"I will have no magic on the Dark Shore?" Jyoti asked.

The witch queen shook her head. "None."

"And I will not suffer from the brightness of the Abiding Star?" Mary inquired.

"Correct." Lady Von removed her arms from their shoulders

and withdrew from under her robes an amber power wand wrapped at the middle in conjure-wire and bearing nodules of hex-rubies. "Each of you grasp one end of this amulet. This will only take a moment, and when I am done, I decree that neither of you will be foreign in your new homes. Each of you will belong to the dirty reality of your own world."

RECONCILED AMONG THE STARS

ON EARTH, AT DOCKSIDE OF THEIR TROPICAL BOAT RENTAL AND Tour office in the Darwin marina on the northwest coast of Arnhem Land in Australia, Jyoti sometimes thought about Irth. The sun sparkles among the many hues of the bay reminded her of hex-gems. Shimmering from the horizon in water shades of sapphire through emerald to the most lucid diamonds of sunshine in the clear water that fronted her office, the jeweled light had the beauty of Charm. But inevitably this reverie transported her to sad memories of her lost brood and Arwar Odawl, and she shunted them aside to make room for her new work and her new life.

Wind and cloud received most of her attention now that she had boats and tourists to protect from storms. Periwinkles and pink conchs bordered the sand yard in front of her office, and beyond that, bougainvillea blossomed in red and orange sprays over white pickets and a low stone wall of jasmine that fronted the quai with its berths of bobbing boats. Reece came from there along the sand road, back from mooring the tour boat.

She went out to meet him, and they strolled together through the feathery ironwood trees to the strand that flanked the marina. Hard sun and a high wind sheared cumulus to swift tufts that flung shadows over the glittering bay, and they read the weather together and knew it would rain before twilight. They waded back to the waterfront office, happy with the prospect of an early night and eager to balance the accounts for that day's business and close the shop.

At midnight, after the rain had returned to sea, they sat on the beach under the ironwoods and the shining band of the galaxy. "Would you ever want to go back?" Jyoti asked, probing to see if he was as happy as she was on the Dark Shore.

"And miss marlin fishing season?" He leaned back against the giant and gentle tree and fixed her with a reassuring smile. "Forget it."

And she did, happily. For both of them, Irth had a dimness of recollection that paled within the vivid immediacy of their lives. The witch queen's magic had touched them with Charm to help them blunt the jagged edges of the most painful memories—and then she had taken away their amulets. Without Charm, memories faded. As the years went by, they would do less recollecting, for their lives had become full and would fill even more when the children arrived and the business expanded.

The same was true across the Gulf, on Irth, in the sea-cliff city of Saxar. Mary Felix and Brick spent most days working in their executive suites at Dig Dog Ltd. They enjoyed the challenge of helping connect the city's factories and charmwrights with buyers in cities of every dominion, and their company flourished in the prosperous eras of reconstruction and expansion that followed.

At night, sitting together under puzzle trees in the park off Cold Niobe at the crest of Everyland street, they watched the planets sliding majestically among the star vapors and talked about their work together and their future. Once in a while, their thoughts turned to the Dark Shore and the adventures that had brought them together. Dogbrick glowed with satisfaction that his trials had won him the unalloyed humanity he had always believed was his. And Mary Felix felt grateful to have found a life of Charm far from the cold world of her exhausted years on Earth.

"You know I can't even remember what he looked like," Brick said, squinting with the effort to recall. "Reece Morgan—he was stocky, blunt nosed, I think. I can't really see him in my mind anymore."

Mary nuzzled against his shoulder and traced her finger against the clean line of his jaw. "The city archives must have a likeness. Search under magus."

"I've tried. The archives have no record of his involvement in the Conquest." He spoke softly, as from the boundary of a dream. "The official histories of all the dominions claim that Hu'dre Vra was slain by Margravine Jyoti, the last of the Perished Odawls. And they say that she died less than a thousand days later, in the firestorm that devoured New Arwar."

Mary amplified the Charm flowing from her amulet-shawl, clearing the static of anxiety that his words set behind her breastbone. "Lady Von was right then to warn us not to speak of this to anyone." She sat up and gazed wistfully through the angular branches at the incandescent fumes of star exhaust silhouetting the curved rooftops of Saxar's affluent heights. "The Sisterhood of Witches and the Brotherhood of Wizards are determined to once again hide the truth of the Dark Shore."

"And for the best, I say. We were lucky to get away at all." Brick pulled her close to him again. "Do you miss Earth?"

She floated with him in a fullness of Charm and an emptiness of all discomfort. "Earth was a completely different lifetime— on a dim and sad world. I never much think about it. And when I do, I feel unhappy for everyone who must live and die there, on the Dark Shore."

"I just wish I could remember what Reece really looked like." Brick pinched the bridge of his nose. "I have this vague memory of a block of a man with a square-cut face. But I don't see his features." He shrugged and offered a soft laugh. "It's easier for me to simply remember him as Ripcat. Those are beastmarks I'll never forget!"

Charm helped their bad memories fade. As the years went by, Brick and Mary Felix would do less recollecting, for their lives had become full and would fill even more with their election to the Peerage and their expanding role as trading giants among the dominions of Irth.

Afterworld

IN A HIGHER WORLD BEYOND WORLD'S END, INSIDE THE SILVER CO-rona of the Abiding Star, life went on simpler and happier yet. The pixies who had trespassed the lady's garden to look at her bathing her swollen belly in the garden's marble pool had been tricked by the dark father to descend into his consort's dream.

They had thought they would be trapped there forever and had acted ferociously to protect themselves—not realizing that the way out of that cold reality was the simplest solution of all: through the heat of the Abiding Star. When charmfire consumed them, they awoke from the dream, once more in the twilit garden under drifts of golden leaves.

Against a tapestry of birdsong, splashings from the pool, and distant dulcimer music, they heard the dark father's laughter. Black and green butterflies scattered from the flower beds where the returning exiles sat up, startled. The pixies shared looks of amazement, jubilation, and fright, and they leaped to their feet, frantic to flee the twilit garden and the nightmare that had once devoured them.

Scores of pixies darted between the pillars, frightening horned lizards and doves from the flower-laden trellises. Scores more pixies clasped their petal caps and twine-bound leaf britches and fled past blooms and fronds that dimmed beneath the slantwise shadows of enclosing night.

Beyond the garden's hedges, mauve horizons of twilight stretched over hay-dust fields and clover meadows, and the dear ones ran in their hundreds toward freedom, laughing faces shining with thrilling lucidity. They knew their place now in the waking world, learned hard in a cruel trance, and were grateful for the lesson and its hints of myth.

Laughter and song returned with them into the fields.

Overhead, evening's purple bleared into violet, fading toward the ultratones of the invisible, and within the utter black of the void no stars glimmered, no moon glided, only shoreless depths of emptiness ranged—like the spiteful forgetfulness of a dream.

the dominions of Irth

Saxar

Zul

the Qaf

Andeje Crag

Keri

Malpais Highlands

the Falls of Mirdath

Lake Apocalypse

Spiderlands

Mjoodrun

Old Shard

Dorzen

Ux

Mount Szo

Elvre

Rainbow Forests of Bryse

Arwar Odawl

Drymarch

Sharna-Bambara

Floating Stone

Mere of Goblins

cloths of Heaven

Palace of Abominations

the Reef Isles of Nhat

JB 96